DARIUS

GRACE BURROWES

sourcebooks
casablanca

Published by Sourcebooks Casablanca, an imprint of Sourcebooks, Inc.
P.O. Box 4410, Naperville, Illinois 60567-4410
(630) 961-3900
FAX: (630) 961-2168
www.sourcebooks.com

Printed and bound in Canada
WC 10 9 8 7 6 5 4 3 2 1

This book is dedicated to anybody who has ever made a poor choice and felt overwhelmed by the consequences. Maybe you can't overcome all those consequences today, but never give up hope. Someday, things will be better, and positive change may come from the direction you least expect it.

One

"IF ONE KNOWS PRECISELY WHERE TO INQUIRE, ONE hears you provide favors to a select few ladies in exchange for the next thing to coin."

William Longstreet—the Fourth Viscount Longstreet, no less—delivered this observation without so much as a quaver to his voice. His veined hands were rock steady, and his tone cordial as he held his glass out to his host. "Just a touch more, perhaps? The wind is bitter, even for November."

And Darius Lindsey, veteran of more unnerving moments, stiff beatings, and bad luck than any earl's younger son ought to have endured, took his guest's glass to the sideboard and filled it with another finger of cognac—a scant finger.

Lord Longstreet was known as a shrewd politician, capable of quietly negotiating compromises between embattled factions in the Lords. He'd sent around a note asking to make a call privately, after dark, and Darius had accepted out of curiosity.

A curiosity he was apparently going to regret at length.

Darius crossed his arms and leaned back against the

sideboard. "You're repeating rumor, my lord, and slanderous rumor at that. Just what did you come here to say?"

"Blunt." Lord Longstreet's faded brown eyes gleamed with humor. "Suppose you've learned to be, and that's all to the good. Excellent libation, by the way, and I notice you aren't keeping up, young man." Longstreet raised his glass with gentlemanly bonhomie, while Darius wanted to smash his drink against the hearthstones—not that he had the coin for even such a small extravagance of temper.

"You needn't confirm or deny these rumors," Lord Longstreet went on, shifting a bit in a chair more sturdy and comfortable than elegant. "I have no intention of recalling the information or where I came by it once I leave you tonight."

"Gracious of you, when you're repeating the kind of insinuations that can get a man called out."

"Involving as they do, the honor of several ladies," Longstreet rejoined. "*If* one can call them that."

Darius didn't rise to the bait. Tonight was not a night when he was expected elsewhere in the wee hours—thank a merciful God—and in deference to his guest's age, Darius had for once built up the fire to the point where his quarters were cozy. This also resulted in more illumination cast on threadbare carpet, scarred furniture, and a water stain high up on the outside wall.

"Ah, good." Longstreet's amusement was in evidence again. "You don't rile, and you neither gossip nor disparage the women. This comports with your reputation as well."

Darius set his drink aside while foreboding and distaste—for himself, his guest, and this topic—roiled in his gut. "While I am pleased to have your approval for mere gentlemanly reticence, I must ask again if you troubled making my acquaintance only to banter gossip. You are an important man, both politically and socially, while I am the proverbial impoverished second son, making my way as best I can. What errand brings you to my doorstep, my lord?"

Longstreet nodded, as if acknowledging that opening arguments were over. "Lady Longstreet—"

"*No.*" Darius paced off to the door, wanting to pitch the old man onto the stairs.

"I beg your pardon?"

"I will not be procured for your wife's entertainment," Darius said, "or for yours, or yours and hers. Finish your drink if you must, and I'll show you out."

"I would far rather you heard me out. Had I any other alternative, Lindsey, believe me I would be pursuing it."

Darius turned his back to his guest and resisted the urge to slam his fist into the wall. "Despite what you've heard, my lord, there are limits…"

"You don't swive them," Longstreet said briskly, as if conceding an otherwise unimpressive mount had good quarters and a sane eye. "You won't, in fact. Which is why you find me here, because any other man—any other *young* man with a need for coin and the ingenuity to go on as you have—would have taken what was offered and considered it his revenge on the feckless women throwing their money at him."

Darius turned a granite stare on his guest, even

knowing the man had the ear of the regent. "I find this conversation exceedingly tedious."

Longstreet met that stare. "Lindsey, do sit down. *Please*. I am older than your braying ass of a father, and this is difficult enough without your wounded pride added to the general awkwardness."

"Did she put you up to this?" Darius took the other chair—the one that rocked slightly, though it wasn't supposed to—and didn't touch his drink.

"She would never do such a thing. Vivian is a lady in every sense of the word."

"Though you are procuring for her." Darius said it flatly, as nastily as he could, for this scheme Lord Longstreet was about to propose, it purely, rottenly stank. For all involved.

"I have my reasons, and Vivian understands them."

For the first time, Longstreet's patrician features showed a flicker of sentiment. Whatever the man's motivations, there was nothing prurient about them, and his lordship was very determined on his goal.

"As best I recall, you have two sons, my lord. What need have you of a... gallant for your wife?"

Gallant. A euphemism that loomed larger than the stain behind his lordship's head.

"Aldous died at Waterloo, and his older brother lost his life on the field of honor this fall." Longstreet ran a hand through thinning sandy-gray hair, then stared at his drink.

"I'm sorry."

"God, man, so am I," Longstreet replied, shifting his gaze to stare at the cheery blaze Darius really could not afford. "We put it about that Algernon eloped to the Continent, but he lies in the family plot at Longchamps. Some creative tale will be woven when the other fellow's family has recovered a bit, for each of the young fools managed to kill his opponent."

Darius pushed aside pity—burying two sons merited pity—and focused on practicalities, something he was good at. "So you seek somebody not only to bed your lady, but also to get her with child? If so, then I am assuredly not your man."

"That would be part of the bargain." Longstreet's voice did not betray a hint of shame about this proposition. "Hear my reasons before you make an old man face that bitter wind."

A lady's honor was to be compromised, but an old man was to be spared the nippy weather. This was what Darius's life had come to.

"Make your words count, my lord. While I am sensible of the dilemma you face, surely there must be cousins or nephews somewhere who can solve the problem by inheritance and spare your lady this unseemly contrivance you contemplate."

"There are none. If I die without legitimate male issue, then the entire estate reverts to the Crown."

Spare me from titled old men and their petty conceits. "This has happened in many a family, and you will be dead, so what does it matter to you?"

Longstreet shifted again in his chair, though Darius suspected that was a seasoned parliamentarian's delaying tactic.

"Were it simply a question of my needs, young man, you'd be absolutely right. However, upon close examination, I find the Crown could make a credible argument that there is virtually no personal estate. My wealth is significant, but the Crown's lawyers will twist matters such that none of that wealth is personal, but rather, all attached to the title. The regent would get everything, and Vivian would be literally a charity case."

"Your wife has no dower portion?"

"None worth the name. I am pained on her behalf to be so honest, but ours was not a romantic match. She needed marrying rather desperately, and I could not abide to see her taken advantage of by those who prey on women in such circumstances. I suppose I needed a bit of marrying too."

Darius sipped his drink, angling for time to absorb his guest's words. Usually, a woman desperately in need of marrying had conceived a child desperately in need of legitimacy. Lady Longstreet's difficulty was the absence of children.

"I cannot agree to anything without knowing all the facts, Lord Longstreet."

His lordship ran a bony finger around the rim of his glass. "Fair enough. Her stepfather would have sold her to any grasping cit with the coin," the older man said wearily. "Vivian deserved better than that. She was my first wife's devoted companion for the duration of Muriel's illness. Vivian and I became friends, of a sort, and when Muriel died, there was Vivian's stepfather, ready to snatch her back and auction her off."

"And she wasn't of age, that she couldn't avoid such a fate?" Darius frowned, because this sounded all too much like his sister Leah's circumstances, though the Earl of Wilton himself was the one intent on procuring for his older daughter.

"She was not quite twenty-one, so she was not of age in the sense you mean. Then too, Vivian lacks the… animal cunning to thwart her stepfather's schemes. She'd kill a man outright, but never by stabbing him in the back. And as you well know, a woman's lot in life leaves her little enough discretion regarding her choice of mate, particularly a woman raised in Polite Society."

Apparently Lord Longstreet was familiar with Leah's circumstances too, which notion brought no comfort. "So you've convinced Lady Longstreet to secure her future by disporting with me," Darius concluded. "How flattering."

Longstreet set his drink down with a thump, the first spark of temper he'd exhibited in a quarter hour of fencing. "You should be flattered, by God. Vivian chose you from a set of candidates I selected for her. There were precious few left on the list once I started discreet inquiries, but you were the one she chose."

"Am I to know why?"

"You can ask her," Longstreet replied, showing the guile of a seasoned politician. "She's a damsel in distress, Lindsey, and you have it in your power to provide her a lifetime of security and to preserve a fine old title from the maw of the regent's bottomless appetite."

Darius felt relief as insight struck. "That's what this is about, isn't it? You don't favor Prinny's politics or priorities, and you're loathe to see centuries of Longstreet wealth poured onto his side of the scales."

Lord Longstreet's brow knitted. "I wouldn't like that outcome, no."

"And even less would you like it known you'd

schemed with your wife to avoid it by consorting with the likes of me."

"Shrewd." Longstreet blew out a breath. "You must see that as much as you desire my discretion, I need yours. I've worked for nigh fifty years for the good of the realm, Lindsey, and between the lunatic Americans, the equally mad King, and the greedy, mad Corsican, it hasn't been an easy fifty years. If word gets out I sent my wife off to some impoverished younger son, like a mare to the breeding shed, then nobody will recall the votes I won, the bills I drafted, the riots I prevented. I will simply be a greedy, unpatriotic old fool."

Darius reluctantly, and silently, admitted that Lord Longstreet's reasoning made a peculiar sort of sense. "You don't mind the old fool part, but the unpatriotic hurts abominably. Again, my lord, I do sympathize, or I would if the nation's fate interested me half as much as my own, but I cannot help you."

"You haven't heard the entirety of my proposal, young man." Longstreet held out his glass for a refresher, buying himself a few more minutes. Darius understood the ploy and allowed it only because of the pile of unpaid bills silently mocking him from the corner of his desk.

And the other pile in the drawer, aging not half so well as William Longstreet had.

"I'm listening," Darius said, foregoing any further drink for himself. "For the present."

Longstreet shoved to his feet in a succession of creaky moves: scoot, brace, push, totter, balance, then pace. "First, you and Vivian must spend enough time together that there is a reasonable likelihood of a child. Second, I'd like you sufficiently invested in the child's life that you will not, for any amount of money, divulge the facts of his or her paternity."

"If I may," Darius interrupted. "The chances are even any child born would be female, in which case your impoverished viscountess is left to support not only herself, but a girl child, which can be an expensive proposition."

Longstreet's gaze turned crafty as he propped himself against the mantel. "That would be the usual case, except my title is very old, and only in my great-grandfather's day was it elevated from a barony to a viscountcy. Nobody has looked at the letters patent in a century, save myself, and while the viscountcy carries a male entail, the barony can be preserved through the female line."

"You're sure?"

"It's that old. When the Black Death came through, there was pressure on the monarchy to liberalize its patents, as tremendous wealth was reverting when family after family lost its male line. Mine is one of the few surviving more liberally drafted letters, and thus the barony—and the estate wealth—will be preserved regardless of the gender of the child."

This scheme was madness—thoroughly researched, carefully considered, potentially lucrative madness. "The barony will survive if there is a child. If I agree to your terms."

"Stop putting that bottle up, young man. Having heard this much, I think there are terms you'll agree to, do we apply ourselves to their negotiation in good faith."

"Good faith? You're attempting to cheat the Crown, procure the intimate services of a worthless bounder for your lady wife, perpetrate a fraud on your patrimony, and you speak of good faith?"

"You're young." Lord Longstreet resumed his seat in another succession of creaks and totters, this time popping a knee joint as well. "You can afford your ideals. Imagine what might befall your family were your father to lose the Wilton title, his lands, his wealth—how might your sisters go on, if not in some version of the oldest and least-respected profession?"

Darius leveled a look at him such that Lord Longstreet flushed and glanced away.

"So you beat your sisters to it," he surmised. "Your father isn't just a braying ass, Lindsey, he's a disgrace to his kind."

"And yet it's his line you'll be grafting onto your own—if I agree."

It took two hours, the rest of the cognac, and very likely some of the toughest negotiating Lord Longstreet had seen in half a century, but in the end, Darius agreed.

❧

"William will not be joining us."

In addition to lustrous dark hair done up in a prim coronet, Lady Vivian Longstreet had a low voice, a contralto, laced with controlled tension.

"I beg your pardon?" Darius succeeded in keeping the irritation from his tone, but only just. This civilized dinner *a trois* had been one of Lord Longstreet's terms, and Darius had grudgingly acceded to the older man's desire to see his wife politely introduced to her... what? Darius couldn't bring himself to apply the word *lover*. *Stud* was too vulgar, if accurate, though worse terms came to mind.

"William is under the weather," Lady Longstreet said. "May I take your coat? The servants have been dismissed for the evening, and yes, I truly mean he's feeling poorly. William is capable of diplomatic illnesses, but I'm sure if he told you he would be here, he meant to keep his word. It's just..."

"Yes?" Darius turned slightly, so she could lift his coat from his shoulders, her touch conveying hesitance, even timidity, as she did.

She smiled slightly and hoisted his coat to a hook in the alcove. "I don't mean to babble. William is much involved in the Lords, and it tires him. I assured him we'd manage, but if you'd rather reschedule this encounter, we can."

Begin as you intend to go on.

"We'll manage." Darius offered his arm, noting with disinterest—*professional* disinterest—that Lady Longstreet was quite pretty. He'd put her age at around five-and-twenty, the same as his sister Leah. Her smile was polite, and her countenance was serene.

That serenity brought lovely features into submission—a perfectly straight nose, slanting dark eyes, full lips, and classic cheekbones—when a more animated expression might have rendered the same face arresting.

She was hiding her beauty, maybe even from herself.

He laid his hand over hers where it rested on his sleeve. "My business with Lord Longstreet has been concluded, my lady, leaving only my dealings with you before you can be shut of me."

"And you'll be relieved when that's the case?" She was barely, barely tolerating his touch, for all her calm expression.

Could he be intimate with a woman who disdained to touch even his sleeve? "Now how will I answer that?" He glanced down at her as they made their progress through the house, not sure if he was irritated with her or for her. "If I say yes, I'll be relieved to complete my obligations with you, you'll be insulted. If I say no, you'll think I relish a bargain I, in truth, regret."

She turned velvety brown eyes to him, her expression curious. "Why?"

Lady Longstreet was brave—martyrs were supposed to be brave—and despite the circumstances, she truly *was* a lady. The realization made Darius pause, and not happily. He was most comfortable when the women with whom he consorted intimately shared with him a kind of mutual resentment and scorn. They used him, he used them, and each could look down on the other's neediness and pretend the other party was the more venal, the more vulnerable. Lady Longstreet would not fit the same mold.

Perhaps she wasn't of any mold.

He resumed the thread of their discussion. "Why what?"

"Why do you regret this bargain? I regret that it can't be William's child I bear, but it will still be the child William gave me, in a sense. I can live with that."

"You're very sensible," Darius said as they entered a small dining room. The hearth at one end was blazing, bringing blessed relief from the unheated corridor.

The table had been set à la française, with the various dishes covered and waiting over warming lights.

"William is the sensible one," Lady Longstreet said. "Practical to a fault, his wife used to say."

"You're his wife."

"I meant his first wife," Lady Longstreet corrected herself without a flicker of irritation. "The woman he was married to for thirty-some years, the woman who bore him two sons. Shall we be seated?"

The table was positioned near the hearth, their two places set at right angles to each other so it couldn't be said there was a head or a foot to the table. William's absence allowed that, and Darius had to wonder how honest the older man was with his composed young wife.

Darius seated her and gestured to the wine breathing in the center of the table. "Shall I pour?" The question seemed absurd, and yet, with such a woman, what else was there to do but continue the pretense of civility?

"I hope you like it." Lady Longstreet's smile was gracious. "We often entertain diplomats, and there is universal accord that a hostess gift must be either wine from one's own country or sweets. The sweets are invariably consumed while the company is present, though we've acquired an interesting cellar."

Darius peered at the label. "German?"

"We're working our way across the Continent," his hostess replied. "Tell me, have you traveled much?"

The meal was… odd, because Darius of late spent little time around women whom he wasn't obligated to deal with. He loved his two sisters, but they still put demands on him. And the other women… They put demands on him as well, demands he was compensated for meeting but would as soon forget.

Dinner with Vivian Longstreet had nothing of overt obligation about it, but rather, was a pleasant encounter with a woman whose mannerliness was such that she could draw him out in conversation, ply him with excellent food and good wine, and make him forget for a time why it was their lives were briefly entangling.

Her ladyship eyed the remains of the fruit and cheese nearly an hour later. "I wasn't sure quite what we were supposed to do with each other this evening, but William insisted that ours is a civilized bargain for civilized ends, and we should begin it on a civil note."

"I'm not sure I'd agree with him." Darius sliced her off another bite of cheese and put it on her plate. He'd never realized how intimate sharing a meal could be and wasn't sure he liked the revelation. She'd be sharing a damned month of meals with him if they kept their bargain.

"You agreed to this." Lady Longstreet's hand waved over the table. "Hasn't there been benefit to you in sharing this meal?"

He'd eaten every bite offered to him, though he sensed she wasn't alluding to that. "Some. I'm not as hungry, and I've made the acquaintance of three very respectable German wines." To his own ears, he sounded a tad... churlish, though *not* petulant.

"One vintage was Rhenish. Aren't you also a little less uncomfortable with what lies ahead of us, Mr. Lindsey?"

"Are you?" Her answer mattered, when it should

not. The bills stacking up apace on Darius's escritoire had to be what mattered most.

She lifted the slice of cheese, eyed it, and set it back on her plate. "I see what you mean, about giving answers that can be either flattering or honest. I've said I will do this for William—he posited this eventuality as a condition of his proposal, though at the time both of his sons yet lived. I will honor my word to him, but it is… odd."

"Yes. Odd."

"Not as odd as we think." Her smile was fleeting, impish, and entirely unexpected. Not her gracious-hostess smile, it was devilish, full of mischief.

"What does that mean?"

"Lord Longstreet is fairly certain he himself was a cuckoo in his papa's nest, by design. He calls himself a judicious outcross."

Darius grimaced to think what his own father might have made of such a notion. "By design?"

"The Longstreet line has not been blessed with a great lot of male progeny." Lady Longstreet popped the cheese into her mouth. "It helps me to know other ladies in the family have been called upon to serve as I have."

Darius watched her chew. "And the late Lady Longstreet would not object to this scheme?"

The present Lady Longstreet blinked. "I was Lady Muriel Longstreet's companion in her final years, and yes, she would approve. One is to hedge one's husband's bets, or so she said. I think forty years ago marriage was a more pragmatic undertaking. She and William loved each other, and they were most assuredly best friends by the time Lady Muriel died."

"If you say so, but I cannot imagine…"

"Neither can I." Lady Longstreet's tone was a little forlorn. "And in a just a few weeks' time, I won't have to imagine it, because I will be on your doorstep, bag and baggage. Oh, dear."

He smiled, mostly because the double meaning was embarrassing her. "I'll be the baggage, if you'd rather."

"We'll get through this, won't we, Mr. Lindsey?" Now her tone was hopeful, and in her brown eyes, he saw she wasn't at all as poised and certain as she'd have him believe. Maybe it was the German wine or the realization that they were indeed to be intimate when next they met or the quiet all around them, but as he held her gaze, Lady Longstreet's trepidation peeked out at him.

She was anxious as hell, bloody scared to death.

"We'll manage," he said. "It is ever a failing of mine to take things too seriously, and in this case, you mustn't allow it of me."

She nodded solemnly. "Nor you of me. I think you have the right of it."

Darius held out his hand to her, palm up. She glanced down at his bare fingers in consternation then tentatively put her own hand over his. He brought her knuckles to his lips, planted a kiss there, then drew her to her feet.

"We've put off the more delicate subjects," he said as he led her over to the fire. There was a tea service waiting there, a kettle on a swing over the hearth, and two cozy chairs catching some of the fire's heat.

She took a seat, all grace and composure, though his observation had made her eyes widen. "Isn't a month long enough to sort through those?"

He considered what he wanted to ask her—regarding her intimate preferences, toys, games, fantasies—and then realized her elderly husband was likely asleep on the next floor up, and really, the discussion could wait.

"We can talk more later. If there is a later. You need to know I won't hold you to this bargain."

"What does that mean?" She motioned him into a seat and prepared the tea, her grace as soothing as the warmth of the hearth. "I'm to be your guest in Kent for a few weeks, but you'd take William's coin and deceive the man?" She wrinkled her nose. "I won't lie to my husband just for your gain, Mr. Lindsey. If I'm that unappealing, you need only…"

He leaned forward, placed a single finger to her lips, and shook his head.

"You appeal." He could say that sincerely, which wasn't necessarily a good thing. "You'd appeal to any man with red blood in his veins, but I'm suggesting a lady can change her mind."

"Change her… Oh." She looked intrigued then resigned. "Not this lady." She added cream and sugar to his tea and passed it to him. "I've given my word, and if you change your mind, I'll simply have William contact the next possibility on the list."

"Who might that be?"

The name had him raising his eyebrows, because the man was a fortune-hunting bounder with no decorum when in his cups, which was nightly. "And if he won't serve?"

"Is this necessary?"

"Yes."

"Then we're prepared to ask another, and another, because William is intent on his plans, and there is no force of nature equal to William Longstreet when he is determined on his goals."

Or Lady Longstreet, her tone implied, when she was determined on William's goals.

"Then I will see you in Kent around the tenth of December." Which was soon. Very soon. "I'm not sure if you should be insulted or reassured, but at least part of me will be looking forward to it."

She sipped her tea delicately. "Part of you?"

"A man doesn't seek to earn his coin in such a fashion, Lady Longstreet." Darius rose rather than belabor what ought to be obvious. "Were I to say all of me looked forward to seeing you at my farm in Kent, then I'd be admitting I've not even a scintilla of gentlemanly honor left, wouldn't I?"

She kept her seat, for which he accorded her tactical points. "Perhaps you would, but we weren't going to be overly serious about this, were we? And in that regard, don't you think you could call me Vivian?"

He reached down and traced his finger over the curve of her jaw, a slow, lingering touch he'd been imagining since he'd taken her hand in his at the table. Her skin was as soft as it looked, as smooth and pleasing to the touch as her soft daffodil scent was to the nose or her perfectly configured features were to the eye. And her hair would be…

"Vivian suits you," he said. "Vivid, alive, vital. I will see you in a few weeks, but you have my direction should you change your mind."

"I won't change my mind," she said, setting her tea aside and getting to her feet. "I will lose my nerve and fret and dread and argue with William, but I won't change my mind."

"Taking it seriously already, Vivian?"

She went still at the sound of her name, and he could see in her expression genuine misgiving threatened her calm. *A damsel in distress, indeed.*

"A kiss for luck," he suggested, bending his head to brush his lips across hers. He'd surprised her—and himself—when their entire evening had been politely correct, without flirtation or overtures of any kind. And he hadn't meant this as an overture but rather as a reassurance. He was just a man, she was just a woman, and it would be… just sex.

Except it wasn't just a kiss. She went up on her toes and slipped a hand through his hair, around the back of his head. She wasn't as tall as she seemed, he realized when she tucked herself closer and brought her mouth back to his. She used the same slow, brushing approach he'd just shown her, but she lingered as their mouths joined, then sighed a little into his mouth.

Her body sighed too, sinking against him enough that he could feel her curves and planes and softness. He resisted the urge to hold her, to do more than let her press her mouth to his as if she couldn't puzzle out what came next.

When she stayed just there, poised between ending the kiss and seeking more from it, he took the initiative from her and turned his face slightly away, so he could inhale the fragrance of her hair even as his arms came around her.

"It's so odd," she said, leaning into him. "I'm cheating on William, you're poaching on another man's preserves, but we're… not."

He tried to focus on her words, not on the soft, trusting abundance of her resting in his embrace. She sounded as bewildered as he felt, for her words were true.

He was crassly bought and paid for, a stud to service a highbred filly, a cicisbeo in the most vulgar, unflattering sense. A dancing bear of a sort, exploiting his own lusty nature for the simple expedient of coin.

But that kiss… it had been neither expedient nor crass nor vulgar.

He withdrew from her embrace, bowed punctiliously, and met her eyes, putting as much distance into his gaze as he could.

"Until I see you in Kent." He left her standing there in her cozy little dining parlor, her index finger brushing at her lips, her eyes troubled.

She clearly sensed possibilities too, and in his gut, Darius knew he should bow out of the agreement. What should have been tawdry, or at best flirtatious, had been lovely, and no amount of sophisticated humor, good luck, or pragmatism was going to get them through this without somebody getting badly hurt.

Two

VIVIAN LET HER GUEST SEE HIMSELF OUT—A RUDENESS she sensed he'd forgive—and retrieved her half-finished glass of wine from the table.

The meal had gone as well as it might have, right up until she'd given in to a building curiosity about what intimacies with Mr. Lindsey would feel like.

Oh, she knew the mechanics. Her older sister, Angela, had made sure of that before Vivian was even of an age to marry, for it was imperative a girl keep the blunt realities in mind when choosing a husband.

But of the actual getting through the business... Angela had said her wedding night with Jared had been sweet and comfortable. Vivian had seen Mr. Darius Lindsey several times in the park in recent weeks and watched him closely on each occasion—spied on him, really.

Tall, intense, dark, lean, even striking, was how she'd describe him, but he was in need of coin, and he'd be discreet. For those reasons, he'd been her choice for this scheme of William's. The other candidates...

There had been only two others, men raised as

spares—William's requirement—who resembled the youthful William in some particulars, who could be counted on for discretion and honorable behavior toward the child, if any resulted. For her conscience, Vivian had wanted plain, unremarkable candidates. For his vanity, William had insisted on good-looking young men. He claimed no child of his name was going to be burdened with merely average looks, and Vivian—as she usually did—acceded to her husband's wishes.

Mr. Lindsey would keep his handsome mouth shut; of that, Vivian was as certain as she could be, and he'd put William's coin to good use. But having seen Darius Lindsey across ballrooms and parks and streets, having assessed him at some length, she was now concerned she'd just bid too high on a horse she might like watching in the auction pen but never be able to control confidently under saddle.

Darius Lindsey wouldn't merely behave honorably toward a child, he'd be fiercely protective. Vivian knew his sister Leah, knew the lengths Lindsey had gone to in his sister's interests, and knew what a hash of scandal and misery Lindsey had dealt with—still dealt with—on behalf of a mere sister.

For a child, he'd fight to the death, and for that reason—for that reason only—he'd been Vivian's choice.

She had chosen him as a father to her child, and if that meant she had to endure him briefly as an intimate partner—the word *lover* seemed too sentimental by half—then endure him she would. But it wouldn't be sweet or comfortable. Not with him.

❧

"You've seen our guest out?" William looked up from his reading to see Vivian standing in the doorway. She'd dressed modestly for the evening, which he'd expect of her. Vivian Longstreet was that rara avis, a good girl. Muriel had been right about that. Muriel had asked William to look after Vivian, but as his second marriage had matured, William suspected Muriel had put Vivian up to looking after him, too.

How he missed his Muriel, and how she'd delight in the way matters were unwinding at the close of William's useful years. He'd often told Muriel she should have been a man, and Muriel had thought it a fine compliment.

"Mr. Lindsey was a charming if somewhat reserved dinner companion." Vivian closed the door to William's sitting room. "How are you feeling?"

"I am all curiosity." William patted the place beside him on the sofa, but Vivian pulled up a hassock and angled it around to face him. "You have that look about you, Vivian, as if you've been thinking something to death."

"How ill are you, William? Should I be worried?"

The question was insightful, and he should have anticipated it. "I'm not ill in the sense you mean. I am sick to death of Hubert Dantry's stupid parliamentary bills, and weary of life, but I'm not contagious. What does it mean, that Mr. Lindsey was reserved? If he offered you any unpleasantness whatsoever, Vivian, I'll have a talk with him he won't forget."

"He was as pleasant as a serious man can be." Vivian looked preoccupied rather than offended. "And you've talked with him quite enough, thank you."

"Now he's serious and reserved both." William grimaced, thinking of the tedium of schemes that came unraveled. "Did he offend, Vivian? Make you doubt your choice?"

"Doubt my choice, yes. I'll be doubting my choice when your son takes his own bride, William Longstreet. I know if I let you, you'll list any number of cronies and familiars who raised children conceived by similar schemes, but I can't like it."

William set his letters aside. "I know you don't like it, and it isn't my preferred choice either, but you've met the man. Is his person offensive?"

"He's taller than I thought. Bigger."

"Believe it or not, child, back in the day, I was an impressive specimen, though perhaps not quite as tall as Lindsey. He tends to his toilette adequately?"

"He's clean, and he uses some exotic scent."

"Oil of fragrant cananga," Lord Longstreet said. "I find it pleasant, incongruously so, given his saturnine personality. You know, Vivian, you needn't spend much time with him when you're down in Kent. Bring your books and journals, have the *Gazette* sent down, ride out when the weather allows. You can limit your dealings with him to fifteen minutes at the end of the day."

"William…" Her tone was as repressive as it got with him, so he paused to consider her. Young people today were both overtaken with sentiment and constrained by propriety. It was an odd world, and William, for one, was glad he wouldn't be spending much more time in it.

"Vivian." His tone suggested marshaled patience, as

he'd intended it to. "You are young. He's comely and willing. For God's sake, enjoy him."

"It doesn't seem right. You're asking a lot of me, William, but do you realize what you're asking of him?"

She *would* raise this. "I'm asking him to have his pleasures of my pretty wife for several weeks and be paid handsomely for it," William said a trifle impatiently. "This isn't a grand tragedy, Vivian, it's a little holiday in the country that will solve many problems for people who are neither better nor worse than most of St. Peter's clientele, provided you catch."

"There is that detail." She rose, pausing to tuck his lap robe more snugly around him. "And that much, at least, we can leave in the hands of the Almighty, in whom we are regularly exhorted to trust. I'll see you at breakfast."

"Sweet dreams, my dear." William smiled absently as she left and returned his attention to the letters Muriel had written him when he'd first gone off to Vienna without her. Within minutes, he had mentally turned back the clock thirty years, when the world was a less complicated, more exciting place, and wives understood that loyalty was a far more meaningful asset in a spouse than simple-minded fidelity.

⤳

"Join me in a nightcap?" Trent Lindsey held up the decanter so the brandy caught the firelight.

Darius nodded, shrugging out of his greatcoat. "I'm surprised you're still awake."

"Laney's cutting a new tooth." Trent yawned then poured them each two fingers.

"I thought she already did that." Darius accepted his drink and sank onto the sofa facing the fire. Everybody, it seemed, could afford adequate heat except him.

Trent settled in beside him. "She has been doing that since just before we buried her mother. I'm told she's particularly good at it."

"It has been a year since Paula died, hasn't it?" Darius lifted his glass an inch in a personal salute to a long, hard year all around.

"Just this week. Suppose we can take down the black, though I'm dreading it."

"You *dread* putting off mourning?"

"I do." Trent thunked the stockinged version of two large male feet onto the low table. "I do not want to remarry, Dare. Not ever, but these children need a mother."

"You're managing," Darius said, but in truth, Trent looked like hell. He was as tall as Darius and even more robust, typically, but since his wife's death, Trent had been slowly wearing away, losing muscle and life, and, Darius feared, the will to go on.

"I'm managing." Trent yawned again. "You must be deranged to be out sporting around on a night like this."

"I had a dinner engagement." Darius sipped his drink, finding it inferior to what he himself stocked, which was puzzling. "How much do you know of Lord William Longstreet?"

"Viscount Longstreet is one of the senior members of the Lords." Trent crossed his feet, getting comfortable with the recitation. "He has at least ten years on our sire, maybe closer to twenty, and he's universally respected."

"What about the wife?"

"Second wife," Trent said, suggesting the heir to the Wilton earldom still bothered to keep himself informed of these things. "He married his first wife's companion, but rather than be considered a pathetic old billy goat, he was regarded as a white knight. The girl's family was unable to provide much of a send-off for her, and the daughters of earls marry where they must."

"Daughters of earls?" Vivian was a lady then, had been from the moment of her birth. The notion... rankled.

"The title was..." Trent frowned, sipped his drink, then shook his head. "I can't recall, but the fellow died, the title and means went to some cousin, and the countess remarried one of those grasping younger sons who enjoys flaunting his titled wife. He had plans for the daughters, and actually matched the first one up with some... a printer, I think, or publisher. I forget which."

Darius set his drink aside rather than consume inferior spirits simply for their ability to dull his senses. "Teething makes a man forgetful. And the other daughter?"

"She upped and went into service when she was eighteen." Trent closed his eyes. "That's how Lord Longstreet met her. Damned lot of work, if you ask me, taking on a wife young enough to be one's granddaughter."

"She'd be done teething."

"Not if she were my granddaughter." Trent settled a little more heavily against Darius's side. "So why were you keeping such august company, Dare? You thinking of running for a seat?"

"Assuredly not. It's all I can do to manage my one little farm and keep up with Leah's social schedule. I have no coin to campaign on."

"I'm out of mourning now," Trent said sleepily. "I can help with squiring Leah about and so forth."

"You'll need new evening finery. You must have lost two stone, Trent."

"Teething." Trent nodded, not opening his eyes. "What are you doing for the holidays, little brother? Will you join us here?"

A pang lanced Darius's chest. He adored Trent's children, though he ought not to be permitted around them.

"I'll bide in Kent. I can use the peace and quiet, and you've reminded me you'll be free to escort Leah about, should she need it, for a few weeks."

Trent opened his eyes and frowned. "Why doesn't Wilton take his own daughter about?"

"You'd wish him on Leah? The only time she gets out from under his eye is when she has an invitation to some ball or musicale."

"She's received, then?"

"She's received. Not exactly welcomed."

"Society has a damned long memory," Trent groused. "The poor thing has been back from Italy for several years now."

"But a duel was allegedly fought in her honor, and the only thing that allows her admittance at all is our father's title. She's also too old and too self-effacing to threaten anybody's darling daughter."

"Makes one want to fight a duel in truth and blow the ears off Polite Society."

"You're teething," Darius said charitably. "We'll make allowance for that remark."

"See that you do." Trent was soon snoring gently on Darius's shoulder, a comforting, warm weight on a cold, confusing night. Darius rose without disturbing his brother, covered him up with an afghan, and departed for his final stop of the night. This one would take some time, unfortunately, but it provided the coin he needed to go on. So... despite the cold, the dark, and the bitter resistance in his soul, he let himself into the back gate of Blanche Cowell's townhouse, used his key, and silently slipped up to her room. As he divested himself of his coat, hat, gloves, and scarf, he heard her stirring behind her bed curtains.

"You are late."

"Be glad I fit you into my schedule, Blanche." He sat to remove his boots and stockings, unbuttoned his waistcoat, and went on with the routine of undressing in a woman's bedroom while she watched.

"Stop." Blanche emerged from the bed, a flannel night robe belted tightly around her waist, her red hair cascading about her in disarray. "Light more candles first."

He obeyed. He was paid to obey—up to a point. Blanche delighted in defining that point as unpleasantly as she could.

"Shirt next." Blanche walked around him, considering the merchandise as she did. "Breeches last."

Her bedroom wasn't cold, thank God, because Blanche Cowell—*Lady* Blanche Cowell—wasn't about to be uncomfortable while seeking her pleasures. Darius stood naked while she perused her human toy; then her eyes landed on his semierect cock.

"You pretend indifference, Darius, but I can see you're only half succeeding." She smiled a little while she said it, and Darius's heart sank. He hated it when she smiled, but to show anything besides indifference would violate both common sense and the rules of their game.

"I am not at all indifferent to your coin." He scratched his chest and yawned—his niece was teething; he was entitled to some fatigue. "If you intend I earn it tonight by simply letting you gawk, then gawk away."

"You are so arrogant." Blanche advanced on him, and only as she came into the light did he see she had a riding crop in her right hand. It was a short, heavy-handled jumping bat, and the sight of it gave him relief. Blanche's dithering over their choice of activities was more tedium than he could bear at this hour.

In his mind, he had names for her various diversions. Tonight they would play Naughty Pony, one of her less demanding inventions.

"On your hands and knees, Darius." She caressed his thighs with the crop then flicked the lash over his most vulnerable parts. He permitted it long enough to make the point that she was not intimidating him, then dropped to his knees before the fire.

"You were late," she repeated, drawing the tip of the crop down his spine. "And that's bad."

She started whaling on his buttocks, telling him what a disappointment he was to her, how she'd make him pay, and all the while, he brought to mind the images that would encourage arousal. The skill of separating his physical and mental realities was one he'd learned early and well, and one result was he could conjure an erection almost without noticing it. Blanche wanted to believe she was sexually stimulating them both with her antics, and thus Darius accommodated her.

It was a salable skill, and every pony needed at least one trick if he wasn't to end up going to the dogs at the end of the knacker's rope.

❦

"You're restless tonight," Lady Leah Lindsey commented as Darius shifted on the carriage seat beside her.

Restless was one way to describe his condition after last night's outing. "Sometimes it's hard to be comfortable in one's own skin," Darius replied.

Leah studied him with a sister's casual curiosity. "And yet, you seem to do this so effortlessly. The teasing repartee, the dancing and flirting. I don't know what I'd do without you, Dare."

Neither did he, particularly when he considered Leah was still living under their father's roof. "You'd manage, and you'd bring Trent out of hiding perhaps."

"He's put off mourning at least."

"And he says he'll be squiring you about more." Which would be a considerable relief, not that Darius begrudged his sister an escort.

When they arrived at their destination, Darius watched Leah swan off to the ladies' retiring room while he scanned the assemblage for those who would treat Leah with less than perfect courtesy. The company was bland enough that he could relax, until a voice at his elbow had him clenching his jaw.

"Mr. Lindsey." Lucy Templeton, Lady Milne, smiled a brittle, knowing smile. She was in some ways much more trouble than Blanche. "Won't you sit with me?"

"That won't be possible." Darius's smile didn't reach his eyes, not when Lucy was breaking one of his most steadfast rules by approaching him in decent company. "I'm here with Leah."

Lucy scanned the crowd while she sipped her punch. She was arrayed in gold tonight, and while the color did not flatter her blond hair, the symbolism was appropriate.

"Your sister will be behind the ferns, as usual. One does wonder what happened all those years ago with the Frommer boy. Lady Leah is the least noticeable woman ever to claim she's looking for a husband."

"She's not looking, and you'll excuse me."

"Until tonight," Lucy said, quietly. She knew better than to risk more, but even that much was pushing Darius to the limits of his patience.

And she knew that too, and no doubt enjoyed his disquiet thoroughly.

"Not tonight," Darius replied just as quietly. "Perhaps tomorrow night. I have responsibilities to my family that preclude accommodating your plans."

She didn't like that one bit. Darius saw her displeasure in the thinning of her lips, the narrowing of her eyes. "Do you think you can tell me what to do, Darius?"

"I honestly wouldn't bother." Darius's smile

should have been visible at twenty paces. "It's the behavior of your pin money I'm interested in. Until we meet again."

He strolled off, feeling daggers in his back from Lucy's expression. She was getting bolder, less willing to abide by the terms they'd struck months ago. In her way, Blanche was the more biddable of the two—she was merely miserable and taking out on Darius the temper she ought to be turning on her somewhat dense, negligent husband.

Lucy, though, had a true mean streak. Something in the woman wasn't quite right, wasn't... sane.

And dealing with her, with his grieving brother, with his nasty excuse for a father, and his forlorn and vulnerable sister, was beginning to drive something inside Darius past reason as well. This mix of woes and worries had been his primary motivation for accepting Lord Longstreet's scheme—there was coin involved, a great deal of it. Enough to free Darius from the Lucys and Blanches of his life, to provide a small dowry for Leah, to look after Darius's responsibilities in Kent.

Relief of that magnitude was worth thirty days of dropping his breeches for Vivian Longstreet. Darius had dickered and bargained and feinted and sparred with the lady's husband at such length because he'd been convinced Lord Longstreet's plan was his last shot at righting the things off balance in his life.

Before he did something he wouldn't live to regret.

～∞～

Tomorrow, Vivian would travel to Kent, there to bide with Darius Lindsey until after the New Year.

If anybody asked, William would say she was at Longchamps, and at the end of her month in Kent, to Longchamps she would go.

But as her town coach took her home from a visit to Angela's busy, noisy townhouse, those thirty days loomed like a prison sentence. In retrospect, she could see she hadn't used her dinner with Mr. Lindsey very well. She should have been setting out terms— *hers*—not the dry, legal details William had no doubt focused on, but the pragmatic realities.

She didn't want Lindsey intruding willy-nilly at any point in her day. She wanted him confined to certain hours or certain parts of the house. In truth, she didn't want to take meals with him, but to refuse would be insulting.

She didn't want him entertaining her as if she were a guest, expecting her to ride out with him, risk meeting his neighbors, or God forbid, attend services.

She didn't want him in her bed, in fact. They'd have to limit themselves to his chambers or maybe a guest room.

And she most assuredly didn't want him kissing her again. Kissing was by no means necessary to the mechanics of conception.

And she didn't expect to have to… entice him…

"Blast." The coach came to a halt in the Longstreet mews, and Vivian's heart sank further when she saw a groom walking a handsome bay gelding with four white socks. The day needed only a visit from Thurgood Ainsworthy, perpetual stepfather at large.

"Speak of the devil," Vivian muttered as her butler took her wrap. "Has he been served tea?"

"He virtually ordered it, my lady." Dilquin's tone was disapproving. "The knocker has been down since his lordship left yesterday, but that one... Shall we bring a tray?"

"No. Ainsworthy will linger as long as he can over a mere pot of tea. If you could interrupt in about fifteen minutes, I'd appreciate it."

Dilquin's lined face suffused with relief, and his gaze went to the eight-day clock in the hall. "Of course, my lady. Fifteen minutes, precisely."

Vivian spared him a smile then squared her shoulders and prepared to meet her stepfather. It was easy to see—still—why her mother had fallen for the man. Even now, Thurgood was handsome—tallish, though not so tall as Darius Lindsey, say—with soulful brown eyes and blond hair going to wheat gold. He had a superficial charm he put to good advantage when consoling a new widow, and he was clever.

Too clever to underestimate.

"Daughter." He took Vivian's hands and drew her close enough that he could kiss her forehead. By sheer force of will, Vivian endured it without flinching. "You look tired, my dear. Should I be concerned?"

Vivian had to discipline herself not to bristle visibly at his avuncular tone.

"I got William off to Longchamps yesterday, and I'll finish up closing the house today, then follow him myself tomorrow. Moving households is always tiring. Shall we sit?"

He took the chair William usually favored, closest to the fire, and watched while Vivian poured.

"You shouldn't have to fuss over him like this,"

Thurgood said. "He's a grown man, and since when does the wife close up the house and follow? The ladies are supposed to travel at leisure while the head of the household tends to the more demanding matters."

"William and I are content with our arrangements." And if Thurgood were the model, the head of the household *never* tended to the more demanding matters. "How is Ariadne?"

"Your stepmama sends her love, though I couldn't encourage her to be out in this miserable cold. I had to see for myself you were doing well since William has left your side."

"I'll see him the day after tomorrow." Vivian told the lie easily. "How is young Ellsworth?"

"Your stepbrother would send his love as well, did he know I was calling upon you." *Such* a look of regret. "But he's a lad, and what passes for cogitation at his age doesn't bear mention. There is something I wanted to discuss with you, something I've been meaning to bring up for quite a while. William is always hovering, though, and a man can hardly find a moment of privacy with his daughter."

The words *I'm not your daughter* remained firmly clamped behind Vivian's teeth. Ariadne wasn't her stepmother, she was merely Thurgood's fourth or fifth wife, and Ellsworth the Waddling, Whining Wonder Child was no relation to her at all. But better to let Thurgood have his say and be done with it—for now.

Vivian sipped her tea and presented a placid exterior. "I'm all ears, Steppapa."

"William is a good man," Thurgood began, the soul of earnest concern, "but he's going to shuffle off this mortal coil, Vivian, and you must think of what awaits you then. His parliamentary cronies and titled confreres aren't your friends, and they'll do nothing to look after you when William's gone. You need to assure me now you'll not try to manage on your own through those unhappy days. Your mother would turn over in her grave were you to live anywhere but with Ariadne and me, letting us protect and guide you in the time to come."

I must not toss my tea into the face of my guest. "That's kind of you, and generous, but I couldn't possibly make that sort of decision without consulting William, and then too, Angela and Jared might be able to use my help with the children."

Thurgood's face lit with a credible rendition of indignation. "You must not consider it! That Jared Ventnor would have you as some kind of unpaid nanny for Angela's pack of brats, and you an earl's daughter."

"That pack of brats has an earl's daughter for a mother."

"But you could do so much better," Thurgood insisted. "Angela hadn't your looks or your poise or your grasp of political affairs. For you, we could aim much higher."

Just as Vivian's patience was threatening to snap, Dilquin's discreet rap sounded on the door.

"Beg pardon, your ladyship, but Mrs. Weir is insistent that you come to the kitchen to supervise the sorting of the linens and spices. Cook claims Longchamps's inventory is lacking, but the matter requires your attention if she and Mrs. Weir aren't to come to blows."

"I'll be right there." Vivian rose, while her stepfather

tried to hold his ground by staying seated—a subtle betrayal of his upbringing and his true agenda.

"Give me your word, Vivian, that you'll let me be your haven when grief comes calling. You and I have grieved together before, and you know I'll have only your best interests at heart."

His thespian talents should have made him a fortune. "As I said, Thurgood, I can't make such a decision without consulting my very much alive and well husband. It's good of you to call, but I must leave you for my domestic responsibilities."

He affected his Wounded Look, which meant his You'll-Regret-This speech was not far behind, and his frustrated rage not far behind that. Vivian ducked out, directing that Thurgood's hat and coat be brought to him.

There was no squabble in the kitchen, of course, just as Thurgood hadn't grieved the loss of Vivian's mother for more than a few weeks before he'd been busy courting Ariadne's predecessor up in Cumbria and trying to pawn Vivian off on some wealthy, desperate old lecher with no sons and fewer wits. Thank God, Muriel had offered employment, and thank God, William had a protective streak.

Which he seemed to have misplaced, or at least allowed to take an eccentric twist. Vivian reflected on that conundrum all the way down to Kent the next morning, wondering if William hadn't concocted this scheme not for the continued glory of the House of Longstreet, but for *her*, to prevent her from becoming that poor relation at the mercy of Angie's nursery or Thurgood's next moneymaking project.

All too soon, she was being handed out of the coach by the object of her musings. Mr. Lindsey seemed larger than ever, but perhaps not quite as serious.

"My lady." He bowed over her hand. "Welcome to Averett Hill. I hope your journey was uneventful?"

"Considering the roads are frozen and we could have snapped an axle at least a half dozen times, yes, it was uneventful."

"Let's get you out of this cold." Mr. Lindsey drew her toward a tidy Tudor manor. "I have food and drink waiting, unless you'd like to see your rooms first?"

Vivian opted for the truth—several truths. "Something hot to drink sounds good. I sent William to Longchamps in the traveling coach, which means he got the hot bricks while I got the lap robes."

"We can send you back to him in the relative comfort of my traveling coach," her host replied.

She halted in her tracks. "Not if it's recognizable, we won't."

His expression remained... genial. "There's no coat of arms. I wouldn't have made the offer of it if there were."

Vivian had the grace to know she'd been abrupt. "My apologies, I'm just…"

He waited, while she cast around for a way to not make an awkward situation even worse.

She met his gaze and knew she was blushing. "I'm at sea here, Mr. Lindsey. Are we going to enjoy a spot of tea and then repair above stairs, there to…?"

"We can," he said, amusement lighting his dark eyes, "or we can get out of this cold, and while we get you that something hot to drink, discuss how you'd

like to go on." He offered her his arm, and Vivian realized he was standing around in the bitter cold without
a proper winter coat on. His fingers were ink stained,
and his dark hair was riffling in the breeze.

She took his arm, unable to quell the thought that
poor William would have been wrapped up to his
wrinkled brow in such weather, while on Mr. Lindsey,
the cold hardly seemed to make any impression at all.

Three

DARIUS LED HIS GUEST INTO THE STURDY, UNPREPOS-sessing manor house he called home, a little surprised Vivian hadn't cried off. She was nervous, maybe still scared—as he was—and her discomfort sparked some sympathy for her.

A little sympathy, though she was even prettier by day than she had been in the candlelight of her husband's townhouse. Or maybe she was prettier when her natural curiosity had her looking all around at new surroundings rather than listening for the sound of her husband's tread on the floor above.

A long month awaited, for Darius and his guest.

"May I make you a toddy?" Darius asked when they reached his study.

"You burn wood." She approached the hearth, sniffing the air as she pulled off her gloves and extended her hands toward the fire. "I don't know what's worse, the stench of London in winter or in summer. A toddy would be lovely, especially if you'll join me."

"Be happy to." Darius started pouring and mixing

at the sideboard, having made sure the fixings were to hand. "How did you leave Lord Longstreet?"

"Reluctantly."

When Darius interrupted his concocting to approach her, she shrank back against the fire screen then turned her head to the side.

He frowned down at her, feeling a blend of amusement and exasperation. "I am not in the habit of pouncing on unwilling women." He unfastened the frogs of her cloak, which she'd claimed to have kept on in deference to the cold. When he stepped back he heard her exhale and knew a moment's consternation. With Lucy, Blanche, and their ilk, a man had to be the one to pull away, to long for a little more finesse and consideration.

"Do you prefer nutmeg, cloves, or cinnamon?" He laid her cloak on a chair and spoke to her over his shoulder.

"A little of all three?" He heard her rubbing her hands together near the fire.

"My own preference." Darius poured his recipe into a pot and hung it on the pot swing to heat. Beside him, Vivian was staring at the fire as if she could divine the future in its depths.

He laid the backs of his fingers against his guest's cheek. "You are chilled. Shall I order you a bath?"

She flinched at his touch then shook her head. "Mr. Lindsey." She took in a breath and still didn't face him. "I don't think I can do this."

"This?" He used a wooden spoon to stir the butter into the toddies, seeing no reason to give up his place right beside her before the fire.

"Spend this month with you, conceive a child.

Doesn't a woman have to be relaxed to conceive? My sister said…" She broke off and wrapped her arms around her middle, tightly, as if holding in words, emotions, everything.

Darius eyed her posture. "I am not undone by a woman's tears. If you'd like to cry, I come fully equipped with monogrammed linen and a set of broad shoulders."

"I don't w… want to cry," Vivian replied miserably. "Your toddies will boil off."

He swung them off the fire, put the spoon in the pot, and turned her by her shoulders to face him.

"I seldom want to cry either." He urged her against him. "The tears come anyway."

She wasn't very good at being comforted. Darius concluded this when she remained stiff against him for a long moment. Or perhaps she wasn't used to being held, which he could understand better than she'd think.

"Maybe it's your menses bothering you," he suggested, resting his chin on her crown. "You started when, today?"

"Yesterday," she muttered against his collarbone, and Darius felt her relax. "I hate that you know that."

"It's worth paying attention to, if you want a baby." He let his hand trail in a slow caress over the bones of her back, pleased when she didn't bristle further. "And it's nothing to be ashamed of. I have two sisters, and they take great glee in informing a fellow when they're crampy and blue and feeling unlovely."

She stepped back, taking his proffered handkerchief. "It's hard to think of you with sisters, cousins, aunts."

"You'd rather I come with a sniveling leer, pinching the maids and telling bawdy jokes?"

"I don't know what I'd rather," she admitted, sinking down onto the raised hearth. "I'd rather William gave up on this whole ridiculous scheme."

"I thought all women wanted children." Darius sat beside her—which caused her another little startlement—and poured their toddies.

"I do want a baby." She closed her eyes briefly. "When one takes vows, one assumes they mean the children resulting will be those of the husband and wife."

"That's implied but not spelled out," Darius said, wondering how sheltered from the doings of titled society she'd been. "There's that obeying part though, and it's very explicit. I think that's what you're having trouble with." Darius tasted the spoon. "I would too. Try your toddy. It might brighten your outlook."

"You're being charming," she accused but sipped her drink. "Oh, my… winter just became a more bearable proposition."

The hint of mischief graced her smile, which yielded Darius relief from the cold far greater than any toddy offered.

"I'll write down my secret recipe for you." Darius poured his drink and stirred the spices in briskly to encourage the soothing—expensive—aromas of cinnamon, nutmeg, and clove. "I came by it in Italy, got it off an old priest who said he got it from a gypsy witch."

"You lived in Italy?"

They sat there, side by side on the hearth, and gradually, Lady Longstreet thawed. She smiled as

Darius recounted being unable to keep up drink for drink with the local clergy, and some of his own more brilliant mix-ups with the Italian language. A maid brought in a tray of sandwiches, and those disappeared, and still they talked, until Darius's guest had finished her second toddy.

She peered up at him. "So you've put me at my ease—or your toddies have. Now do we get to the pouncing part?"

"By no means." Darius took her empty glass from her and set it on the sideboard, along with any notions he might have entertained involving pouncing in the immediate term. "You are indisposed, and will be for several more days. There will be no pouncing, unless it's Waggles bothering the mice."

"Waggles?"

"A younger relation lives with me here," Darius said, gauging her reaction. "His cat is named Waggles. Don't ask me why."

"Is he your son?" She rose and moved away, starting on an inspection tour of the room. That she would conclude a man available for prurient purposes might have a by-blow shouldn't have been a surprise, and it wasn't—she thought exactly what Darius intended people to think.

Though it was a disappointment.

"He's a relation," Darius said, watching her perambulations. "He's dear to me, though, and I'll tolerate no insult to him."

"I know." Lady Longstreet nodded, even as she picked up a jade-handled letter opener and held it point-first toward her sternum. "It's why I chose you."

"Why is that?" He ambled over and took the letter opener from her hand.

"You will protect this child, if it comes to that," she said, meeting his gaze.

"How could you know such a thing?" He didn't like her reason. He'd rather she had picked him because he was a handsome toy, reliably discreet, naughty by reputation—not this other nonsense.

"I'm of an age with your sister, Lady Leah. I attended her come-out ball. Lord Amherst led her out for her first set, but you danced the supper waltz with her."

"That had to be… eight years ago, at least. Why would you recall such a detail?"

"Because you and your brother Amherst weren't dancing with her from duty. You were genuinely proud of her, and you hovered all evening and monitored her dance card and how much champagne she drank and so forth."

He recalled Leah's come out very clearly—she'd been so happy. How could he not? "I am no longer that man. I'm sorry if you think I am."

"We all change. I am no longer that girl, either."

"One hopes not." Darius considered her, casually denouncing youth while beaming inexperience in every direction. "How would you like to proceed with me this month?"

"I'd like"—she subsided onto the couch—"to put a sack over my head, stuff cotton wool in my ears, and hum some good old Handel while you do the *going on*. You can let me know when I've conceived."

"Interesting approach." Darius couldn't help a

slight smile. "One surmises you'd be more comfortable in darkness then."

"You're going to get mortifyingly personal now, aren't you?"

"A little personal. Not pouncingly personal."

"When does that start?" She wrinkled up her nose, as if they were discussing liming the jakes. Nasty business, but necessary.

"It can start now." Darius settled in beside her uninvited. "Except given your indisposition, that might be untidy. It's up to you."

"I didn't know one could…" She let the observation trail off and turned her face away, though he could see the blush creep up the side of her neck.

"Copulation now isn't likely to result in conception," Darius said, wondering just how much of their bargain William had shared. "That can be part of its appeal."

"How do you know these things?" She studied her hands where they lay in her lap. They were lady's hands, fine-boned, clean, soft, the nails tidily manicured and free of color.

"I'm naughty," Darius said, for once finding it useful, not merely expedient. "Women who disport with me are usually bent on not conceiving, as any childbirth is dangerous, and most are at least inconvenient."

"Are there many women disporting with you?"

Some women knew how to wallop a man broadside with no warning—and Darius had the sense Vivian hadn't even meant to.

"Right now, there's only the one, and she has forbidden me to pounce."

"I have." She nodded, relief evident in the way her shoulders gave. "How do we manage for the next few days?"

"As we please." Darius took one of those hands in his and laced his fingers with hers. "As I see it, I'm a stranger to you, and you to me. While I might be used to dealing intimately with strangers, you are not. I think you'd be better served were we to use the time to become acquainted."

She frowned at their joined hands. "You make it sound logical, while I'm not sure this getting-acquainted business is wise. We're going to have to get thoroughly unacquainted in thirty days, and stay that way."

"I know, Vivian." He patted her knuckles with his free hand. "You need have no fear I'll appear at your balcony, spouting poetry. We have a month, and then, nothing."

"Right. Nothing, except—possibly—a baby."

❧

William Longstreet regarded his son over the chess board, knowing the man was only pretending to consider his next move. Able wasn't an intellectual giant, but he tried to observe the civilities, and he had common sense, for which a father could be grateful.

William stifled a delicate yawn. "My concentration is not what I'd wish it to be. Perhaps I'm still fatigued from traveling."

"It's too damned cold for a man of your dignified years to be shut up in that drafty old coach for hours." Able straightened away from the board. With his lanky frame, brown eyes, and sandy hair, he could have been William forty years past, at least physically. "How about a nightcap?"

William glanced at the clock, wondering idly if Vivian were at that moment bouncing on the sheets with the handsome Mr. Lindsey. William did not envy young Lindsey the effort, which was a sad testament to the effects of great age.

"A drink is in order," William said. "So tell me, Able, how fares my son?"

"I'm well." Able poured them each a couple of fingers of brandy. "The estate had a better harvest this year than last, and as bad as this winter is, it hasn't yet equaled the past two for sheer miserable cold."

"Have you given any thought to running for the local seat?"

Able smiled thinly and resumed his place across the chessboard. "We've had that argument, your lordship. It's generous of you to offer, but I'm not cut of the same parliamentary cloth as you are."

"I wasn't either, the first few years." William held his drink without taking a sip. Not until Muriel had gotten hold of him had he really started to enjoy his parliamentary work. "But the Lords is going to have to cede some power to the Commons. It's inevitable, and the longer they put it off, the worse the struggle will be."

"You're no doubt right." Able usually agreed with his father. "I'm surprised Vivian didn't join you here for the holidays this year."

"She'll be down in a few weeks." William glanced at the clock again. "Her sister, Angela, is expecting a fourth child, and Vivian is a doting aunt. Then too, every couple needs a little breathing room if polite appearances are to be maintained."

"Portia would have my head were I to suggest such a thing." Able's smile was more fatigued than humorous. His drink had disappeared in very short order.

"She seems in good health." One could not say Portia Springer was in good spirits, ever. The woman had a decidedly pinched view of life despite the embonpoint quality of her frame.

"She's sturdy, my Portia. How long can you stay?"

The question wasn't really appropriate, since William owned the home and was technically the host, though Able lived at Longchamps a great deal more than William ever had. Still, the inquiry wasn't mean, but more likely one Portia required an answer to and hadn't had the nerve to put to William directly over dinner.

"I'm not sure." William eyed his drink. "Depends some on Vivian's preferences, since she doesn't particularly like Town life."

"She doesn't?" Able seemed surprised by this. "All that entertaining, all those titles gathered around at her dinner parties, she doesn't enjoy that?"

"Rather dreads it." How was it his wife and his son were no better acquainted? "She's a good sport though, and now that she's figured out most who vote their seat are more interested in the Catholic question than in gobbling her up, she's gotten much better at it." She'd never be quite the hostess Muriel was, but that comparison was hardly fair.

Able crossed back to the sideboard to refill his

drink. "You'd think she'd be here, though, with you, instead of lingering in Town."

"Meaning?"

Able shrugged. "She's young and larking around Town without your supervision, but then, she's not my wife."

"She is mine." William sipped his drink placidly, enjoying the heat more than the flavor. "I've never had reason to doubt her, Able. Not once, not in the use of her pin money, not in her consumption of spirits, not in her choice of social companions. Vivian is a lady."

"Of course, she is."

William saw the comparison with Portia hit its mark. He didn't envy Able his wife. Nobody would.

"You can douse most of the candles," William said, settling in a little more comfortably in his reading chair. "I'll keep my nightcap company here for a bit in solitude."

"If that's your preference." Able dutifully blew out the candelabrum on the table. "I'll bid you good night, your lordship."

William lifted a hand. "Thank you for the game, Able. I promise I'll be in better form tomorrow night."

Able left, no doubt to be interrogated by his wife, while William had to admit he truly missed Vivian. She would have had a lap robe tucked around him, her chess was interesting and sometimes brilliant, her conversation laced with humor, and her form easy to look upon.

Lindsey, to his credit, hadn't even asked about her appearance, though he'd asked a damned lot of other questions—when were her menses due, had she ever miscarried, what had her sister's deliveries been like, what about her mother's? They were the questions of a surprisingly shrewd man, but also the questions of a man who cared about his womenfolk.

With any luck, that number would someday include Vivian. On that cheering thought, Lord Longstreet let himself doze off, because he hadn't lied: he was utterly worn out.

∽

Vivian looked up from her book—a volume of Byron, whom William declared a disgrace on countless levels—when a single knock landed on her door.

"You still awake?" Darius Lindsey strolled into her room, stopping a few feet from the bed. "Now, now, none of that. You look at me like I'm the invading French army. I brought you a nightcap."

"Did you ever consider buying your colors?" Vivian asked, only a little alarmed when he sat on the end of her bed and lounged back against the bedpost. She accepted the drink he passed her, but didn't sip it just yet.

"I did not." He scooted to scratch a shoulder blade on the bedpost, an informality if ever there was one. "My father was not kindly disposed toward my sister Leah. If you're of an age, you probably know that much, so I considered it my responsibility to stick close to her rather than defend King and Country. Then too, until my nephew Ford was born, I was the Wilton spare and obligated to keep body and soul together as a result. Don't forget your drink."

She dutifully sipped but couldn't think of a thing to say to the handsome man regarding her from the foot of her bed.

"What are you reading?"

She eyed the book. "Byron. William would snort with derision."

"Byron himself does a good job of deriding just about everything. Shall I read to you?" He picked up the book where it lay facedown on the counterpane and ran his finger down the page. When he started in reading, Vivian realized the poetry was better for being rendered in the voice of a young man, one jaded, but not quite bitter, and just as unimpressed with Polite Society as the poet was.

"You read well," she offered between verses.

"Better than you finish a nightcap," he said with a slight smile. Vivian took another sip. It was potent stuff, burning a trail down her throat to her innards.

She eyed the little glass dubiously. "What is this?"

"Cognac." He set the book aside. "I favor it in winter. I had another purpose for coming up here."

"You're going to pounce?" She had to ask. He was without cravat or coat—in dishabille by polite standards—and by candlelight, at his ease on her bed, he looked even larger than he had at dinner.

Also… handsomer, plague take him.

"No pouncing for me, delightful as the prospect might be. I haven't been given permission."

"You don't have to do this, you know." She set the drink aside, only to have him move up the bed and take a sip of it himself—from the same place on the rim she'd just put her lips to.

"Do what?"

"Be so… considerate. I'll manage. Earlier, down-stairs, it was just a weak moment. If our good queen could bear fifteen children to a man she'd never met before her wedding day, I'll manage."

"I'm not offering a kingdom in return," Darius said. "Not in the traditional sense."

"What does that mean?"

"I can offer you pleasure, Vivian, or I can be as perfunctory and undemanding as you wish."

"This is an increasingly uncomfortable discussion." Vivian tucked the covers more tightly around her. "Not one I am prepared to have."

"Consider this a discussion of how you want to be pounced upon. You need to decide whether pleasure and duty are mutually exclusive, Vivian. If they are, I'll come to you only when the candles are out and you're under the covers. We need not see each other, in fact, for the duration of this month."

"And if pleasure and duty can coincide?" She knew she'd taken the bait, as he'd intended, but the question was exactly what had been bothering her. Where had her resolve not to socialize with him gone, and why had it seemed so important?

"If duty and pleasure are to coincide, then you have to trust me at least a little to make this a seduction, a pleasure for us both."

"Which would you prefer?"

His eyebrows rose, and that caught her attention, suggesting he wasn't used to being asked his prefer-ences. She stored that realization away for later, and lengthy, consideration.

"My first reaction is to say it makes no difference to me," he said. "I am being paid good coin to achieve a specific end, but I'd rather do that in the manner least upsetting to you. If I had to be honest though…"

"Yes?"

The look in his eyes changed, became slumberous in that instant before he lowered dark lashes and veiled his soul from her scrutiny.

"You are lovely, Vivian, and deserving of pleasure."

He wasn't telling her everything. A man who romped with society women as he did was capable of discretion, of keeping his own counsel. Silence crept up between them and expanded as Vivian considered him. He took another sip of her drink then raised his gaze to hers.

"I propose an experiment," he said, putting her book on the night table. "To help you make up your mind."

The look in his eyes was naughty and entrancing. "What kind of experiment?"

"A good-night kiss. I won't touch you with anything other than my mouth, and you decide whether you like it or not."

She scooted back against her pillows. "Kissing is very personal."

"Just my mouth, Vivian. You simply turn your head and wish me good night if you don't like it. Kissing is not pouncing, not by any stretch. I kiss Waggles."

Surely she could keep up with the standard set by a fat, lazy tomcat?

"Here's my dilemma." She folded the edge of the counterpane into a precise one inch hem. "I don't want you to laugh."

"To laugh?" She could tell he was laughing already.

"I just confessed to kissing a cat, and you think I'll laugh at you? I thought we weren't going to take any of this business too seriously."

"*You* weren't," she corrected him. "You know what you're about."

"Vivian, all I'm proposing is a kiss," he began, but she stopped him with an upraised hand, needing to get this part of the conversation behind them.

"William isn't a… demanding husband."

"I see." The smile spreading across his face was at once beatific and diabolical.

"What do you think you see, Mr. Lindsey?"

"I'm sitting on your bed after dark sharing a drink with you. Don't you think you could call me Darius?"

"I don't want to."

"You're not torn up with conflicted loyalty," he accused, pleased as punch. "You're afraid of yourself, afraid you'll enjoy yourself just as old William so generously intended you to."

"Afraid…" She narrowed her eyes at his hubris. "You're likely afraid I won't, and then where will your swaggering, pawing image of yourself be?"

"Good shot, Vivian." He nodded, still grinning. "But best pucker up, as I'm still here."

In contrast to the great good humor of his words, his kiss was serious. He just leaned in and laid his lips over hers, giving her a moment to startle and breathe and then settle in. When she'd managed all that, he moved his mouth softly over hers, pulling her lower lip between his teeth and sucking gently, then turning his head an inch and tracing his tongue along her lips.

She startled again and thought she heard him chuckle, so she retaliated by using her tongue the way he'd used his to… taste his lips. That earned her his sigh into her mouth, fruity and sweet from their nightcap. And then she felt herself being pressed back against the pillows, until she was lying on her back and Darius Lindsey was balanced over her, braced on his hands.

And it was her turn to sigh, more slowly, more of a bodily sigh or relaxation of her defenses, because in this kiss, he would take care of her.

"Better," he murmured, shifting to cruise his lips over her features. He nuzzled and nibbled and grazed and tasted, her jaw, her forehead, her chin, and then back to her mouth, until she was happily melting into the bedclothes, ready to concede that duty and pleasure could disguise each other thoroughly.

And then the real kissing began, as his tongue stole past her lips, into her mouth, and began to insinuate beautiful, naughty, wonderful, previously unimaginable notions. She tried to follow his lead, until she realized her hands were tangled in his thick, dark hair, pulling him down to her, and her body was…

"Merciful heavens." She turned away by force of will but kept her hand wrapped around the back of his head, inviting him to rest his forehead on her collarbone.

"That is a little taste of option A," Darius said, sitting up.

Why was any effort at all involved in letting him go? "And option B?"

He leaned in again, and when she'd inhaled in

anticipation of another rousing, lingering, soul-stealing kiss, he put a brotherly peck on her forehead.

"Good night, Vivian." He rose, took her glass from the night table, and turned to leave.

"That's it?" She struggled up to her elbows. "Good night, Vivian?"

"Good night, Lady Longstreet?"

"Get out." She tossed her book at him. "Just go, and I hope you sleep miserably."

He stopped at the door to blow her a kiss, still smirking, and Vivian realized she was smiling too. Awful man—how was she supposed to sleep after that?

Which, she reflected, had likely been the point of his experiment.

⤞⤟

Darius took himself to his bedroom, resisting the urge to stand outside the door and listen for the sounds of Vivian Longstreet going to bed. She'd be methodical: banking the coals, replacing the fireplace screen, snuffing each candle, and in all likelihood, locking her door. Her place in her book would be carefully marked with a bookmark—no dog-eared pages for her naughty Lord Byron—and she'd kneel beside the bed to say her prayers, no matter how drafty the floor, no matter how her knees might ache.

William Longstreet had taken a perfectly lovely young woman to wife and made her elderly, as well as deaf, dumb, and blind to her own appeal.

Darius had been more honest than she'd known, when he'd said she deserved pleasure. She deserved heaps and hoards of it, years of it, but instead she'd gotten duty. As he readied himself for bed, he had to wrestle with a question: Vivian deserved a romp, a frolic, a few weeks decadently rife with flirtation and sexual gratification. He was in a position to give her that, but as she'd said, then what? A virtual spinster, she'd be ill equipped to deal with the attachments that formed when two people were physically intimate.

Except, he could teach her that too. He could teach her to flirt and carry on and enjoy herself, and part with a sigh and wave before moving on to the next enjoyment. Clearly, Lord Longstreet had urged her in that direction, but Vivian had been too timid to dip her toe in the waters of dalliance.

Or maybe, she had been too wise.

By habit, he checked on John before turning in, finding the child fast asleep in his bed, the tomcat blinking slowly as Darius closed the door to the boy's room.

He could fathom pleasuring Vivian, could imagine it all too easily, but far more difficult was the idea that she was eager to bear his child. He'd seen it in her eyes—she wanted a child, and to his surprise, he wanted that for her as well.

And this, he reasoned as he climbed between cold sheets, was why he didn't allow other women the intimacy of coitus with him. It made a simple situation complicated and had him wishing all manner of impossible things, when he really should be too tired to give a damn.

Vivian Longstreet should be a means to put a new roof on his stable, a duty, a convenient source of revenue, and here he was, offering to escort her past reason into the land of sexual pleasure and harmless dalliance. Offering her a choice had been rash, and upon reflection, he wished he could recall his words and sneak into her bed of a night, pretending by day her body had been shared with some other man. That would be smarter—better, at least for him.

But by breakfast, Darius had come to a decision: if she allowed it, he was going to pleasure Vivian Longstreet out of her clever, nimble, ladylike mind.

Four

THE DRESS MADE UP DARIUS'S MIND, A SHAPELESS, NO doubt warm atrocity in a color that put him in mind of calf scours.

"Good morning, Mr. Lindsey." Vivian smiled at him shyly when Darius seated her at the breakfast table.

"Good morning." He let himself lean in for a little whiff of her, catching the scent of daffodils. Lemon verbena might have been more retiring, but only just. "I trust you and Lord Byron slept well?"

Her smile widened. "I wouldn't presume to speak for him. I slept like the proverbial baby."

"I've wondered where that phrase came from." Darius poured her tea. "My experience with babies suggests they are better at waking entire households than sleeping. May I fix you a plate?"

"Thank you." She accepted the tea. "You've had the raising of your... relation since infancy?"

"I've had exclusive responsibility for him since shortly after his birth."

"How old is he now?"

"He'll join us shortly." Darius focused on sorting

through the ham slices to find one he deemed thick enough for her. "You can ask him yourself, but be warned, he can talk nonstop for days."

"Not a typical male." Vivian frowned at the plate he set before her. "I can't possibly eat all of this."

"Especially"—Darius took a slice of bacon off her plate—"if you stare at it until it gets cold. You start, and when you've had your fill, you stop."

"But that's waste…" He stuffed a bite of bacon into her mouth between syllables, and finished the strip himself.

"I like it crisp like this," she said. "William likes his thicker than I do, and oh, you've had cheese cooked in the eggs, you shameless man."

Darius nodded complacently and sipped his tea. "That would be me." Did Longstreet even realize what a treasure he shared breakfast with each morning? Did he see her or merely disappear behind *The Times* and consume his soggy bacon?

"Is this the lady?" a small voice piped.

"Good morning, John." Darius smiled at the lad who hovered in the doorway. "Make your bow."

"Good morning, my lady. John Cowperthwaite Lindsey, at your service." He bowed dramatically and came up grinning. "You're our guest, so I'm on pro… I have to behave."

"Probation." Darius hoisted the child onto his lap. "If you're on your best behavior, you can have breakfast with us, and perhaps we'll go riding while Lady Vivian is here."

Lady Vivian, not Lady Longstreet, because Darius intended to exercise as much discretion about her visit as he could.

"Do you like horses?" The look John aimed at Vivian suggested this was *the* pressing question of the day.

"Very much. Do you like bacon?" She held up a crispy slice.

"Darius?"

"You may."

"Thank you!" John took the slice of bacon and was away from the verbal starting line at a gallop, waving his bacon around minus one bite as he spoke. "I have a pony. He's old but sturdy, and his name is Hammond. He doesn't like Waggles, because Waggles is sneaky and hard to see in the dark, which is good for hunting mice, though there aren't any in my bedroom 'cause Wags sleeps with me. May I please have another piece of bacon?"

"I'll fetch you a plate." Darius rose and sat the child in his own seat as John went on about how cold weather made his pony harder to groom, but friskier, which was good.

"Would you like to go riding?" John raised brown eyes to Vivian, and Darius swore the boy was batting his lashes at her.

"It's too cold for riding today," Darius warned. "We can introduce Lady Vivian to Hammond, if she's amenable."

"What's amendable?"

"Amenable," Vivian corrected him. "Willing, which I am." As he put a plate before the child, Darius shot her a naughty smile—the opportunity was too good to let pass. "Willing to meet your pony, that is."

"Capital!" John started on his eggs. "I visit him

every day before my lessons. Darius says the company of a horse starts a gentleman's day off right, and I take care of him all by myself, except sometimes Dare helps. What's your horse's name?"

"I don't have just one," Vivian said. "When I want to ride, the lads tack up a mare and off I go."

John frowned as Darius gestured to the child to put his serviette on his lap. "But what's her *name*? You have to know your horse's name, so you can say, 'Whoa, Hammond,' or 'Good boy, Ham.' You know, her name?"

"One of them is named Pansy, or I've heard the lads calling her that, so it's probably her nickname."

John devoured his breakfast, peppering Vivian with questions as his eggs, toast, and most of Vivian's bacon disappeared, while Darius sat back and watched.

"John, you need to put on your boots and collect a carrot or two for your steed," Darius said when the child's plate was clean. "Lady Vivian needs another cup of tea, and then we'll meet you in the kitchen."

"Yes, sir." John scooted off his seat then paused abruptly. "Sorry, I forgot. I am still on proba… Whatever that word was?"

"Probation," Darius supplied. "You caught yourself, and having such a pretty lady at table is distracting, but let's do it right, shall we?"

John resumed his seat and met Darius's eye. "Sir, the meal has been very good, but I'd like to visit my pony now. May I please be excused?"

Darius smiled. "Well done. You may."

"Thanks for the bacon!" John dashed off, leaving the door to the breakfast parlor banging in his wake.

"What a delightful little boy," Vivian said in the ensuing silence. "You must be very proud of him."

"I am, and I'll be just as proud of you if you finish your toast."

"I told you I couldn't possibly…"

He passed her a half slice, slathered with butter and jam. "It's cold out, and you'll need your sustenance." He held it to her mouth, and her hand came up to cover his. She took a bite and sat back.

"Raspberry." She munched away. "My favorite."

"Let me guess." Darius put the rest of the slice on her plate. "William prefers some bitter old marmalade, and you haven't had raspberry jam since you married him."

"Of course I've had it." She picked up her toast. "At my sister's I have it all the time. My brother-in-law knows I like it, so he keeps it on hand."

"Your brother-in-law knows your favorite type of jam, but your husband does not," Darius observed, pouring her another cup of tea. "Why aren't I surprised?"

"What's your favorite kind of jam?" Lady that she was, Vivian wasn't going to argue with him, but Darius found it heartening she didn't try to defend dear Lord Longstreet.

Darius added cream and sugar to her tea. "As of this moment, it's raspberry."

He switched their plates, finishing the last of her eggs without her permission as she enjoyed her toast and tea. When they'd made their way to the kitchen, Darius insisted on tying the fastenings of her cloak and winding a scarf around her neck.

"Bonnets might be fetching, but they aren't warm, and they obscure a lady's lovely face."

"But this is your scarf," Vivian protested as he led her across the back gardens.

"How can you tell?"

"It has your scent," she said, then apparently realized what she'd admitted. "And what is your scent, by the way?"

"It's Eastern and mixed to my order and used to scent my soaps, lotions, and linens, and that is one of the first things we're going to address, Lady Vivian."

She slipped her arm free of his. "Address?"

"You have been languishing in your husband's care." Darius opened the barn door for her. "It's time you took yourself in hand."

"I do not follow your meaning, Mr. Lindsey."

"Take your dress." Darius paused to remind John, gamboling ahead of them, not to run in the barn. "Who in his right mind made a dress out of that fabric?"

"It's very practical." Vivian glanced down at her skirts, expression puzzled. "I got a superior bargain on the entire bolt."

"Because it's the exact color of the results of a young bovine having intestinal distress," Darius countered. "You should not be allowed in public in such a color, Vivian. Trust me on this."

Her perfectly arched brows knitted. "Why should I trust you? You're a man."

"Who appreciates women with particular intensity. That dress is going to the maids, and you are going into the village with me, where we have a passable seamstress who no doubt is lacking for work this time of year."

"You're *dressing* me?" Vivian stopped, clearly bewildered at such a notion.

"And we're going to find you a scent, play with your hair, experiment with cosmetics," he went on. "And for God's sake, why don't you have a personal mount?"

"What are you going on about? I have as many horses to ride as I wish."

Darius crossed the barn aisle to a loose box. "This is my personal mount. His name is Skunk, and he's a good fellow."

"Peculiar coloring." Vivian held out a gloved hand to the horse whose black and white coat was reminiscent of a milch cow. The gelding left off eating his hay long enough to sniff delicately at her fingers.

"His plebeian coat pattern is why his steady disposition, perfect conformation, and good bone were overlooked," Darius said. "He suits me and we get along and he's *my* horse. Nobody else rides him, and he's always available for me. You need a personal mount, a fetching steed who takes your welfare seriously and isn't just anybody's hack."

He wasn't merely talking about horses, and Vivian was astute enough to know it.

She held out her hand to John. "Introduce me to Hammond. And is that a cat I see?"

Darius watched as John explained in painful detail how he groomed his pony. Vivian asked the right questions, and was graciously granted a turn with the soft brush, while Darius wondered what it was he was feeling.

She was good with John, and that solved a looming problem in itself. A month was too long to send the child off with the servants, and yet, Vivian might have resented sharing the household with a bastard child, particularly given the point of her stay at Averett Hill. She didn't resent John, just the opposite.

She'd be a good mother, which was part of what had Darius's insides unsettled.

"Let me introduce you to Bernice," Darius said, interrupting John's chatter.

"She's a mare," John provided helpfully. "So you can ride her."

Vivian gave the pony's shaggy neck a final pat. "She's to be my mount?"

"If you'd like," Darius said. "She's very gentle, but she'll take care of you. She's not... passive, like some horses are. She'll think of your welfare."

"You've ridden her?" Bernice was a good-sized dapple gray with big eyes and an inelegant pink nose.

"I have," Darius said. "I wouldn't put a guest, much less a lady, on a horse I couldn't speak for personally."

Vivian frowned at him then turned to the mare, stepping into the horse's stall for a closer introduction. "She's larger than the horses I usually ride."

"You're taller than many women," Darius replied, fishing a piece of carrot out of his pocket and passing it to Vivian. "You need a horse in proportion to your seat and leg. I thought Bernice would fit you."

"She has a kind eye." Vivian fed the horse the carrot. "Wonderful manners."

"Consider her your personal mount for the duration,"

Darius said. "John will offer to walk her out for you, and if you don't mind, I'd allow it."

"She's that docile?"

"He's that comfortable with horses, and Bernice is a lady, or I wouldn't have paired her up with you."

"You're flirting somehow."

"Stating a fact," he said, leading Vivian from the stall. "John, if you groom that pony any longer, he's going to fall asleep. Get you back up to the house, and I'll expect to hear at least three perfect Latin verbs at teatime."

"Will Lady Vivian hear my Latin?"

"I will," Vivian said, "and I will be on my extra good manners at tea if I know there are to be two gentlemen present." She shot an arch look at Darius. "We can all be on probation together."

"Capital!"

⁂

Vivian missed her husband. Missed the steady, dependable, boring routine of their life together. Missed knowing the answers before the questions were asked. She'd fallen asleep the night before, secure in the conviction that the next day she could explain to Mr. Lindsey that she'd choose Option B. William had said she could limit her dealings with the man to fifteen minutes at the end of the day, and Mr. Lindsey himself had acknowledged as much.

That way would be safer for everybody. Simpler.

But then… that child had joined them at breakfast, and Vivian's heart had started beating harder in her chest.

Darius Lindsey loved that boy. He'd die for a child who had clearly been cast off by his parents as an embarrassment. And Vivian wanted to see more of the man who'd taken in the boy and raised him to be such a charming little gentleman. The difficulty was, the man who noticed that a child's manners needed praising was also a man who'd noticed Vivian's husband didn't know her favorite jam.

Vivian herself had nearly forgotten.

She glanced down at her dress, running her hand over the nappy, plain fabric. It was warm, sensible, durable, economical…

And *ugly*. The same color as calf… diarrhea, he'd said.

A metaphor for her life, maybe.

She wished her sister were on hand to talk with, wished she had anybody to parse with her the dilemma she faced. Darius Lindsey was dangerous, and not just because he loved the child in his care. Vivian glanced out her window to see it was already dark, nigh teatime, when a knock on the door interrupted her musings.

"Are you cavorting with Byron again?" Darius asked as he eyed her sitting on the bed.

"We're through, Lord Byron and I. He's fine for a passing amusement, but the man lacks depth."

"Thus speaketh Polite Society about one of its own," Darius replied as he lowered himself beside her. "Do you shrink away from me out of habit, or are you afraid I'll end up sitting in your lap by accident?"

"I don't…" She stopped and tried for honesty. "You're very informal. I'm not used to it."

"Doesn't William touch you? I thought that was

one of the blessings of marriage, that one had permission to touch and be touched, not just in bed."

"I touch William. I'm forever tucking in his lap robes, holding his jackets for him, tugging off his boots."

His smile became knowing. "I'll bet he still has the same valet he had when his first wife was alive."

"He does. William is frequently required to wear formal attire, and a valet... what?"

"My brother is heir to an earldom, and he sacked his valet as soon as he married. Many men do upon marriage, unless they're exceedingly toplofty."

"Muriel was too ill..." Vivian fell silent.

"Even when she was still cutting a dash," Darius guessed, "her husband had his valet."

"What is the point of this digression?"

"You are a married spinster," he accused quietly. "For this, I cannot forgive your dear William, and neither should you."

"I am not a married..." She closed her eyes, and her shoulders slumped. "What do you mean?" Though she could guess. She could guess all too easily.

"Come here." He rose and tugged her to her feet, then slipped his hand around her wrist to pull her over to the full-length mirror. "You're a beautiful woman, Vivian Longstreet, but look there and tell me what you see."

She shrugged, unwilling to look in the mirror. "So the dress is unprepossessing."

"Look." He stood behind her, his hands on her shoulders trapping her before him. "Look, Vivvie, and see."

Purely to make him hush, she regarded her reflection. "An ugly dress. A serviceable, plain, ugly dress."

"An atrocious dress," he rejoined, "an abomination in calf scours yellow that obscures a luscious feminine figure. You're also sporting a bun my granny would disdain to wear in public, lips pinched with disapproval that should be rosy with kisses and laughter, and eyes dull with boredom that should sparkle with mischief."

"You're to give me a child, Mr. Lindsey, not a lecture."

She'd turned her face, but because he still held her, that only put her cheek against his fingers where they'd settled on her shoulders.

"I will do my damnedest to give you that child, Vivvie." He turned her, keeping his hands on her shoulders. "Consider allowing me to give you a little more than that. Let me give you a few weapons to use when William isn't there to protect you."

"What manner of weapons?" And why would she much rather stare at him than her ugly dress?

"The weapons every female needs to know how to use if she's to move in polite circles safely. You need to see yourself as you could be, as you need to be."

His thumbs made little circles on her shoulders as he spoke. Impossible-to-ignore little circles. "Need for whom?"

"You're the Viscountess Longstreet," Darius said, exasperation creeping into his voice. "If you bear this child, who will be his or her guardian in the event of William's death?"

"I'm not sure. William will make provision, I know, and he's in good health, so that day can't be near at hand."

"Vivvie." Darius peered down at her. "You need

to have a frank talk with your spouse, but whoever the guardian is, you're going to have to handle him to your own satisfaction."

"What do you mean, *handle* him?" She put the question to him with equal parts dread and curiosity.

"What if he wants to send your son off to public school at age seven?"

Vivian's brows shot up. "Seven? I thought I'd just get tutors and governors and so forth. *Seven?*"

"Seven. Little boys go into men's hands at seven, and for many, that means boarding at public school. What if this guardian wants your son to spend summers and holidays with him, rather than with you?"

"Surely William wouldn't allow that?" Vivian's fingers touched her lips. "He could make stipulations, couldn't he, in his will?"

"Not that anybody would enforce. Unless William lives to be a hundred, you're going to be the only parent this child has, and between the guardian, the solicitors, and the tutors, your say will count little, unless you make it count."

Foreboding took up residence in Vivian's middle. Why hadn't anybody pointed this out to her? Why hadn't William told her what the provisions of his will were? Why was she trying to have a child without having thought these considerations through?

"So what would you have me do?" She turned back to the mirror. "Who would you have me be?"

"The mother of my only child," he said softly. "A lioness no man would tangle with willingly. A lady who isn't afraid to fight for what she believes in and knows to be right for her child. I can't be there in any noticeable way. William can't be there. You're the child's only champion, Vivvie, and you need to start now to step into that role."

She met his gaze in the mirror. "The dress goes."

"For starters."

"For starters," she agreed, standing taller on the strength of the words alone.

❧

Within three days, Vivian knew what it was to hate a man. Oh, she despised her stepfather, but Ainsworthy was simply venal, his schemes and ambitions predictable and mundane. He was evil, but in a sense, he couldn't help himself.

Darius Lindsey, by comparison, was ruthless, cunning, and relentless. He'd put her through one tribulation after another.

At the modiste's, he'd dressed her from the inside out, choosing nightgowns, chemises, stockings, *everything*, from laces and trims to dress fabrics and patterns. He suggested alterations, sketching creations Vivian never would have dreamed of.

"You need to accentuate your height," he insisted on their way back to the manor, "not try to hide it. William is tall. You're not going to embarrass him if you dress well at his side. Stop fidgeting."

"Stop touching me. You handled me in that shop like I was some… prize hound, my conformation and coloring shown off for company." And thank God the modiste had been French and not the least dismayed by his behavior.

"You're not a hound, though you're definitely a

prize. A treasure, a gem of surpassing beauty. And I've about had it with your bun."

"My *bun*? You've had it with my bun?" She drew herself up on the seat of the phaeton, prepared to reel with righteous exasperation, when a rut in the road pitched her against him. "Bother."

Darius smiled over at her. "Did you even think of lingering there, leaning against my side before you pokered right up again?"

"Why would I lean against you when I can sit perfectly well unassisted?"

"Lean against me, Vivvie, just a little."

She gave him a look intended to put him in his place—several counties distant.

"Come here, Viv-vie," he singsonged. "Just a little lean on a deserted lane, as if you're a touch cold or tired or in want of a cuddle."

"You are ridiculous," she spat, except she *was* cold and tired and maybe that other thing he'd said.

He slipped the reins into one hand and tucked an arm around her waist, drawing her closer to his side.

"Were you truly ambitious," he murmured, "you'd allow me a hint of the side of your breast against my arm, just in passing."

"Whyever would I do that?" But she stayed leaning against him, strictly because he was warm and solid.

He smiled at her, a charming, naughty smile. "To scramble my wits, sweetheart. Then you could slip in a little observation about how the green velvet walking dress might look just as fetching in a dark brown with green trim, and next thing you know, I'd be offering to order it for you in both green and brown. Given what William is paying me, I can afford to indulge you in one more frock."

"You want me to... *wheedle*?"

"I want you to have what you want, however you have to exert yourself to get it," he said, turning them up the lane to the manor. "You're willing to disport with me to get a baby, Vivian. Why not a little wheedling to get something simpler?"

His version of reasoning would scramble *her* wits in short order. "I know nothing of this wheedling. It sounds tedious and demeaning."

"What's demeaning is having to depend on others to meet your every need, because you can't use the strengths you have to do it yourself."

Vivian kept her voice low by sheer self-discipline. "*What* strengths? I'm a married female. I have no rights, no property, no wealth. I can't hire or fire my own staff, I can't enter into business ventures unless I inherit them from family once I'm widowed. I can't even name my own child, does my husband forbid it. What damned strengths?"

"That's a start," he said slowly, smiling over at her.

"You have me using foul language. Cursing is not an indication of strength, but just the opposite. And that reminds me, Mr. Lindsey, when am I to conceive this baby you're always going on about? I've been here four days, and you've run me ragged to milliners and cobblers and modistes and had me reading all manner of scandalous tripe and riding the countryside in this weather, and *none of that is in aid of conceiving a child*."

Let him argue that.

"Are you inviting me to your room tonight, Vivvie?"

He drew the vehicle to a halt in silence, jumped down, then came around to lift her off the seat. As the groom led the horse away, they stood in the stable yard, Darius's hands on her waist.

His expression was no longer teasing, nor was it even flirtatious. He stood there, regarding her almost solemnly.

She bit her lip. "Maybe not tonight."

He studied her expression for a moment then turned her under his arm and led her toward the house. "Still untidy?"

"Some." She was blushing, drat it all to perdition. Drat *him*. "Not much longer."

"I'll come to you," he said, holding the back door for her.

"But I thought…"

"Trust me." He dipped his head to kiss her cheek as he untied the frogs of her cloak. "I won't do anything you don't agree to, and as much trouble as I've had convincing you to try a few fripperies on, we won't get very far in a single night."

"I don't want…" She glanced around the deserted kitchen.

"What don't you want?" He hung her cloak and his coat on pegs, then swung the kettle over the fire and began assembling a tea tray. "Tea?"

She moved to stand beside him. "I dread this."

"You've yet to tell me how we're to go about it," he reminded her. "My brother favors Darjeeling, so I keep some around, but I'm more partial to a mild oolong. What about you?"

"What about me?" Tea and copulation in two

consecutive sentences. She was going to end up in Bedlam. "I like mine with cream and sugar."

"Vivvie." He tucked an arm around her waist. "You are a disgrace." He made it sound like an endearment though, and Vivian dropped her head to his shoulder.

"How we're to go about what?" she asked, though she knew exactly *what*.

"Do I merely service you," he asked, moving away to get down mugs, not teacups, "or will you let me pleasure you?" He retrieved the cream from the cold box at the window, apparently able to discuss one appetite while preparing to fulfill another.

"Is this how these things are decided?" She watched him moving around the kitchen. "Between trips to the pantry?"

"Come here." He backed toward the dark confines of the pantry, tugging her with him. "I've been wanting to do this for days."

"Do…?"

When she was sharing the small, orderly confines of the pantry with him, he settled his lips over hers and wrapped her close against the warmth of his larger body. The heat of him felt heavenly, and Vivian knew with a sudden certainty the weight of him would feel just as good.

She'd learned a little in their two previous kisses, and tasted his lips with her tongue before he got around to offering her the same gesture. She felt the pleasure and surprise go through him, felt it in the way he gathered her closer, and in the way his body seamed itself to hers.

"More." He whispered it against her neck, and

the sensation of his breath on her skin sent tendrils of pleasure curling through her vitals. His hand slid down her back and cupped her derriere, urging her more closely against him. "More, Vivvie, please…"

Vivvie… when had he started calling her that?

When had she decided she liked it?

She opened her mouth beneath his and invited him in for a taste, squirming against his chest when his tongue came calling. When she moved, her breasts pressed more snugly against him. This relieved some vague discomfort welling up from her middle, so she did it again, more slowly.

"That's my girl…" His hand traveled around from her hip, up to her waist, then her side, and then, glancingly, along the side of her breast.

"You…" She broke the kiss to look up at him. "You're wheedling."

"Not yet." He nuzzled her neck, and Vivian was abruptly aware of a different pressure, nuzzling against her abdomen. He rocked against her, ensuring she'd know what that rigid length was, setting up a slow, naughty rhythm that made her insides hum.

"Now." He closed his eyes and kissed the side of her neck. "Now, I'm wheedling." He kept up that slow rocking, until the teakettle whistled and Vivian stepped back, bumping into the shelves behind her.

"The tea…" She glanced out into the kitchen.

"Answer me first, Vivvie love." He let his hand slide down her arm then trail away. "Pleasure or duty? You decide."

She gave him a look, feeling undecided, torn, aroused, and miserable.

"Both."

She bolted into the kitchen, having used up her entire store of courage in a single syllable, and didn't see him grinning like an idiot while he adjusted a raging erection behind his falls.

Bless her, she'd lit on the one and only correct answer.

Five

SEVERAL HOURS LATER, VIVIAN WAS DEBATING HER FATE from the soapy, fragrant confines of a steaming-hot bath.

The bath Darius Lindsey had ordered for her.

The knowledge he had of women was... disquieting. Vivian considered his insistence that she join him here in Kent as her menses began, and realized from the moment she'd laid eyes on him, he'd known something more personal about her than her sister generally knew. More personal than William *ever* knew, except this once.

From the moment Darius had laid eyes on her, the exact cycle of her body had been shared between them. Such knowledge was appallingly intimate, the sort of thing Vivian suspected Jared and Angela might both know but never discuss.

With Darius Lindsey, whom Vivian had known less than a week, the topic had been discussed. Everlasting God.

She rinsed her hair a final time and stood, letting the water sluice off her body as she reached for a thick, warm bath sheet.

He understood a lady's comforts, and the idea made her shiver in anticipation. She hadn't known this about him when she'd chosen him. She'd known he was fierce, discreet, and in need of coin. William hadn't questioned her choice though, and that had to mean something.

A knock on the door as Vivian shrugged into a dressing gown had her heart speeding up, but it was only Gracie, the maid of all work. She seemed to manage easily despite a slightly withered arm, balancing a tray on her hip while she pulled the door closed.

"Master Darius sent you up a toddy," Gracie said. "I'm to brush out your hair so it dries before bedtime. If you're decent enough, I'll have the tub taken away."

Vivian took a seat at the vanity, trying to recall the last time somebody else had brushed out her hair. Her lady's maid—formerly Muriel's maid and not a young woman—had never volunteered for the task. "Why do you call him Master Darius?"

"Habit," Gracie said, turning down the sheets on the bed to warm, then going to the door. "Come on, you lot, and step quick, as there's leftover toddy still on the hob in the kitchen."

A procession of servants—the scullery maid, the boot boy, a footman, and the groom from the stables—made quick work of removing the tub, buckets, and screens, leaving Vivian to sip her toddy before the fire.

"Let's get you seated," Gracie said, pulling the dressing stool over by the fire. "And my heavens, you've more hair than I've seen in a while."

"Are there footmen in this household?"

"Oh, sometimes." Gracie started gently toweling

Vivian's hair dry. "Master Darius hires us and gives us coin for our labor. We don't fret too much about who wears which jobs when the work piles up. The grooms will help out with the chimneys. The footmen will muck a stall come summer. We do pretty much as Pitt directs us."

"Mr. Pitt is the butler?"

"On his good days." Gracie switched to brushing, starting with the ends of Vivian's hair. "Pitt used to work at Wilton Acres, but he got too old, and Lord Wilton turned him off, so here he is."

The toddy was wonderful, another comfort, courtesy of her… of Darius Lindsey. "Wilton turned off a loyal retainer without a pension or character?"

"Wilton's like that. We're not to speak ill of our betters, but that Wilton is a scandal. Let's turn you a bit, shall we?"

"What about the other brother, Lord Amherst?"

"Master Dare dotes on him," Gracie said, expression brightening. "Loves those kiddies, too. A child never had a more devoted uncle than Master Dare."

"John loves him," Vivian said, sipping her toddy.

"And we all love our Master John. Turn again, milady."

"Did you all work at Wilton Acres?" This was prying, shameless, unladylike prying, but no more personal than having to tell a man about the very rhythms of one's body.

Gracie paused to work at a tangle. "We don't all come from Wilton, but we worked somewhere, and most of us were let go through no fault of our own. Word gets out, though, when a man's willing to take a chance on people. Master Dare puts us to work, and if we've a mind to move on, he writes the best characters and lets us know he appreciates our loyalty."

This toddy had a particularly lovely mixture of spices—something blending the cinnamon, clove, and nutmeg together. Something subtle and exotic—cardamom? Allspice? An extravagance, surely, and one Darius Lindsey had expended on *her*. "How long have you worked here, Gracie?"

"Years. Most wouldn't hire me, 'cause of me arm, but it hardly slows me down a'tall, and Master Dare knows that. Turn."

Vivian sipped her drink in silence, considering what Gracie had said. It was true. Servants in the better homes were expected to be attractive—whole, fit, and comely. She'd not considered this before, because William's residences had been fully staffed before she'd married him.

But in five years they'd had some turnover—and the butlers or house stewards had hired the men, while housekeepers hired the maids.

And the lady of the house did exactly… what?

"There you go." Gracie stepped back. "Can I fetch your book, milady, so you can stay here by the fire while your hair finishes drying?"

"I'll get it." Vivian took one last, scrumptious whiff of the dregs in her glass and stifled a yawn. "Are there really leftover toddies in the kitchen?"

"Master Dare's toddies are legendary. I had a taste as he was putting in the spices, to make sure he got it right."

"It was lovely," Vivian said, handing over the glass. "No more for me, or I'll be asleep on my feet."

"Good night, then, milady. Pleasant dreams."

"Thank you, but, Gracie?" Vivian hoped neither her tone nor her expression gave away the depth of her curiosity.

"Milady?"

"Does Mr. Lindsey have other guests here, other ladies?"

Gracie met her gaze for the merest instant. "Never overnight, milady. You'd best be asking him about that directly."

Vivian nodded, understanding that Gracie had just passed along a tidbit, one woman to another, that came up against but did not cross the boundaries drawn by a devoted employee. Vivian was still sitting on the hearthstones, trying to puzzle out if she wanted to know of Darius's other associations, when he knocked once and stood in her doorway.

"You're letting in the cold air," she said.

He pulled the door closed behind him. "Your hair is even more lovely than I'd imagined, and longer."

"You're not supposed to see it down," she groused, stifling another yawn. "And the toddy was a masterful touch. Should I take my clothes off? I'd rather climb under the covers first."

He smiled slightly as he prowled into the room. "Are you tipsy?"

"Maybe a little. I drank it quickly. I don't do this sort of thing, ever, you see, and… what are you doing?"

He'd picked up the hairbrush and was advancing on her, but she kept scooting around to face him.

"Vivvie, I can't brush your hair if you won't give me your back."

"Oh." She angled slightly so he could sit behind her on the raised hearth.

"One braid or two?"

"One, over my left shoulder. How did you bathe if I had the use of the tub?"

"You can tell?" He smoothed her hair over her shoulders, and Vivian shuddered at his touch. He repeated the gesture, making it even more of a caress.

"Your hair is damp and you smell good," she said. "Maybe I am tipsy."

"You're nervous." His hands settled on her shoulders and kneaded slowly. "It's too soon to be nervous, Vivvie. Nobody will be taking any clothes off tonight except possibly myself."

"Why would you do that?"

"If you asked me to, I'd do it." His thumbs traced circles on her nape then up the sides of her neck.

"Do you do this to other women?"

"Massage their necks, no." His hands disappeared, making Vivvie want to curse her tongue, but she felt a need to drive him off, to establish some breathing room. "Nor do I allow them coitus, but I do enjoy the company of the occasional understanding woman, and I've been known to allow ladies other privileges for sufficient consideration."

"Allow them coitus." Vivian said the words, frowning but not arguing, because she had to conclude that, very likely, *coitus* with Darius Lindsey would be a privilege.

An expensive privilege, and it hurt to think about that.

"I have many faults, Vivian." His voice was tired as he put the brush to her hair. "I do not lie."

"My stepfather lies," she said, wondering where the words had come from. "He's like a little boy, expecting me to believe he cares for my welfare, when in truth, it's his purse he's concerned about."

"Which is how you ended up married to William?"

"Oh, that…" The rhythm of the brush was soothing, and Vivian closed her eyes, to rest them at the end of a trying day. "Muriel made me promise I'd look after him, and I suspect she extracted the same promise from William, and so there we were. That feels good. I loved Muriel. William did too. Still does."

Behind her, Darius said nothing while his hands were in her hair, dividing it into three thick skeins.

"I think William misses Muriel more than he wants to live," Vivian went on. "He thinks of death not as the end of life, but as the way he can be with her again. It's sweet."

"It's ridiculous," Darius countered softly. "William can be with you, and he's pining for a dead woman."

"They were married forever. Are you going to take your clothes off now?"

"What is this obsession you have with disrobing, Lady Longstreet?" He flipped a fat rope of brown hair over her shoulder. "Would you like me to take off my clothes?"

She shook her head but kept her back to him, and when the silence stretched and stretched, she felt her nerves humming.

"Darius?"

"Come to bed, Vivvie," he said. "You're tired and the sheets are warm and it's too late to argue with me."

His voice was no longer directly behind her, so Vivian rose and turned, only to see him stretched out on the bed.

Without a stitch on.

✌❀

Vivian abruptly turned her back to him again. "You are unclothed, sir."

She put a load of consternation into four words.

"You were going to ask me but lost your nerve."

"I was?"

"Vivvie." Darius sighed mightily and not entirely for effect. "You are making this far too complicated. Your clothes are on, and I expect they'll stay that way for tonight, while mine are off. You might as well see what you're getting."

She peeked over her shoulder, face flaming, and Darius wanted to laugh, except that would unnerve her further.

"I can't be such a horrendous sight as all that," he said, holding out a hand. "You'll make me lose all my manly confidence if you stay over there much longer."

"You want me only to look?"

He nodded, holding her gaze. "For starters." She crossed the room, step by step, never taking her eyes from his face. "The dressing gown can come off, madam. Your nightgown could house regiments."

"It's warm," she protested.

"So the nightgown stays on," Darius said, "but I'm warm too." She stood by the bed, unbelted her robe, and then carefully folded it at the foot of the bed. When she looked like she was planning on blowing out the candles, Darius circled her wrist with his fingers.

"Come here, Vivvie, now. Please."

She nodded, swallowed, and climbed on the bed, then settled back against the bolstered pillows, keeping her eyes front. "Now what?"

The possibilities were myriad, though none of them exactly in keeping with his preferences. "I don't know. I could discuss with you the Christmas traditions at Longchamps or maybe exchange childhood Christmas memories with you? But if that holds no appeal, there's a spot on my back…" He sat forward and crossed his legs tailor fashion. "I can't reach it, and when the weather is cold, it itches damnably."

"I know the one." She risked a glance at him, and when he felt her looking at him, Darius slid over onto his belly.

"Maybe you'd give it a scratch, hmm? Ladies have the most effective fingernails for that sort of thing."

He lay there, facedown, naked as the day he was born, offering himself to her in a way he'd never offered himself to her more avaricious predecessors. Offering himself and hoping she'd accept what he offered.

"Here?" Vivian's nails raked lightly in the middle of his back.

"God, yes, and a little higher."

She obliged, her touch becoming more confident. "Like that?"

"And lower." She moved her hand down the length of his back. "Lower still."

"But that's your…" Her hand fell away. "Does somebody *beat* you?"

"Regularly." He shifted up onto his side and cursed himself for being forgetful. "You very nearly had your hands on my backside, Vivvie. Well done."

"Get back on your stomach."

He obliged, slowly, dreading what was coming but unwilling to dodge it.

"This must hurt," she said, her hand skimming over his buttock. "And these are not fresh marks. Darius, why does someone beat you?"

"For diversion." He rolled to his back, wishing she weren't who she was, not wanting her to be anybody else. "For profit. It isn't something you need to fret about, and they never go at me very hard—they haven't the strength to do real damage. How about if I tell you I have an itch on the front of me, Vivvie?"

"No doubt you do," she said with some asperity. "You're a man, after all." But her eyes strayed—finally, finally—to his groin, where his parts lay quiescent against his thighs. "You don't."

"I have a lot of control." He smiled at the puzzlement on her face. "I have enough control that you can tell me, at any time, for any reason or for no reason, to leave you in peace, and I will. Touch me."

"I just did," she said, her gaze remaining on his genitals.

"Touch me where you want to, not where you feel safe touching me."

She shook her head.

"Pleasure, Vivvie. It takes a little courage to allow yourself pleasure, and all I'll do is lie here." He folded his arms behind his head to emphasis how harmless he intended to be—for her.

"I'd rather you were blindfolded."

He considered her words and understood them. She was not asking to control him, so much as she was asking to protect her own privacy and dignity.

"So blindfold me. The belt of your robe will do, or there's a handkerchief in my pocket."

"You'd let me do that?"

He got off the bed, fished in the pocket of his discarded breeches, and handed her the handkerchief. She took it, frowning, but when he sat on the edge of the bed, she tied it securely over his eyes.

"On my stomach or my back?"

"Your back. May I touch you?"

He climbed across the bed and settled on his back. "Wherever you please, however you please, but if I feel you get off the bed, I'll know you're blowing out the candles, Vivvie, and that's not allowed."

She went still and muttered something in unlady-like tones under her breath.

"Naughty, naughty, Lady Vivvie. Give me your hand."

She did, and he placed her palm on his chest.

"Consider this an adventure," he suggested, finding *he* considered it an adventure. Of all the times he'd been in bed, with all the bored wives, merry widows, and fast ladies, they'd none of them required coaxing or reassuring or any real thought. Vivian was genuinely shy, and the novelty of it was peculiarly challenging— almost touching, in fact.

Still, he'd not permitted himself even the beginning of an erection, lest he spook her. He was gener-ously endowed, he knew it, had heard it from too many pleased women to doubt it, and took perverse glee in denying both Blanche and Lucy the use of his cock.

"Your chest is so different from mine." Vivian's palm smoothed over his sternum then up across his collarbones.

"Not so different." He exhaled slowly. "I can't nurse a child, but my nipples are sensitive, just as yours are."

"Sensitive, how?"

He trapped her fingers in his and used the tip of her third finger in a light, glancing circle on one nipple.

"Give me your other hand," he said, arching up into her touch. Her fingers laced with his. "Keep touching me."

He settled her free hand on his groin, over the soft length of his cock, and held it there when she would have pulled away. In silence, she slowed the movement of her finger on his nipple, and he knew she was watching his flesh contract.

"Don't stop, Vivvie," he whispered. "This is merely another little experiment."

"Can I switch sides?"

"Switch sides, use your tongue, bite me, but don't stop yet."

Under her hand, his cock was coming to life, filling and lifting, becoming sensitized just from her single finger circling so lightly on his nipple. He felt her breath on his chest and wondered if she were having a closer look or considering the use of her…

Oh, *Jesus*. Her tongue, soft, warm, wet, swiped over his other nipple.

"Did I hurt you? You gasped…"

"Again," he whispered. "Nice and slow, take your time."

She took direction well, to his consternation and delight. Her tongue was slow, sweet, and tentative at first, then bolder, and then—holy, ever-loving Christ—she suckled at him, gently, curiously, and Darius felt his pulse begin to beat steadily in his cock.

"Look at this." He shifted her fingers, to wrap her hand around his length. "You did this, with your mouth and your hands, Vivvie. You gave me this much pleasure."

She sat back, and the loss of her attention to his chest was a grief, but he could feel her gaze on his cock, so he let his hand fall away and he lay there, keeping his hands at his sides by sheer will.

"May I touch you—here?" She did not address him by name, a minor, telling frustration he stored away for further study.

"You may touch me if you bring the candles closer to the bed first." He felt her hop off the bed and congratulated himself on a second lucky guess.

"How does this feel, to you?" She was sitting at his hip, and though she wasn't touching him, she was arousing him with her curiosity.

"I'm blindfolded, love. You'll have to touch me if I'm to know what part you're asking about."

"This." One whisper-light drawing of her finger up the length of his erection. "It can't be comfortable."

"The feeling is one of yearning. It can be sweet or sharp, it can be nearly soothing, or burn. Touch me more, and I'll tell you how it feels."

She held still for a moment, and then around the edges of his blindfold, Darius felt the light get stronger.

Her fingers circled him, measuring his girth.

"I like that," Darius said. "I like a firm touch, especially around the base. Move your hand up, along the shaft, and just there, under the tip. The tip is particularly sensitive, and that spot, more sensitive still."

"What do you mean, sensitive?"

"Easily aroused."

"Like your…"

"Nipples," he said the word slowly, teasingly. "My balls are sensitive too."

"These." She slipped her hand down, and he raised his knees and spread his legs to give her room to maneuver. He did not dare tell her he was proud of her boldness.

"Those." Darius sighed at the pleasure of it—she was unfailingly, beguilingly gentle. He'd missed gentleness in bed desperately and not even known it. "One good, hard squeeze, and you'd have me retching on my knees. They're that sensitive."

She didn't squeeze, she caressed, a soft, fondling pass of her fingers that learned the shape of him as it pleased as it... stirred.

"So odd, your manly bits." He couldn't see her smile, but he could feel it. "This is all very interesting, but now what do we do with it?"

"We needn't do anything." He lifted his hips though, for she'd gone back to sleeving his cock with her fingers. "I just wanted to acquaint you with my equipment, so to speak." Because William, in five years of marriage, apparently hadn't bothered.

"I have a question."

"I won't hurt you." He found her hand and brought it to his lips. "You're wondering how this will fit, how it will work, and I can assure you, you'll enjoy it."

"Give me leave to doubt," she said, wrapping her hand around him. "I think your dimensions have increased even while I've been touching you."

"You're built for bearing children. I won't hurt you." He was taking a vow, whether she comprehended it or not.

"I'm built for bringing forth children in pain," she reminded him. "Angela says Scripture does not exaggerate."

"And how many children does your sister have?"

"Three." Her hand paused. "With another one on the way."

"This won't be awful, Vivvie." He arched into her touch again. "I'm not moving my hands."

"I didn't say you were." She stroked him again while her other palm passed over his nipple, and he had to fist both hands hard to keep from dragging her over him. "Why do women spank you?"

"How do you know it's women?"

"All right." She caught a rhythm, her hands synchronizing on the respective parts of his body. "Why do you let anybody hurt you?"

His wits had been ambushed by honest arousal, and he lacked the mental focus to dodge her question. "It makes them feel good, and it's profitable. And it doesn't hurt that much."

She fell silent, thank a merciful god.

"If you keep that up," he whispered, "I can spend, Vivvie. You don't have to do this."

She didn't stop, so he tried again.

"If you just want to play"—his hips were moving in counterpoint to her hand—"I can hold off, but…"

"It's sharp now, isn't it, the yearning?" she said, her tongue grazing his nipple.

"And sweet." His hand ached to caress her hair, to smooth the curve of her shoulder, to guide her breast to his mouth. "Very sweet."

"Spend," she whispered the word just before she

passed her tongue over his nipple once more, and though he forced himself to hold off a few moments more, that was truly all he could manage. His balls drew up tight, his spine tingled, and pleasure, hot, fierce, sweet, and achy welled out from his groin as he came.

"Jesus... God..." He shivered with it, bowed up, pushed hard against the snug pressure of her fingers, and let it drown him, the sheer relief of it bringing a lump to his throat even as his body went limp and sated against the bed. "For that, you have to kiss me."

She let go of his cock. He felt her balance on her hands and knees over him then give him her mouth. It was good this way, with her above him so he could sip and kiss and take from her while his heart slowed its pounding and his breathing calmed. And the blindfold comforted too, giving him a kind of privacy, keeping his eyes and the secrets they'd reveal safe from her scrutiny.

"Darius, are you all right?"

For that question, he gave her a little of his heart. There was concern in her voice, and her hand smoothed his hair back, the first spontaneous caress she'd offered him. God, she was dear...

"I'm undone. Wonderfully undone, but my blindfold could be put to use elsewhere, if you'll allow it."

"Of course." She sat back, and he missed the proximity of her without even being able to see her. He sat up and felt her untying the knot at the back of his head.

"Water?"

She passed him a glass from the night table, and he dribbled some onto his stomach then used his handkerchief to wipe himself clean.

"That's your seed?"

"It is," he said, recalling that he was abed with a curious, wonderfully ignorant woman. "And I've lost my erection, thanks to you."

She looked worried, and he had to smile. "Don't worry, Vivvie, it will come back any time you want it to."

"That's normal, isn't it?" She worried her lip, regarding the softening length of him with a frown.

"Of course." He kissed her cheek, just because he could. "And it's normal to cuddle up for a bit afterward." For some lucky people, in any case.

She looked uncertain, and Darius had to wonder what was wrong with William Longstreet. Even if the man couldn't get his wife pregnant, even if his elderly vanity required the candles snuffed on every occasion, surely he wasn't denying the woman all the marital intimacies?

"Normal for me," he clarified, and her expression eased, then her brow puckered again. "No." He drew a finger down the middle of her forehead and over her nose. "I am not going to get dressed just to climb into bed with you, silly woman. Let me bank the coals, and we'll talk, if that's what you want."

He hoped she wanted to talk, wanted to have discussions with him she'd not had with anybody else, including her brilliant statesman of a dim-witted husband.

She shifted to let him off the bed. He knew she was watching him as he hunkered naked before the hearth, poked the logs to the back of the andirons, and secured the fireplace screen. She was watching as he ambled back across the room, and she watched him as he blew out the candles one by one.

"I can hear you thinking," he mused as he blew out the last candle. "I'm not a diviner of thoughts, Vivvie. What has your mill wheel turning at such a great rate?"

"Do you intend to sleep here?"

"Ah." He scooted across the bed and drew the covers up over them both. "We can negotiate this if it bothers you, but yes, I think that makes the most sense."

"I'm not sure I'll be able to go to sleep with you here."

"Naked, don't you mean?"

She yelped as he drew her into his arms and hauled her back against his chest.

"You'll sleep," he assured her, kissing her nape. "You'll sleep a lot better without this lawn tent between us."

"I get to keep my lawn tent for tonight," she replied. "What are you *doing*?"

He'd spooned himself around her, settling one hand over her breast, snugging his groin up to her buttocks.

"Cuddling." He bit her neck this time. "And, my God, you are a delight to cuddle with."

"Don't do that."

"What?" He gently squeezed her breast again. "This?"

"That." But she sighed after she said it, giving herself away.

"All right." He relaxed his grip. "You've had an adventure, after all, so I should let you get some rest."

"Yes, you should."

He took pity on her, rubbing her back, her neck, even her scalp and buttocks until he felt her slipping away into sleep. He lay with her in his arms for the longest time, marveling at the peace he felt, in his body, and in his mind—and a little wary of it too. Sex had become a commodity for him, something he traded in, up to a point, for gain. Vivian couldn't approach it like that, hadn't the sophistication to see it thus—yet.

But she felt wonderful in his arms, her curiosity and inherent integrity a refreshing change to a man too used to trading in dark and spoiled emotions. She was right: Duty and pleasure could overlap, delightfully so.

In the morning he might pleasure her, he thought as he drifted off, might bring her the same glorious relief she'd given him. It would be his duty, and the sporting thing to do.

They passed the night easily enough, sleeping in tandem, with Vivian sometimes burrowed against his back, sometimes cradled against his chest. She was a natural at sharing a bed, another thing to like about her. He drifted off on that thought and slept for hours, peacefully for a change.

As a cold, gray light filtered through the curtains, Darius rose to awareness slowly, feeling the heaviness in his groin he usually began his day with, but also a sweet, feminine warmth against his body.

He propped himself on one elbow, brushed the hair back from Vivian's brow, and kissed her cheek. "Arise, Lady Vivvie. Sweet Philomel calls us from our beds."

Vivian's eyes opened, focused, then narrowed. "What, may I ask, are you still doing here?"

Six

EVERLASTING GOD, SHE HAD TO GET HIM OUT OF HER bedroom—out of her bed. And there he lay, scratching his chest and stretching like that worthless cat.

"Good morning to you too." He offered her a sleepy smile and flipped back the covers to cross the room in all his oblivious nudity. Vivian turned away, but not before she caught sight of his arousal, and she had to swallow back a howl of sheer… upset.

William must hate her, to put her into the keeping of a man built like that. In the cold light of morning, she saw there was no way she could couple with Darius Lindsey and not be rent asunder. Women bore children, true, but they also *died* bearing children, probably the children of great, oversized, handsome louts like him.

He moved behind the privacy screen, but his height meant Vivian knew exactly where he was, and her ears told her exactly what he was about.

"So, Vivvie," he said around a mouthful of her toothbrush. "I take it you aren't a morning person?"

"I *am* a morning person." She hiked the covers up

to her chin. "I am not a waken-to-find-your-hands-on-me person."

"You're shy in the morning," he concluded, not sounding at all disconcerted. "I used to be, but then, I am in charity with life today, and you can't bring quite the same good cheer to the morning I can."

"And why is that?"

"You're frustrated." He shrugged, his smile sweet as he—*all of him*—came into view. "While I've been recently sated, after a fashion. Shall I relieve your frustration?"

She nodded firmly. "By leaving this room."

She thought he was going to oblige when he ambled over to the door in all his glory, but he merely stuck his head into the corridor and bellowed instructions to the house at large. When he strolled over to the bed, it was obvious his interest in the day was still… aroused.

She spared his erection a shuddering glance. "Can't you do something about that?"

"I'd rather you do something about it." He yawned again and climbed in beside her. "I suppose you being shy in the morning, that's a little much to ask for our first time."

"Will you leave me in peace?" She hissed it, and some of her upset must have gotten through to him, because his smile faded.

He tucked the covers around her shoulders. "Here's how I see it, Vivvie: the more often we couple, the more likely you are to conceive. If we're to achieve your goal, then you should be pestering me for my attentions every few hours for the next three weeks."

"Every few *hours*?" She huddled down into the covers on a moan of horror.

"Sweetheart." He scooted closer. "Talk to me. I can't address whatever's bothering you unless you tell me what it is."

Just when Vivian thought she'd die of mortification, a knock sounded on the door, followed by Gracie's cheerful presence bearing a tray.

"Morning, all." Gracie beamed in the general direction of the bed. "Looks to be snowing out again, and Master John's already up and about."

"I'll take the tray, Gracie." Darius reached out long arms. "You see to the fire."

"I take it milady likes to sleep in." Gracie eyed Vivian, who had all but scooted under the covers.

"I wore her out."

Vivian poked her head up enough to catch his smile, whipped a pillow from under her head, and smacked him with it.

"Wakes up cranky," Darius said, shielding the tray with his body. "Best be quick, Gracie, if you don't want to be the victim of violence."

Gracie winked at Vivian. "Smack him again, milady. It's the only way with the cheeky ones." The maid was gone before Vivian could fashion a reply, and then Darius passed her a cup of tea.

"She'll leave us in peace until we leave your room," he said, pouring his own cup and setting the tray on the nightstand. "Now what are these maidenly vapors about?"

The tea was hot and strong and as much fortification as she was likely to find anywhere.

"Every few *hours*?"

"'Fraid so, love." He sipped calmly. "I'm looking forward to it more than I thought I would."

"You're looking…" She finished her tea in two gulps, feeling a sudden empathy for foxes set upon by hounds. "I cannot do this."

"You haven't even tried, Vivvie." His tone was chiding, and he was right, damn him. "Don't you want a baby? A wee little fellow to cuddle and coo at?"

"Yes, I want a baby." She set her cup aside, because he was right about this too. "But I'm… scared."

"Ah." He set his cup next to hers, and Vivian wasn't sure that was a good thing. "Then we'll put your fears behind us tonight, and you'll see it won't be so bad. I promised you pleasure, remember? I'll take care of you, Vivvie. I'm good for that, if nothing else."

And what was that supposed to mean?

"Come here." He looped an arm across her shoulders and pulled her to his side. "Relax. Last night, you slept like a soldier after a forced march."

"You wear me out." She sighed at the feel of his hand massaging her scalp.

"Just distracting you from your imagined fate." His lips grazed her temple, and Vivian had the oddest notion it had been a kiss for comfort—her comfort. "You like to cuddle, you know."

"I am not in a position to argue." She was, in fact, plastered to his side, her cheek pillowed on his chest. "I can hope it's a passing tendency."

"I gather William isn't a cozy type of husband?"

"How would I…?" She closed her eyes and turned her face into his warmth. "William is dignified."

"Dignity in the bedroom is almost impossible to imagine. You're afraid I'll hurt you?"

She nodded, relieved he could say what she couldn't.

"I've never physically hurt a woman, Vivian." His grip shifted to her nape, where he was squeezing the tension right out of her. "Never, nor will I."

"But you let them hurt you," Vivian pointed out because it bothered her, exceedingly.

"A few whacks with a crop is hardly worth quibbling about, and they enjoy it sufficiently to make it worth my while. It's of no moment."

The teasing tone was gone from his voice, and Vivian had the sense she was now in bed with the real Darius Lindsey, not the strutting, teasing, flirting facade he'd offered her earlier.

"Do you bring them here?"

"We're not going to discuss this." He kissed her cheek this time, in apology for his words—she hoped.

"I don't want to be like them, Darius." She felt him closing himself off from her, and surprised herself—him too, based on his expression—by hiking a leg across his thighs then straddling him. Her nightgown made the whole business more complicated, but when she was snuggled down onto his chest, the effort had been worth it.

His arms came around her, and his cheek rested against her hair. "How is it you don't want to be 'like them'?"

"You let them take advantage of you," she said. "If they weren't whacking at you, they'd just find some other man to abuse. You aren't a person to them."

"Another naughty pony," Darius said. "Perhaps."

"Not perhaps." She nuzzled at his sternum, then

shifted up and slipped a hand around the back of his head. "I want to beat them with a crop for treating you thus." She clasped him to her chest and put a name to what she was feeling: protective. Protective of a great, strapping lout with no sense whatsoever.

"Vivvie." He wrestled her away a little. "Look at me."

She turned her face from him—she was straddling him, and nightgown or not, there was nowhere to hide.

"Look at me."

He brushed her hair back with such tenderness she wanted to cry, but then he anchored his hand in her hair to turn her face back to his.

"You have to learn, Vivian Longstreet, not to let your heart get tangled up in the physical sensations. We're going to be repeatedly, gloriously intimate. I've promised you pleasure, and I can assure you I'll be sharing in it abundantly. But you have to decide right now it's only pleasure, like an ice on a hot day, a good gallop on a fall morning. It means nothing more than that. It can't."

"You decide that," she accused, "or those beatings would have significance you can't allow them."

"Hush." He brought her back down to his chest. "You're disconcerted and tenderhearted, and you'll see the sense in what I'm saying."

He fell silent, and Vivian lay there in his arms, listening to the steady beat of his heart and wanting to cry—for herself, but also, incongruously, for him.

❧

"For pity's sake, Able, you have to ask him." Portia Springer set her teacup down with the sharp bang of fine porcelain used roughly.

"You're ghoulish, Portia." Able rose from the kitchen table. "I can't ask my own father what's in his will."

"Whyever not?" She rose too, and paced behind him across the kitchen. "You've managed this estate for him for years, Able, and shown one handsome profit after another, and the land is entailed. *Entailed.* You're his only living child, and it would be the work of a moment to legitimate you. Truly legitimate you."

"Not the work of a moment." Able rinsed his cup off then went back to the table for hers. "The work of several moments, felonious, expensive moments, and I am not in the habit of forging marriage lines. The person providing that service would be in a position to blackmail me and all my children, Portia—your children."

Which they were unlikely to have, the silence around them declared, as long as she was so parsimonious with her marital favors.

"I'm twenty-eight," she spat. "There's plenty of time for that."

"I'll not see thirty-eight again," he countered, using a thumbnail to scrub at the sugar stuck to the bottom of her cup. "I'd like to be on hand to raise my children, Portia. I've no doubt William has left his current viscountess in peace, in part because he understands the need for a father to raise his own children."

"You'd raise his children," Portia muttered, though Able knew by her tone she was regrouping.

"He hasn't any other children left. This is a moot discussion, and I cannot relish the task of raising half siblings four decades my junior. Leave it, Portia, please."

"If the land goes back to the Crown," she started up again, fists propped on ample hips, "you have nothing. Twenty years of slaving for that man, and nothing to show for it."

"If the land goes back to the Crown, somebody still has to manage it, and we've money set aside, Portia. I'm a good steward, and there's work to be had for such as me, and for thirty-eight years, my father has provided either directly or by means of furnishing me a livelihood."

"Like hell." She shifted to block his exit, and Able knew for the thousandth time some sympathy for men who beat their wives. "Stewards are invariably poor relations, and that old man is the only person you're related to, and he's looking worse each year, Able Springer. Each season."

Able couldn't argue that, not when his father was indeed showing his considerable age. "He has been generous with us, Portia, and you'll not be pestering him now regarding his will. His lordship has had enough of death and grief these past few years."

"Not so much he couldn't remarry well before his mourning was up," Portia snapped. "You must get all that strutting and pawing in the bedroom from him."

He was torn between the urge to lay hands on her and the urge to emigrate to the Antipodes—alone. "Portia, dearest wife, if I could recall the last time you permitted me the pleasure of strutting and pawing in the bedroom, I might comprehend your remark, but for a woman who's intent on inheriting a title and wealth, you're doing precious little to secure the succession."

He departed on that volley, not sure he'd know

what to do if she did allow him intimacies. Eight years ago, she'd seemed like such a catch—practical, knowledgeable about the running of an estate, and comely enough for a man of his station. He'd hoped they could be friends.

His father hadn't commented on his choice of wife, and a few years later, Lady Muriel had succumbed to the illness plaguing her. He'd liked Lady Muriel, and thought Portia might share a few of her more interesting qualities. More fool him.

He found his father in the breakfast parlor, noting again the older man's gauntness, and felt a sweeping sense of loneliness. They didn't know each other well, but, by God, they were the last of their line.

"Good morning, your lordship." Able took a seat at the table. "I trust you slept well?"

"I slept." Lord Longstreet's smile was fleeting. "As one ages, that becomes a practice of dozing between trips to the chamber pot."

"You miss your wife," Able said. "Perhaps you'd sleep better in her company."

"Vivian?" Lord Longstreet's eyebrows rose. "One can hardly imagine such a thing. When are you and Portia to present me with some grandchildren, Able? It's been what, six, seven years?"

"About that." Able topped up Lord Longstreet's teacup. "The Lord hasn't seen fit to bless us."

Lord Longstreet stirred his tea. "Is it the Lord being stingy, or your lady wife?"

The morning was to be a series of interrogations. "Is there a reason for such blunt inquiry?"

"An old man's nosiness. A father's nosiness. The

male line in our family is not known for its fecundity. You might have to work at it, do you want children, if you're like I was."

"You had three sons. Many families make do with less than that."

Lord Longstreet took a sip of his well-stirred tea. "Is she hounding you?"

"My lord?"

"Portia, is she hounding you regarding the estate?"

Able studied his tea—into which he had not put even a dash of sugar.

"You never call me father, Able."

"You've never invited such familiarity," Able said, wondering if everybody in the household had gone daft. "And you do not call me son."

Lord Longstreet considered him from across the table. "You are certainly acknowledged. You always have been."

"I'm not your heir, and I never can be." Able addressed his teacup. "I understand that."

"Though Portia would have it otherwise," Lord Longstreet concluded. "She has the ambition I found in Muriel but not the integrity."

Able bristled, because indirectly, it was a harsh judgment of him—and accurate in all its implications. "That's an unflattering conclusion about a woman you barely know."

"I've thrived in the Lords for half a century, Able, because I am an astute judge of character. Not as astute as Muriel, but she taught me to see what most men miss, and Portia is becoming bitter. She likes being lady of the manor, pretending to be the viscountess, but she's the steward's wife. That's all she'll ever be, and it tears at her."

"The bastard's wife," Able said. "I was the bastard when she married me, and not even the regent can change that. I do comprehend my station, my lord."

"And I comprehend your worth, Able." Lord Longstreet rose slowly, mostly by bracing his knuckles on the table and pushing. "You may assure your wife of this fact and refer her to me should she doubt it. It looks like we're in for more snow."

"Snow means it can't be all that cold," Able said, rising out of respect. "Would you like to ride out with me today?"

"Ride out? I haven't ridden the land here for what, three years? Suppose we could bundle up, take a flask or two?"

"Of course." Able smiled as much at the prospect of escaping the house as at the twinkle in his father's eye. "And maybe drop in at the Hot Cross Bun for a scone."

"Haven't had one of their scones for years." William smiled in remembrance, and Able knew, he just knew, the last time William had dropped by the local bakery for a treat, Lady Muriel had been the one to jolly him into it.

"Let's be off, then," Able said. "Before we're caught and forced to spend the day with the ledgers—or worse."

❧

Vivian Longstreet was proving problematic— interesting, but problematic. A month wasn't going to be long enough to unravel the blend of shyness and determination Darius sensed in her, and a month was going to be too long to have her underfoot.

He glanced at the note from Blanche Cowell complaining of his month-long absence from Town. Because her husband would require her at the family seat for at least two weeks of that month, Darius hardly spared her a thought.

Lucy Templeton was similarly discommoded by Darius's absence, and her missive promised predictable retribution for his not coming when she snapped her fingers at him.

Darius set her note aside as well, anticipating a game of Spoiled Puppy when he returned to Town. She'd spank him until her hand hurt, and "let" him put his nose in her lap for his reward when he was sufficiently contrite. It was beyond tedious. If Lord Longstreet provided the remuneration he'd promised, Lucy Templeton, Blanche Cowell, and all of their ilk might soon be nothing more than bad—very bad—memories.

"So this is where you hide?"

He glanced up from his desk to see Vivian standing in the door of his study. She was attired in the closest thing he'd seen on her to an attractive dress—a soft brown velvet creation with a raised waistline, suggesting it was years out of date, though it looked comfortable.

"This is where I shovel my way through the reams of correspondence that must occupy a man involved in commerce."

"Commerce?" She advanced into the room, glancing around. "I thought you were a gentleman farmer."

"A farmer, in any case." He tossed his pen down.

"I haven't enough land to raise corn and livestock in any quantity, so I raise those goods that can be easily sold in Town."

"And those would be?"

"I'm still figuring it out." He rose and gestured to a pair of reading chairs near the hearth. "I've done well with garden vegetables thus far, mostly because I take inordinate care in their transport. I eschew the practice of hauling manure out of London in the same wagons I use to haul the vegetables in. The flavor benefits as a result. Eggs are easy to produce in quantity, chicken manure is valuable, and the feathers can also be sold, to say nothing of having a steady supply of chicken for the table. Eggs are hard to transport, though, and most everybody with an alley can keep a coop themselves in Town. Some keep their chickens on the rooftop, much like an old-fashioned dovecote."

"William once said something about homing pigeons being a profitable venture."

"I hadn't considered them." Darius took his seat after Vivian had taken hers. "It would require time, because the generations born on my land would always home to me. I'd have to sell breeding pairs, though I assume it can be done."

"The government is using them more and more," Vivian said. "They used them to get word of the victory at Waterloo, and it was faster than any horse or packet."

Darius considered her, seeing not only beauty and grace, but also intelligence—and wondering if William saw any of it. "I didn't know that. What else does William have to say about British commerce?"

"We need finer wool," Vivian said. "There are Spanish sheep that produce a much higher grade of wool than our farm breeds, but we stick to what we know, when pretty much every country on earth can grow its own sheep."

"His Majesty had some of these Spanish sheep, didn't he?"

"William bought some in the dispersal about ten years ago, and they've been producing little sheep at Longchamps all the while. They're… distinctive, but very soft to pet."

"Like you."

She smoothed a pleat in her dress. "And here we were doing so well, Mr. Lindsey."

For her fortitude, Darius returned to the matter at hand. "So William thinks we need to focus on competing with other nations?"

"Of course. The Americans have more space to grow corn of all kinds than we'll ever have, the Antipodes can grow sheep, and the shipping is getting faster each year. You think of competing with other vegetable farmers to get your goods to Town, but soon you'll be competing with the French table grapes, the Spanish citrus, and so forth."

"You've learned a thing or two, being married to Longstreet."

"And what fascinating stuff it is." She smiled, though the result was sad around the edges.

"To a man strapped for coin, it is fascinating."

She apparently took him at his word. "Whatever you have, there's demand for it on the Continent. The Corsican saw to that."

"What do you mean?"

"His Majesty's troops were usually provisioned by design, with quartermasters and contracts and a whole supply line set up by the military as the armies moved from place to place. The Russians and Germans operate similarly. Napoleon relied on what he called foraging, and what we would call pillaging, even in his own territory. Any place the Grand Armée passed through was devastated. Crops, goods, livestock, entire buildings were torn asunder in a night to feed the campfires—they'd even burn the fodder for the livestock in their campfires. You could export lumber, had you a wood. You could export anything, and there'd be a market for it there somewhere."

Darius frowned at the fire, because this conversation was the furthest thing from flirting—and he was enjoying it. "How to get my goods to that market? And how to retrieve one's coin?"

"That's easy." Vivian rose and went to the window. "You hire one of the half-pay quartermaster's officers who campaigned from Portugal to Poland, and he'll be happy to live cheaply on the Continent while taking a little coin to see to your business. Most of them picked up enough of the languages, they still have contacts, and a few have wives of foreign extraction."

"You've thought about this?"

"I listen." She turned, that slight smile still in place. "Hour after hour after hour, I listen to my husband and his parliamentary associates debating everything from soap taxes to window taxes to reform of every stripe."

He could see her doing it too, quietly keeping the servants organized, the guests happy, and the conversation flowing—while William expounded on soap taxes. "What is there to debate about a soap tax, for pity's sake?"

"If soap were more affordable, the general populace might put it to more frequent use and avoid some of the pestilence plaguing them. We'd then have a healthier work force and could tax what they create, rather than the soap they can't buy now. Similarly with the tax on windows and fresh air in tenements and factories."

She looked lonely over there by the window. Remote, though she was only a few feet away. "And we'd all smell better. This is what you and William discuss over dinner?"

"William and I rarely dine together privately. We entertain a great deal, or we did until this fall. Losing two sons has taken a toll on William."

"It would take a toll on any man." Darius rose and crossed the room to stand behind her. "Except possibly my father."

"I don't know the man."

"Count yourself fortunate."

She cocked her head in a manner Darius was learning meant serious study, so he distracted her by scooping her up and settling with her in his lap.

"You said you'd wait until tonight." She sounded wonderfully tart in her disapproval, even as she cuddled into his embrace.

"I'm not under your skirts, Vivvie." He nuzzled her breast, closing his eyes. To his consternation, she threaded her fingers through his hair and cradled him against her, as if he were a tired boy.

"Tell me about your father."

"He's awful." Darius resisted the temptation to tell her they weren't going to speak of this either. The topic was harmless enough—though distasteful. "If I learned to tolerate a beating anywhere, it was at his hands. My brother, Trent, was his particular project, which was no privilege, believe me, and my mother staked me as her personal favorite."

"I gather your parents were not congenial."

"They were at daggers drawn. Part of the reason I can countenance this scheme of William's is because there is reason to doubt the paternity of at least one of my siblings. My mother was that angry with Wilton, that desperate."

She stroked his hair absently. "One shudders to think of it, years and years of battle, and all within the one place that's supposed to be a haven from strife."

He fell silent, because her caresses were mesmerizing, which made no sense. "Shall we take a nap, my lady?"

"You gave me until tonight," she chided, her hand pausing. "Is your father's example why you're so careful with John?"

"I'm not sure what you mean." And he didn't want to pursue it, so he nuzzled her breast again, rubbing his cheek deliberately over her nipple.

"You're trying to distract me. Let's take a walk, and you can show me some of your land."

"There's nothing to see." He did it again. "It's all under snow."

"So we'll kidnap John from his studies." She pulled away, but only a little. "We can make a snowman."

"He'd like that." Darius frowned while she traced his eyebrow with a finger. *He'd* like it too. He'd made snowmen before, for his sisters' entertainment, mostly. Emily was more than a decade his junior, and she'd been in need of playmates. There was no point to a snowman, but a man could do only so much paperwork.

Vivian rose off his lap. "Then we can have a toddy before dinner."

"You like my toddies?"

She smiled at him, not only with a curving of her lips but also with her lovely brown eyes. "The entire household likes your toddies. But yes, I do. I never knew this about myself, but I could become over-indulgent in them."

Darius rose, feeling bemused. "And I won't be on hand to see the effects of my bad influence." Neither would he see her great with child, and that... bothered him. "Come, and do not think of wearing a bonnet when the wind could kick up at any moment."

"Imperious." She took his arm. "It's fortunate you're competent with a toddy."

"Among other things."

He got the last, leering word, pleased to have restored the tenor of their dealings to harmless flirting. Talk of his father, making money, and commending Vivian back into her husband's keeping was not... comfortable, and at least in his own home, a man should be comfortable.

❧

Vivian had eaten as slowly as she could, though she'd known all the while Darius was watching her with a speculative, assessing eye. Had she gotten tipsy? Oh, likely. Would she regret it? Invariably.

He'd treated her to a game of chess after dinner, beating her eventually, but she'd at least made him work for it. The difficulty was, lingering over the chessboard made the effect of the spirits wear off, and here she was, bathed, nightgowned, and tucked up in her bed, awaiting her fate.

When the clock struck ten and still Darius hadn't joined her, Vivian had had enough.

She yanked open her door, intent on searching him out and demanding he be about his intended purpose, only to find him lounging across the hall in the chair she assumed was reserved for a footman.

"Good evening, Lady Longstreet."

"What are you doing, sitting there?"

He rose and prowled toward her, giving Vivian the sense he'd been gathering his nerve, of all things. "Are you sure you want this, Vivian?"

She nodded and tucked her lawn tent closer. It was colder than Hades in the hallway, and God knew how long Darius had been sitting there.

"Because to want this baby, you're going to have to want me."

"Come." She tugged him by the wrist down the hall.

"Where are we going?"

"Your bedroom, which I've yet to see. I want my bed to be for me, your bed for other things."

"What if I don't care to share my bed?"

She shot a peevish look over her shoulder and

towed him along. Of course he'd want his privacy. He probably needed it desperately, in fact. "Then we'll go to a guest bedroom."

"One isn't made up, much less warm."

"Darius." She stopped and peered up at him. "Do you want William's coin? Because if you do, you're going to have to want me, and I intend to be in your bed."

"I want William's coin," he said, gathering her braid at her shoulder and staring past her head. "I do want that."

"So, where will we do this?"

Well, everlasting, merciful God, so what if he heard the tremor in her voice? But when he looked at her, some of his characteristic amusement was evident in his eyes.

"Wherever you please, Vivvie." He slipped his fingers through hers. "I'm yours to command."

"Of course, you are." She *hated* the detachment behind his humor. "Where is your room?"

"Come." He slid his arm over her shoulders. "It's nice and cozy. I've languished in there at my bath for most of the evening."

Interesting. Vivian had drawn hers out until the water was cold too.

"I don't get to keep my lawn tent tonight, do I?"

"We can worry about that later."

"I want to worry about it now."

He opened the door to his bedroom and let her pass through before him. Vivian put aside their argument to take in his most personal surroundings. She was relieved to see the bedroom wasn't a monk's cell, which she could have easily seen him inflicting on himself. The room was comfortably masculine, with odd little touches.

"Flowers?"

"They're made of silk and paper," he said. "A curiosity, but pretty enough to fool the eye for the months when I can't afford hothouse flowers."

"You don't have a hothouse?"

"I do, but it's taken up with growing food," he said, letting her amble around as she chose.

"Why does it smell good in here?"

"There's cinnamon in that little pot by the hearth." He shrugged out of his jacket. "Occasionally, I'll burn a scented candle. Then too, I make lavender and rosemary sachets to sell in Town, and my linens and wardrobe are scented with both."

"You're very enterprising," Vivian said, studying the room rather than the man removing his clothes so casually. The bed was huge, as it would have to be for a fellow of his dimensions, and raised up one step, for warmth. The bed hangings were a rich green velvet, the linens snowy white, and the entire thing looked far too comfy for what was going to happen there.

"If I'm to have any comforts at all"—Darius was pulling his shirt over his head—"then enterprise is necessary. What did you decide about the lawn tent?"

"It's up to me?"

"It's up to you." He sat on the raised hearth to tug off his boots.

"Why are you so casual about disrobing?"

"I don't think of it as disrobing." His stockings

followed. "I think of it as getting into my livery. The fit is superb."

She did not want to smack him, *never* that. "That's awful."

"It's honest." He rose, wearing only his breeches. "In truth, Vivvie, I want to be naked for you. I want you to desire what you see. I want to please you."

He was slipping further into his role as seducer, and Vivian wanted to howl at the shift. His eyes became slumberous, the pitch of his voice dropped, and his spine curved a bit, to let him strut rather than walk toward her.

"Stop this immediately."

Seven

He halted his progress toward her, holding her gaze. "Stop what?"

What words could she use? "I don't want to be a job, a task, an obligation."

His expression darkened. "You've known me for a week, Vivian. This is business. Pleasurable business, one hopes, but business. I *am* being paid for what happens here, and you are being compensated too, with a lifetime of motherhood."

"I know." She sat on the bed, disgruntled, impatient, and not at all willing to be seduced. "But sometimes people can be friends when they've business to transact. William is friends with his cronies from the Lords. They argue, fight, and scheme against one another, but they're friends."

"Interesting form of friendship." Darius lowered himself beside her. "I can't have you getting silly notions, Vivvie. When you leave here, we're done."

"You've said as much."

"It has to be that way, for the sake of the child." He took her hand, which was some consolation. "You cannot have this child raised with rumors regarding paternity. Whispers like that haunt a person. I know, because they've haunted my sister Leah her entire life and excused all manner of poor behavior on my father's part."

"That is dreadful."

"More dreadful for her, but you comprehend that when we're done with this little winter idyll, Vivian, we're strangers again. Worse than strangers, because a man of my reputation would seldom cross your social orbit unless I'm escorting my sister."

"I don't believe that." She leaned against him, resenting his insistence on this discussion. He was an earl's spare, and they often became MPs, and she entertained MPs in quantity at William's table.

"Believe it." He petted her hand. "The people I keep company with late at night would make you cringe, Vivvie. They've turned being mean into a hobby. You don't want them getting wind we were connected."

She stayed silent—she could hardly argue this point—until he leaned over and kissed her cheek. "This is not lighthearted conversation, and flirtation should be lighthearted, my lady."

"Is that what you call it?"

"I honestly don't know what to call it." He rose, his tone both impatient and amused. "I intend to pleasure you tonight, Vivvie. So make your decision about the lawn tent."

He stepped out of his breeches, folding them over a chair with the rest of his clothes, then got the warmer, filled it with coals, and ran it over the sheets. Something about the matter-of-fact, any-night-of-the-week nature of the activity gave Vivian courage. If he could consider this a passing romp, so could she. She dragged the lawn tent over her head and stood by the side of the bed, clutching it to her chest.

Because then again, she had no notion of what a romp, *any* romp, entailed.

"Brave Vivvie." He set the warmer aside. "Your courage will be rewarded."

His smile told her how much he approved as he crossed the room in a few slow, easy strides. He stood right next to her, naked, reminding her of how tall and muscular he truly was, but thank Jesus and the angels, he didn't tug the nightgown away.

He leaned down and ran his nose along the curve of her shoulder. Because her hands were full of nightgown, she could only stand there and let him inspect her naked person with his nose.

"Relax, Vivvie." She felt him tugging on the nightgown gently. "The bed is nice and warm, we have all night, and you're going to enjoy it."

She nodded, but his nose tickled where he ran it over her shoulder. Then his lips settled at that spot where her shoulder joined her neck, and Vivian comprehended what it meant when a woman's knees went weak.

"Hold on to me, Vivvie," he coaxed, and she did, with one hand on his bicep and the other clutching her nightgown to her chest. He pushed her with his chest until she was sitting on the bed, him looming over her, kissing her cheek, her jaw, her temple, and sending heat cascading out along her limbs. He stood between her legs, denying her his mouth on hers until Vivian let the nightgown go and used both hands in his hair to hold him still so she could kiss him properly.

Improperly, she corrected herself, opening her mouth immediately under his. But still, he was damnably coy, only teasing her with his tongue before skating away to press a kiss to her cheek or take her earlobe into his mouth.

She flinched. "That tickles."

"Behold." He held her gaze with amused solemnity. "She drops the nightgown." He went to his knees between her legs and wrapped his arms around her waist before Vivian could recover her shield. "You're as lovely as I imagined you'd be, and your nipples are the exact right shade of pink."

"Hush," she managed, but he was pressing his cheek to her exposed breast, ignoring the nightgown pooled in her lap. "I want the candles out."

"You won't, later," he promised, taking one nipple in his mouth. And just when Vivian's back arched into the heat of that mouth, he rose abruptly and began blowing out candles. "Though I've no doubt we'll both be too weak to leave the bed, so maybe blowing the candles out now is a good idea." He paused between candles to give her a brooding look. "Safer."

But it did not help, not one bit, to see his lean, naked flanks gilded by firelight, to see the red highlights in his sable hair, to see the night shadows on the handsome planes of his face.

He came back to the bed and considered her. "How about if we fold this"—he raveled up her nightgown—"at the foot of the bed?"

She let him have it, one handful at a time, knowing her blush was obvious even in subdued light. She turned her face away when he had the entire garment, and sat naked before a man for the first time in her life. He took an eternity to drape the nightgown across the bottom of the bed, and when he turned back to her, Vivian could see the beginnings of arousal stirring his…

She nodded at his parts. "What does one call this?"

"I'll tell you later. Touch me, Vivvie."

She knew it was probably not what came next, but she put her arms around his waist and pressed her face against his flat stomach. Yes, she could feel him, feel the soft mass of his genitals against the rise of her breast, but she hadn't the courage to do more than hold him, hiding her face against his ribs.

His hand came down on her hair, starting a slow massage at the back of her head, and she realized he'd give her all the time she needed to find her way through this.

She realized something else: All night wasn't going to be nearly long enough.

❧

She was throwing him completely off stride, with her modesty, and her… inexperience. For a lady married five years, Vivian had no sense of herself as a woman, and Darius felt a passing irritation for her. Older men might lack resilience, but they were experienced, for God's sake. William should have been considerate enough out of sheer gratitude to have given Vivian some confidence.

But here she was, twined around his waist in an embrace so odd and dear he didn't know quite what to make of it.

And having her wrapped around him was arousing. Usually, his degree of arousal was completely within his control, a matter of willing a response to occur, or willing it not to occur. Some men could throw darts with deadly accuracy, others sang beautifully even when sober; Darius could muster a cock stand on command.

Or not.

He bent over her and tugged on her hair to bring her face to where he could kiss her on the mouth. She slid her arms around his neck, urging him closer, and the shy command in her behavior made him smile against her lips.

"Get into bed, Vivvie," he whispered, "where you can have your way with me."

He pressed his cheek against hers for an instant, wanting to feel her blush heat his skin. She scooted back and was under the covers before he could peek at much of anything, but he'd seen enough already to have his cock on the rise.

And for once, he hadn't had to think his way to an erection. It was just there, along with a growing sense of happy anticipation.

Until he recalled: he was being *paid* for this.

"Now what, Mr. Lindsey?"

"Whatever you please." Darius followed her onto the bed. "The kissing was just getting started."

"You like to kiss?"

"Hmm." He kissed her again, lingeringly, loving

the way her arms came around him of their own accord and her fingers got tangled in his hair to tug him this way and that for her delectation. "I might."

With her, he did, and there was a small shock in that. He used his mouth on Lucy, frequently, and occasionally on Blanche, and they certainly put their mouths on his body and each other's, but he didn't kiss them on the mouth. An unspoken rule, one he hadn't understood at the time he'd made it.

He understood it now. Kisses were to be given, not bought.

"I like kissing you," he admitted, seaming her lips with his tongue. "I like it a lot."

"Mmm." Which, he supposed translated to "As do I" when considered in conjunction with the way she was sighing into his mouth. He angled his body half over hers, half along it, and slipped an arm under her neck. She paused in her kissing and turned her face into his shoulder.

"Now what?"

"Do you think there's a list somewhere, Vivvie?" He slid a hand down her thigh and tugged her leg over his hip. "Kiss three to five minutes, fondle at least two minutes. Mount, thrust, spend, wait nine months, name baby?"

She blinked up at him in the firelight, and he could see her trying to think. The way passion slowed her busy brain and softened her eyes was lovely.

"Here's my list." He nudged at her belly with his cock. "Kiss her until she's mindless with it, feast my hands on the glory of her body until she's begging for my cock, swive her until she explodes with pleasure more times than she can count, repeat steps one through three until she lies sleeping and sated in my arms."

"Begging?"

"Begging." He kissed her temple, more than a little surprised that all this blather was the honest truth. "Pleading, demanding, praying for me to give her what she craves."

"Gracious, everlasting God."

"Kiss me, Vivvie," he whispered in her ear then drew her earlobe between his teeth. He shifted so he was over her, but kept his cock off of her lest she become too... rushed.

Hell, lest *he* become too rushed.

And, by God, she'd gotten the knack of kissing him. Her tongue was bold and teasing, and just when he thought maybe it was time to slide down her body and show her what else a mouth could do, she bit his earlobe, and then his neck, and he had to retaliate by slipping a hand over her breast and tugging at one ruched nipple.

"Darius." She whispered his name on such an exhalation of longing that Darius heard it in the throbbing tip of his cock. She laid her hand over his and closed her fingers. "More, please."

Please was not begging, but it was importuning of a sort. He obliged, experimenting with the pressure and grip she liked, until she was arching her back and rolling her hips against him.

"Tell me what you want, Vivvie." He levered up and twisted to get his mouth on that nipple.

"More, please, Darius... God." He suckled the one

and kept his fingers busy at the other, and she shifted restlessly beneath him, her hands trailing along the muscles of his back, into his hair, over his face, over *his* nipples.

He'd wanted to make her come a few times before they joined, out of pride, some, but also out of consideration for her. She'd been hesitant, and nothing overcame hesitance like pleasure, except his first plan didn't seem quite… necessary.

"Darius?" She'd arched up against his cock and gone still, then he felt her hand, carefully shaping him.

The expedited approach was going to have to serve, pride be damned. He moved over her, nudging at her damp sex with his shaft.

"Kiss me." He lowered his head, but she'd turned her face, so he concentrated on finding the entrance to her body.

"I'm not sure…" she began when he'd settled his mouth on the side of her neck, a spot he already knew made her melt, and her words trailed off until he'd found his target.

"Just relax, Vivvie," he said, because she'd gone abruptly tense and silent. "Relax so I can bring you pleasure." He pushed against her gently, feeling the sweet, wet warmth of impending bliss. The urge to thrust hard, to go *home* in her body was strong, but she tugged stoutly on his hair.

"I don't think…" She inhaled again and held her breath, waiting.

He wasn't hearing "no," so Darius pushed again, more gently, and she stiffened even more.

"Darius, wait. I can't…"

"Vivvie?" He rested his forehead against hers, his intellect telling him very clearly the lady was having second thoughts, while his body shouted with equal certainty this was no time for *thoughts* of any kind.

"I can't do this."

Well, of course. Last minute nerves, conscience, whatever. This was Vivvie, and nothing was simple with her.

"Am I hurting you?"

"You're going to."

"You're not comfortable?"

"I'm very uncomfortable."

"Here?" He gave a small but productive thrust, gaining him the first real increment of penetration. She yelped, and her body closed against him.

And not in passion.

"You see?" she muttered, teeth clenched.

He realized as he stayed poised just inside Vivian's body that William's disservice to her went deeper than he'd thought. In his infirmity or inconsideration or pure blind devotion to a dead woman, William Longstreet hadn't shown Vivian even the barest consideration due between any two people sharing intimacies—on those few and distant occasions when he'd availed himself of his marital privileges at all.

"I won't hurt you." He smoothed a hand down her hair but could see even by the firelight she didn't believe him.

"This won't work," she insisted, her expression miserable. "I'm sorry."

"Vivian." His tone came out more harsh than he'd

intended, but the control he'd bragged of so easily was costing him. "Vivvie, don't you want a baby? A child to hold, to love, to treasure?"

"I want a baby," she said, near tears, "but I'm not suited to this... I just... I can't..."

"Hush." He kissed her forehead and withdrew. "We'll go with another approach."

"Another approach?" She sounded not at all reassured, even when he shifted to his back and held out his arms.

"Come here."

She cuddled against him, apparently ready to be comforted, but he lifted her to straddle him, smiling at her surprise.

"What are we doing?"

"We're getting you that baby," he said, settling more comfortably on his back. "Mount up, my lady."

"Mount...?"

He fished between their bodies to position himself, then arched up so she could feel his cock against her sex.

Her expression changed. "One can conceive like so?"

"Two can. You'll have to kiss me back into the mood." Which was a patent lie. His blood was nearly sizzling with the need to be inside her, to swive her silly.

"Kiss you." She eyed him speculatively. "I suppose that will work." She leaned down and brushed her lips over his.

"That's it." He slipped a hand over the ripe fruit of her breast. "This position has all sorts of advantages, now that I consider it."

"Such as?" She brushed her lips over his again, and Darius thought she might have pressed the slightest bit down on his cock.

"I can fill my hands with the abundance of your lovely breasts." He demonstrated, teasing at both nipples simultaneously. "If you like it, you should reward me, Vivvie."

"Reward... you?"

"Give me a little more of what I crave." He arched up minutely, and she didn't resist. "What I need."

He dug deep for mental and physical reserves he hadn't had to draw on before, and let her nibble and tease her way down his cock. One kiss, one fondle, one sigh, one suckle, one nuzzle at a time.

He buried his hand in the hair at her nape, holding her over him several fraught, luscious minutes later. "I want to move, love."

"Move?" Her voice was lazy, distracted, as if she were listening to some internal melody, and he hoped to God she was.

"Here." He gave her one slow, controlled roll of his hips. "Let me move, Vivvie, please."

"Do that again, slowly." She looked thoughtful. He was inside her, not as deep as he'd like to be, but not just begging at her door, either. She sighed as he moved cautiously, and dropped her head.

"Just be careful."

"Oh, I'll be careful." He gathered her close, meaning it. "So careful, but kiss me, Vivvie. Your kisses will help me take you slowly."

Another lie, for her kisses had become languorous, lazy, decadent imitations of coitus that had him bowing up to devour her mouth even as his cock began to ply her with slow, *careful* precision.

"You're all right, love?"

"Mmm." She hung over him, and he took her nipple in his mouth, not willing that she be just all right. He suckled, teased, and stroked into her, letting himself go a little, but only a little.

"This is… different, Darius."

"Not painful?"

"Uncomfortable."

Damnable word. He went still. "You move, then. If it hurts, you show me what you're comfortable with."

"I didn't say it hurt." She tried a slow glide along his cock, and Darius nearly shouted with the pleasure bolting up his spine. "It's… unsettling."

"Arousing?"

She didn't answer, her expression suggesting she was too inwardly focused.

"Don't think so hard, Vivvie." He brushed his fingers over her serious expression, unable to recall when bed sport had required so much talking. He didn't ask her permission but shifted on a slow roll in counterpoint to her movement.

"Oh… my… gracious."

"You like that?" He offered her a tad more and prayed for fortitude.

"It… helps. I think."

"How about that?" He let another inch of the reins slip through his mental gloves. "Does that help more?"

"Mmm." She folded down, depriving him of the sight of her face should her eyes go soft with further arousal, depriving him of the sight of her breasts, rosy from his attention, begging for more. But she anchored herself on his chest, telling him he was free to pleasure her with his cock—pleasure them both—so he spent a few minutes easing her along, getting her used to the push and drag of two bodies intent on one goal.

"Hold on to me, Vivvie," he whispered, sneaking in a kiss to her temple and fitting one hand around a full breast.

She clung, and he kept his tempo slow but purposeful, until he could feel her losing her grip, shifting from considering the sensations gathering in her body to being swamped with them.

"Let it happen, Vivvie." He anchored an arm across her back and thrust deep. "I owe you this. Let me give it to you."

"Darius…?"

He'd wanted a pleasant little appetizer orgasm for her, an introduction to further pleasures as a way to gain her trust, like the promenade at the beginning of a ball. But the way she was panting and meeting him thrust for thrust told him she was going up fast, hard, and hot.

"Darius… what? Oh, Jesus save me…"

"I've got you." Darius felt her body begin to flutter and grab at his cock. "Let yourself go, Vivvie. I've got you." He held her tightly, curling up into her embrace even as he thrust deeply into her, seeking heat.

And he hadn't meant to let himself come, but she convulsed around him hard, then harder still, and in the part of his mind not incoherent with pleasure, he heard the words, "Give her a baby."

Bliss rippled up from their joining and washed out

over his body in long, hot pulses, until he lost the sense of where his skin separated him from Vivian, or any other aspect of creation. He heard himself moan—he never moaned—and felt himself clutching at Vivian more desperately than he sought his next breath. His body gave itself up to drenching spasms of pleasure, until he realized that harsh, grating sound was his breathing, and he was going to suffocate Vivian if he didn't turn loose of her.

"Jesus." He echoed her earlier prayer. "Holy Jesus."

She pushed up to peer at him. "Was that how it was supposed to go?"

He smiled at her, loving the earnest concern in her expression, the rosy flush of pleasure on her chest. "It will do for a start."

"You're teasing me." She settled down against his chest, content, and he was content to have her in his arms. More than content, God help him.

"Did I hurt you?" He was smug, intent on his point, and he emphasized it with a soft push of his flagging erection.

She lifted her face again to consider him, and there wasn't any humor in her eyes.

"I didn't know it would be like that."

She was asking him a question. He kissed her nose and dodged, partly. "I didn't either, love."

"It changes things."

"Conception could be considered a change." He congratulated himself on the nimbleness of his feint. A little honesty went a long way under these circumstances. "We won't know about that for a few weeks."

"Gracious. Weeks." She subsided, laying her cheek

over his heart, and he was grateful for her silence, because the magnitude of the possibility was hitting him in a way it hadn't earlier. This little romp—this excursion into pleasure—very well could result in a life, an innocent life, full of potential for good and ill. The notion stilled the humming pleasure in his body but ignited a different kind of warmth where Vivian lay gathered against his chest.

He couldn't recall the last time he'd let himself come in a woman's body. He'd had the experience, of course, with… some pregnant baroness, or the Italian equivalent thereto. He wasn't sure which, but it had been years ago, before he'd become so desperate for coin, before his sister's safety and welfare had been thrust into his youthful and impoverished hands.

And now Vivian was in his hands, trusting him to get her a baby and not break her heart in the process.

He could do that. He'd make sure of it. The only real question was whether he'd survive when his own was broken instead.

❧

She was going to cry, and Vivian was certain that wasn't comme il faut. The sensations were overwhelming, the pleasure beyond description, and the emotions… She silently apologized to William, who'd no doubt shared years and years of these kinds of feelings with his Muriel. Feelings Vivian would never have been able to compete with, never have been able to match.

And what of Darius? How did he do this, hire himself out for coin when the consequences were so intimately devastating?

Or were they?

He held her tenderly, his hands on her back leaving a trail of slow, sweet pleasure where he traced her bones and muscles. He'd shown her consideration of a magnitude Vivian had never imagined—was this why Angela loved her husband? Was it the promise of that kind of care that had seen her own mother giving in to Thurgood's smiles and caresses?

Vivian was witless to puzzle through it, but her best guess was that Darius wasn't witless. He was used to this. He'd said as much.

Like an ice on a hot day, a good gallop on a fall morning. Nothing more. Not even when it started a precious new life, not even when it meant a woman he hardly knew would be financially secure for life.

She felt him slipping from her body, and then he was patting her backside. "Slide up, so you're over me."

"I'll make a mess."

"A small mess. On me, rather than on the sheets. Up you go."

Another gentle pat, and she complied, mortified to feel his seed leaving her body along with him. And then he was casually holding a folded handkerchief to her sex, preventing the mess but completing her sense of embarrassment.

"You're blushing." He kissed her cheek and dabbed at her gently. "There's no need for that."

"Blushing isn't a matter of need." She dropped her face to his shoulder and felt him using the handkerchief low on his belly. "Shall I go back to my room?"

"Is that what you'd like?"

He tossed the handkerchief aside and passed her a

glass of water. When she sat up to drink it, she realized she was still straddling him, and she was naked, and he was…

Well, of course he was looking at her, smiling up at her a little… *tentatively*. The light from the banked fire was dim, but Vivian was certain she'd never seen that exact smile on Darius Lindsey's face. She passed him the water, and when he'd finished, she set it on the nightstand.

"I'm sleepy," she said, "and your bed is warm."

"Never say I sent a lady alone to a cold, dreary bed." He stroked the mattress beside him, and she climbed off him and cuddled up.

"So is that something they pay you for too?"

"I beg your pardon?" There was amusement in his tone, also something else—bewilderment? *Hurt?* She would certainly have paid him for it, paid him a great deal.

"The ladies who pay for your favors? Do they pay you for the pleasure of cuddling?"

"They do not," he replied, sounding displeased. "Nor would I allow it. Now hush." He settled his chin on her temple, and Vivian was all too willing to hush. She hurt for him. Hurt that he had nobody to cuddle with, that the only child in his life was likely his brother's by-blow, and he must sell even his kisses to keep his household intact.

She resolved to ask William why this should be so. Most earldoms came with fat, old estates, capable of supporting younger sons to at least some modest extent. But as her body went boneless in Darius's arms, and sleep seeped into her brain, Vivian considered she might not bring this up with William, ever, for what passed between her and Darius was somehow precious and private, business arrangement or not.

◈

Darius knew the moment Vivian gave up and let sleep claim her. He'd been prepared for her to fire off more of her pithy observations about his lifestyle, if not his lovemaking, but she'd succumbed, and now he could wallow in the pleasure of simply holding her.

How long had it been since he'd held a woman for the uncomplicated pleasure of it? He could tell himself he wanted to swive her again in the morning—increase the chance of conception, that is—but right now, all he wanted was to hold her, to keep her and her tender, inexperienced sensibilities safe for as long as he could.

He missed Italy, where the women understood what a cicisbeo was and what he was not. He was a friend, an appreciated friend. And he missed the way Italian men were demonstrative with their ladies. They didn't show they cared for a woman by blowing another fellow's brains out on some foggy meadow strewn with sheep dung. They wrote poetry to women and sang to them and toasted them before open company. And the ladies blew them kisses in return.

In England, the last thing Darius could be was a friend to the likes of Lucy or Blanche. They took their power too seriously, dealt too much from weakness and need, not generosity and pleasure.

He hadn't been willing to let himself think this way, not until the prospect of Lord Longstreet's coin loomed closely enough at hand that Darius could consider becoming a gentleman farmer in truth.

And how nice it was going to be, to have another three weeks to toss ideas back and forth with Vivian over the breakfast table. To see her dressed appropriately to her station, and to know of all men, he—without coin to speak of, or expectations—had given her her heart's desire.

In sleep, Vivian stirred then settled, but her hand had slipped lower, from Darius's waist to rest over his groin. Her fingers flexed, brushing his cock— forbidden territory to all other women—and he went still then shifted slightly under her hand. She brushed her fingers over him again, patted him sleepily, then subsided.

And for that, for that simple, sleepy, affectionate little pat on his soft cock, he gave up another piece of his heart to her.

Eight

ABLE REGARDED HIS FATHER, WHO SAT IN THE STIFLING library swaddled in blankets and scarves. "I never should have put you up to riding out with me. You've been ailing ever since."

"Ah, but it did me good, my boy." William's eyes held a twinkle. "To treat myself to a hot scone or two, a nip from the flask, a trot through the village. It reminds me what it's all for, you know?"

"All what?"

"The scrapping about in the Lords, for one thing. You think it's fun, to listen to the same old arguments over the Catholic question? To hear Prinny whining for yet still more money while the streets of London are littered with men who gave limbs and eyes in defense of King and Country?"

"You're sounding suspiciously liberal, your lordship." Able drew up a chair before the blazing fire, because it wasn't often he and his father just talked.

"Not liberal, exactly. I believe the monarchy in the hands of a wise and just ruler is still government as God intended," William said, setting aside some faded correspondence. "But the people aren't sheep, and we've seen what they can do when they decide revolution is their only recourse."

"England isn't France."

"Hunger is hunger," William countered, sitting up straighter. "Bad harvests can happen anywhere, and Louis was ruling an abundantly blessed and happy nation, and then, in just a few decades, all is chaos and murder."

"I suppose you're in a better position to appreciate that than most. Not many have your perspective."

William smiled thinly. "I'm too damned old, you mean. God knows I feel it."

Able did not argue the point, for William was venerable indeed. "We should send word to Vivian that you're ailing. I can put a note in the post tomorrow."

"You'll do no such thing," William said with a touch of asperity. "She'll be galloping down here, wielding vile concoctions, putting plasters on my feet, and clucking and fussing until a man can't get any rest. I have a little cold, is all, and there's no better place for me to be recovering than in the company of my family, at my ancestral home."

Able smiled at the reference to family. It wasn't much, but they weren't demonstrative men. Coming from William Longstreet, it was something, to be called family—as clearly, whatever she was, Vivian wasn't included in that designation.

❧

Darius grinned down at Vivian. "I made it to Edward the Martyr that time."

"I beg your pardon?" Vivian thought her tone was impressively crisp, but she spoiled the effect entirely by brushing his hair back from his forehead and slipping her fingers over the curve of his ear. She knew he liked her to touch his ears, and his hair, and his...

"You know, Alfred the Great, Edward the Elder, Athelstan, Edmund, Edred... when you tempt me to lose control, I recite them in my head."

"And all the past kings of the realm help you withstand my charms. I'm impressed." She was impressed that she could have this discussion—*any* discussion—when her body was still throbbing with the pleasure Darius visited upon her.

"I've never even gotten as far as Canute," he confessed, still clearly pleased with himself. "You're a siren, Vivvie."

And didn't that just prompt a woman to be pleased with herself, too? "I'm a hungry siren." She stroked his ear again.

"It's been a taxing week. Undo us, sweetheart."

"Why is it my job?" she groused, but she carefully extricated his waning erection from her body, because he preferred she be the one to do it. Vivian suspected Darius just wanted her to become at ease handling him, as God knew, he was at ease handling her. In a week's time, she'd learned all manner of naughty, wonderful things from him, and she suspected he was only bringing her along slowly so as not to shock her.

"You like having your hands on me," Darius said as he shifted off of her. "I'm humoring you."

"Of course, you are." She pushed him to his back and rolled off the bed to fetch a damp cloth from the basin on the washstand. "Every proper English schoolboy learns the royal succession so he can humor the ladies." She swabbed off his cock, comfortable now moving him this way and that. He hiked his knees and spread his legs so she could make a pass at the inside of his thighs, his belly, and groin, and then the part she suspected he liked best, when she'd carefully tend to his balls.

"You are like that tomcat." She dabbed at herself, set the cloth aside, and climbed back on the bed. "Your physical pleasures are dear to you."

"All of God's creatures like to feel cared for." Darius ran a hand down the side of her face, a caress that had her nigh purring. "It's how you show your appreciation for all the care I lavish on you."

"Forcing me into new gowns, slippers, gloves, and bonnets isn't care, Darius Lindsey, it's your idea of entertainment."

He wrapped her in his arms. "Ungrateful wench. You love it when I make you read Mrs. Radcliffe and dance with me in the library and try decadent desserts with each meal."

"Except breakfast."

"I just served you your breakfast dessert, unless you'd like to nibble on my parts? No? Well, perhaps another time."

"You keep suggesting this. I can't believe you're serious."

"Of course I'm serious." He slid a hand over her breast. "Though you won't let me nibble on you. I'm attempting to get a child on a spinster, and it's trying, to say the least."

He teased like this mercilessly, making Vivian wonder if all couples were so free and affectionate with each other.

"You're trying to shock me, sir, but I need a nap, so hush and rub my back." She rolled over, because in this at least she was in complete earnest. Sharing a bed with Darius Lindsey was exhausting.

Darius smiled and did as she ordered. As Vivian dozed off, he made a bet with himself that she'd be giving him more explicit orders long before their month was out. She was or soon would be fertile, and her natural sense of curiosity was making quick inroads on her inherent shyness.

Day by day, and night by night, she was shedding one inhibition after another. She now insisted the candles be kept burning when he made love to her; she didn't gasp and stammer when he accosted her in the study or her own bed or the broad light of day. He'd jammed a saddle rack against the feed room door just the day before, and hiked her skirts for a little ride at midday in the chilly confines of the barn. His thighs still ached pleasantly from the exertion of thrusting at just the right height.

When Gracie tapped softly on the door, Darius quietly bid her to enter. The maid took one look at Vivian, thoroughly tousled and cuddled even in sleep against Darius's side, and shook her head.

"You wore the poor thing out," Gracie said, passing Darius a cup of tea. "Best be careful, Master Dare."

"Of?"

"She'll take a piece of you with her."

"And leave thirty pieces of silver," Darius replied.

"Which we can use around here." Though a child would be a piece of him—maybe the best piece.

"You know, when he'd got his silver, Judas hung himself from a tree." Gracie poked at the logs on the hearth. "And what good will you be to any of us, swinging in the breeze that way?"

"She's leaving, Gracie." Darius's hand passed gently over Vivian's head. "She'll be gone in two weeks, and then it won't matter what happened between us. We'll be strangers again, and my obligation will be met."

Gracie rose from the fireplace and turned a pitying expression on him. "As if the woman who breaks your heart can ever be a stranger to you. Have a care, sir, or you'll be picking out your tree."

Darius offered her a lopsided smile. "Be gone with you, Gracie. When I've tired this one out, I'm coming after you."

"I've got one good hand, Master Dare." Gracie swept toward the door. "That's plenty enough to paddle your naughty backside into next week for such foolish talk. Mind you order that woman a soaking bath, or she'll be too sore to walk."

Gracie closed the door softly on that whispered reminder, and Darius made a mental note to do just that. Were it not for the need to consider Vivian's inexperience, he'd be going at her twice as often as he did, and twice as hard.

Just once, he'd treated her to a hard, fast coupling, and she'd come like a house afire before he'd even found his rhythm.

And then come again when he had.

But he hadn't used her so hard since, aware that

their goal was conception, and frequent coupling was conducive to that end. This kept him gentle with her, considerate, mindful of the need to savor and conserve when he might have otherwise plundered.

As he lay back on the pillows, sipping his tea and petting Vivian's hair, he considered that with a woman like Vivian, marriage might not be the trap he'd envisioned it being. With Vivian intent on a child, they were having exactly the kind of unrestrained, frequent sex newlyweds might have.

And it was... overwhelmingly sweet, a backhanded gift from fate that he, a man who never allowed women the intimacy of intercourse, never allowed them to kiss him, should have all that given to him in such unstinting abundance—from a woman to whom he'd have to become, just as he'd said, a stranger in the new year.

He set his tea aside, slipped down into the covers beside Vivian, and drew her into his embrace. She went into his arms trustingly and gave him her warmth without even waking.

❧

The weather moderated, and Vivian found herself riding out with her... with Darius. He loved his estate fiercely, and she concluded fierceness was a part of him, part of the boy who'd grown up between battling parents, finding his purpose befriending his brother and protecting their sisters.

As they rode over his muddy acres, Darius told her his plans for this field and that pond. Trout could be raised like a crop, she learned, and it would improve

Darius's crop yields if he set up a system of irrigation and flood control for the water on his property.

"Why not raise flowers? You don't need a hothouse for them, much of the year, but you could easily sell them in Town."

"Townhouses all have back gardens."

"Bachelors buying flowers for the ladies do not have gardens," Vivian said. "No single townhouse or mansion has enough flowers on hand to decorate for balls and entertaining. There is demand, and you could specialize."

"In?" He was bringing the same focus to this topic that he brought to every topic, including how best to bring her pleasure. The notion left a lady somewhat breathless, even as her horse merely ambled along beside his.

"Fragrant flowers?" Vivian tossed out the idea. "Exotic flowers, I don't know. It would be easy enough to see what's in short supply and provide it."

"And then when fashion dictated that fragrant flowers were no longer all the rage?"

"You diversify," Vivian said as Bernice stepped around a puddle. "Just as you have already. You excel at it, with your chickens and sachets and... other things."

"My whoring." He cocked an eyebrow, looking pleased to have an opportunity to shock her with bad language.

"Your enterprise. I suspect you feel sorry for those women, Darius."

"Vivian..."

"Don't scold." She kept her tone mild, but this aspect of his life bothered her increasingly. "No matter what they pay you, you have to feel a little something for them, or you'd just sell more chickens."

"Chickens produce only so much income. The ladies pay very, very well, and they cost me nothing."

"They cost you dearly."

"I'll race you to that stone wall."

He nudged Skunk with his heels, so Bernice cantered more forward as well, and Vivian knew the point he was making: sexual pleasure, or pain, mattered only like a good gallop on a crisp day, nothing more. So she let the subject drop and let the mare have her head for the next half mile, but when she woke in Darius's bed on Christmas morning and saw a small, wrapped box on the breakfast tray, the cost of Darius's enterprises with the ladies came to mind again.

She nodded at the box. "Why is that there?" William gave her presents, on their anniversary or her birthday. Little things—a book of old verse, a pair of ear bobs, nothing unique to her, but thoughtful gestures nonetheless.

"Happy Christmas, Vivvie." He poured her tea and passed it over to her, the same as he had every morning for more than a week. "Open your gift."

"I thought you told me my gift was hiding under the covers on your side of the bed?"

"You've already enjoyed that gift." He sipped his tea placidly, though there was something… grave about his demeanor, or watchful, so Vivian took a fortifying gulp of tea, passed the cup back to him, and reached for her present.

"This had better not be naughty, or I'll leave it here, and you'll be reminded of your…"

Inside the box was a small, elegantly cut glass bottle holding about four ounces of golden liquid. She lifted the stopper and sniffed delicately.

Her nose woke up, and she sniffed again, finding something that started off a little like the scent Darius himself wore—soft, soothing, a little sweet, a little spicy—but then the fragrance took off in a more mysterious direction, carrying notes both floral and spicy in a blend that intrigued and promised and drew interest on a purely sensual level.

"It's lovely." She sniffed again. "What is it?"

"I had it blended for you," he said, watching as she continued to inhale through her nose and consider, then take another little whiff. "The recipe is under the lining, as is the name of the *parfumier* who blended it for you."

"You had this made for me?" She was still trying to analyze the fragrance as she frowned and whiffed. "Did it turn out as you'd planned?"

"Scents are tricky." He set the breakfast tray on the night table. "You think you know what will go together, but then the ingredients react with one another, and with the wearer, and sometimes it turns out better than you planned, but not always."

"This is fascinating." She passed him the bottle, and he took a cautious, glancing sniff, held the bottle away, and repeated the move several times.

"It's what I wanted for you," he decided, "maybe a little richer." He tipped the bottle against his finger, then replaced the stopper and set the bottle aside. "Hold still."

With his wet finger, he touched the sides of her neck then drew a line from her throat to her cleavage.

"We'll see how it takes on you, assuming you like it?"

"I love it. Thank you very much."

He wrapped an arm around her shoulders and drew her against his side, and for the moment, Vivian was content to lie against his warmth, the lovely scent subtly spreading over them as they drowsed together.

"I'll miss you." Vivian's words came out without any warning, to her or him, and Vivian felt Darius stiffen beside her.

"Vivian…"

"Don't Vivian me." She hitched her leg over his thighs, as if he might toss back the covers to escape her. "I've been married five years, and never once has William given me a gift this thoughtful. This personal. I've known you two weeks, and you give me this… and frocks, gloves, and waltzes, and… I know, it means nothing to you, but to me…"

"To you?" His face was unreadable, but he wasn't telling her to hush or to finish her tea, nor was he lecturing her about ices on hot days.

"I was a married spinster—you were right. Not so much in my dress and choice of reading material, but inside, where no one sees. Where no one cared to see."

"It can't mean anything," he said sternly, as if he were reminding himself and hoping it was true.

"Too late, Darius." She closed her eyes and relaxed against him. "What you think you mean, is that the sexual business means nothing. What you really mean, is you want Darius Lindsey to mean nothing to me. The two are not the same, and you won't convince me they are."

He kissed her into submission, gently, slowly, entrancingly, and she let him sweep her away again, because he'd at least let her have her say, and she owed him the fair hearing he was demanding with his hands and mouth and body.

But what was wrong with the man, that he'd try to convince them both such tenderness and caring meant nothing at all?

She bided her time and waited until the night before the New Year to counterattack. By tacit agreement, they now slept together in his bed, and on a few occasions, had fallen asleep without having intercourse. On those occasions, Vivian would wake up to find Darius making love to her sometime in the middle of the night. She had cuddled up with him and let sleep overcome her, because he'd exhausted her once again with final fittings, riding around the property, a rousing argument over the Catholic question, and a long chess match, which she'd won.

When she was sure he'd fallen asleep, she got up, built up the fire, and then gently eased the covers back to reveal Darius's naked form.

Everlasting God, he was beautiful. The whip marks had faded, leaving only smooth, burnished skin over hard muscle and powerful bones. She knew his body now, knew the scents and textures, the sounds and touches. Tonight, she wanted to know the taste of him.

"Vivvie?"

"Here." She curled down to rest her head on his stomach, and felt his hand stroking over her hair. Heaven help her, when did his touch create in her the desire to purr? Her hair, her hands, her shoulders, anywhere and everywhere on her body, she wanted his touch and missed it on some level when she didn't have it.

She curled her fingers over his shaft, and his hand went still.

"Vivvie, no…"

"You hush," she chided as she touched her tongue to the tip of his cock. "For once, Darius Lindsey, you hush, and you let me."

His fingers laced through her hair, and Vivian was sure he was going to gently deny her this—deny himself this, more significantly—but then his palm cradled the back of her head, and she heard him sigh.

He said nothing, verbal surrender being too much to expect, and Vivian settled in to explore him with her mouth. He was religious about his personal hygiene and typically bathed before retiring. There was a lingering fragrance of lavender about his person, but something beneath that unique to him, and just as distinctive. Cautiously, Vivian used her tongue to wet the length of him, feeling his erection grow as she did.

When she concentrated her attention on the silky-smooth head of his cock, she felt the jump of arousal in his stomach where it lay under her cheek. She suckled gently, and his fingers tightened in her hair.

"Let me," she whispered again, rubbing him against her cheek and easing off to stroke the wet length of him with her hand while she held the head of his cock in her mouth.

"You don't owe me this," Darius whispered, his voice oddly tight.

"Hush." She emphasized her command by drifting

her fingers over his balls, and he sighed and arched toward her. He liked her hands on him. He'd never said as much, but he'd told her nonetheless, and so she explored him with leisurely thoroughness, using her tongue and lips and fingers to map him over and over again.

His cock was magnificently hard, his hips moving in small, slow undulations when he again attempted to tug her away.

"Darius, no." She returned to the spot under the tip of his cock and applied a hint of suction. "Let me, please."

He went still, and she drew on him slowly, feeling arousal coil up more tightly in him, though his hips weren't moving. She knew his struggle: This wasn't merely an ice on a hot day, not merely a brisk gallop on a cool morning. There was nothing merely *anything* about letting himself have pleasure like this.

Holding him carefully in her mouth, Vivian reached over and found Darius's free hand. She slid it up his torso until his fingers rested over his own nipple, and then she retrieved her hand and wrapped her fingers around the thick base of his shaft again.

The sound he made was low, pained, and soft, but when Vivian began to stroke him, he moved slightly in counterpoint. She caught the rhythm and gradually got her mouth, his hips, and her hand synchronized, until it was as if she could feel his arousal building in her own body.

"Vivvie…"

She neither paused nor sped up, but kept at him with the sort of determined patience he'd shown her time after time. His pleasure was the object of this exercise, and she would neither relent nor show him mercy. She'd learned that from him, that to pleasure another person took discipline and self-sacrifice and genuine caring. When she felt the tension in him drawing impossibly tight, she realized he was holding off, purposely, maybe trying to hold off altogether.

She drew on him, strongly, and when he would have pulled her away at the last moment, she held her ground and kept him in her mouth, where she could force pleasure upon him more, longer, deeper, than he'd intended to allow. His body had its revenge for all his discipline, and his release had him groaning as he bowed up, shook, and bucked against Vivian's mouth and hand.

When he finally lay quiet on the mattress, breathing harshly, his hand loosely tangled in her hair, Vivian was still unwilling to relinquish him.

"God, Vivvie…" He sounded bewildered and spent. "Why?"

She closed her lips around his softening length, so he'd feel himself being drawn gently from her mouth, and got off the bed to fetch the wash cloth. As she tidied him up and offered him first crack at the water glass, she considered his question.

She'd done this because, in some regard, she'd come to love him. She'd wanted him to have something of her that was unique, something she'd never share with another. She had a need to give to him she couldn't question at that moment, and it had felt right to do this with him.

But that answer would hardly serve, not with him already in full retreat. When she bundled in beside him, he obligingly wrapped an arm around her, but his touch was cautious and… withholding.

"Why?" He reiterated the question, sounding more in possession of himself and not particularly happy.

"I wanted to know I could," she said, thinking it was a version of the truth. "I wanted to know what it was like."

"Don't do it again." He kissed her temple; his tone was relieved. "Not with me. We're supposed to be getting you a baby, if you'll recall."

She nodded, knowing if she didn't do it with him, she wasn't going to do it with anybody else. Not ever. Not because it was vulgar and base, as he no doubt thought, but because with Darius, it was sweet and lovely and unbearably intimate. She'd given this to him, but to demand one iota more would be more than his damaged image of himself could sustain.

⁂

Darius lay awake, his arms around Vivian, the weight of a thousand regrets on his heart.

Why on earth had he permitted this? None of them, not the laughing barmaids at Oxford, not the good-hearted ladies in Italy, not the scheming bitches he consorted with now—not one of them had been allowed what he'd just permitted with Vivian. Bad enough he was her stud, worse yet that he'd taken a hand in her wardrobe and appearance, worse still, he'd admitted to himself it was going to be hard to send her back to her William, but this…

He told himself he didn't trust Lucy or Blanche not to harm him, did he allow them to French kiss him.

Putting his cock between a woman's teeth was an act of trust, no matter what else a man might say or boast or brag regarding the experience. With those two, it was unthinkable.

With Vivian, it had been impossible to deny her.

So she'd been curious, and he'd obliged her. That's all it was. A small erotic experiment, quickly concluded and not to be repeated.

He dropped off into sleep on that thought, but when he woke and Vivian wasn't with him, he was almost relieved.

Or so he told himself.

❧

"So the smallest one, who could climb higher than any of the other kittens, went way, way, *way* up into the tree, until his brothers could see only his tail twitching among the branches, and from there he could tell them exactly in which direction the castle lay. All four kittens made it home by dark, and every other cat in the castle envied them their great adventure."

"Did they live happily ever after?" John stifled a yawn, and it was clear he'd kept his eyes open by sheer determination.

"They did," Vivian said, "although the smallest one grew up to become a great, lazy black tomcat who spent his time protecting his favorite little boy from mice."

John smiled sleepily and scooted farther down under his covers. "Wags does that. Will you stay until I fall asleep?"

"Of course." Vivian tucked the covers in more

closely around the boy, kissed his forehead, and resumed her seat at the foot of his bed.

"Darius sings to me sometimes, when I've had a nightmare," John said, eyes drifting closed. "I like the one about the lady with the green dress."

Vivian took a moment to translate, but then she started in on a quiet version of the folk song "Greensleeves," switching to a soft hum as John fell back to sleep. When she looked up, Darius was standing in the shadows by the door, arms crossed, regarding her from across the room. She rose, and he held out a hand. "Nightmare?"

Vivian tucked herself under his arm. "Gracie came to get you, but I heard her knocking, so I let you sleep. Does he get them often?"

"Yes." Darius ran a free hand through his hair. "I think he dreams of his mother, of the few months of his life when she was extant, and then wakes up, and she's not here, not anywhere."

"But you're here." Vivian leaned up and kissed his cheek. "And he goes right back to sleep, the same as any child."

"You think so?"

"I have two nephews and a niece. The boys are eight and five, and I can assure you they have had their share of nightmares, and their mother has never been farther away than the next hallway."

He looked relieved, which made her realize how deeply he fretted for the boy.

"You're doing a good job, Darius. John is a delight, and he loves you."

Something shadowed crossed his features, but

they'd reached Darius's bedroom, and Vivian let him tug off her nightgown and bathrobe, then wrap himself around her in the middle of the bed.

"You love that child," she said softly.

"I do." Vivian couldn't see his face in the dark, but she knew the admission cost him. "He wouldn't love me, did he know all the circumstances of his situation here."

"Yes, he would." She laced her fingers through his where they splayed over her midriff. "Children can be very forgiving, and you're doing the best you can for him."

He gathered her closer and began to make excruciatingly tender love to her without saying a word.

That night marked the turning point in their dealings, with the date of Vivian's scheduled departure drawing inexorably closer. They teased less, spoke less, and loved with a quiet desperation neither acknowledged. On the final night, Darius left her in peace to take her bath and tuck herself up in bed.

Near midnight, after much useless gazing into the fire in his study, he found her asleep in his bed for the last time and decided not to wake her. She'd become subdued these past few days, but so had he. When he'd found her tucking John in after a nightmare, something inside him had broken. Of all the burdens he carried, the burden of raising that child alone was the heaviest and the lightest. John was goodness, innocence, and all the hope and potential in the world.

John deserved to be loved and protected, and Darius died a thousand deaths every time Blanche tooled out in her coach and the servants hustled

John up to the third floor, there to remain until Lady Cowell took herself off hours later, lighter in the pocket and none the wiser about the composition of Darius's household.

He hated—*hated*—entertaining her under his roof and insisted on using a guest room at the back of the house to see her. Lucy, thank God, wasn't inclined to stir so far from Town in search of her pleasures, but rather, delighted in demanding that Darius go always to her at the hour of her choosing.

"Darius?"

"Here." He curled around Vivian's back, fitting his groin to her derriere and snugging his arm around her waist. "Go back to sleep, love."

"Where were you?"

"Making sure you're packed." He kissed her nape. In truth, he'd been sitting among her things, touching them, lifting them to his nose and wishing. Pathetic, but after tomorrow, the opportunity to be pathetic wouldn't be within reach, so he allowed it.

"Gracie helped me." Vivian brought his hand up to her lips and kissed his knuckles. "Have you any advice?"

"Name the baby William," Darius said on a sigh.

"My menses should have started by now. I'm not myself of late, so perhaps they're just delayed."

"You'll be sure William tells me if there's a child?"

"Yes." She tucked his hand over her naked breast. "I won't have to make him. William keeps his word."

"Do you know what to look for?"

"Regarding?"

She wouldn't just ask him. "Conception. You'll be tender here." He gently closed his hand over her breast. "You might be sleepy, queasy, or faint. Your sister can tell you more."

"How do you know these things?"

"John's mother was under my roof for much of her pregnancy. I became familiar with her various complaints."

"I envy you that." Vivian shifted to her back and hiked a leg over Darius's hips. "You know more what to expect than I do. Will you write to me?"

"Of course not."

"And I'm not to write to you?"

His finger traced down the side of her face. "You know we cannot, and it wouldn't be kind, either. Neither to you, nor to me, nor to William. Mostly, it wouldn't be smart."

"Because this means nothing, you mean nothing, I mean nothing."

"You're learning." Darius leaned over and kissed her mouth, but it wasn't to shut her up; it was gratitude for not belaboring the miserable point.

"Darius, I really, really want you to stop dealing with those women." She scooted so she was right up against his length, on her back and able to regard him by the firelight.

"You don't get a say, love." He kept his tone light. "It won't be of any moment to you after tomorrow, because we'll rarely see each other."

"Rarely?"

"I'm to attend the christening if there's a child, and I'll be squiring my sister around this year's Season, which means our paths might cross."

"You don't want me to say this, but I'll look forward to that."

"Vivvie." He rose up over her and braced himself on his arms. "You can't. You *cannot*. You should be relieved to be getting back to the safety of William's arms. Relieved to be done with such a one as I. You can't go... getting sentimental on me."

"If you didn't want me getting sentimental, then why create a perfume for me? Why let me meet John, why insist on sending Bernice along home with me? Why, Darius Lindsey?"

"Because you are a lady," he said, lowering himself to his forearms and gathering her in his embrace. "You were supposed to be a damned new roof, and you turned out to be a lady. One doesn't treat ladies with less than consideration."

"And you are a gentleman." Vivian stroked his hair. "And yet you let those infernal women beat you and humiliate you, and I cannot abide it, Darius."

"It isn't yours to abide or not," he said softly, kissing the side of her neck. "I don't want to argue with you, Vivvie."

"Yes, you do. You want to insist coin alone is adequate justification for letting them abuse you. I could just shake you."

"If you meet me at some Venetian breakfast, Vivvie, you're to look down your lovely nose at me, as if I'm a bug on the walkway, and ignore me thereafter."

"Ignore the father of my child?"

"Ignore the conniving bastard who took coin for swiving you," he whispered, letting her feel his growing arousal. "The man who got a child on you and walked away without a backward glance. The idiot who..."

But he stopped himself by sealing his mouth over hers, and for the last time, sliding himself home into her body. He wanted to rush, wanted to pound into her so she'd recall him for the rest of her life, so she'd never make love again without remembering what it had felt like with him.

For her, he held himself back. For her, he went slowly and tenderly until she was begging and writhing and her nails digging into his back with a sharp, sweet little pain. When she was near tears, he let her come, joining her one last time in the sexual pleasure that he, love-struck idiot, had tried to insist was of no more moment than a cold ice on a hot day.

And when the tears came, he kissed them away and started all over again, but in the morning, he would send her away just the same.

Nine

"So you're just going to put the poor thing in the coach and wave her on her way?"

Darius scowled at Gracie, who had brought the usual morning tray while Vivian slept on beside him. "I'll have the bricks heated first."

"You were never cold before, Master Dare." Gracie busied herself at the hearth. "I'm not proud of you, you know."

Before this month with Vivian, he'd been cold all the time. Darius kept his voice to a whisper, lest Vivian wake up any sooner than necessary. "If you must know the truth, I'll be relieved to get shut of her. It's past time she was back in her William's loving arms, and I can get back to my usual routine."

If a man told a lie often enough, he might begin to believe it.

"Some routine." Gracie snorted. "As if it was making you happy, to lark about in low places, consorting with those creatures."

"Happy matters little compared to solvent." Darius glared at her, and she had the grace to withdraw without further comment. He sipped his first cup of tea in silence, wishing he could put off the chore of waking Vivian and spare her their parting. She seemed to understand his warnings but not to take them to heart, and he mused in silence for some minutes on how, in truth, he was going to bear putting her into his traveling coach.

Vivian stirred sleepily beside him. "Tea?"

"Here you go." He passed her his cup. "Slowly, as it's hot."

"Gracie's been here."

"Making trouble, as usual." Darius offered her a smile. "Shall I pleasure you once again before you leave this bed?"

"Shut up, Darius." Vivian sipped her tea.

"Cranky again, I see." Darius's smile faded. "My apologies."

"You can stow that too." Vivian set her cup aside. "I already hate this day, and you don't need to be irritating to get me through it." She flopped down onto her side. "It isn't even snowing."

"Why should it be snowing?"

"So I don't have to leave you, you idiot." Vivian settled her head against his thigh on a grumpy sigh.

His hand moved slowly on her hair, treasuring the silky feel of it. "Here's how that works, Vivvie. You think this will be dreadful, this parting, which is very flattering but entirely unnecessary. You wish we could spend an indefinite amount of time romping like bunnies and oblivious to the rest of our obligations, but this is better."

"Better?" She bit his hairy, muscular, male thigh,

but not hard. "How can it be better to spend hours in a freezing cold coach, to be greeted by my elderly and dignified spouse, while I await the delivery of your child and you treat me as a perfect, and perfectly forgettable, stranger?" She turned her cheek against his leg and closed her eyes. "It's going to be dreadful."

"No, it is not." Darius focused on the feel of her cheek against his thigh. "This day will be a nuisance, getting under way, and then putting up with the roads, but you'll be in your own bed in Town tonight, and then on your way to Longchamps tomorrow. You think you'll miss me, but you'll be relieved to have this child conceived, Vivvie. William will be overjoyed, and the longer you're parted from me and back to your own life, the less you'll even think about me."

"You're sure about this?"

"Utterly."

"Ass." She nuzzled his cock. "I will miss you until my dying day."

"No, you shall *not*."

"Will too, and you know you want to send those women packing. You do. They have no business in your life, much less under the same roof as that dear child. You know this." She swiped at him with her tongue, and he didn't stop her.

❧

Vivian stood in the freezing January air, while outside the stables, Darius's traveling coach, complete with heated bricks, toddies, and a full hamper, waited for her.

"My lady." Darius offered her his arm, but to her surprise, he walked her back into the barn and not up to the coach. She was wearing one of the new cloaks he'd had made for her, velvet, fur-lined, warm and lovely. Under that, her dress was one he'd designed, more velvet, a rich brown trimmed with green that felt as comfortable as it was elegant. Around her neck, though, he'd wrapped his cozy wool scarf, because she'd brought none of her own.

"I don't want to go," Vivian said, holding his gaze and swallowing against the pain in her chest. "You can't make me want to go, Darius. That much, at least, I insist on."

"I can't, but I can warn you again, Vivvie. We're strangers after this. Nothing but strangers. If you see me in the park, we'll need to be introduced before you can acknowledge me, and I will all but cut you, for the sake of the child."

"Oh, of course." She knew he was trying to be decent, misguided lout that he was. "Unlike a few dozen other young men, you can't be bothered with a little old bluestocking parliamentary wife like me for a passing acquaintance. I'll recall that."

"See that you do," he warned, his voice stern. "Recall this as well, Vivvie. If you need anything—anything *at all*—you will discreetly apply to me."

"I have a husband," she said a little stiffly.

"For now, but during this child's lifetime, you at some point likely won't, and then you've only to ask, Vivvie, and whatever you need, if it's within my power, I'll see to it for you."

"While you treat me like a stranger?"

He nodded, looking again like the grave man who'd joined her for dinner a lifetime ago in London.

"I want your promise, Vivvie. This is likely the only child I'll have, and you have to let me do what I can, should the need arise."

"This should not be your only child, Darius." Of that she was certain, though she assuredly did not want him procreating with anybody else. "If I'm even pregnant."

"You're carrying."

"How can you know that?"

"I just do." His smile was smug and sad. "You are, and that means more coin for me, so well done, Vivvie Longstreet."

"We'll see," she said, wanting to screech at him for bringing up their mercenary bargain yet again. "Was there anything else?"

She glanced at the coach, feeling as if it were some sort of hearse, only to find herself pulled into his arms and kissed, gently, fiercely, and thoroughly.

"Damn you." She wiped a tear from her eyes with her new gloves, and went up on her toes to kiss his cheek. "Damn you, Darius Lindsey, for that kiss and the lectures and all of it."

He winked at her as he escorted her out to the coach. "May I roast in hell, and so on. That's the spirit." She smiled, and he looked relieved and desperate and dear as he handed her in.

"Godspeed, Vivvie, and from the bottom of my jaded and worthless heart, thank you." He banged on the door, and the coach pulled out before Vivian could stop crying long enough to wonder what on earth he was thanking her for.

❧

Darius's traveling coach was comfortably conducive to crying, which was fortunate, because Vivian was disposed to indulge. She knew Darius had purchased the vehicle for a song, and probably kept it for himself because it was as luxuriously appointed on the inside as it was carefully unremarkable on the outside. She wasn't a weeper by nature, but gracious, almighty, merciful, everlasting God...

She buried her nose in his scarf and missed him and hated him for his effortless savoir faire, and loved him for the excruciating tenderness with which he'd made love to her just two hours earlier. He hadn't said a word; he'd just started in with the kissing and touching and loving, and she'd been... lost.

What was *wrong* with him, that he'd insist they part on such cool and rational terms, and what was wrong with her, that she couldn't see the wisdom of his logic?

The trip into Town took longer than she'd liked, in part because she'd needed time to use the facilities at various inns along the way, but also because snow had started to fall—too late to do her any good, of course. When the coach gained the Longstreet town-house, midday had come and gone and Vivian decided to allow herself a short nap while her trunks were being unloaded.

The idea of going back into William's house, the one he'd shared with Muriel for several decades, was daunting. In just a few weeks, Vivian had become terribly attached to a man she'd met only once previously. How much closer must William and Muriel have become, making love, raising children, sharing his career...

Things she would never have. Not with Darius,

not with anybody. A fresh wave of grief rose up to clog her throat, and Vivian went inside and accepted Dilquin's solicitous greetings. She kept her new velvet cloak though, claiming the house was chilly, which it was. An hour later, her personal maid found her asleep in her own bed—without a stitch on, God have mercy—and with the velvet cloak spread over the counterpane for extra warmth, and a brown scarf jammed halfway under her pillow.

As Vivian slept away her afternoon, the unloading of Darius's coach proceeded without incident, except that it was observed by one of the coach's former owners. Thurgood Ainsworthy had had the thing built to order in one of his wealthier marriages, and it was a traveling coach fit for a man whose social life required a good deal of both discretion and mobility.

Thurgood had loved that coach and loved owning it. He'd seduced more than one lady in its cushy confines, and had only bet the thing because he'd been in his cups and unfamiliar with his gambling opponent. It had been years ago when he'd made the mistake of thinking some cocky younger son was acting as if his hand were poor, when in fact the bastard had been holding a full house, queens over knaves.

Rotten luck.

Apparently the younger son had come upon rotten luck now too, because Longstreet must have purchased the thing for his darling Vivian.

But as Ainsworthy watched, the coachy wheeled the empty vehicle not around to the alley that lead to the Longstreet carriage house, but rather back out into the street and off toward the nearest coaching inn.

❧

Darius heard his traveling coach clatter back up the lane and realized he'd failed to drink himself into oblivion. Well, it was only just past dark. There was time for that.

"I miss her." He passed that admission along to his great and good friend, the brandy decanter, which sat loyally guarding his right elbow where he sprawled before the fire in his study.

"I miss her in bed," he began, finding his usual tolerance for pain serving him well. "I miss her over the dinner plates. I miss her out riding. I miss her arguing with me over stupid political questions nobody cares about except the bloody Lords. I miss her teasing John—I miss that a pissing damned lot. John misses her, God help us."

He took another contemplative sip and regarded his companion.

"I miss having somebody, anybody, to talk about John with, and she was so kind." He mentally relaxed before he could wind up for the next blow. "She was *reassuring*, telling me I'm doing a good job with the boy, when I've exposed him to all manner of depravity. I'm a grown man, and I've been raising that child for years. When did I sprout this need for *reassurance*?"

He veered off that perilous ditch and took off in a more familiar direction.

"She deserves so much better." He was mumbling now, mumbling around the ache that had been in his throat for hours. "She says I deserve better, silly wench. And she smelled lovely, always. How did she do that?"

That question brought to mind the scent of stale powder and singed hair he associated with Blanche and Lucy. He was going to have to do something about those two. Vivian was carrying—carrying *his* child—and that meant the first and second installments of William's payment would come due. The first one should be on its way as soon as Vivian rejoined William at Longchamps, and the second when she'd missed her second menses. The third, if there was a third, would arrive when she was safely delivered of a child, and then, by God, Darius's finances would be in the closest thing to good repair he'd ever known.

"And then what will I do?" He scowled at the decanter. "Raise bloody pigeons to bill and coo their way across England while I grow old selling pigeon shit?"

Such a question signaled inebriation, even Darius knew that, as unaccustomed as he was to over-indulging. He rose unsteadily, saluted the decanter, and went up to his room. He spent the night fully clothed in a chair by the fire, alternately missing Vivian and cursing his stupid, useless, pointless life.

◦❦◦

Vivian took an extra day in London to regain her energy, though her energy wasn't very cooperative. Her clothes were repacked, the townhouse closed up, the baggage loaded, Dilquin and her lady's maid loaded with it, and off they went.

And with each mile, Vivian's emotions grew more confusing and unhappy.

William greeted her with a smile and a kiss to her cheek, then took her hands and stepped back to study her.

"You're well?"

"I am in good health," she said, not wanting to remove her cloak. Reluctantly, she undid the frogs herself—thank goodness William would not be so presumptuous—and passed the garment to the waiting footman. "And yourself?"

"Getting over a little cold, my dear." William's eyes skimmed over her new dress and the way she'd styled her hair with a part down the middle, not pulled straight back into a governess's bun. "Will you join me in a cup of tea?"

She didn't want to, but she kept her expression pleasant.

"Of course, William." She took his proffered arm as she had a thousand times before, but missed, badly, the strength of Darius's escort as she did. William's arm was a prop. In truth, she supported him more than he supported her.

They sat down to tea in the library and began the ritual conversation that signaled each of their various reunions over five years of marriage. William was polite, Vivian was polite, and it was all... wrong.

"Shall we speak of your time in Kent, Vivian?" William had waited until the tea tray was removed and they were guaranteed privacy. "Or would you rather we pretend you were merely visiting your sister while I passed the holidays down here?"

His old eyes held nothing but a banked, patient kindness when Vivian finally met them. "I wouldn't know what to say, William."

"The trip did you good. You might not see it yet, but it did."

"If you say so." Vivian wished the tea tray were still

there, so she could at least occupy her hands. William missed little, and his scrutiny weighed on her.

William patted her knuckles. "It's all right to be infatuated with the man, probably better, in fact."

She looked away, feeling her throat closing. "William, hush."

She'd never told him to hush once in five years, but he was apparently able to weather the shock. He passed her his handkerchief.

"Vivian, you're young, and he will be the father of your child," William said. "We didn't choose him because he was the Scourge of the High Toby. Lindsey is comely, he has a certain dash, and he no doubt charmed you. Some feelings for him were inevitable."

"I said hush." She let the tears come, not realizing William had shifted until the familiar scent of bay rum grew stronger and she felt his arm around her shoulders. He said nothing, but for the first time in her marriage, she merely tolerated his embrace, finding no comfort in it at all.

She wanted to smack him, in fact, and shout at him to stop *reasoning* with her.

"You are angry with me," William said. "I'm sorry for that, but you won't be so angry when you hold that child, Vivian. I promise you."

"I know." She agreed out of a need to shut him up. They'd never been this personal with each other in all their years of marriage, and she wasn't about to start now. Maybe not ever, given what had passed in the last month.

"Can I assume your lunation is late?"

"You can." She blotted the last of her tears and

folded his handkerchief into a small, tidy square. "Just a little."

"That's enough for now." William rose off the arm of her chair. "We'll not speak of your visit in Kent again, for it upsets you, and we must take the best care of you now, Vivian. Early days can be chancy."

"Yes, William."

"You're tired. Shall I send Portia to you?"

Vivian rose, though fatigue and sadness dragged at her. "Everlasting God, please, not that. I'll see her at dinner, and we can trade veiled barbs over a decent meal." Except Vivian had no appetite. "I think I'll take a walk while the sun is at least shining."

"As you wish." William stepped in and kissed her forehead. "You know, Vivian, I do realize what a toll this has taken on you, what a toll it will take, and I am appreciative."

"As I am," she said, "of all you've done for me." She withdrew, wrestling with her first-ever bout of anger at William Longstreet. Oh, she'd been exasperated with him in the past, irritated, cross, annoyed—they were *married*, after all—and he was two generations her senior, but she'd never felt this burning, resentful rage at him.

So she took her walk in the cold sunshine. A long walk was an excuse to wrap Darius's scarf around her neck, and the pretty, warm cloak he'd bought her around her body, and to be alone with his scent.

❦

"I need the name of a good solicitor." Darius put the question to his older brother, who was for once looking reasonably well put together.

"I thought you used a firm you were happy with," Trent replied, pouring his guest a cup of tea.

"I do, for my commercial interests. This is personal, and requires… discretion."

"Anything I can do?" The question was posed with studied casualness, but the offer was sincere, and Darius knew a pang of… something. There was loneliness in it and love for his brother and despair.

"A small matter"—Darius's lips quirked at the private joke—"requiring a delicate hand. I won't get my ears blown off though, so you needn't worry."

"One does, you know." Trent sipped his tea with the equanimity Darius had long associated with him. "In your absence over the past couple of months, I've had to do the pretty with Leah a time or two, and I'd forgotten how exhausting it is."

"It's not so bad. You learn to bow and smile and twirl down the room without putting anything into it." And you looked for the well-padded chairs, of which Trent's modest library sported an adequate number.

"Well, I haven't yet acquired the knack. Your return to Town is most welcome. In terms of solicitors, I use Kettering. He's young, but absolutely discreet and shrewd as hell."

"He'll not go tattling to Wilton?"

"I'd shoot him on sight if he did," Trent said, no smile in evidence. "And likely miss. The man is quick in every sense."

Darius studied his brother, who was drinking tea for a change. "You seem to be a little more the thing. Maybe you needed to put off mourning."

"Having to go out with our sister on my arm required a certain reestablishing of my own routines."

Routines, Darius surmised, like having one's hair trimmed, shaving regularly, putting together a proper suit of clothes, and getting them on one's person. Making conversation, those sorts of routines. Well, bless Leah's social calendar, if it had given Trent a toehold on regaining his balance.

"Uncle Dare!" A little dark-haired boy shot across the library, his face wreathed in glee.

"Nephew Ford!" Dare barely set down his teacup in time to snatch his nephew into his lap. "Is my best nephew in the whole world ready to go riding?"

"I'll get my boots and my coat and my hat and my gloves too!" He was off at a dead run, the library door slamming shut behind him.

"You don't mind?" Trent asked, setting his teacup aside. "I could go with you, but I'd have to take Michael up before me."

Darius smiled. "Droit du Uncle, to fuss over one child at a time. Michael and I can plot an outing on some fine spring day when it won't send his nurses into the vapors to think of him in the nasty cold air."

Ford came charging back into the room, once again banging the door in his wake. "Ready, Uncle Dare!"

Darius scooped his nephew into a piggyback perch, and soon had him up on the pommel of Skunk's saddle. The day was cold but sunny, and there was little wind, so a short ride through the park was a pleasant outing for uncle and nephew.

"Papa's not mourning anymore," Ford reported.

"How do you know this?"

"His breath doesn't always smell like brandy when he kisses us good night. Are the ducks cold?"

"They waddle about with featherbeds on, so no, I don't think they're cold. They even go swimming, for pity's sake."

"Maybe they have to, to eat."

"We all do things we'd rather not when it comes to the necessity of eating."

"Why, Mr. Lindsey!" A soft female voice cut through Darius's musings. "Won't you introduce me to your handsome companion?"

And there she was, just like that, as if sprung from Darius's constant, unhappy thoughts. Except Vivian looked... wonderful. She was wearing one of the fur-lined cloaks he'd bought her, and her face was lit with a soft, eager smile. She sat Bernice like a princess, and beamed a sense of joy at all she surveyed.

"Madam?" Darius was relieved his tone was civil— merely civil—when his heart was thumping in his chest like a kettledrum. "You have me at a disadvantage."

"Lady Vivian Longstreet," she supplied, though around her eyes, her smile faltered, and Darius's thumping heart skipped several miserable beats. "My husband introduced us last fall."

"Your husband?"

"Lord William Longstreet," Vivian countered gamely, and Darius knew the meaning of self-hatred in a whole new way. "We're back in Town for the opening of Parliament."

"You'll give him my regards, then. Good day." Darius tipped his hat just as Ford spoke up.

"I like your horse. Good bone and a kind eye."

He sounded just like John, and Darius saw the hurt that did Vivian.

"I am remiss," Darius said, knowing it was a Bad Idea. "My lady, may I make known to you my nephew, Fordham Lindsey."

"Good day, Master Fordham." Vivian's smile expanded to include the boy. "You sit that big horse quite well. I'm sure your uncle is very proud to be seen with you before him."

Ford sat up straighter. "I'm the oldest. Skunk likes me."

"I can see that, but it's chilly out." She shifted her gaze to Darius. "I mustn't keep you, or your mama will fret."

"She's dead." Ford didn't seem the least concerned about this. "We're not mourning anymore."

Vivian's brow puckered. "My condolences."

"My sister-in-law did not enjoy good health," Darius said, and then, because his chest hurt ferociously to think he'd nearly snubbed her, he added, "But you do?"

"I do, Mr. Lindsey. The very best of health." Her smile became radiant, and Darius realized he'd trumped his Bad Idea royally, for that smile would haunt him into his dotage.

"Well, good day, then, my lady. Safe journey home."

"Safe journey to you, too, Mr. Lindsey, Master Fordham." She nudged her mare along, still beaming as she and her groom passed out of sight around a bend in the bridle path. This told Darius two things. First, she was still safely carrying, which was a good thing. Second, she wasn't going to exercise plain common sense and ignore him when their paths crossed, which was a bad thing. A very bad, stupid thing, which pleased him far more than it should.

⁂

"Can you keep a secret?" Vivian kept her voice down, though she and Angela were alone.

"I am the mother of three," Angela replied, not even glancing up from her embroidery hoop. "I can keep secrets, though not from my husband."

Vivian smiled at her sister, whose impending addition to the family was growing increasingly apparent.

"I believe I am in an interesting condition," Vivian said softly, eyeing the closed door to the family parlor. "Though not yet very far along."

Angela set her hoop down. "How not very far along?"

"I likely conceived around Christmas, so about six weeks." Perhaps five, perhaps seven, possibly as much as *eight*. "I know that's early, but I haven't had any real trouble."

"Oh, Viv…" Angela rose and hugged Vivian hard. "I am so pleased for you and for William. He must be over the moon."

"I think he's relieved, but pleased too, for us both. The thought of a baby has eased his grief over Algernon's death. I'm hoping it will chase off the last of the cold he brought back from Longchamps."

"Best watch that," Angela said, resuming her seat. "A cold can become a lung fever, and then you're a widow with a baby on the way."

"You will cease that grim talk, Angela Ventnor." Vivian poured them both more tea, though lately she had come to loathe the stuff. "I'm weepy enough as it is."

Angela grinned. "That's quite normal, as is casting up your accounts, weaving a little on your feet, and taking naps at the oddest times. Jared says he suspected we were carrying again when I started needing more cuddling."

We were carrying... Angela had been married for ten years, and Vivian could not recall her sister ever previously referring to her husband and cuddling in the same sentence. Impending motherhood was indeed an interesting condition.

"Your husband notices more than I thought he did."

"You must let William spoil you too, Viv." Scolding came naturally to the mother of three. "For once, let him take care of you, and not just the other way 'round."

"Yes, Mother." Vivian smiled but tried not to consider her sister's words too closely. William wasn't the taking-care-of kind of husband. He was considerate, when he wasn't out all evening arguing with his cronies, or up late reading draft bills and correspondence, or distracted because it approached the anniversary of his marriage to Muriel, or her death, or Algernon's death, or Aldous's...

As Vivian saw her sister out, she admitted to a sense of furtive relief that she could again seek the solitude of her bedroom. Ever since she'd run into Darius in the park with that little boy who looked like him, and like John, Vivian's attempts to forget her winter idyll and move on had been completely unsuccessful.

She didn't want to forget; she wanted to *remember*. She kept Darius's scarf in the back of her wardrobe and took it out to sniff it at least once a day. She wore her new wardrobe, admiring the woman in the mirror far more than she had the one she'd seen last November. She visited with her mare first thing in the day, because it was a good way to start the morning, even when they couldn't get to the park for a brisk canter.

And she missed him.

She didn't flatter herself he missed her, but she hoped, in a small, honest, very private corner of her heart, he at least thought of her from time to time.

She climbed onto her bed, knowing a short nap was in order—another short nap. Maybe next time her path crossed with Darius's, there wouldn't be a curious child underfoot, and they could even exchange a few more words.

Ten

IN THE TWO WEEKS AND THREE DAYS SINCE HE'D SEEN Vivian in the park, Darius had become a master at the game he privately called "What I Should Have Said." This game consisted of endless mental rehashings of his short encounter with Vivian and endless variations on the winning answer: he *should* have said not one damned thing; he should have cut her utterly.

He'd failed that round and admitted in hindsight that such a purely coldhearted approach was beyond him, so he'd graduated to Round Two anyway, which he thought of as "What I'll Say Next Time."

Knowing full well there couldn't be a next time.

"There you are." Lucy's voice was low and hard. "You're late again, and believe me, I have about had it with you, Darius."

"I am abjectly sorry to have discommoded you," he drawled. Her eyes widened in astonishment then narrowed in what he recognized as anticipated pleasure. "Domestic obligations called that couldn't wait." Then too, William's first payment had yet to show up, and a man inured to disappointment had to accept that it might never arrive.

"Insolent." She looked him up and down. "Get up to my room and have yourself on my bed in five minutes."

"As my lady wishes." His tone was even more indifferent than he'd intended, and Lucy's eyes took on an unholy gleam. As he made his way to her room, he felt a crushing fatigue radiating out from his middle, almost as if he were wrung out from a stomach flu or a long footrace over steep terrain. He quickly shed his garments and got comfortable facedown on Lucy's bed. He was careful to put his clothes where he could see them—he didn't trust Lucy not to hide them or damage them, and they cost a pretty penny. He also unlatched her balcony doors before she arrived, because locking him in would seem a fine game to her in her present mood.

He knew this waiting period was intended to create anticipation in him, or anxiety. For Lucy, the two were closely related, but for him, the temptation to steal a catnap was taking precedence. He'd been out past midnight with his sister at one of the few early balls that would crop up until the Season began in earnest. It was three in the morning—a full hour later than Lucy had summoned him—and he wouldn't see his own bed until dawn.

Lucy swished into the room and secured a silk scarf around his wrist. "So what have you to say for yourself, Darius?" She pulled it tight and knotted it to the bedpost. "You disappear and leave no word when you'll return. You ignore my first two notes and then show up tonight an hour *late*?" She gave the second scarf a yank on the last word, and Darius realized she expected an answer.

"One usually spends the holidays with family, Lucy." Darius made a show of yawning. She'd tied his hands, and he couldn't politely cover his mouth. "You are not my family."

"I'm not," she agreed, disdaining to secure his feet. "Crouch up."

He complied—Lucy had a fascination for his fundament, God help him.

"You've been rude." Her hand came down hard, a stinging, loud slap of flesh on flesh that Darius found not as bracing as it usually was. "You're inconsiderate, your manners are atrocious, and you'll regret this lapse." She whaled on him in a similar vein, and Darius turned his attention to the task of producing an erection for her entertainment. When she untied him and spread herself for his further attentions, she'd expect to see a nice hard cock. From her perspective, the idea that he wasn't allowed to swive her with it made his suffering more intense, which meant his remuneration was earned.

So…

For the first time in his memory, Darius had to work at gaining an erection. He succeeded only by using the friction of the bedcovers against his skin as a stimulus, for sheer determination gained him little. He writhed convincingly against the silk sheets, relieved when his flesh eventually rose at the simple glide of the material over his groin. Fortunately, Lucy's hand had delivered all the punishment it was capable of, though Darius was required to wear the scarves around his neck like a collar and leash. By the time he'd brought her to her first orgasm, his erection had faded to a brief memory. By her second, he realized Vivian had been right, and he truly could not do this again. By her third, he was nearly asleep on his knees.

∽

"It's a financial matter." Darius watched Worth Kettering tidy up an oddly elegant French escritoire. The desk looked like it would crumble to gilded and lacquered matchsticks if Kettering simply banged a fist on it. Kettering himself was large, dark, beautifully attired in various shades of dark blue, and possessed of curiously tidy mannerisms.

"Most matters entrusted to solicitors are financial," Kettering replied, lacing his fingers and settling his hands before him on the desk. Big hands, though clean and capable looking.

"Let me be blunt." Darius rose and went to the window. "If my father gets word of this, he'll use it to destroy me."

"Your father being Wilton, whom Lord Amherst had the misfortune to be sired by as well?"

"The same." Darius's mouth quirked up at one side at Kettering's honesty.

"I understand the need for discretion, Mr. Lindsey, and can assure you your brother wouldn't have sent you here had he any reason to doubt me."

"He told you I'd inquired?"

"Mentioned you might be around, and warned me to attend to your situation personally, without clerks, juniors, or other intermediaries."

"Older brothers meddle."

"Younger brothers prevaricate."

A short, considering silence all around, and then, "I want to set up a trust for a child." Darius turned his back to the other man, as if watching a beer wagon snarl up traffic in both directions was of great moment. "The child has yet to be born."

"A conditional trust, then." Kettering's voice gave nothing away. "What will the contents of the trust be?"

On the street below, the swearing and insults began in earnest, complete with raised fists. "Coin provided by the lady's husband. Substantial coin." The first installment of which had arrived by unliveried private messenger, to Darius's shamefully intense relief.

"I see." A pause. Darius heard papers being shuffled. "I don't see. You're setting up a trust for another man's child?"

"Legally, yes." Darius turned from the farce below and watched as Kettering parsed the realities.

"Is the child's legal father to know?"

"I don't care if he knows. I care only that Wilton doesn't and Polite Society doesn't. My sisters need spouses, and this is the kind of juicy little aside that could queer their chances."

Kettering took up a quill pen and began stroking his fingers over the white plume. "How much coin are we discussing?"

Darius named a figure, and Kettering's brow shot up. "Not such a little aside after all. I'll need details."

"Here are the most pertinent details: you will not have the trust document copied by a clerk, will not leave the file where the clerks can find it, will not tell them I'm a client of yours."

"My staff is trustworthy, but yes, if those are your conditions, I agree to them."

"Those are some of my conditions." Darius went back to his window, hating the necessity of discussing Vivian's personal life with anyone, even Kettering, who was rumored to rival the tomb for his ability to keep confidences. "Another is that I pay you in cash, not bank draft, and I deposit the contents of the trust in your hands, also in cash."

"That is a deuced lot of cash. Why not use bearer bonds?"

"I'm being paid in cash." Darius felt the silence behind him grow and intensify as Kettering no doubt put the puzzle pieces together.

"Why didn't you just have the husband put funds into a trust?" Kettering spoke from Darius's elbow. For a big man, he'd moved without a sound, sneaking being perhaps a required talent for his kind.

"Because the funds had to leave the man's estate." Darius rubbed a hand across the back of his neck. "A man's life can end at any moment, so the funds had to be legally transferred into other hands, lest they become tied up in his affairs and subject to scrutiny upon his death."

Kettering snorted. "Scrutiny? You mean controversy, and likely hung up to dry in Chancery for all the world to see for years on end as a result."

"It's your profession, not mine."

Mr. Kettering refrained from commenting on what Darius's profession must be, and began asking the questions Darius knew he had to answer. Names, dates, exact amounts, and conditions. The document would be straightforward enough, leaving a tidy sum in Vivian's hands, or in Kettering's hands for the benefit of Vivian and her firstborn child, should Vivian remarry. The trust was revocable only by the creator, that worthy soul being Darius, and the principle invested, some in the five percents, some in ventures of Kettering's choosing.

Hashing through all the what-ifs and in-the-event-ofs took two hours, but Darius left satisfied he'd done what honor demanded.

He couldn't claim he'd behaved without self-interest—not that he'd expect that of himself. Some of William's first installment had gone to liquidation of immediate debts, and some of the second would go to enhancements at Averett Hill. If there were a third installment, a portion of that sum would go to a trust for John, because Trent's money was largely tied up in trusts for his children, and Darius never wanted John scrabbling for necessities, as Darius had been for his entire adult life.

❦

Vivian wasn't lying in wait for Darius, exactly, but she did make it her business to quietly learn where his quarters were, and to frequent the shops closest to his neighborhood. She also went riding as often as the weather permitted, which was hit and miss, at least for most of February. She listened rather more carefully than she had previously to idle gossip when she made calls on the wives of William's various associates.

She heard no mention of the Earl of Wilton's younger son, though she did hear the older was out of mourning, and perhaps once again in search of a bride.

By the time March rolled around and Vivian's menses were absent for the third time, she'd all but given up hope of seeing Darius again by chance. Still, she'd gotten in the habit of taking Bernice out for a hack in the park, and in another few weeks her riding habits wouldn't fit. So when the weather moderated a trifle, Vivian was again hacking along the Ladies' Mile when she spotted a pair of riders ahead, moving along at the walk.

She knew that piebald gelding—or thought she did.

The rider was female, petite, blond, and unfamiliar to her, though there on the big chestnut sat none other than Darius Lindsey.

This hurt, physically and emotionally, to see him with a young lady—a very young lady—smiling and enjoying a day that whispered of spring. Whoever she was, she was on Darius's personal mount, the one reserved for him, always available to him.

Now Vivian understood why Darius hadn't wanted them to run across each other: not because he wanted shut of her, necessarily, but because even though he *was* shut of her, he sought to spare her sensibilities.

Vivian drew Bernice down to the walk and made as if to pass the pair, when the mare decided to turn up friendly. She whickered at Skunk, who stopped, planted his hooves, and turned a curious eye on the mare.

The blonde offered a cheerful smile. "Good morning. You will excuse my mount, but he has a mind of his own, much like his owner."

"Good morning." Vivian would have edged Bernice forward, but the way the horses were positioned, that would have meant brushing stirrup to stirrup past Darius.

"That's a lovely mare," the blonde said. "I told my brother I'd get along better with a mare."

"Tell your father," Darius said. "It's his stables that lack a suitable lady's mount and require that you borrow my horse if you're to go for a safe hack."

"A generous brother." Vivian addressed her words to the blonde, lest Darius see the relief in her smile. "You must be Lady Emily."

Emily turned a questioning glance on her brother. "Darius? Where are your manners?"

"Lady Longstreet, I believe?" Darius's expression was bored, as if he'd rather be home reading *The Times* than indulging the ladies in their socializing. Vivian nodded rather than address him, and Darius continued with the introductions.

"Dare, you and Arthur lead on, and I'm sure Skunk will follow along." Lady Emily ordered her brother around with apparent confidence in his compliance, and he maneuvered the chestnut back onto the path ahead of the ladies.

"How do you know my brother, Lady Longstreet?" Emily's expression betrayed simple curiosity and maybe even some friendliness.

"In truth, I've known your sister longer," Vivian said. "We came out the same year. I trust she's keeping well?"

Emily's lips thinned. "Leah will be setting her cap for a husband this Season, or my father will know the reason why, but as wonderful as she is, the men ought to be lining up to offer for her."

"A loyal sentiment, and one that takes the perspicacity of men as a given." Vivian's mouth kept making words, despite the dictates of prudence. "That, I'm sad to say, is likely a mistake."

"I heard that." Darius drew rein until his horse was even with the others. "Though where Leah is concerned, I'm afraid I have to agree. It will take a special man for each of my sisters."

"Spoken like an overprotective older brother." Emily was not offering a compliment.

"Spoken like a wiser older brother," Darius said. "Watch your whip, Em. You don't want it bouncing along on Skunk's quarters like that. But tell me, Lady Longstreet, how are you faring?"

"I'm in good health." Vivian fiddled the reins to hide her smile. "William caught a cold while at Longchamps, and he's not quite shaken it yet."

Darius considered her, and she felt his gaze travel over her in a quick—perhaps reluctant?—perusal. "Spring will likely take care of that. You will give my regards to your husband?"

"Of course." Vivian glanced up to see him watching her. There was a guarded tenderness in his eyes that pierced her to the bone with its veiled warmth. Her lips turned up, and without willing it, she was smiling *at him*, a smile full of longing and remembrance and hope.

"Emily." Darius called to his sister more sharply. "If we take this turnoff, we can be back on the street and heading home. Lady Longstreet, good day, and... take care."

"Lady Emily, Mr. Lindsey." Vivian nodded her

farewell, and just like that, he was gone, muttering something to his sister about keeping her hands closer to the horse's withers and looking where she was going.

Vivian hardly knew where *she* was going, but Bernice must have, for they were soon towing their groom back to Longstreet House. How wonderful to have seen Darius, though to Vivian's eyes, he'd looked tired and a trifle drawn.

And how… hard, to see him and not be able to touch him and truly talk to him. This time, Vivian had been lucky—he'd been with his sister. But if there was a next time, and she came upon him in the company of one of his fast women? She'd had the impression he didn't openly socialize with them, but what if she were wrong?

She handed the reins to the stable boy and was trying to sort through her jumbled feelings, when Dilquin appeared at the porte cochere.

"My lady, his lordship is home early from Westminster, and he's asking for you."

≈

"She seemed very amiable to me," Emily said, and though her tone was casual, her eyes held the overly discerning curiosity of a sister whose instincts have been piqued by an older sibling.

"I hardly know her, Em." Darius let his considerable fatigue show in his tone. "Leah could probably tell you more about her. Her husband is quite a bit older."

Emily grimaced. "A May-December wedding. Meaning no disrespect to my father, but I can't see the appeal."

"Even if it's a Duke of December or Marquis of Early November?" Darius asked, but good God, Emily was sixteen, a child, and here she was considering marriage. It made him feel old, and... lonely. Trent and Leah had both dipped their toes in matrimonial waters. If Emily soon followed suit, Darius would be the only one of the siblings not to do so, and yet, how could he?

And why would he?

"I want to marry for love," Emily said, giving Darius a start. "Mama and Papa were an arranged match, and look what a farce that turned out to be."

"You're too young to be so cynical, Em." She made a lovely picture on his gelding, a lovely adult picture if a man weren't her older brother. "Hands lower and eyes up."

"I'm not cynical." Emily corrected her riding while she spoke. "I don't want to become cynical, and a love match seems better suited to that end."

"Or perhaps, a love match gone sour creates more cynicism than a more practical union that's allowed to grow into a cordial alliance."

Emily rolled her eyes, looking a great deal younger. "Bother that. You sound like Trent, and you can't tell me he and Paula had a cordial anything."

"They cared for each other."

"They secured the succession," Emily retorted. "I don't want to be cared for, Darius. I want to be loved, and I want that for Leah, and you and Trent, too."

So young, and so convinced of her position. "Dreamer. Don't let your father hear you talking that way."

"I don't." Emily's expression sobered while the

horses clip-clopped along the street. "He's your father too."

"An unfortunate circumstance, in his opinion," Darius said, "and in mine, but for the siblings it's brought me. Heel down."

"How can you tell? It's on the other side of the horse from you."

"Your seat is less secure, and you're tipping forward," Darius said as they turned into the alley that led to the Wilton House stables. "You'll make my excuses to Leah?"

"Of course, but she'll miss you."

"She'll see me tomorrow night at some damned ball or other."

"It's starting up, isn't it?" Emily patted the horse, who'd been a perfect gentleman for her—the traitor. "The Season has begun and so has Leah's hunt for a husband. Lord Hellerington was closeted with Papa yesterday for more than an hour."

"Hellerington?" Darius couldn't hide his reaction. "We can only hope he isn't feeling the need for a bride—again."

"Leah didn't say anything, though I know she's worried."

Darius dismounted and came around to assist his sister. "You see entirely too much. I liked you better in pigtails and pinafores."

"I liked you better when you smiled more, Dare." Emily kept her hands on his biceps even when she'd gained her feet. "You're too somber these days, and you always look tired and preoccupied to me."

"It's all the late hours." He hugged her briefly and kissed her cheek. "Escorting a sister around is taxing work."

"It's only going to get worse," Emily cautioned. "Papa has said Leah must accept every invitation."

God in heaven. Though maybe if he were sufficiently exhausted, Darius might forget Vivian Longstreet, or at least stop fretting for her. "Nobody expects Leah to be at every entertainment."

"Tell that to Papa," Emily said quietly, for the grooms were at hand.

"You can leave the horses," Darius said, swinging up on Arthur and taking Skunk by the reins. "Shall we do this again, Emily?"

"Yes, but can we at least trot next time?"

"Ladies riding sidesaddle primarily walk and canter," Darius informed her. "But yes, we can trot. You'd best have a soaking bath this evening and another tomorrow."

"How one suffers for the cause. Send a note around when you've another afternoon free, and Trent can lend us his gelding."

"As my lady wishes." Darius saluted and clattered back into the alley at a trot. He had to drop off Trent's gelding, Arthur, then grab some rest, or he'd be asleep where he stood tonight when he'd need all his wits about him.

And he would see Vivian today, of all days.

Most nights, he saw her in his dreams, if his schedule permitted him any sleep. He'd been fortunate that Lucy Templeton's mother had requisitioned her presence at the family seat for a few weeks, leaving him to contend with only Lady Cowell. That lady's husband was between mistresses, and because he was a randy beggar, Blanche had not been free to impose on Darius for much of the past month either.

But tonight she'd summoned him, and tonight he'd go—to explain to her that their dealings were at an end. Lucy would be the trickier situation to extricate himself from, but she would come into line if he held firm.

He hoped.

As he returned to his rooms and fell onto his mattress, he had to wonder what drove a woman to enjoy beating on a man's naked ass. It was difficult to comprehend that Lucy and Blanche weren't as bored with and tired by the whole business as he was. He lay down and hoped to soon be drifting off, once again dreaming of Vivian and the nigh-unfathomable miracle that she should be bearing his child.

Eleven

BLANCHE LAY ON THE BED, REPLETE AND ROSY, watching Darius while he got dressed as quickly as he could without giving away how desperately he wanted to be away from this place and this woman.

"Lucy won't stand for this," she said, twiddling a bed tassel around her finger. "She'll be wroth you'd even think of ending our arrangement."

"She'll be wroth whether I end it or not." Darius wrapped his cravat around his neck once, rather like a linen noose. "She was born unhappy, Blanche, and the less you have to do with her, the more likely you are to find some peace in this life."

"Peace is boring." She rolled up on her side and regarded him through slumberous eyes. "She'll make you think twice about throwing us over."

His temper would not be silent. He turned and glowered at her. "Are you threatening me?"

"I'm warning you, Darius." For once, Blanche looked like the tired, nearly middle-aged woman she was. "Lucy doesn't see straight where you're concerned. I can understand if you're bored with the whips and bindings, and I'll speak to Lucy, but she won't give you up without a fight."

"I'm not a juicy bone to be scrabbled over." Darius yanked on his boots. "And you are exactly correct: I'll have no more of the bindings, whips, and stupid games. I'm done with it, and done with Lucy's airs and pouts. You may kindly tell her for me to go swive herself if she can't accept that."

Blanche sat up and shrugged into a dressing gown. "She'd rather be swiving you. As would I."

"No, you only think you would. You want to believe you're wicked, naughty, and sophisticated in your pleasures, but you're not, and neither is Lucy. What we do is nothing short of pathetic, and I'm through with it."

"You're not. You're not done until Lucy says you're done."

Darius barely resisted offering her a rude gesture, but instead bowed and took his leave, the long walk in the chilly night air serving to calm him only marginally.

Sleep, unfortunately, eluded him, leaving him to the torment of his thoughts. He didn't want to think about Vivian; his mind felt too dirty for even her mental presence, but she beckoned to his thoughts like a siren.

How was she feeling?

Was William taking good care of her?

Was she anxious over the prospect of giving birth?

Did she think of Darius?

He flattered himself she did, as her obvious pleasure in their two chance encounters suggested, but this was not a good thing at all for several reasons.

Having had hours to ponder his dealings with

Blanche Cowell, Darius concluded he'd tactically erred, and this could eventually devolve to Vivian's detriment.

Lucy Templeton would be on notice now that Darius was abandoning the kennel where she'd tried to tie him. She'd have time to plan her counter-moves, which meant the element of surprise was on her side. Stupid of him, but he'd been so damned tired lately...

He fell into restless slumber then, and dreamed of Vivian making snow angels with John while Wags sat on the fence, licking his paws.

§

"You have to rest." Vivian crossed her arms and prepared to lay siege to William's stubbornness. "You're just over that cold, William, and you've been pushing yourself ever since you got back to Town."

"We've been here weeks, Vivian. Months, in fact." William's smile was patient and pained. "I am resting. I do little else but rest."

And read Muriel's old letters and diaries. That, more than his pallor or the persistent weakness dogging him, alarmed her. She knew her husband occasionally communed with his first wife's personal effects, but it had become a nightly ritual, and she suspected he carried one or two of Muriel's letters around with him too.

"You work," Vivian said, hands on hips, "and while we aren't entertaining as much, you attend one supper meeting after another, William."

"It's my duty." He met her gaze only fleetingly, twitching at the blanket over his knees. "There's a sense of urgency, Vivian, when one feels time is running out."

"Hush." She poured him a finger of brandy and brought it to him. "You're simply tired and fretting over me and the fate of an entire nation. Fret a little for yourself, William Longstreet. I've no wish to become your widow."

"You fret enough for both of us." William sipped the brandy, but Vivian sensed it was more to placate her than because he enjoyed it. "There's something else to fret about in the mail today, Vivian."

"Anything serious?"

"One hopes not. Portia has taken it into her head to come up to Town for the Season."

Gracious, everlasting, immortal, avenging God. "Portia is to be our guest?"

"I'll refuse if you insist." William's tone was noncommittal. He did not want to refuse—did not want Portia's enmity, probably. "Nothing must be allowed to upset you now, Vivian. Nothing."

"You upset me." She softened her words by patting the back of his veined hand. "I can't face having this child without you, William, so no more late nights, and no more tearing around the city at all hours on foot. Please."

"If you insist, my dear."

Vivian's alarm notched up at his complacent tone. "Don't humor me, William."

"I'll be a good boy, Viv." He smiled at her, a sincere smile that hinted at the charm he'd traded on as a younger man. "With Portia underfoot here, it will be hard not to haunt the offices of government."

"She can help me sew baby clothes."

William's smile widened. "That's diabolical. Muriel would have approved. You're feeling well?"

He asked often, and she replied the same as she always did. "I'm fine. A little more prone to fatigue, but even that's passing."

William eyed her. "What does the physician say?"

"First babies show later." Vivian busied her hands by poking at the fire. With Darius, she had discussed bodily functions and female biology openly and often. "In all other regards, things appear to be progressing normally."

"Shall I convey that sentiment to young Mr. Lindsey?"

Vivian set the poker back on the hearth carefully, so as not to make a racket—also to buy her an instant to hide any reaction. "William?"

"I was young once too, Vivian." William peered at the rejuvenated fire. "In his place, I'd want to know that my firstborn child, however conceived, was being carried in good health."

Vivian's conscience pricked her hard every time she kept her encounters with Darius to herself. There was no reason to tell William, even though there was no reason not to, either.

"You must do as you see fit, William." Vivian rose from the hearth, considering William. Considering *her husband*. "If you think it would be kind, then pass along what you must. I honestly don't know if he'd prefer to know or be left in ignorance. He'll know when the child's born, and perhaps that's enough."

"I shall ruminate on this." William took another sip of his brandy. "Ruminating is one activity my great age leaves me suited for."

"Don't ruminate too hard." Vivian tucked his lap robe around him and took herself to her chambers, knowing William would spend the shank of the evening reading Muriel's letters and diaries, while Vivian dreamed of Darius Lindsey.

❦

Before he opened his late wife's diary—he was up to old George's second bout of madness, about which Muriel had written plenty—William Longstreet gave some thought to his present wife.

Vivian had fallen hard for the Lindsey rascal, and since coming to Town, she'd contrived to run into the man at least twice that William knew of. Dilquin wouldn't peach on his mistress, but the grooms were mostly up from Longchamps, and they were loyal exclusively to William.

Lindsey had behaved with perfect propriety toward Vivian on both occasions. No covert letters were being exchanged, no tokens dropped, no steaming glances or bald innuendos passed around.

Young people didn't realize how quickly years slipped away, and then there you were, sitting alone with a brandy you didn't want, laboring for each breath, and trying to recall the laughter of the only woman you'd truly loved in all your days on earth. It was sad and lonely, and made the prospect of death almost a comfort—almost a reward.

One he couldn't claim just yet, not with the young people being so buffle-brained about what should be perfectly obvious to any save themselves.

❦

"Darius says Reston's coming back to Town for the Season." Blanche offered that tidbit in hopes of placating Lucy, who was stomping from one end of her boudoir to the other.

"What interest would I have in that great, strutting lout?"

Blanche's mouth curved. "You had an interest once, Lucy. As did I."

"Reston is fine for a simple romp," Lucy conceded. "I graduated from simple romps years ago, and so did you."

"A simple romp has its place." Blanche set her teacup down—the taste was off, as if the leaves had been reused and the tea boiled. "At least with a man built like Reston. I wish Cowell understood even a simple romp."

"He still bothers you?"

"We have only the one son." Blanche went to the window and regarded the wet, cold day outside. "I'm not that old."

"One must occasionally tolerate a husband to cover one's tracks, so to speak." Lucy turned to regard her. "I'm sorry, Blanche. I'll bring Lindsey to heel for you, see if I don't."

"Maybe I'm bored with him." Blanche felt Lucy's arm go around her waist and leaned her head on the other woman's shoulder. "He's so… ungracious. Mercenary."

"You still want hearts and flowers, my girl. That's not what men are for."

"So you say." Blanche slipped away. "What have you in mind for Darius?"

"Just a little pressure, applied in the right places.

You said his sister is up for a husband this Season, and we can queer her chances easily enough."

Lucy in a plotting mood was unpredictable. Brilliant, but unpredictable. "Some have mentioned Hellerington in context with his sister."

Lucy's smile broadened. "A truly dreadful specimen. Wasn't there some scandal involving the sister years ago? She must be quite the antique."

"She's younger than we are by a decade," Blanche chided. "But yes, she ran off with a younger son, and there was rumor of a duel and then a long stay on the Continent."

"How do you learn these things?"

"Her papa is hard on the help," Blanche explained. "The help will talk, if induced sufficiently, particularly when they've been turned off without cause and a quarter's wages wanting."

"So Darius comes by his sour nature honestly. Well, don't fret, my dear. Darius will be eating out of our hands once again, so to speak. He just doesn't know it yet."

"Don't go to any trouble on my behalf." Blanche sat on the bed and began to peel down her stockings. "He's just… the thing you cleanse your palate with between the substantial courses. Inconsequential. Largely decorative."

"What a lovely analogy." Lucy sat beside her and stroked Blanche's hair back with a slow caress. "But what does that make me?"

❧

"If there is a benefit to all this socializing," Darius informed his sister Leah one cool April evening, "it's that you at least get out of that house and away from Wilton. Where are we off to tonight?"

"The Winterthurs' ball," Leah said, fluffing her skirts as she settled into the Wilton town coach.

"You look fine," Darius assured her. "You'll be fine."

"I'll be whispered about." She might have leaned against him on that sentiment, but Darius's sister was not complaining. "You'll dance with me, and a few other stalwarts will, but it will mostly be an evening to endure."

"I saw Val Windham standing up with the ladies the other night. He wouldn't make a bad husband."

"He's a duke's son." Leah smoothed her skirts again. "He can do much better."

"Dance with him anyway. He's decent company, and it can't hurt to be seen on his arm."

"Suppose not, and it passes the time. What about you? Any prospective brides on the horizon?"

Sisters knew exactly how to turn the tables on a fellow. "A bad joke, Leah. I'll leave the hunting to you and Trent."

"And Emily," Leah added. "She's making lists, scouring *Debrett's*, and ranking prospects by title."

"A right little scientist. Has Hellerington pestered you?"

"He's too infirm to dance," Leah said, though her eyes narrowed tellingly. "So far, he just breathes on me, ogles me, and hints he's in discussions with Wilton."

"Which he well could be."

"How do you know this?"

"Men talk." Darius studied the passing street lamps, hoping Leah would accept that explanation. He'd put

Kettering on to keeping an eye out at Hellerington's solicitors, and clerks talked over a pint more than old women at a quilting party.

"Should I be worried?"

He wanted to offer her reassuring platitudes, about providing for her no matter what, dowering her if necessary, but he'd gotten another summons from Lucy Templeton, and the tone was overtly threatening. Before he took on his siblings' troubles, Darius admonished himself to put his own house in order.

"You should be cautious," Darius said, but that increased the anxiety in her eyes, which called for a change in topic. "What do you recall of a Vivian Longstreet? She said she came out with you."

And thank the angels, the trepidation in Leah's gaze became curiosity. "You ran into her in the park with Emily last month. I knew her as Lady Vivian Islington. She's an earl's daughter, and we're of an age, so we were thrown together a great deal. We lost touch, though, when I went to Italy. I recall her as quiet, kind, and more sensible than the average debutante. Pretty too. Why do you ask?"

Darius did not take his sister's hand, though he wanted to—to comfort her, but maybe also to comfort himself. "She was kind to Em, and a girl making her come out can use every ally. Speaking of allies, shall I remain at your side tonight?"

"Only if you spot Hellerington. I'll find a place among the wallflowers and dowagers, and be content enough."

Darius shot her an exasperated look. "You have to at least try. You're pretty, intelligent, you run Wilton's household on tuppence or less, and you'd make some fellow a wonderful wife. A husband would be an escape from Wilton and from whatever mischief he plans for you."

Leah rummaged in her reticule, extracting a pair of long white evening gloves and slipping them on. "I'm used goods. Wilton has seen to it the world knows what low esteem he holds me in, Darius, and yet, you're right: I should at least try. If I don't, that will be reported to Wilton as well."

"True enough."

He danced the opening set with her then gave in to her pleading when they'd seen no sight of Hellerington, and left her among the companions and chaperones.

"Mr. Lindsey? Ah, it is you. A pleasure to see you again."

Darius turned slowly, not initially placing the dry, aged voice. William Longstreet stood near a pillar under the minstrels' gallery, looking pale, alert, and... genuinely friendly.

"Lord Longstreet."

"A little bird told me that you might be interested in raising pigeons at your estate in Kent. Might we repair to the card room and discuss such a venture?"

Darius wanted to ask the old blighter what he was up to. A challenge lurked in Lord Longstreet's rheumy eyes, a suggestion of a dare.

"May I fetch some punch for you first, sir?"

"For God's sake, Lindsey, I'm old, I'm not doddering. That punch is for giddy children and tippling companions. Now, have you ever done contract work for the military?"

The question was peculiar enough to have Darius's entire concentration, which explained why, when a soft, beguiling scent crept into his awareness, it took him a moment to realize that right at his elbow, a woman—

"My lady." He bowed, while William turned a smile on Vivian.

"Dearest Vivian, I was wondering if Lady Chinwag was ever going to turn loose of you. I was interrogating young Lindsey here about raising pigeons for His Majesty's military. Intriguing notion, and one we can pursue later, Lindsey."

"Lady *Chinwag*, William? You are being curmudgeonly, and in public too." Vivian's smile for her husband was perfectly sweet, while her figure was...

Some queer sensation thrummed through Darius's chest at the sight of Vivian in a high-waisted gown of shimmering brown velvet. Her hair was half caught up off her neck, half tumbling over her shoulders, while her bosom...

Carrying a child did marvelous things for a lady's décolletage, though Darius could hardly allow himself to appreciate those things with William Longstreet looking on. And it wasn't just the fullness of her breasts Darius noticed. Vivian had a glow about her, both a softness and a new substance that made him want to... linger in her ambit, though that was a thoroughly, exceedingly Bad Idea.

William cleared his throat, which turned into a fit of dry coughing. Vivian patted the old fellow's back,

Darius found him a glass of champagne, but William waved them both off.

"Perhaps you will take pity on an old man's frail bones and take Vivian for a turn on the terrace, Mr. Lindsey? While the warmth of the ballroom might be stifling to you young people, the night breezes hold no appeal for me."

William's expression was saintly, a definition of the absence of guile, which suggested strongly to Darius that guile was at work. Vivian's gaze was trained on the parquet flooring—no help would be forthcoming from her. Knowing it to be a Worse Idea Yet, Darius winged his arm.

"Come along, my lady. The ballroom is indeed stifling."

Without so much as a backward glance at her husband—should Darius be pleased or alarmed?—Vivian laced her fingers over Darius's arm.

"Do you think William is pale?" she asked when they'd left William to banter politics with a crony. The honest concern in her tone was a bracing reminder of the realities.

Vivvie—*Vivian*—was married to William Longstreet and cared for him sincerely. "I've met his lordship on only two occasions. He didn't strike me as any more pale tonight than he did months ago."

They exchanged no more words until they'd reached the relatively quiet terrace overlooking torch-lit gardens.

"The moon is about to come up," Vivian said. "Shall we find a seat?"

Darius gave up cataloguing what an ill-advised turn the evening was taking and escorted Vivian to a stone bench in a shadowed corner of the terrace. Shadows were appropriate for them, and always would be.

The thought steadied even as it frustrated.

"How do you fare, my lady?"

She scuffed her dancing slipper against the flagstone, and though they were sitting, she did not disentangle her arm from his. "I am growing fat, Darius Lindsey."

"You sound pleased enough with this state of affairs." She sounded smug, in fact. Wonderfully, femininely smug.

"I am…" She turned her face up to the stars. "There are not words, Darius."

Mr. Lindsey. He needed to be nothing more than Mr. Lindsey to her.

"Tell me anyway."

"I'm a little worried, of course. Things can go wrong."

Darius stroked his fingers over her knuckles. If she'd been worried, he'd been nigh cataleptic with concern. "You will have the best doctors. William assured me of this."

"It's a bigger worry than that. I worry the child won't be healthy, that I won't know what to do, that I'll drop him, that he won't like the names William chooses."

Darius wanted desperately to pursue that topic— what would his child be called? He hadn't the right. But he did have the right to offer Vivian comfort, even as his heart broke for what he could not offer her.

"You will be a wonderful mother, Vivvie. You'll be a lioness, and all will know that your child has his mother's love and devotion." Or hers. A daughter with Vivian's smile and her tender heart… Darius snapped that thought off like an errant daisy growing among thorny roses where it had no business being.

He'd apparently found the right thing to say, though. Vivian went silent, but perhaps—just perhaps—she leaned a little more heavily against his arm.

He'd taught her that. The thought was both a comfort and a torment. While he pondered the subtleties of the torment, the moon crested the horizon.

"The light of a full moon is so beautiful," Vivian said. "There's peace in it, benevolence. It comforts one just to behold it."

She was trying to tell him something, something sweet, painful, and well intended. "It's the most beautiful sight I've seen in several months. I thank you for showing it to me, my lady. I would have missed it otherwise."

A lean. A definite lean of a full, soft breast against his arm. He cherished the torture of it. "Give me your hand, Darius."

He'd taken off his gloves in anticipation of playing some whist. Her excuse for being barehanded was a mystery. He let her take his left hand in her right, but nearly shot off the bench when she settled his hand, quite firmly, low on her belly.

"I'm fat, getting fatter by the day."

He said nothing, too stunned by the shape of her. She wasn't fat—of course she wasn't—but where her waist had been was a soft bulge, a change, a whisper of movement.

"*Good God*. The child has quickened."

She kept her hand over his. "In the past couple of weeks. I lie down at night, and for half an hour, I simply marvel at the sensation. It's like… a soft breeze fluttering my insides."

The little breeze came again and again. The feeling at once unmanned him and made him want to conquer armies barehanded for the woman beside him. He wanted to go down on his knees, to bow his head, to pen sonnets and ballads and proclaim them from every street corner.

"I am happy for you, Vivvie. Profoundly, indescribably happy." Not enough, but a truth, nonetheless. He brought her fingers to his lips, offered her a kiss, and withdrew his hand.

"I wanted you to be happy too, Darius."

So she'd put William up to this outing, engineered a stroll on the patio, and utterly ambushed Darius's best intentions. He loved her for it, even as he knew the rest of his life wouldn't be adequate for him to recover from the emotions her sharing of happiness had engendered in his breast.

⁂

Vivian had composed all manner of foolish speeches once she'd decided Darius ought to know his child was thriving in the womb.

She and Darius could be friends—she was friends of a sort with some MPs who shared William's politics.

She and Darius could be cordial—she was an earl's daughter; he was an earl's son. No one would remark it, *much*.

He might call on William just to be polite, and Vivian would pour. She'd poured a thousand cups of tea in aid of lesser ends, such as the good of the realm and the glory of old England.

Only to find, when Darius said not one word but

merely shared a moonrise with her—the most beautiful thing he'd seen in months—that Darius had the
right of it. They could be nothing cordial, friendly, or
polite to each other. He might have the savoir faire
and stamina for it; she did not.

William had said a little infatuation was acceptable,
to be expected even, but part of Vivian's wonder at
her pregnancy had to do with becoming a person
William knew not at all. For the first time, she had a
privacy in her marriage to rival what William had in
his memories of Muriel.

She respected his privacy now more than she had,
and William extended to Vivian the same courtesy.
He was all those things Vivian had tried to tell herself
Darius could be—cordial, friendly, polite—which was
fine. Vivian loved her husband, was grateful to him,
and wished him only the best.

But for Darius Lindsey, the father of her child, her
feelings were so much more complicated, inconvenient, and precious. She would accept every instance
when their paths crossed and treasure the pain and
delight of each meeting, for in Darius Lindsey, she'd
found not just a man to respect and appreciate, but a
man whom she could love.

The moon was clearing the horizon, spreading
light in all directions even as its size seemed to
diminish, when a woman's laughter sounded out in
the shadowed garden.

Beside her, right immediately beside her, Vivian
felt Darius stiffen. Before he could make some polite
comment to reestablish the picket lines, Vivian slipped
her arm from his and rose.

"Shall we go in, Mr. Lindsey? The best of the moon's display is over, and I would not want to cause my husband undue concern over my absence."

His eyes widened, suggesting Vivian might have overstated her point. "I would never want Lord Longstreet to worry unnecessarily. A lady is always safe in my care."

Safe. The slight emphasis on the word made it clear Darius would not use tonight's shared moment to encroach in the future—which ought to be a relief rather than a cause of sorrow. The laughter came again from the garden, a raucous taunt, reminding Vivian that she'd gotten more than she'd bargained for in this rendezvous.

And much less.

"Shall we go in?" Darius managed to put some pugnacity into the way he offered her his arm. In no time at all, Vivian was back at William's side, and Darius had disappeared into the smiling, bejeweled crowd.

"How fares Mr. Lindsey, Vivian?"

William's question was kindly, his expression suggesting concern for Vivian—and even some for young Mr. Lindsey.

"He is all that is correct, William."

William patted her hand and said nothing while the orchestra took up a gavotte. When the knot in Vivian's chest was threatening to choke her, William said, without glancing down at her, "I'll have the carriage brought around."

Twelve

BLANCHE COWELL WAS LOOSE ON THE GROUNDS—
Darius would recognize her laughter anywhere—and
all Darius could think was that he must not allow her
to see him with Vivian. By the time he emerged from
the safety of the card room, Vivian was nowhere to be
seen, heard, or sniffed.

And neither was Leah, until he spotted her leaving
the supper buffet on the arm of none other than
Baron Hellerington.

The old goat must have come late and kept out
of sight until he could accost his prey. As Darius
made his way around the periphery of the ballroom,
Hellerington parted from Leah with a bow and a
damp, lingering kiss to her hand.

"Are you all right?" Darius peered down at Leah in
concern. She had the indefinable stillness of a woman
coping with internal tumult. "You look pale, and
you've been thinking too hard."

"Hellerington is going to talk to Papa."

"God." Darius ran a hand through his hair. "It
would have to be him."

"He's titled, and he has some blunt, Dare." Leah was tapping her foot, though not in time to the music. "And he's desperate, which are the requisite qualities for any match Papa finds for me."

"But Hellerington." Darius spat the name. "It isn't to be borne, Leah."

"He and Papa will dicker," Leah said, sounding as if she were trying to convince herself. "Something might develop while they do."

"We live in that hope, feeble though it is. I do not like leaving you here to be preyed upon." He scowled down at her to emphasize his point.

"I am largely ignored, Darius." She put a touch of frost in her tone, enough for him to realize she'd like privacy to collect herself rather than more of his badgering presence. "And if you don't ask that Windham girl to dance, the Season will be half over, and you'll be wishing you had."

He curbed the temptation to lecture and rant, bowed over her hand, and departed. He wasn't about to dance twice with any woman he wasn't closely related to—the notably single Lady Jenny Windham, for example—but he took himself off anyway, mostly to cool his temper.

The ball was well attended because the Season was officially under way, and among the crowd, Darius saw that indeed, Lord Valentine Windham's friend, Nicholas Haddonfield, Viscount Reston, had deigned to join the fray. The man was noteworthy for his great height and the physique of a Viking blacksmith, and for his enthusiasm regarding women of a certain ilk.

Easy women, naughty women, even decent women

seemed to enjoy Reston's attentions. Now why couldn't a fellow like that take Leah on as his wife? There was an earldom in the offing for Reston, the rumor being he'd promised his ailing father he'd marry this Season.

And when Darius handed his sister into the coach, he was quietly surprised that it was about Reston she inquired. Well, she could do worse. And if Hellerington's coin spoke loudly enough, she *would* do worse. Darius dropped Leah off then walked the few blocks to his destination, hoping the crisp night air might help him marshal his wits for the coming ordeal.

It did no good. Lucy was a snake, and she could strike from any angle, and Darius, God help him, was her prey of choice these days.

"Don't tell me." He seized the offensive as he strolled into her bedroom. "I'm late. My apologies, but Leah is bound to attend her entertainments until at least after supper, and I am bound to escort her."

"Let your brother Amherst do it," Lucy spat. "He's the damned heir."

She was in sufficiently rare form that he decided he'd placate her first—one last time—and take permanent leave of her thereafter.

"Trenton is only recently out of mourning, Lucy. He does his share. Then too, the matchmakers will swarm him should he show his face among decent ladies."

Lucy's expression moderated. "While you, they leave to the likes of me. Clothes off, Darius. You'll pay for your divided loyalties, and dawdling won't help."

Darius shrugged out of his coat, wondering if Lucy realized his loyalty was to her coin. "As tired as I am, any excuse to get into any bed sounds appealing. How is your husband?"

She slapped him for that, which woke him up nicely.

"Been ignoring you, has he?" He saw the next blow coming and seized her wrist in a grasp not quite intended to hurt. "Hold, Lucy. Your puppy has run off, and in his place is a man unwilling to pleasure you for coin. I'm done with your beatings, whippings, and spankings. Take your ire out on Blanche or the footmen or the damned stable boys, but attack me again, and you'll regret it."

"I'll regret it?" She wrenched free and came at him, nails and teeth, fists and feet, until Darius had her pinned beneath him on the bed.

"Enough, damn you." He bounced her wrists hard against the mattress for good measure. "Be still."

"Fuck me," Lucy ordered, arching up against him. "If I can't have the fun I want, the least you can do is swive me."

"You know the rules, Lucy." He did not make the mistake of letting her go. "No one runs the risk of pregnancy, and I don't have to worry about a glove across my face."

"As if Templeton would bother." She tried to wrest free again, but Darius was too big, too strong, and too damned sick of her nonsense. The singed scent of her crimped hair alone was threatening his digestive control.

"I can hold you here all night," he said through gritted teeth. "Or I could offer you the gratification you pay me for. Rather than do either, I will, for once, do exactly as I please and walk out of here, not to return."

And, God in heaven, the words felt wonderful.

"Damn you!" She made another futile attempt to regain her freedom, and Darius waited it out as patiently as he could. He perceived a new difficulty all too easily: though she tried to hide it, Lucy enjoyed being overpowered, probably even more than she enjoyed hurting him with her silly games.

"Do I have to bind you, Lucy?" He gritted out the question with a sinking feeling in his gut. He'd thought there was nothing worse than being her plaything, hers to tie up, beat, humiliate, and toy with, but pretending she was his plaything had to rank far beneath that.

"Yes," she panted. "Bind me hand and foot, and then, by God, you'd better exert yourself, Lindsey, or I'll ruin that sister of yours, see if I don't."

"Ruin *her*?" Darius whipped off his cravat and used it to secure her right wrist. "And how will you manage that, without being ruined yourself?"

"Oh, no." Lucy shook her head, and her smile was a thing of evil. "You won't tell a soul, Darius, not about these little trysts of ours. Do that, and your whole family suffers. Blanche is well informed regarding your sister's little contretemps five years ago, and we can remind all and sundry of the details."

Temper and seething frustration turned the edges of his vision red. Leah had been through enough, and yet Lucy would derive savage glee in destroying the remains of Leah's marital prospects.

He used the sash of Lucy's night robe to tie her other wrist, and made it a point not to tie her tightly or to yank her wrists uncomfortably as he did. It was petty revenge against a renewed sentence of misery at Lucy's hands, but all he could manage.

"As if anyone in this town ever forgets a scandal." He sat back and eyed her, realizing his clothes were on, and his complete lack of sexual interest in this woman was at least his to privately savor.

"Get busy, Darius."

"No." He moved off the bed and considered pleasuring himself while she was bound and helpless to do anything but watch. She'd hate that.

He'd hate it more. He tugged off his boots, rolled up his sleeves, and poured himself a drink of fine old brandy from the decanter on the sideboard, knowing Lucy was watching his every move.

Another swallow, while he rolled the alcohol around on his tongue and eyed her on the bed. God above, he needed to be drunk for this.

"I want it to hurt," Lucy said. "Blood would be good. On the sheets."

"You're sick." Darius set his glass down and approached the bed. "I should pity you."

"You should fuck me."

"No." Never had a single word held so much pleasure for him.

"Shut up." Lucy closed her eyes and lifted her hips. "Just shut up and get your mouth on me."

He reversed direction and brought his glass of brandy to the night table.

"You want it to hurt, Lucy?"

She glared at him. "I want it to start."

"I can make it burn," he said, taking another swallow of brandy and climbing onto the bed.

She spread her legs and became docile as Darius did, indeed, make her burn, while his own torment involved flames of conscience rather than desire.

∽≈≫

How had his life come to this?

Lucy had paid him with a choker, of all things, of topaz and emeralds. The piece was pretty, and as he'd taken it to the little shop on Ludgate he discreetly patronized, it occurred to him the jewels would go well with Vivian's coloring.

Where in the hell had that ludicrous notion come from?

Now, more than ever, he needed to put thoughts of Vivian from his mind, and now, more than ever, his imagination returned to her like a lodestone. She was a beacon of pure goodness in his otherwise sordid existence, and as spring advanced to its full glory, Vivian kept invading his mind and pushing darker thoughts aside.

So he squired Leah about, and took Emily for the occasional quiet hack, and popped down to Kent to check on John, and dreaded the next summons from Lucy or Blanche. They'd backed off, and Lucy at least seemed content to be cast in the role of victim, but it wore on Darius like being her abused pet never had.

As if he could enjoy hurting any woman, even her, even for her pleasure.

"Looking for me?" Blanche appeared at his elbow and wrapped her arm around his, pressing her breast to his bicep. He nearly gagged in response.

"Lady Cowell." He eased back and sensed this was to be his punishment. Lucy and Blanche might allow him to recast his part in their games, but they'd have their revenge for his attempted escape, and accosting him in public was a good place to start.

"I have a few dances free." Blanche reattached herself to his side. "I'm told you're grace itself on the dance floor."

Darius turned to pick up his drink and managed to dislodge her again. "For that, you need to dance with Lord Val Windham."

"The pianist?"

"The same." Darius kept his drink in his hand, for Blanche wasn't about to risk spilling something on that gown of hers. Ye gods, it was barely decent.

"I'd rather dance with you." She eyed him as if he were a hanging ham and she a starving bitch. "Later tonight, as a matter of fact. On my sheets."

Vivian. The thought of her circled in his mind like a tired old prayer, a child's futile wish, a forlorn hope. He opened his mouth to put Blanche off when rescue came from an unlikely quarter. His sister approached, the tallest man in the room at her side. Leah began on introductions, but her escort cut her off.

"We've met." Nick Haddonfield smiled blandly, while his piercing blue eyes assessed Darius closely. "Lindsey, a pleasure to see you in Town. And Lady Cowell, a pleasure as well."

"Nicky," the woman clinging to Darius purred, "always a pleasure to see you, but I don't know as I've met your young lady." She added a particular female emphasis to the word "young," the slightest, nasty little inflection, so in the way of unkind women, it implied its opposite.

"My sister." Darius spoke up and shifted to shake Blanche off his arm once and for all. "Lady Leah Lindsey. Leah, Lady Blanche Cowell." Darius was amused to see Leah did not curtsy but merely inclined her head.

Reston winged out an arm thick with muscles no amount of finery could disguise. "Blanche, perhaps you'd favor me with a few minutes of your time. It has been at least since the holidays since our paths crossed. Lindsey, Lady Leah." He offered Leah a slow, deep bow, one unmistakably intended to convey respect, and took his leave, Lady Cowell on his arm.

Darius nodded at Reston's retreating back. "So where did you meet that?"

"I met *him* in the park with Emily," Leah said. "Where did you meet her?"

Swimming in the Channel with a school of sharks who will cheerfully destroy you.

"She's frequently at the same functions you are," Darius lied, oh, so easily to his dear sister. "She travels in a slightly less genteel circle."

"Lord Reston apparently frequents the same set."

"You needn't sound so offended." And to anybody but her brother—any of the hundred or so people milling around the ballroom with them, she probably wouldn't have. "I doubt either of them will be joining us for supper." He'd run screaming into the night if Blanche presumed that far.

"I think we might see more of Lord Reston. He seems to have taken an interest in Emily."

The topic was now familial, so Darius took his sister's arm and steered her toward the corner of the room reserved for chaperones, companions, and other wallflowers. "And Wilton will probably allow it. The man's heir to an earldom, though birthing his get will likely kill little Em."

"You don't like Reston?" Leah asked, her curiosity evident.

"I like him well enough, though I can't say I know him."

"What do you know *of* him?" Leah asked, and Darius was reminded she'd asked about Reston before.

"He's a favorite with the ladies, at least the ladies like Lady Cowell," Darius said meaningfully. "He pays his bills, looks after a herd of younger siblings, and is quite the horseman. Not sure what else there is to tell, except that he's the largest titled lord I've seen, and his papa, the earl, is old as dirt. Haven't I said as much previously?"

"And his papa is not in good health," Leah added, causing Darius to study her more carefully.

"Is he trifling with you, Leah?" He'd flatten the man if he were. Leah had troubles enough as it was, and a good bare-knuckle fight would fit on Darius's schedule with appalling ease.

"He most assuredly is not. Is Lady Cowell trifling with you?"

Sisters knew how to shut a man up. "I am not going to dignify that. Shall I lead you out or find you a place to hide?"

"Leave me in peace."

Because Hellerington hadn't been again in evidence, Darius acceded to her wishes. He danced with his share of wallflowers, kept an eye on Leah, and saw her

later sharing supper with Reston. Wouldn't that spike
Wilton's guns, if Reston were courting Leah and not
angling for little Emily?

When Darius loaded his sister into the coach, he
tucked an arm around her shoulders, and she budged
up with a sigh of relief.

"Do I tell you often enough what a good brother
you are?"

"I'm not a good brother," Darius replied, thinking
of John hidden away in Kent and Lucy threatening
what little peace Leah enjoyed. "But I am a noticing
brother. What was that business with Reston and
the strawberry?"

"The strawberry?"

"He sequestered himself with you behind the ferns,
Leah, and in the course of sharing supper with you, fed
you a strawberry from his own hand."

"He was flirting." Leah yawned. "Nick likes to flirt."

"Nick."

"Lord Reston." She straightened up, but Darius
gently pushed her head back to his shoulder.

"You said he might be trolling for Em," Darius
reminded her. "What if he's trolling for you?"

"He might offer, just to wave Hellerington off."

"He might hurry Hellerington up, if he offers."
Darius frowned into the darkness. "Do you need me
to speak to him?"

"No." Leah sounded firm on that. "If there's
'speaking to' needed, I can address the man directly."

"That's unusual, for you to be forthright with a
man other than me or Trent."

"He's an unusual man." Leah's voice was dreamy,

and Darius wished there were enough light that he could assess her expression. "He said to warn you off that woman all but humping your arm."

The description left no room for confusion. "Blanche is a casual acquaintance."

"If Nick said to beware of a lady, and Nick makes no bones about enjoying women, mind you, then you need to take heed."

"Nick, Nick, Nick."

"Lord Reston."

Darius jostled her affectionately. "Keep telling yourself he's Lord Reston, but to me, it looks like he's already gotten to first names, strawberries, and God knows what else."

"And if he has?"

"Marry him," Darius said flatly. "He's big enough and man enough to face down Wilton, Hellerington, me, whomever." *Lucy and Blanche*. "You could do much worse, Leah, and he'd take care of you. If he's courting you, he has my endorsement."

It wasn't something he'd been able to say before, not about the puppies who had sniffed about her skirts five years ago, not about her would-be elopement partner, not about the few men who'd shown an interest so far this year.

"Don't tell him that," Leah said on a weary sigh. "He's arrogant enough as it is."

"Not arrogant," Darius said, almost to himself. "Reston is self-assured, and that's a different thing entirely."

When Leah was dozing on his shoulder, he let the conversation lapse but sent a prayer up to whatever God listened to creatures such as he that Reston took on the problem that was Leah and her situation, and please, heaven, let it be soon.

❧

"You are kind to think of me." Vivian accepted a cup of tea from Portia, knowing it would lack sugar, for Portia deemed sugared tea unfit for breeding women. Since learning of Vivian's pregnancy, Portia was a veritable font of odd ideas regarding childbearing, and even child rearing.

"Public school builds the character," Portia announced. "Look at Able, and he's a product of Rugby."

Look at Able? One could barely see the man for the way he avoided his wife's company. Able had stayed about a week then hared back to the country, there to plough and plant and enjoy his wife's absence, no doubt.

"And what will you name this child?" Portia inquired as she sipped her own tea—heavily sugared.

Lindsey Longstreet had a nice sound and would fit either gender—she'd yet to suggest this to William. "I assume William will want a family name."

"And good heavens, what if it's a girl?"

Portia's own gender must have temporarily escaped her notice, so great was her dismay at this possibility. "We'll love any child God sees fit to give us, Portia."

"But a girl can't inherit the viscountcy, and then where will we be?"

"We'll manage, Portia."

Except Vivian wasn't going to manage another minute of the woman's conversation.

"I'm for a little shopping," she decided, though what she'd shop for was a mystery. "How about you?"

"Shopping?" Portia's eyes took on a gleam, and Vivian realized she should have been more devious. "I might need to pick up a few things."

"You must accompany me then." Though invariably, Portia needed something at every shop they browsed, and somehow, Vivian ended up paying for it. Portia's maid forgot her pin money, or her reticule, or didn't think to bring quite that much with her. The excuses were as endless as they were lame.

No matter, every outing was a potential opportunity to cross paths with Darius.

Vivian recalled shopping with him, the way he'd managed the proprietors and clerks, the eye he had for quality, and the way he'd teased, reasoned, and cajoled her into everything from embroidered underthings to new gloves. His name stood for the ache in her heart and the empty place in her bed and the life growing in her womb. She missed him and missed him and missed him, and worse, she sensed William knew it.

She'd see Darius at the christening, and for more than the space of a single moonrise. He'd said as much, and if there was one thing she'd believe about Darius Lindsey, it was that he'd keep his word.

Thoughts of him had her nipping up to her bedroom to retrieve a little slip of paper from her vanity. She was still kept waiting a good ten minutes before Portia joined her at the foot of the stairs.

"Shouldn't we take a footman or two with us?"

So Portia could collect more purchases? "They have enough work. It's a pretty day, and I can use the exercise."

"We're not taking the carriage?"

"I need to stretch my legs. Shall we be off?"

Portia gave her a peevish look but linked arms and marched off with Vivian into a lovely spring day.

"Well, Vivian," a male voice called out when they were nearing Green Park, "won't you introduce me to your pretty companion?"

The benevolence of the spring day muted. "Thurgood." Vivian stopped abruptly, so lost in her ruminations she hadn't seen him on the sidewalk before them until he'd spoken. "A pleasure. Portia Springer, may I make known to you the gentleman who used to be my stepfather, Thurgood Ainsworthy. Thurgood, Mrs. Portia Springer, late of Longchamps, Oxfordshire, where she is the wife of William's hard-working steward."

Hell would freeze over before Vivian would discuss her husband's illegitimate son with the likes of Thurgood.

"Ladies." He bowed low over each of their hands, holding Portia's—of course—a moment too long. "May I escort you somewhere, or are you returning home?"

"We're off to Bond Street," Portia caroled, batting her lashes.

"All the way to Ludgate, actually," Vivian said. "I need to pick up a bottle of scent made to order. But it's kind of you to offer."

"Nonsense." Thurgood slipped his arm through Portia's, and Vivian wasn't at all surprised to note Portia had turned loose of Vivian without a second thought. "Lead on, Viv, and let me be your gallant escort."

There would be no getting rid of him, not when he was having such a good flirt with Portia, and Lord, wouldn't William laugh to hear of this. Portia was handsome, true enough, but girlish coquetry on her looked about as believable as spectacles on a flying pig.

Thurgood insisted on fetching a hackney, so they arrived to their destination shortly where, thank a merciful deity, Thurgood made his excuses.

"Mr. Ainsworthy." Portia held out her hand again. "It has been the most sincere pleasure. You must call on us at Longstreet House."

Heaven help me, I shall kill her. Portia had no business extending such an invitation.

"I'd be delighted. My dear daughter and I always have a great deal to talk about." Thurgood gave Vivian one of his indulgent smiles, and Vivian smiled back, trying not to choke. He'd been enough of a pest lately, with his carping about grieving together and William's failing health. Everlasting God, the man was a disgrace.

Once in the shop, surrounded by a blend of lovely scents, Vivian was possessed of an immediate sense of well-being. She felt closer to Darius here. He'd had this shop mix up her personal scent for her. She'd come here only once since Christmas, but she wore the scent every day and never wanted to run out.

"What a handsome specimen you have for a step-papa." Portia took Vivian's arm as they strolled the shop. "You never said, Vivian."

"I don't think of him as handsome or ugly," Vivian said, though she did—he was as ugly as a week-old sheep carcass in high summer. "He's a terrible flirt, Portia, so mind yourself around him."

Portia's nose tipped up. "He's not a flirt. He's gallant, and that's something else altogether."

Vivian gave her order to the clerk then started

on a round of the shop, sniffing idly at this and that scent. She was hunting for the one Darius used, but suspected he had his custom-made as well. And then she caught it, a little hint of his scent, as a woman's voice drifted across the shop.

"Really, Darius," the lady drawled, "rose is too juvenile, and lavender doddering. You can't expect me to wear those *in public.*"

He was there, leaning in to say something quietly to the woman, speaking right into her ear. She laughed softly in response, and her bosom was positively mashed against his arm.

Vivian had ached over Darius Lindsey, and cried a bit, and sighed and wished and wished. Those tender sentiments paled to nothing when between one heartbeat and the next, her heart broke, leaving both anger and sorrow to flood into the breach.

"Perhaps in *private* then," the woman said, loud enough that others could overhear. Darius straightened, and whatever he'd been intending to say died on his lips as he realized Vivian was standing only a few feet away.

Gaping, like a stupid cow. She shut her mouth and turned with brittle dignity. From behind the woman's shoulder, though, she caught Darius mouthing the words, "cut direct."

What was he trying to say to her? Cut him? Prepare to be cut by him? And there was Portia, catching sight of Darius and his companion as if they were the most fascinating entertainment since the coronation of Mad George.

Darius touched the woman's arm. "Excuse me, Lucy. I see an acquaintance. An old acquaintance."

He prowled over to Vivian, his entire manner exuding a kind of mute swagger, but his eyes held a plea Vivian still couldn't fathom. He sidled up to her and picked up her hand, bowing low over it.

"My lady." He kept hold of her hand, just as Thurgood might have, until she snatched it back. "A pleasure to see you again."

"Sir." Vivian's voice shook. "I believe you have me at a disadvantage, and I would like to remain there. Portia, it's time we left." She walked out without retrieving the perfume the clerk had brought from the back, but then she had to wait at the door of the shop for Portia to join her.

"Another satisfied customer, Darius?" The woman's voice held amusement.

"Hardly." Vivian heard him dismiss her without a backward glance. "If you don't like the single-note fragrances, Lucy, you should try the blends. Over here…"

Portia came huffing up to Vivian's side. "What was that all about? I was about to make a purchase."

"I needed some air." Vivian put a hand over her stomach, for reassurance, to steady herself, to quiet the pounding of her heart. "Shall we be on our way?"

"But we just got here." Portia glanced back at the shop with longing. It wasn't a cheap place to spend money. *And Darius had so little of it to spend.*

"We're going home, Portia." Vivian's tone was for once sharp. "We can come back later."

"Who was that man?"

"I haven't the least notion," Vivian replied, walking faster, and her words were true. That fawning, droll, insouciant tramp was not her Darius, and that woman… how could he bear it? To be intimate with such as that? Had he taught that creature how to press up against him? Was she going to leave the shop with a personal blend chosen by the handsome Mr. Lindsey?

Or was the better question how Darius had borne being intimate with Vivian? She was unsophisticated, retiring, and more knowledgeable about Corn Laws than quadrilles, and it hurt, terribly, to see how she compared with Darius's usual fare.

It hurt for her, and worse, it made her hurt miserably for him.

Thirteen

HOW HE GOT BACK TO HIS ROOMS, DARIUS DIDN'T know. Lucy had ambushed him on The Strand, and that was how they played their game now. She and Blanche both insisted he acknowledge them when they met in public. And lately, he'd been running into them far too much for it to be mere happenstance.

He felt stalked, hunted, like a wee mouse in the shadow of the hawk.

And then his worst nightmare, a potential encounter between Vivian and Lucy.

Between good and evil, between his dreams and his deserts.

Vivian had looked so stricken, seeing him with Lucy on his coattails, and well she should have. Her thoughts had been clear enough: she'd been comparing herself to Lucy and finding herself wanting. And that, *that*, was what hurt the most, that his lovely, sweet Vivian should doubt herself.

Though wouldn't Lucy have a fine time shredding Vivian's reputation? Leah had been through the worst treatment gossip and scandal could cause, had dealt with heartbreak, grief, and a load of earthly woes. Lucy could hurt Leah, but she could *destroy* Vivian.

So Darius had dealt what he hoped was a survivable blow first, and now he had to do something, had to make amends to Vivian lest she fret and brood and doubt herself further. He owed her an explanation and an apology, and that was that.

He was about to put pen to paper when a knock sounded on his door.

"Mister Darius Lindsey!"

Darius opened the door to find a running footman panting on his doorstep.

"I'm Lindsey."

"I know." The man bent over to ease his breathing. "I'm to give you a message from Reston. Your sister is at his place, and she's right enough, but you're to come. Don't tarry or discuss your plans, and I've told your brother the same. I'm off to the grandame's when I get me wind."

"Grandame?"

"Lady Warne." The man straightened. "Reston's grandame."

"Leah's all right?"

"She be fine." The man's gaze slid away, and Darius could only guess Leah wasn't quite so fine.

Darius caught up with Trent, whose toilette had likely required some attention before he could call on Reston even casually. Together, they arrived to find a teary Leah burrowed against Reston's side, a visible bruise rising on the side of her face.

Reston explained that their sister had nearly been abducted from the park, and further ventured his suspicions that it was likely Hellerington's doing. To Darius's thinking, the near tragedy was a blessing in disguise, as it put any notion of Reston's offering for Emily off the table.

Leah wasn't just comfortable with Reston's touch, which would have been noteworthy enough, she was positively clinging to him, and Reston was damned near clinging right back. On a man of his size, the behavior was oddly sweet and… dear.

Which was fortunate, for Reston announced his intention to marry Leah, and from what Darius could see, Leah was going to allow it.

Arrangements were made for Leah to be chaperoned under Reston's roof by his grandmother until a special license could be procured. Reston was confident he could handle Wilton, and so Darius was left to stroll home in the slanting twilight with Trent. Later, he'd troll in low places for clues regarding his sister's would-be abduction; for now, he'd see his brother home.

Trent shook his head. "Just like that. We're fretting over her being dragged into Hellerington's clutches one day, and she's marrying Bellefonte's heir the next."

"I like him."

"You know him?"

"Some. Not as much as I should, but Leah trusts him, and that has to count for a lot."

"How can you tell?"

Darius cocked his head at his brother. "She was wrapped around him like seaweed, Trent. You had to have seen that."

"I *saw* him whispering at you in the corner and looking alarmingly ferocious when he did."

Nick Haddonfield looking ferocious was a sight to give any sane man pause. "He was suggesting, as a wedding present to our sister, I leave off associating with certain women of questionable character. Reston delivers a very convincing scold."

Trent delivered a very convincing look of fraternal disappointment, which suggested Darius's public encounters with Lucy and Blanche were being noticed.

Bloody, sodding hell.

"I will not waste my breath echoing Reston's sentiments, but I will point out that our situation with John will be considerably complicated if Leah marries Reston. He's not stupid, Dare, and if he's part of the family, sooner or later, he'll pop in on you at Averett Hill."

Darius stopped walking. "Good God."

"Beg pardon?"

"He's my bloody neighbor." Darius blew out a breath. "Not two miles up the lane, and closer as the crow flies. Reston, that is, down in Kent. This is going to get tricky, Trent."

Trent kicked at a loose piece of cobblestone, sending it skittering and bouncing down the lane. "I hate tricky. Perhaps he'll be at the family seat now that his papa is sticking his spoon in the wall."

Darius resumed walking at a more brisk pace. "Not Reston. He hops around like a great flea, and I've seen him often enough on this or that huge horse to know he'll be in evidence around the neighborhood. As will Leah."

"Give it time," Trent said, his tone grim. "They're

not married yet, and even when they are, we'll want to see how they go on. Reston's no saint. He'll be decent about John, and he'll keep his handsome, smiling mouth shut."

"We could send John to Crossbridge." Trent's estate, one where he'd spent precious little time in recent years, and more distant from Town and all its gossip than Averett Hill. The notion of sending John away to strangers left Darius feeling sick in the pit of his stomach.

"I'll write to my staff there," Trent said, though the way he wrinkled his nose suggested the idea of moving John had no appeal to him either.

"It's just a thought. There's no need for any hasty maneuvers yet." And, Darius reminded himself, he had a letter to write too.

❧

Darius tried to write the letter, the *brief* note to Vivian, and it kept escaping him. Instead of a simple, innocuous apology, he'd trail off into admissions that he missed her, worried for her, regretted their encounter, but didn't regret it either.

He stared at the little bottle of scent she'd left behind. He sniffed it repeatedly, and he missed her.

He worried for his brother, took Emily riding, and missed Vivian. He kept to his rooms lest Lucy and Blanche have more opportunities to accost him in the broad light of day, as lately they'd grown miserably bold and uncaring of appearances. It was as if they had put a collar and leash on him in truth.

Reston's papa died, and Darius considered popping

out to Kent to attend the funeral, just to get away from London. He discarded the notion because Leah needed privacy with her new husband, not Darius hovering at an awkward time.

And the truth was, Darius could never again be with Vivian the way he had been in Kent. The pain of that was sobering and checked his need to spend time with her again. So the silence between him and Vivian lengthened, until Darius was at a bookshop, looking for a gift to present to Emily on the occasion of her seventeenth birthday.

He caught Vivian's scent first, then the sight of her, back turned to him, but it had to be Vivian. He knew the nape of that neck, knew the curve of that spine, and the soft, muscular swell of those glorious female buttocks.

"Vivvie."

He'd spoken softly, for there were other patrons elsewhere in the shop. She went still at first, so he said her name again, and what a pleasure that was, just to say her name out loud. "Vivvie, look at me."

She turned slowly and looked at him, and over his shoulder and everywhere else.

"I'm alone," he assured her, closing the distance between them slowly, as if she might spook and bolt did he move too quickly. Except she was visibly, wonderfully pregnant, and bolting was likely beyond her. "You're well?"

He stood as near to her as he dared. Seeing her up close was intoxicating, sending currents of pleasure and longing out over his limbs and down into his gut.

"Say something, Vivvie. Please." He'd been paid

to beg, but now, here, in this public place, he had to struggle not to go down on his knees. "Laugh me to scorn, ring a peal over my head, kick me anywhere you need to, but please don't—" He fell silent.

Her gaze held his, and in her eyes, Darius read a wealth of conflicting emotions: wariness, hurt, confusion, and—thank you, Jesus and the holy saints—longing.

"I'm well, Mr. Lindsey. And you?" Her hand settled over the bump where her waist used to be, and he had to touch her. He reached out and traced his fingers over her knuckles where her hand rested over her tummy.

"I'm…" *Miserable.* Miserable for want of her, for worrying about her, worrying about Trent, dodging the female predators he'd invited into his life, fretting over John… "I'm glad to see you. I've wanted to explain, to apologize for our last encounter."

"You needn't." She turned from him, as if to study the shelf of books at her eye level.

"I need to," he corrected her and leaned in close enough to whisper, close enough to inhale her fragrance. "The woman I was with would hurt you and enjoy doing it."

Lucy and Blanche would hurt Leah, Trent, John, anybody Darius was foolish enough to allow within their ambit.

Vivian shook her head, and when she looked up at him, her eyes were glistening.

"I can't understand it, Darius." She stared at the books again. "I can't understand what the attraction of such a woman is to you, but I must conclude you have a talent that serves to provide you coin, and where you exercise that talent matters little."

"It's not like that," Darius protested in a whisper. "It *wasn't* like that."

She pierced him with a gimlet gaze, and Darius slipped his arms around her. This was dangerous, stupid, and utterly irresistible. He had to touch her, had to feel her embrace again. For a moment, she was stiff and resisting, but then, ah, then...

Vivian's hands slid around his waist, and she pressed her face to his sternum. "I tell myself not to miss you. I should not miss you."

"Hush." He held her, rubbed her back, and breathed her in with his every sense. Her shape had changed, delightfully, so the baby rested between them, and he knew a flare of desire for her, even there, in public, with her upset and him needing to soothe her. He noted it, noted that it was the first bodily stirring to visit him since the last time he'd seen her, and then firmly ignored it.

Though he needed to kiss her, to soothe himself by kissing her. She startled a little—he remembered those little shocks and how they felt radiating through her body—and then she groaned softly into his mouth and kissed him back.

Ye gods and little fishes... He'd never kissed like this, with all the longing and tenderness he possessed, with all the apology, despair, and hope. He wanted to be better for her, but he was only Darius Lindsey, and she was married to William Longstreet, and so the kiss was a prayer too, for forgiveness and for time and for...

The kiss was not about any sexual passion on his part, though for her he had that in abundance. As he gloried in the sheer feel of her, what welled up in Darius's soul was a passionate wish for her happiness, for her well-being, and that in some way, he might contribute to both.

"Vivian?" A shrill female voice carried from over the next set of shelves. "Where have you gotten off to, my dear?"

Slowly, Darius let her go, feeling as if a cold wind had pierced the first sunshine his soul had seen in months.

"I have to go." Vivian rose up and kissed his cheek. "Stay well, Darius."

"You too." He watched her go, but it was the hardest thing he'd done. Harder than dealing with Lucy and Blanche, harder than handing Leah off to her giant viscount, harder than knowing John was lonely and inadequately supervised at Averett Hill. She moved off with that rolling gait common to women approaching the later stages of pregnancy, and Darius imprinted the vision of it in his imagination.

"Vivian, really, you shouldn't go off like that by yourself," he heard a woman complain. "What if I'd wanted to purchase something?"

"My apologies, Portia." Vivian's voice was softer. "One gets distracted by all that's on offer. Have you found something to take back to Longchamps with you?"

The women moved off, while Darius kept to his niche in the back of the store, trying to think his galloping emotions into submission and letting the gladness in his heart and mind subside. He'd seen her, he'd held her, they'd spoken, and his cup was running over with relief. He waited until they'd left the shop then waited another fifteen minutes lest he run into them on the street.

He didn't wait quite long enough though, because as Darius quit the bookshop, a purchase for Emily in his hand, he saw Vivian and her companion emerging from the shop across the street. He couldn't help but smile like an idiot when their gazes met fleetingly across the distance. He was still smiling a moment later when a voice at his elbow snapped him out of his reverie.

"I've never seen you look that way," Lucy Templeton mused. "Not at your sister, not at Blanche, and certainly not at me. Who is she?"

❧

Portia Springer did not want to return to Longchamps, but William had spoken. Not loudly, for William was a gentleman, and Portia wasn't stupid. He'd merely suggested London in summer wasn't healthy and he'd appreciate it if Portia would repair to Longchamps and ensure all was in readiness for Vivian's confinement.

Portia had never had a child, so the request was a transparent excuse to send her packing. Ainsworthy knew it; Portia knew it. If nothing else, Ainsworthy felt a grudging admiration for old William's deft maneuvering.

"I don't want to go." Portia settled against Ainsworthy in blatant invitation. "You smell ever so much prettier than Able. But then, you're a gentleman, and Able is a glorified farmer."

"I don't want to let you go," Thurgood crooned.

"Though I'm sure your husband must be mad with missing you by now." He shaped her generous breast lingeringly, and she let out the predictable sigh.

"Love me, Thurgood." She pushed herself more tightly against him.

"Of course." Love being the ladies' preferred euphemism for a jolly good fuck. He opened his falls, rucked her skirts, and obliged her on the closed lid of his wife's piano. Portia liked to feel naughty, Thurgood liked to swive, so it was a good bargain all around. Five minutes later, Portia was drowsing on his shoulder, their clothing back to rights, and her nimble female mind apparently on other things.

"I have those documents," she said, kissing the side of his neck. "Thank you ever so much for letting me know whom to go to."

"The occasion arises where every person of enterprise has need of same." Thurgood patted her breast, which he truly would miss until his next pigeon came along. "When can you come back to Town?"

"Once William dies." Portia's eyes took on a different kind of gleam. "With these documents in hand, we'll have Longstreet House and all that goes with it. I'll live here in Town, and we can be together as often as we like."

Thurgood produced a somewhat honest, rueful smile at the complications inherent in having dear Portia permanently underfoot. "As if you'd limit your attentions to me. When you dwell here in Town, what's to stop Vivian from simply rusticating at Longchamps? She'll have a child to raise, and that's the family seat."

"I'll stop her." Portia's smile was wicked. "If Able wants the child, he's welcome to it, but Lady Vivian will be cast into the loving arms of her stepfather, and what you do with her will make no difference whatsoever to me."

Thurgood beamed at her. "Portia, my love, you are a woman after my own heart."

He undid his falls again and filled his hand with the soft abundance of her breasts. She truly would be a woman after his own heart, if he had one.

~

The note made no sense.

> *My Lady,*
> *You left this behind. I trust, having seen it into your keeping, our paths will not cross again.*
> *Lindsey*

The little bottle of scent sat on Vivian's dressing table, silent and mocking. Darius had been so… loving in the bookstore, and now this. Whatever game he was playing, Vivian wanted no part of it. Maybe he enjoyed the torment, maneuvering, and manipulation he indulged in with those other women, but it left Vivian feeling sick, sad, and heartsore.

The baby shifted, no longer the little fluttering sensation of months ago but a noticeable movement that applied a passing pressure to her innards.

Darius Lindsey was the father of her child, he'd brought her more pleasure and more joy than any other man, and he was hurting her in equal proportions.

For the sake of their child, Vivian resolved to forget Darius Lindsey, to put him from her life, her mind, her hopes.

That kiss… and now this.

If he liked playing hot and cold, come here and go away, he could play it with his other women. Vivian had seen him a handful of times in the past five months, and he'd been cool to her on all but two occasions, and now this.

Enough. She had a child to think of, a husband in ailing health, and better things to do than hope she caught Darius Lindsey in an approachable mood.

❧

Darius had felt a moment's panic when Lucy had accosted him outside the bookshop.

"Portia Springer," he'd said, thanking a gift for recalling details. "She isn't up from the country often. Her husband is steward to a large estate."

"She looks like your type." Lucy's frown was thoughtful. "A little used but holding up, and intent on getting what she wants. Can a steward's wife afford to pay you well?"

She would ask that. Darius turned a frigid stare on her right there in the street. "None of your business, Lucy. I suppose since you've taken to following me, you expect me to escort you somewhere? It will give me a chance to tell you I'm off to Averett Hill and wish you a pleasant summer while I'm at it."

"Why go there now?"

"Because London in the summer is pestilentially hot. Because I need to tend what few acres I have, and it's almost time for haying. Because I damned well please to go."

She attached herself to his arm and minced along beside him. "I forbid you to go."

"Too damned bad," he muttered, feeling her stiffen with outrage beside him. "Lucy, you do not own me, and my sister is safely married to Bellefonte, so sheathe your claws."

"You have another sister," Lucy snarled. "She can be tarred with the same brush."

He resisted a flood of curses, because this vulnerability had not occurred to him. "Emily is as pure as the driven snow, and Wilton would call you out, did you offer her insult."

"Wilton is an ass. Maybe Hellerington can be persuaded to take an interest in Emily. He likes little girls."

Merciful God. "Go to hell, Lucy." Darius pried her fingers off his arm. "And take Blanche with you."

He left her there, glaring daggers at his back in broad daylight, but then he'd gone home and written the most difficult note he'd ever penned, and it hadn't even taken a single rough draft to get it right.

The confrontation solidified a resolve Darius had felt growing ever since he'd tucked Vivian into his traveling coach bound for London. She'd seen clearly what Darius himself only now grasped: The price of disporting with Lucy and Blanche was not his honor, but rather, his soul. Every single person Darius cared for—John, Leah, Trent, Vivian, and even the child she carried—was imperiled by Darius's association with two women who regarded him as nothing more than an animated toy.

He had the determination; he had the courage; he had the desperation. He lacked only one final resource to see his plan set into motion, and he knew exactly where to find it. The time had come to ransom his soul back from hell.

❧

So vast and varied were London's commercial offerings that one no longer needed to make with one's own hands each and every item a baby required. Vivian had embroidered receiving blankets and caps, knitted booties and shawls, and sewn dresses upon dresses for the unborn child, but there were a few things she had yet to procure.

A rattle. Every child needed a rattle, or several rattles.

A baby spoon, something in silver, not too ornate, but sized for a tiny mouth.

A little baby cup, also in silver, so it could be engraved upon the occasion of the child's birth.

These purchases were of sufficient import to justify delaying a remove to Longchamps—these purchases, a growing concern for William's health, and a reluctance to share a household again so soon with Portia.

That Darius Lindsey might yet be in Town was of no moment—unless Vivian were alone in her room late at night, sharing her bed with a particular brown scarf.

Vivian's gaze traveled across a shop she'd patronized frequently to where a gentleman and a clerk were in conversation near a handsome bay hobbyhorse. The hairs on her nape prickled before her mind identified the speaker.

"The boy has been riding since I took him up before me as a babe. He needs…"

Vivian spoke up, though clearly Darius hadn't spotted her yet. "He needs books, full of excellent stories about dragons and witches and trolls. He needs things to draw with, and a basket with a great fluffy pillow for his cat."

Darius turned to her, expression inscrutable. "Madam?"

Today he was cool-Darius, though not cold-Darius. For an instant, she considered trying to be cold-Vivian

Then discarded the notion. He looked thin to her, and tired, but not… she didn't know what, but he was different. "Mr. Lindsey, isn't it?"

"At your service, Lady Longstreet." He bowed, and Vivian was very much aware of the shopkeeper watching their exchange.

"How old is the child you're shopping for, Mr. Lindsey?"

He relaxed at her civil tone, and why not? His harpies were unlikely to accost him in a shop for children. Vivian would skewer them where they stood if they tried to.

Another queer start attributable to her delicate condition. Darius took a step closer to her then checked himself. "John is rising seven and a curious fellow. I think you'd like him very much. He tries to exhibit the best manners possible under all circumstances."

Oh, not this. Not veiled innuendos backed up by dark, pleading eyes.

"And does he succeed often enough to merit a lady's praise?"

"I pray he does, and I'm sure his lapses are all well intended."

She had no riposte sufficiently clever to convey that

the lady's feelings were slighted regardless of the well-mannered fellow's intentions. When she might have signaled to her maid to gather up her purchases and complete her transactions, Darius took another step closer, and this was her undoing.

Carrying a child caused all manner of havoc with a lady's sensibilities. She might be queasy, light-headed, fatigued, or unduly energized, wear a path to the necessary, and wake up at all hours with odd cravings.

In Vivian's case, she had also acquired an astonishingly acute sense of smell. Darius's unique scent came to her, promising pleasure, comfort, and passion in the middle of a children's shop.

I'm fat, she'd said, quite proud of the fact several months ago. She had the proportions and maneuverability of a coal barge now, and in the space of a moment, she was seized with belated self-consciousness. That he, the only man to see her unclothed, should regard her in this state…

"My lady, are you well?" He took the last step to her side and slipped an arm around where her waist used to be. "When did you last eat, Lady Longstreet?"

Darius as a paramour was a force of nature, an overwhelmingly skilled and astute bed partner who could swamp a woman's sense completely by conjuring pleasure upon pleasure. Darius as the worried father of her child had Vivian wishing she could manufacture a convincing swoon just to keep the potent concern simmering in his dark eyes.

"I had a proper breakfast." A light breakfast, the most prudent way to start her day when the very scent of William's bacon still made her queasy.

"You nibbled dry toast hours ago and washed it down with weak tea. You." Darius waved a hand at the maid. "Her ladyship and I are going for an ice. Take her purchases back to Longstreet House and meet us at Gunter's." He passed the girl enough coin for hackney fare halfway to Paris, and paused to inspect Vivian.

"You're not arguing with me, Lady Longstreet. One is encouraged to think impending motherhood might have turned you up biddable."

He did not sound as if he were entirely teasing, but an *ice*… she'd been longing for a nice tart barberry ice, craving one, and she hadn't even known it. "An ice would be acceptable."

He escorted her from the shop, the picture of a young man performing a friendly courtesy, while Vivian tried to put a label on what she was feeling.

"Cheated."

"Viv—I beg your pardon, Lady Longstreet?"

As they sauntered toward Berkeley Square, the street was not particularly busy, and for some reason Darius appeared willing to stroll along, arm in arm, despite any harpies who might pop out of doorways or passing coaches.

"I feel cheated."

No immediate reply, though Vivian could feel Darius thinking. Then, very softly, "By me, Vivvie?"

He *would* leap to that conclusion. "Not by you, by the circumstances. I should have gone to that shop with you, to choose something for John, to find a baby spoon, rattle, and a silver cup. I should be complaining to you about not being able to see my feet, and I should be wrinkling my nose at your bacon every morning."

He gave her an odd smile as they walked along, suggesting this was not a queer start, it was something else, something dear to him.

"Don't stop there," he said, patting her knuckles. "I should be rubbing your feet and your aching back at the end of the day. You should curse me roundly for costing you your figure and then ask me if you're still beautiful—you are, you know. More beautiful than ever, which shouldn't be possible."

They got the entire way to Berkeley Square, cataloging her inconveniences and insecurities, and the listing of them—to him, only to him—eased something in Vivian's soul even as the entire conversation made her ache terribly for what would never be.

"I positively loathe the scent of William's bacon, but he's gotten so thin I can hardly deny him what sustenance he takes."

"Take a tray in your room before you come down to breakfast, Vivvie. Join him for tea, and he probably won't notice you're not eating."

Good advice. Over two ices served under the maples—one barberry and one vanilla for her, from which Darius poached not a single bite, and one raspberry for him—Vivian learned to put her feet up as much as possible, to use pillows creatively to assist her to more comfortable sleep, and to walk as much as possible to prepare for the birth.

"How do you know these things, Darius? Did you learn them with John's mother?"

His expression shifted, becoming sad.

Why had it never occurred to Vivian that Darius might have been in love with the boy's mother? And yet… something he'd said about Vivian's child being the only child he'd sire came back to her.

"The Continent is a more enlightened place regarding childbirth." He held up a forkful of his raspberry ice. "One bite, Vivvie, to bring the color back to your cheeks."

She obliged, knowing he was distracting her. By the look in his eyes, he knew she knew. For a few minutes, he pushed raspberry ice around with his fork.

"John has gone to spend the summer with Leah and Bellefonte."

The way he said it, softly, as if the words hurt to even speak, broke Vivian's heart.

"Darius, I am so sorry. To send your own—"

He shook his head and set the little bowl of ice from him. "He's not my son, which is what you were about to say, and he's not Leah's or Trent's either." He glanced around, maybe taking inventory of the other customers, maybe looking for courage. "John is a half brother. Wilton mustn't know that, not ever, and Reston—or rather, Bellefonte, now that his father has died—can keep him safer than I can. I did what I thought was best for the boy, at least for now."

He'd no doubt repeated that litany to himself endlessly. The only person he'd allowed close, the person he seemed to love most in the whole world, and now this.

"I need your handkerchief, Mr. Lindsey."

He smiled a sweet smile and waved a little square of linen at her. "You are the dearest woman. John is very happy. Trent is sending his children out to Belle Maison for a summer outing too. I'm promised regular letters."

"But you're *alone*," she said, blotting at her eyes even as the scent on the handkerchief ripped at her composure further. "I hate being in this condition. I have no dignity, I have no airs and graces, I have—"

Cold and sweetness bumped against her lips. "Your ice is melting, Lady Longstreet. It will taste sweeter for thawing a little."

Damn him. Bless him. She took the bite he offered and took courage from the simple affection with which Darius regarded her. "Do not lecture me about queer starts, Darius Lindsey. I will not have it."

"When do you repair to Longchamps?"

The change of subject was intended as a kindness. Vivian wasn't having any of that either. "Are those women still plaguing you, sir?"

The look he sent her was chilly indeed. "I have every confidence my path will depart from theirs very, very soon, though at present I'm told they're each rusticating."

It wasn't what she had expected to hear and wasn't at all what she'd wanted to hear, either. The entire encounter palled, because *very soon* was no comfort at all, and had *those women* not been rusticating, Vivian would not now be enjoying Darius's company.

He sent John away but did not put from him the women who tormented him, and to all appearances, he avoided Vivian except for chance encounters.

She should have him summon a cab immediately and hope they didn't run into each other again for a good long while.

"I'd like another ice. Chocolate, I think, and you're not to steal even a bite of my treat."

His gaze dropped to her belly, and his smile was not sweet in the least. Nor was it cool. "Bit late for that, isn't it, Vivvie?"

He crossed the street to order her a third ice without further comment, only to stop in his tracks as he reemerged from the shop and a stylish lady with reddish hair came swanning up to his side.

"Why, Mr. Lindsey! What a lovely surprise."

He did not even glance at Vivian, seemed determined not to glance at her, in fact. Vivian balled his handkerchief up and stuffed it into her reticule, signaled for her maid, and quitted the square without sparing him a glance either.

The prudent course was obvious: there could be no more meetings with Darius Lindsey, not by chance, not by design, and not by anything in between. Vivian vowed she'd leave for Longchamps in the morning—and stay there.

Fourteen

"THIS IS AN UNEXPECTED PLEASURE." BLANCHE EYED Darius up and down, the way she'd look at a decadent dessert or expensive pair of new shoes. Darius's flesh crawled at her inspection, but no more than it had a week previous, when he'd barely been able to leave Gunter's without ripping her to shreds in public.

And then pelting after Vivian for all the world to see.

"Unexpected, perhaps, a pleasure, most definitely not." He handed his hat and gloves to one of the handsome footmen Blanche insisted on employing and met his hostess's gaze. "You will want to hear me out in private."

"I want you in private," she agreed, "but as for listening to you carp and bark, I think not. You have more worthy attributes than your speaking voice."

Darius let her shut the parlor door behind them, but when she moved to embrace him, he stepped back.

"Playing hard to get has limited charm between well-acquainted lovers." Her tone was reproving, and again Darius felt a spike of nausea.

"We are not," Darius said softly, "nor will we ever be, nor have we ever been, lovers. I accommodated you for a price. Your usefulness is at an end, and I am doing you the courtesy of informing you of this in private. I will do likewise with Lucy Templeton."

"This straining at the leash is ill-mannered, Darius," Blanche said, smiling as if anticipating a rousing argument. "You will continue to accommodate me and Lucy, and whomever else we choose to direct you to. Have you no sense of what Wilton would do to you were he to learn of your nocturnal schemes? Cease your nonsense, or there will be consequences."

Darius crossed the room, his back to her for a long moment while he marshaled his temper and tried to calm the turmoil in his gut. This was what hatred felt like, corrosive, heavy, and lethal.

When he turned to face her, he saw the first flicker of real fear on her face, but it gave him no satisfaction.

"For all intents and purposes, Blanche, I have whored for you, but it is a whore's prerogative to accept or decline the customer or the encounter. Even those rules you've disrespected in your dealings with me. I went to my own kind, to the streetwalkers and courtesans and prostitutes, and found what I needed to enforce the rules."

And not once in the past three days of scouring the city's most depraved haunts had Darius been judged, ridiculed, or scorned. The soiled doves and molly boys hadn't hesitated to share their resources. They hadn't even taken his coin in exchange for what he so desperately needed.

"You have a fourteen-year-old daughter," Darius

said, "growing up in Ireland in the home of your cousin's steward. Most of your jewels are paste, though I made sure the ones you tossed to me were real enough. You're dying your hair—the hair on your head—and I know this because you've made the mistake of keeping the candles lit when I pleasured you."

Her jaw dropped, and Darius felt the surging satisfaction of a well-executed ambush. "Shall I go on?"

"You would not dare."

"I would dare. I dared to take coin for that which no gentleman should, and I would dare to cheerfully ruin you *not* for taking advantage of me—for I was taking some advantage of you as well—but taking unfair advantage, backed up by unconscionable threats to innocents who owe you nothing. We can part without further hostilities, or we can declare war. It's your choice."

He held her gaze a moment longer, making sure she read the resolve in his eyes.

"Lucy was the one who suggested we take your sister," Blanche said, her expression becoming desperate. "I had nothing to do with that. She said the girl was already ruined, and you were getting too difficult."

Darius went still, while he heard a roaring in his ears and his vision dimmed. His hands fisted, his jaw clenched, and he held himself back from throttling the miserable female before him only because he'd kill her if he laid a finger on her.

And he'd enjoy it.

"She came to no harm," Lady Cowell babbled on. "Really, there was no harm done. Reston saw to that. We were just going have her drink a bit of absinthe, set her down in a gambling hell. There's no real harm in that."

Merciful God. Drugged and disoriented, Leah would have ended up in a brothel before dawn.

"You say there was no harm," Darius growled, stalking across the room, "when my sister will never feel safe in the park again." He loomed over her, his voice lethally soft. "You say leaving an innocent woman to the mercy of the pimps, drunks, and bounders would have been *no harm*? I should tell your husband what you've been up to and send word to *The Times* as well."

"Please." Blanche dropped her gaze. "Please. You don't know what it's like."

Darius forced himself to breathe evenly. She had bullied him unmercifully, for her entertainment, for her pleasure. He would not bully her. "Do we understand each other, Lady Cowell?" His voice was even and yet laden with menace. "Answer me."

"We understand each other, and I will make sure Lucy understands as well." She met his gaze long enough to nod once.

"That will not be necessary." Darius sketched an ironic bow. "The pleasure of enlightening your sorry friend and familiar will be entirely mine." He cleared the room so quickly he didn't see the look of stunned horror on Lady Cowell's face, or the way she dropped into a chair and sat staring into space long after he'd gone.

His interview with Lucy Templeton was even more to the point, though he also allowed her the courtesy of closeting herself with him before he threatened the future she'd assumed was secure.

"You accepted payments from French sympathizers to keep certain contraband from coming to the attention of excise men quartered near your husband's seat. The punishment for treason is hanging."

"I would never do such a thing! You lie, Darius, and poorly."

"Now, Lucy," Darius nearly purred as he came to stand too close to her, "I have no reason to lie. I've been a naughty man, true, but I've never paid for the pleasure of whipping children nigh to death. What would your husband think, did he learn of such an excess of temper?"

"My husband is devoted," Lucy said, her eyes venomous.

"Devoted, indeed, to the mistress who bore him two sons, for whom he provides well. He apparently had no trouble functioning with his mistress, unlike his situation with you. All he'd need is an excuse to have you sent to one of those pleasant, walled estates for women with nervous constitutions."

Color drained from her face, and Darius observed with curious dispassion that the woman might have once been pretty, had not vice and bitterness twisted her expression.

But he hadn't yet finished with her.

"And if you truly dispute the charges of treason"—he nailed her with a frigid look—"then charges of attempted kidnapping of my sister might still see you in jail, my lady. Your footmen can be bribed as easily as any, and Reston—Earl of Bellefonte, now—would do anything to see those who threatened his countess brought to justice."

She sank onto the sofa, his words landing with more gratification than well-aimed blows.

"I'll leave you to contemplate your sins, but be warned that Bellefonte's brothers are yet at university, and they will be admonishing their entire forms to avoid the likes of you, and making sure their younger brothers are warned as well. Do we understand each other?"

"We do." Her answering croak was in the voice of a woman who knew when she was… beaten.

"I suggest you and Lady Cowell take a repairing lease somewhere as distant as, say, the Italian coast. Latin men are notably solicitous toward older women. Good day."

⤷

Casting off the pall of association with Blanche and Lucy should have left Darius euphoric. Mightily relieved, in any case. Instead, it was overshadowed by four things that deflated positive feelings considerably.

First, Darius had bid good-bye to the only family member to share his household, the only bright spot in much of his recent years.

Saying good-bye to John when the boy left for Belle Maison had hurt, but not Leah, not Trent, not even John himself seemed to comprehend Darius's loss. Nicholas, oddly enough, had pulled Darius aside for a fierce hug and promised him the child would come to no harm and visit Darius often. That assurance had been so desperately needed Darius had found himself blinking back tears.

Crying, for God's sake, and on another man's shoulder. What did Darius have to cry about?

The second development of great proportions in Darius's life was that Nick had confronted Wilton with evidence of the earl's mishandling of funds—and worse—earlier in Leah's life. Wilton was effectively banished to Wilton Acres out in Hampshire, and the maternal inheritance Darius's father had pilfered from him was being repaid, with interest.

When a man learned to live on next to nothing, a sudden and deserved influx of capital created challenges: What to do with it, how much to invest, where, on what…? It all took time, concentration, and a focus Darius had to force himself to maintain.

The third development was more alarming still, in that Trent, drifting along into a shambling sort of widowerhood, had to be taken in hand. Darius escorted his brother bodily to Crossbridge, the estate Trent owned free of any entail, and set his brother down a considerable distance from the brandy decanter. Trent's children were sent out to Nick and Leah in Kent, and Darius was left to pace and fret and pray that his brother pulled out of whatever malaise had him in its grip.

The fourth development was the worst: Vivian left Town.

The other matters—losing John, maybe losing Trent, being inundated with business decisions—Darius could manage those, relatively. He could not manage losing all contact with Vivian. She would be approaching her confinement, and likely concerned about it, and he…

He had no right to offer her reassurances, no right to comfort her, no right to look forward to the birth with her, and yet, she'd been right: in this regard, they'd been cheated.

He couldn't help himself. When Lord Valentine Windham offered an invitation to rusticate in Oxfordshire just a few miles from Longchamps, Darius leapt at the chance.

❧

Pregnancy scrambled a woman's brains.

Vivian reached this profound conclusion within days of returning to Longchamps. True, London was miserable in summer, but she and William traditionally stayed in the city until Parliament adjourned in August. And William had stayed there, which only proved to Vivian that her wits had gone begging.

William was… failing. *Dying.* She'd admitted it to herself only as he'd deposited her into their traveling coach and she'd seen the way his shoulders were more stooped, his gaze less clear, his gait slower. She was losing him, and now of all times, she didn't want to lose the closest thing she had to an ally.

Still, she'd been so intent on putting distance between herself and a certain Darius Lindsey that she'd left William in Town with no one but Dilquin to fuss over him, and hied herself back to Longchamps.

Where Portia's hovering presence was going to move Vivian to murder. The woman was an atrocity, and Vivian's sympathy for Able grew with each hour. Portia suggested changes to the house, as if she knew William's health were precarious and she planned to take over as lady of the manor when William was gone. Able brushed off her plans and schemes and shared the occasional sympathetic look with Vivian.

But worst of all for Vivian was that distance, which she'd intended to help her get some perspective on Darius Lindsey, was only making his presence in her imagination harder to eradicate.

Would the child look like him? Would Darius come to the christening? Was he thinking of her, or was he sauntering around with one of those horrid women on his arm, in his bed, at his side? Had "very soon" come to pass that he'd parted company with them, or were they still commanding his escort when Vivian could not?

That last question hurt. He'd been honest with her, told her exactly who and what he was, but it still… hurt. If Darius were nothing but a cicisbeo, bought and paid for, what did that make Vivian?

She tortured herself with questions like that, even as she took long walks all over the ripening countryside. To see the crops growing, even as she grew, was a comfort, though her ambling became more and more deliberate.

Darius had told her to walk, to resist the urge to become sedentary as well as gravid.

To escape Portia, Vivian frequently took a blanket and a book—Byron was her most frequent choice—out to the stream running behind the orchard a half mile from the house. The roll of the land protected her from the view of the manor and its outbuildings, and the distance was just right to give her a sense of peace.

Which was disturbed past all recall when she felt something tickling her nose. She batted at it, not quite ready to be done with her late-morning nap, but it returned.

"Shall I kiss you awake?"

She opened her eyes, and her mind told her Darius Lindsey, whom she had not seen for weeks, was on the blanket with her, but she refused to accept such a reality.

Pregnancy scrambled a woman's wits that badly.

"Go away."

"Soon." He did ease away, but not before Vivian saw a light dimming in his eyes. This was a good thing, lest he think he was still welcome to kiss her or hold her or take her hand in his.

But what he did was worse. He shifted to sit a foot away from her.

"How are you, Vivvie?"

Vivvie. His name for her, delivered with unmistakable concern. Unmistakable caring.

"I'm fat," she huffed, making it as far as her elbows, but anything approximating lying on her back was no longer comfortable, so she flailed around until Darius boosted her to sitting, smiling at her shamelessly.

"You're glorious," he said. "Your face looks thinner. How are you feeling?"

She glared at him, arranged her skirts, and felt tears welling. She loved his eyes, loved the way he could communicate intimacy without saying a word, and right now, those eyes were tormenting her with the tenderness they offered.

"I feel pregnant. Ungainly, a little worried. What are you doing here?"

"William is taking good care of you?"

"William is doing his best."

"Vivvie?" He was closer, though she hadn't seen him move. "What aren't you telling me?"

She scooted a little away, the better to see him and avoid his scent, because as pregnant as she was, she wanted to make herself drunk on his fragrance.

"You have no business showing up here and accosting me."

"I've done a great deal more than accost you." The humor was back in his tone. "That gives me the right to at least inquire about your well-being. William stayed back in London, didn't he?"

She nodded, glancing away.

"What can he be about?" Darius eyed her searchingly. "Leaving you out here among the servants to go into your confinement?"

"You think he meant for you to come and inspect his broodmare?" Even Vivian was shocked by the bitterness in her tone.

"Perhaps." Darius's tone gave nothing away. "I was more concerned for the mother of my child. You're cranky, and that's to be expected. Shall I hold you?"

"No."

He shifted, sitting behind her, a leg on either side of her, and drew her against his chest. "I went through this with John's mother."

Vivian felt his chin resting on her crown, and the tears constricted her throat. She should fight him off, but it had been so long, and she was weak with longing for just this.

"She was weepy and grouchy, and so worried for her child she could hardly carry on a civil conversation for the last few weeks. Fortunately, Gracie was on hand, and little moods and snits didn't alarm her in the least."

"You loved John's mother?"

"I pitied her. I do not pity you, much."

"Damn you." Vivian did try to shove him off, but he held her gently.

"Vivvie, calm yourself." He propped his cheek against her temple and kept both arms around her. "John resides with Leah and her husband, Bellefonte."

"You miss him." Vivian sighed against Darius's chest. "You miss John, and you can't pester him to write to you because you want him to be happy."

"Hush." He stroked her back in slow circles, and Vivian felt her eyes grow heavy.

"I'm angry with you."

"I know, love." He brushed a kiss to her hair. "You're furious and disappointed. You have every reason to be."

She dozed off, and he held her, and when she woke up, he was still there, and when she'd managed not to cry for weeks, that made Vivian cry.

☙

Had God in all His wisdom created a sweeter experience than to allow a man to simply hold the mother of his child? Darius hoped Vivian would sleep for hours, but in fact she dozed only for a few minutes.

She was angry with him, but all trust hadn't been destroyed, or she would never have let down her guard to rest in his arms this way. He assured himself this was true, and assured himself she was in blooming good health as he took a cautious inventory of her appearance.

Her face was thinner, more mature, and more lovely than ever.

Her pregnancy was advancing visibly, and the sight was dear and erotic and amazing to him. He locked the eroticism away behind high walls of respect and guilt.

Her breasts were magnificent, her hips voluptuous, and her shape… Slowly, Darius slid a hand over her belly, his patience rewarded when the child shifted slightly, causing Vivian to move in his arms.

Ye gods, ye gods. A child, their child, alive and safe under his hand, under her heart. He had to blink and swallow and blink some more as he prayed Vivian didn't choose that moment to wake up.

He wasn't going to rush his fences this time. Vivian had been hurt enough by all his vacillation, and she wasn't going to give up ground easily. But just to hold her… to hold her and know she was confiding in him and at least allowing herself the comfort of his embrace, it was enough.

It would have to be enough.

Vivian stirred, rubbed her cheek against his chest, then sat up and speared him with a look.

"You have to leave, Darius." She tried to wiggle away. "I can't tolerate any more of your hot-and-cold, here-and-gone treatment. It's good of you to inquire about the child, but I'd appreciate it if you'd take yourself off now."

❧

"Able, not now." Portia shoved him away and slid the letter she'd been writing off to the side—since coming home from London, Portia was doing a prodigious amount of letter writing. "You smell like a stable."

"And here I thought breeding women were supposed

to be affectionate." Able obligingly withdrew, but he'd bothered to wash thoroughly before presuming to kiss his wife's cheek, and the rebuke disappointed.

Portia gave him an exasperated look as she recapped the inkwell. "What do you mean, breeding women? Go maul Vivian if you're attracted to breeding heifers."

Able lowered himself into one of the chairs facing the desk, since Portia appeared unwilling to yield his proper place to him. "I'm not talking about Vivian. How far along are you, Portia?"

Her mouth opened as if to deliver another broadside then snapped shut with a click, and Able realized his wife hadn't been being coy about her condition; she simply hadn't known.

And now that she did, she wasn't pleased.

"This is your fault."

At least she was predictable. "I certainly hope so. The date of the child's arrival will likely shed light on those particulars."

She tidied a stack of green ledgers that needed no tidying. "And just what do you mean by that?"

"We've been married for years, Portia, and you've never caught before. A little trip up to Town, and there's a blessed event in the offing. You don't know how far along you are, do you?"

"I'm not... regular," she hedged. "It's hard to tell."

She wasn't *ir*-regular, but Able saw she was worried, and knew a moment of exasperation with the Almighty. Managing, scheming, grasping Portia might be, but she wasn't enough of a steward's wife to have timed her indiscretion so there was at least some possibility the child was Able's.

"It's all right, Portia," he said tiredly. "Children are easy to love, and Vivian's baby will have someone to call family. That's for the best."

"Vivian's…" Portia's hand went to her throat, then her expression shuttered. "This is for the best, you're right, and the child is yours, Able."

He considered her and recalled she'd permitted him intimacies just before they'd left for London, but not since. If the child were his, she'd be better than three months along, and the signs Able had seen were as much behavioral as visible. She was rounder, in certain places particularly, but that was hardly conclusive.

This child was not likely his. In his life, in his marriage, with his Portia, such a happy occasion was improbable.

"You'll want to warn whomever you dallied with," he said, rising and moving toward the door. "If the child were mine, I'd want to know, even if some other man would have the raising of it."

He left her sitting at his desk, for once silent, the expression on her face detached and calculating. Disappointingly so.

❧

"What if I said I'm not going to leave you?" Darius let Vivian go and shifted to sit beside her. The question was only half in jest. "Would you have William summon the King's man to take me off your property?"

"Don't be ridiculous." Vivian glared at him but ruined the effect entirely when she reached out to brush his hair off his forehead. "You've been in the sun."

Her touch, freely given, eased something miserable

and desperate in Darius's chest. "I'm spending the summer at the Markham estate, which Valentine Windham is hell-bent on restoring to its former glory."

"Markham?" Vivian's brow puckered. "I thought nobody lived there."

"Bats live there. When we started it was barely habitable, but it's coming along."

She plucked clover from the grass and began threading a chain. "So you thought you'd just pop over and see how I'm doing?"

"No." He'd thought he'd lose his mind if he had to face never seeing her again. "I thought I'd beg a berth with Windham so I could make amends for how I treated you this spring."

"I'm a married woman," Vivian reminded him, staring at her clover. "And I love my husband."

They needed to air this linen, of course, but not at length. "I am not seeking favors from you, Vivvie."

"You're not?" The little note of wistfulness in her voice had him smiling again, though he was gentleman enough to try to hide it.

White clover was for promises, so he'd give her a promise and revel in the pleasure of that small token. "You love your husband," Darius said slowly. "I promise to respect that. You would be upset if I sought to dally with you now. It would upset me not to offer you my sincere friendship."

Vivian smiled too and tossed the chain of clover flowers at him. "Everything upsets me. Tell me about Windham's estate."

He spent an hour with her on that blanket, not touching, but talking, and by the end of it, she was talking too. Talking, Darius hoped, as she might have talked to a trusted friend.

"William tries to hide it, but he's not doing well," she finally admitted.

"What does that mean, Vivvie?"

"He's fading." She said it softly, as if it were a relief to share the reality with someone. "He's tired of living, and now that I'm to have a child, he can assure himself my welfare is taken care of."

"You'll miss him." Darius said it for her.

"Terribly. When there was nobody between me and Ainsworthy's vile schemes, William shook off his mourning and married me, facing down scandal and talk and possible political repercussions. I'm grateful to him, but I love him too, and when I asked him to come down here with me early, he shook his head and told me to run along and enjoy being in the country."

She sounded bewildered and forlorn, and in this, at least, Darius could offer a male perspective.

"He has a kind of courage," Darius said. "Not simply the courage of his religious faith, which assures him an honorable life will find a reward in the hereafter, but a courage for living in *this* life, without you, without his first wife, without the faculties he had as a younger man."

Vivian studied him for a moment, while the breeze riffled the branches of the ripening orchard above them and a fat bumblebee went lazily about its business.

"You admire him."

"Of course I admire him." Though he was only now realizing it. "He's put aside his own convenience to do what was necessary to protect you, Vivian. How could I not admire a man with that much practical honor?"

She frowned as she digested this description of her husband. "Practical honor is a good term. William would understand it."

"Remind me who Ainsworthy is."

"My former stepfather."

Darius watched emotions play across her features. "Given your expression, Vivian, I do not care for the fellow."

She retrieved the chain of clover and wound it through her fingers. "When my mother died, he took it upon himself to launch my sister, except I saw what he did to Angela, and I wasn't about to allow him to do that to me."

"I thought you said Angela was happy with her... publisher?"

Vivian stretched her feet out and regarded her bare toes. Darius kept his gaze on her face lest he recall too clearly the taste of those toes when Vivian had been fresh from her bath.

"Angela is married to Jared Ventnor," Vivian said. "They are happy now, but Jared essentially outbid the titles competing for Angie's hand. It wasn't a love match on her part. Angela barely knew her husband when they wed, and Ainsworthy was willing to use any means to secure the match."

"And you." Darius tapped her nose. "You consider your sister resigned herself to her fate so she'd have a household for you to come to when your turn arose."

She frowned at the clover wrapped around her fingers.

"Except I crossed paths with Muriel, who saw what was what and offered me a position as her companion."

The bumblebee came around again, a reminder that time spent on a blanket with Vivian was time bartered for the sustenance of Darius's soul from other responsibilities. "I will remember Muriel in my prayers. Shall I escort you back to the house?"

To make that offer openly and to mean it was a small moment of grace.

"Gracious, everlasting God, *no*. Portia is likely spying out of windows and bribing the servants to report my every move. The last thing she needs is to find some basis for her suspicions that I've played William false."

"You're going to have to explain me somehow." Darius rose and offered Vivian a hand. "I'll show up at the christening, and thereafter, and that is at William's request."

"Then William can explain you," Vivian retorted. She let Darius pick up her book, fold the blanket over his shoulder, and offer her his arm.

Vivian scowled—even her scowls were dear—and accepted his escort. "You can't walk me back to the house."

"Let me see you across the stream." He wrapped the reins of his courage around his wrists, and ambled along beside her. "I'd like to meet you here again on Friday."

"Friday? This is not wise, Darius."

He paused and looked down at her. "Your welfare concerns me. I know you don't trust me, I know you've been disappointed in me and hurt by me. I am sorry, more sorry than you can possibly know. But if you'd allow it, I'd like to be your friend."

To be her friend, a man she could rely upon for kindness, honesty, and decency, was the highest aspiration he'd ever held.

"What do friends do?"

She hadn't ordered him off the property for his presumption. He took heart. "They occasionally pass the time together," Darius said, resuming their progress. "They care for each other, and keep each other's confidences, and they acknowledge each other in social situations."

"Like you didn't acknowledge me. On several notable occasions."

"It won't happen again," he said quietly. "And I am abjectly sorry."

"I believe you, but I don't understand you, Darius. If you detest those women so much, why are they in your life? William has compensated you, hasn't he?"

"We can talk more about that on Friday," he replied, reluctant to explain that he'd used dirty weapons on dirty opponents, and been shown a curious grace by unlikely angels. "Weather permitting. And if the weather doesn't permit, I'll try on Monday, and so forth."

"You're determined on this, aren't you?"

Was she trying to hide a smile—or a frown? "Yes. I am determined to be your friend."

More silence as they approached a little rill babbling happily along toward the sea. "Very well, but for pity's sake be discreet."

"I'll be careful, but my attentions are not going

to be of a nature you'll need to hide," he replied, swinging her up into his arms and carrying her over the stream bordering the trees. "You be well, Vivian, and know I'm thinking of you." He brushed a kiss to her cheek before setting her down and kept his hands on her upper arms for a moment.

"You can leave the blanket here," Vivian said. "I'll send a footman for it."

"Until Friday then." He bowed and smiled at her again, a soft, remembering smile—but a determined smile too.

Fifteen

DARIUS PASSED A CARD TO THE DIGNIFIED LITTLE person who served as the Longchamps butler.

"The Honorable Darius Lindsey?"

"Lady Longstreet came out with my sister, Lady Leah Lindsey, now Countess of Bellefonte." Darius smiled the smile of a man who doesn't owe his inferiors an explanation but might be entitled to sympathy from them in any case. "Women must keep up their gossip, and I am a dutiful brother."

"Very good, sir." The man bowed himself out the door and left Darius listening to the rain on the mullioned windows. He'd ridden the length and breadth of Longchamps in recent days and had seen it was a well-run, old-fashioned estate. Whoever had been tending it for William had done a good job and had been doing a good job for some years. The house was well kept too, not a speck of dust, not a wilted flower, not a dingy window to be seen.

The door opened, and there Vivian stood in her gravid glory, her expression conveying both reluctant pleasure at seeing him and exasperation.

"Lady Longstreet." Darius bowed, not even taking her hand. He had to do this by the rules or he'd lose his nerve—and Vivvie would toss him out on his ear.

"Mr. Lindsey?" She advanced into the room, leaving the door open—of course—and extending her bare hand to him. He bowed over it, resisting the urge to lay his cheek against her knuckles, and straightened.

"I bring felicitations from Lady Leah, now Countess of Bellefonte." He assayed a smile, a cordial smile. "And I can pass along to her the news that you are in great good looks. Greetings as well from Lord Valentine Windham's summer abode, where I am a guest for the season."

Vivian's lips quirked at his formality, but she sailed on, lady that she was. "Please have a seat. I'll ring for tea."

"Tea would be lovely." He gave the last word the barest hint of an emphasis, and added a discreet look at his hostess's person that conveyed what or who, exactly, he thought was lovely. "Is his lordship in residence?"

"No. He remains in London until Parliament adjourns, but I'll pass your greetings along to him. How is your sister, and when did she wed?"

Darius offered a brief and somewhat edited recounting of the odd courtship of Nick and Leah Haddonfield. "There is suspicion that Leah might already be in anticipation of a happy event. May I tell my sister you're well, my lady?"

Vivian dipped her chin, abruptly shy. "You may."

"Vivvie"—he dropped his voice—"we've had this discussion."

"But not"—she glanced around—"not *inside*, with

walls and carpets and a tea tray on the way. What can you be thinking, Darius?"

He'd been thinking that friends called on each other, a precious, prosaic thought. "If I'm not a stranger on the day of the christening, it will be easier to explain my interest in the child." Her eyebrows rose at that, but he wasn't done. "Besides, Leah and Emily have both asked after you. Do you know Mrs. Stoneleigh?"

"The late colonel's widow?"

"She's Axel Belmont's wife now, and not an hour distant in the direction of Town. She's similarly anticipating a happy event."

Vivian studied her hands, upon which, Darius noted, she no longer wore rings. "You know a prodigious number of expecting women."

He could sense the speculation in her observation—a penance he'd serve until he'd regained her trust. He rose and spoke barely above a whisper. "You're the only one expecting my child, Vivian."

"You're certain?"

"Positive." And what a fine thing it was to be able to say that to her with absolute sincerity.

She chewed on his assurances while the tea tray arrived, piled high with scones, butter, jam, cheese, and fruit. The look he gave the tray must have communicated easily.

"Don't stand on ceremony." She passed him a cup of tea. "The kitchen cooks for Able, me, and Portia, but guests are a rarity."

"Because you require peace and quiet."

While he watched, she split him a scone, spread a thick layer of butter on one half and jam on the other, and arranged it on a plate with strawberries and cherries.

"I can pass on the cheese," he said, putting his hand over hers when she'd reached for a few slices. "It figures prominently in our camp fare."

"Camp fare, Mr. Lindsey?" She eyed him up and down, rose, and went to the door to speak with a footman. As she resumed her seat, she aimed a question at him. "What are a duke's son and an earl's son doing subsisting on camp fare?"

He overstayed the requisite social call by half an hour, which a man might do when bringing news from a long-out-of-touch acquaintance, and the same man was intent on demolishing the flaky pastries and fresh fruit before him. In that time, he told Vivvie about his brother's progress down in Surrey, and about Valentine Windham's struggles with the Markham estate, and with the widow Markham as well.

Vivian's brow knitted. "I don't know her. She's a baroness?"

"She keeps a very circumspect existence, for reasons known to her." Darius surveyed the crumbs on his plate. "Valentine will get her sorted out, and she'll sort him out too, unless I miss my guess."

"A summer idyll." Vivian's tone was wistful, and Darius knew he had to take his leave of her before he put his arms around her and offered the kind of comfort an acquaintance would never offer.

Though a friend… "Walk me to my horse?"

"Of course."

He could not resist putting a hand under her elbow and assisting her to her feet. It was dear, sweet, and vaguely worrisome that in her condition such assistance was genuinely appropriate.

"I miss my feet," Vivian said as she took his arm and progressed through the house. "I recall them, though, and trust they are still in their assigned location."

"Appears that's the case." Darius patted her hand as they approached the front door. A footman opened it, and they were in the shade of the front terrace. "I've missed all of you."

He'd kept that admission for when they had the privacy of the out of doors, and for his restraint, he was rewarded with another of Vivian's shy smiles.

"You barely know me," she murmured, but he noticed she wasn't in any hurry to get him to the stables.

"Perhaps you'll allow me to call again. I'm without much civilized company at the Markham estate, and without civilized victuals entirely."

Her steps slowed as they approached the stable yard, and she did not turn loose of his arm. "Your sister would expect me to extend some hospitality to you, so you must not be a stranger."

"Gracious of you." Darius kept his relief at this victory off his face. "And what's this?"

"Some civilized victuals." Vivian eased away from his arm and took the bag from the footman who'd come around from the back of the house. "For sons of the nobility forced to rusticate in primitive surrounds. Is this your horse?"

She patted Skunk with a convincing show of interest.

"Skunk, by name." Darius took the reins from the groom and checked the tightness of the girth.

"Is he from America, then?" She ran a hand down

the horse's neck, a slow, gentle caress that Darius felt in low and lonely places.

"Just his name." He checked the length of his stirrup leathers, which the grooms would have had no reason whatsoever to fuss with. "You might consider calling on Mrs. Belmont. She's been accepting callers since her remarriage."

"I know the Belmont estate. It's very pretty." She stroked the horse again, and Darius told himself to stop dawdling, for God's sake. He leaned in and kissed her cheek.

"You're very pretty." He murmured the words in the moment his mouth was near her ear, and was rewarded with her blush.

"Lady Leah never told me what a flirt you are." Vivian touched her cheek. "I am going to tattle on you, sir."

"Vivian?" Portia's voice caroled from the direction of the garden, from which she was marching forth, a basket of blooms in hand. "Do we have a visitor?"

Of course *they* did not. The steward's wife might have visitors, but Vivian's visitors were not Portia's. Darius did not remark the distinction, but rather, exerted himself to bow and smile and give a convincing impression to Portia of a younger son avoiding work on a hot summer morning.

He made liberal mention of his sister, and batted his eyes at Portia until she was simpering. Vivian took her revenge by stroking Skunk, fiddling with his mane, and scratching gently behind the beast's hairy damned ears.

"I'll take my leave of you both." Darius swung into

the saddle. "My thanks for the provisions. You may be assured a letter reporting all to the Countess of Bellefonte will be in the next post." He touched his hat brim and trotted off before Vivian could run her hand over the horse's flank one more time.

Vivian, for her part, did not watch him go, because Portia was a shrewd observer.

Portia's eyes narrowed on Skunk's retreating quarters. "The man no doubt has haunted Town since coming down from university. He could have called on you there. He's a good-looking devil, if you don't mind all that height and muscle."

"Wilton is tall." Vivian picked up the basket of flowers—forget-me-nots among them, of course. "Lady Leah has the same height and was quite graceful on the dance floor."

"And she's caught an earl."

"You've a good man, Portia," Vivian chided. "We both have good men."

"I suppose." Portia linked arms with Vivian. "This heat makes me peckish. Shall we have a plate to tide us over?"

"Nothing for me, thank you. Mr. Lindsey brought with him a spectacular, if politely indulged, appetite." She lifted the basket. "I'll put these in water. They're very pretty."

Portia's lips thinned. "That Mr. Lindsey was pretty, too. Speaking of attractive men, have you heard anything from your dear steppapa?"

Oh, for God's sake. "Of course. He dutifully writes once a month and conveys that all is well in his household." He also conveyed that William was rumored to be in declining health, and Vivian must resolve to join the Ainsworthy household when the inevitable occurred.

A carriage clattering up the drive interrupted her unhappy musing, and both women stopped to regard the Longstreet traveling coach as it pulled into the stable yard. Vivian set the basket down and cocked a questioning glance at Portia, who merely shook her head.

"William?" Vivian's husband emerged slowly, blinking at the sunshine heating up the humid air.

"Greetings, dear wife." He crossed the few steps between them to kiss her forehead, and Vivian accepted his embrace easily. "I know I should have sent a note, but I bring the best news. Portia, I'm sure you'll be glad to know as well that Mrs. Ventnor has been safely delivered of a daughter. Mother and child are thriving, as is Mr. Ventnor, truth be told."

"Oh, William." Vivian hugged him in fierce joy and profound gratitude for her sister's continued well-being. "You are dear to bring me this news in person, and I have missed you so."

William smiled down at her. "You flatter an old man. I'm a tired old man, too. Come sit with me on the terrace, and I'll catch you up on all the gossip from Town." He did not include Portia in the invitation, which was likely what prompted her to speak up.

"We've some gossip of our own. Vivian just had a caller, an earl's son, no less."

"Vivian has occasionally entertained dukes, no less." William offered his wife his arm, his tone deceptively pleasant. "If there's a title visiting in the area, it was simply protocol for him to look in on my dear wife."

"But Mr. Lindsey hasn't a title," Portia went on, "though I gather his sister and Vivian were acquainted in her youth."

"Vivian is still very much in her youth." William's tone cooled a trifle at Portia's persistence. "My eyesight, thankfully being undiminished, I can attest to this. Portia, would you be good enough to relieve Vivian of these flowers?" He passed her the basket, and a look even Portia should have been able to interpret. "I've missed my wife and would beg a moment to enjoy her all to myself."

Portia took herself off, and William sighed gustily as he and Vivian made their way around to the back terrace.

Vivian peered up at him as they made a slow progress down the walk. "You look in need of a rest and some cosseting, William. You've been working too hard."

"I've been getting too old," he countered good-naturedly. "Clever of Lindsey to recall the connection with his sister."

"You don't mind?"

"Mind?" William took a minute to lower himself onto a cushioned wrought iron chair. "I should have thought of it, but if he's bothering you, Vivian, I'll wave him off. I think it's… sweet, I suppose, that he's doing the pretty."

Vivian signaled a footman for a tea tray, hoping there was still a scone or two in the larder.

"I think it's cheeky," Vivian said, meeting her husband's gaze.

William's expression became thoughtful. "You're

going to need allies, Vivian, and Lindsey is motivated to champion your causes, so to speak. You'd be silly to take umbrage at a perfectly respectable social call. Now, I did not have time to write you and fill you in properly on the fate of Havisham's little bill regarding French soap."

He patted her hand, and launched into a juicy recounting of the maneuvering necessary to distinguish legislatively between French soap and English soap. Vivian listened dutifully, and could probably have repeated much of what William had said verbatim, though her mind was elsewhere. First, she was concerned, for William looked like death, for all his spirits seemed sanguine, and he was actually eating a little of the food before him.

Second, William was not the least perturbed that Darius had called on her. In fact, he'd seemed almost to have expected it.

∽

Darius had nigh expired from surprise when William Longstreet signaled his coach to stop and poked his head out the window to offer a cheerful greeting.

"Lindsey, what a unique mount you have."

"My lord." Darius nodded as a sort of mounted bow. "I bid you good day, having just had the pleasure of doing likewise to your lady wife."

"And how is Vivian?" William's smile became mischievous. "Did she threaten to have you forcibly ejected from the premises?"

"She was all that is gracious." Darius straightened a lock of Skunk's mane that had fallen to the off side. "Mostly. You don't mind?"

"My dear young man, you think I'd mind a social call after what has transpired previously—and at my request? Call all you like. It will be a nice change from all that parliamentary whining, and make your occasional presence at Longchamps in future less of an oddity. You're summering with Moreland's youngest, aren't you? You must come calling when bivouacking with the primitives palls."

He'd thumped his cane on the coach roof and departed with a wave of his hand, leaving Darius to stare at the retreating coach in puzzlement.

He tried to put a name to the expression on Lord Longstreet's face: mischievous, yes, but also amused and even pleased. And of course, Valentine Windham's father, His Grace the Duke of Moreland, would be rubbing shoulders with Lord Longstreet and passing along the occasional piece of family gossip.

Hence, William had known Darius would be in Oxfordshire.

Had William foreseen Vivian's proximity to Darius?

He discarded that notion as patently absurd but had to admit William had seemed blasé about Darius calling on his wife. Blasé, and tired—weary to the bone, perhaps even ill. Vivian had warned Darius it was so, but still, seeing the man was a shock. Realizing Darius would genuinely mourn the old man's passing was a greater surprise yet.

৩

"The Honorable Mr. Darius Lindsey, come to call."

William glanced up from Muriel's 1805 diary—and wasn't that an exciting year?—to find young Lindsey standing in the doorway looking handsome, bashful, and determined.

Relief at seeing that Vivian's doting swain remained well and truly interested vied with an old schemer's pleasure at plans coming nicely to fruition. Lindsey would do—for Vivian and for the child; Lindsey would do well.

"Mr. Lindsey. I see you took me at my word, which is more than I can say for most of the damned Commons." William creaked to his feet and extended a hand toward his guest. "Vivian has abandoned me to make the acquaintance of Professor Belmont's new wife."

Lindsey accepted the handshake, glancing around the study William considered his retreat at Longchamps. The furniture was heavy, worn, and comfortable, and Portia knew better than to trespass in here.

"I wasn't sure you'd receive me in Vivian's absence."

Young men were so relentlessly afflicted with bravery. William glanced at Muriel's diary and hoped she was enjoying the little drama playing out in their home.

"I'm the friendly sort," he assured his guest. "Or perhaps I'm merely bored, as country life is abysmally quiet. Let's find some shade out back. I've been wanting to know how your sister ended up wedded to Bellefonte's heir."

He led Lindsey through the house as he spoke, wanting the fellow to see that Vivian's surrounds were commodious and well cared for. They reached a side door, and William turned to aim a conspiratorial wink at Mr. Lindsey. "We'll have more privacy back here."

To William's delight, thirty minutes later, young

Lindsey was deep in explanations of the Lindsey family's secrets.

"I haven't shared this with anybody." Lindsey looked puzzled as he took a sip of sangria—the man had lived in Italy for a time, and William had chosen their refreshment accordingly.

"It isn't as if I'll be repeating it," William replied.

Lindsey studied him for a long moment while a lovely fresh breeze stirred the leafy branches above them. From the look in the man's eyes, William had the sense Lindsey hadn't had the benefit of much plain speaking regarding his family, certainly not from those whose opinions were unassailably well informed.

When William picked up his drink, his hand shook slightly, so the ice clattered against the side of the glass. His guest ignored that indignity, for which William accorded him points.

Muriel would have said Lindsey had possibilities, and she would have been right, though Lindsey himself might not agree. Fatigue dragged at William, and a touch of regret that he would not see all of Lindsey's potential bear fruit.

Lindsey rose and leaned down as if to offer William assistance.

"None of that," William said, waving him off and pushing out of the chair. "I can still maneuver about, though God knows for how much longer I'll be forced to racket around in these old bones. I'll tell Vivian you called, and she'll be sorry to have missed you. Truly, Lindsey, you've brightened my morning, and you must come again."

"I think you mean that." Vivian's dashing swain

looked bewildered and... humble. Humility was a precious quality in a young man—in any man. "I can't fathom why it should be so."

Lindsey was a bright fellow. In another few decades, he'd understand well enough.

"Be off with you." William waved toward the stables, which lay at too great a distance for a tired old man to contemplate. "I'll expect you back when you have more time to spend socializing."

And then, when he ought to have gone striding off toward the driveway on those young, strong legs of his, Lindsey turned, hat in hand, and speared William with a look.

"Thank you, my lord. Thank you most sincerely."

At least he had the savoir faire not to lapse into specifics, because William knew damn good and well Lindsey was not thanking him for a glass of sangria and some idle talk.

"And my thanks to you, Mr. Lindsey. You must come back soon, and we'll talk further. I never did hear back from you regarding those homing pigeons."

Lindsey took the hint. He bowed, tapped his hat onto his head, and promised he would call again soon.

Muriel would have been pleased.

Vivian would be pleased, too.

✑

Darius had taken to calling at Longchamps on Mondays and Fridays, and for three consecutive visits, he'd found himself entertained exclusively by his host. Lord Longstreet's company was oddly comfortable, and he told Darius a number of stories about Darius's father that supported Lord Longstreet's conclusion that Wilton was a "waste of good tailoring."

Longstreet also talked about commercial policies, and where the trade opportunities were likely to lie if legislation were enacted as he anticipated.

"I'd be discussing this with my son, you know," Longstreet said over one of their pitchers of sangria, "but the man hasn't the head for policy matters. He's a dab hand with the land, though."

Longstreet was old and frail, but he was by no means growing vague. "You speak in the present tense, my lord. I was under the impression you had no extant progeny."

"So Vivian didn't get around to tattling on me?"

"Regarding?" Darius knew his host well enough by now to suspect Lord Longstreet had told him only what he wanted Darius to know when they'd met that long-ago November evening.

"My steward," Longstreet said. "Able Springer is my by-blow. He can't inherit the title, of course, hence your assistance was necessary."

Assistance. Perhaps Longstreet had been more diplomat than politician. "I suppose this explains his wife's presumptuousness."

Longstreet gestured to the pitcher—a ceramic container Darius could lift easily, though he suspected his host could not. "Portia's a managing baggage," his lordship said as Darius refreshed their drinks. "Maybe a child will settle her down."

"I don't think so." And what was it about Longstreet that invited such honesty? "Women like that are bound for trouble, and they don't outgrow the taste for it."

"You speak from experience, but there's little I can do about her. She's Able's wife."

"You can keep her away from Vivian."

Longstreet regarded him steadily, and Darius realized it was the first overt mention between them of any interest Darius might have in Vivian's welfare.

"I can send Vivian back up to Town," Longstreet suggested after a moment. "I'd as soon have her lying in where there are physicians available. I do not want to entrust the Longstreet heir's arrival to some country midwife."

"It's not my place to comment," Darius said, though the idea that Vivian might have none save Portia to attend her was intolerable. "Her sister is in London as well, and if a lady cannot have the comfort of her mother's support at such a time, then her sister might be the next best thing."

Darius withstood yet more scrutiny from faded brown eyes that likely missed nothing. "I don't suppose you're on your way up to Town?"

He was—*now*. Darius rose, sensing the summer heat, the wine, and the time spent in conversation had tired his host. "As a matter of fact I will be soon."

Longstreet pushed himself out of his chair, a maneuver Darius watched with some concern. William was slowing down yet further, having to pause for balance frequently, and looking even thinner than he had a few weeks ago.

He accepted the cane Darius handed him and aimed a look at his guest Darius could not read. "Will you make your good-byes to Vivian?"

"Lord Longstreet…"

"Now is not the time to turn up prissy," his lordship said briskly. "If Vivian thought I'd let you scamper off without taking proper leave of her, she'd skewer me where I stand. She should be back now, though she and the Belmont woman have become thick as thieves."

"They're both facing impending motherhood for the first time."

"While I face death," Longstreet said, "and you face, exactly what?"

Excellent question.

"I've been summoned to my brother's estate in Surrey," Darius said, "and I've my own place to check in on, as harvest approaches. Then too, my younger sister is in Town with Lady Warne, and I should likely make my bow to her."

"You'll be busy, rather than fretting over Vivian," Longstreet observed. "Staying busy helps. Staying drunk decidedly does not."

"One perceives this."

"Then you're a brighter lad than I was. Muriel had to put her dainty foot down with me. Ah, Vivian." Longstreet's gaze traveled to where his wife came around the corner of the house. "You're in time to stroll with Mr. Lindsey before he departs for points south. Don't stay in the sun too long, my dear. It leaves one quite fatigued. Lindsey, safe journey."

Darius took the older man's hand and knew a welling sadness that he might not see William Longstreet again. Nothing but good had come of Darius's association with the man, and that surprised as it touched as it confounded.

"You'll listen to Vivian when she orders you to rest and eat and so forth?"

"Hush, lad." William drew Darius closer and settled both hands around Darius's one. "You'll give the woman ideas, and she's adept enough at fussing and coddling. You'll look after her for me? I'll have your word on this, if you'll humor an old man."

"You have my word, Vivian and the child." Darius nodded and swallowed, and then, with Vivian looking on in broad daylight, clasped Lord Longstreet in a careful hug. The man was all bones, his scent one of bay rum and camphor, but he hugged Darius back with surprising strength.

"Vivian, see Mr. Lindsey along, would you? I'm for a little lie down, and then perhaps you'll send Able to me? The correspondence is piling up."

"Of course, William." Vivian watched him return to the house, concern in her gaze. "What was that about?" She aimed the question at Darius, who was also watching Lord Longstreet's retreat.

"He's dying, Vivvie." Darius said it quietly but couldn't keep the sadness from his tone. "He's not going to last much longer."

She slipped her arm through his. "He talks often about when he's gone, and what I must tell the child of him, and so forth, as if dying comes around every other week. It upsets me, but I think he's simply trying to get me used to the idea. What were you two whispering about?"

"Nothing consequential." Darius patted her hand and led her toward a shady path. "You're feeling well?"

"I'm feeling like a hippopotamus out of water,"

Vivian said, and that confiding this was so easy was a pleasure to Darius, even as he wished he could take all the ungainly, hippopotamus sentiments onto his own shoulders rather than leave Vivian to endure them alone.

Love made a man daft—even a man who was trying only to be a good friend.

"Angela says it gets like this, so you can't wait to be free of your burden, and then you realize you *are* going to be free of your burden, and after nine long months, you want a little more time to get used to the idea."

"If she says that after four children, it's likely true."

They strolled along in silence until Darius spoke up again. "I'm going to have to depart soon for Surrey, but I'm leaving my direction with the Belmonts, and I'll leave it with you as well."

"And then?"

"And then there'll be a christening to attend, God willing."

"Or a funeral," Vivian said softly. She turned into him, and his arms came around her.

"He's ready to go, Vivvie. We don't want to let him go, but he's ready."

She nodded against his chest. "He is, but why now?"

Darius didn't answer, just stroked her back and let her be a little weepy and hoped none of the tears were because they were parting. Again. When she was more composed, he resumed their walk, keeping his arm around her shoulders.

"William thinks you'll be safer delivering in Town where there are physicians at hand."

"I agree. And Angela is there. She'll attend me."

"That's good, then." Darius realized they'd soon be within sight of the stables, and rather than turn loose of her, he drew her to a bench beneath an ancient oak. "I can't write to you, and I can't call much once you're in Town, but know that I'll be thinking of you and praying for your safety."

She nodded, looking down at where her hand lay in his against his thigh.

"We've had an odd summer," she observed. "Becoming friends."

"It's what I can offer you now," he said, wondering at his own words. They were true, so he charged forth into more truth. "I've enjoyed this summer. You are good company, Vivvie Longstreet, and a good wife to your husband."

"Hold me."

She pitched against him, giving him little choice, but he was more than willing to oblige. He loved the ripeness of her shape, the subtle luminance of her skin, the maternal secret lurking in all her smiles. To see her here at Longchamps had been a privilege beyond imagining.

"We're going to get through this, aren't we, Mr. Lindsey?" She offered him one of those smiles now, a little sad, a little pained, but genuine.

"Yes, my lady." He kissed her cheek and drew her to her feet. "We'll get through this too."

When she waved him on his way at the mounting block, Vivian was the picture of serene grace. She patted his horse good-bye and took his hand one final time.

"Leah has enjoyed your letters," Darius said quietly, mindful of the grooms. Vivian's brows rose, and Darius saw she'd taken his point.

"And I enjoy hers," Vivian said, her smile not at all maternal. "Safe journeys, Mr. Lindsey, and my regards to your sister."

He touched the brim of his hat with his crop and nudged Skunk into a canter, knowing if he lingered one more moment, he'd be off the horse, arms wrapped around William's wife, unable to let her go.

Sixteen

"It's a belated lying-in gift." Angela set the little package on the table by Vivian's sofa. "From William, who looks positively beamish these days."

Vivian smiled at the bundle in her arms. "A man his age should look beamish when he has a newborn son. Will you hold the baby?"

"Come here, wee baron." Angela scooped the child up. "I swear he's smiling already, Viv, and growing like a weed."

"I've the sore parts to show for it." Vivian frowned briefly, only to find her sister regarding her with a pragmatic intensity.

"Has the bleeding slowed down?"

"It has stopped," Vivian reported, used to Angela's blunt speech about female functions. "And I'm eating my steak and kidney pies, and drinking a great deal of chamomile tea." She tore at the wrapping on the package and found two books, slim little volumes in Muriel Longstreet's hand.

Angela shifted to sit on the couch next to her sister. "He said they were from Muriel's confinements and her years of early motherhood."

"Oh, Angela…" Vivian traced the leather binding and peered at a random page. "William treasures these, and I can't…"

Angela met her sister's gaze and smiled in sympathy.

"You can," she said. "Our mama is not here to offer her support, but William can give you this much from a woman who took your interests very much to heart. He's still down in the breakfast parlor, if you're thinking to thank him."

"I'll take the baby and give my husband a scold he won't soon forget."

Angela bit her lower lip. "You might consider thanking him instead. William wants you and this child to be happy, and he can't stop what's coming any more than you can."

"He can fight it." Vivian set the books aside and slipped on a pair of house mules. "He can at least pretend having this child gives him a reason to live, not an excuse to die." She stopped and looked away, only to find Angela passing her the handkerchief from her bodice.

"It's like this," Angela said in sympathy. "You think the child is safely born, and all will be well, and it will be, but nothing is the same, and that takes getting used to."

"I'm all right." Vivian dabbed at her eyes then passed the handkerchief back. "How do you manage as if you've five hands, Angela? I'd have dropped the baby by now."

"No, you wouldn't," Angela said with peculiar gravity. "You're his mother, and that means, on some level, you'll never let him go. Now, let William dandle his son, and then I must be back to my own brood."

"You're good to keep checking on me." Vivian

leaned over to kiss her sister's cheek and accepted the baby back from Angela.

"That reminds me: Is Ainsworthy keeping his distance, or does he presume to check on you too?"

Vivian glanced up from the baby. "He presumes. He was here less than a week after the baron was born, carping at me regarding my future, as if my husband weren't alive and breathing under the same roof as my son."

Angela's normally serene features creased with distaste. "Thurgood Ainsworthy is a snake. Another benefit of being married to a publisher is that Jared doesn't mince words, and I probably fell in love with my husband the day he forbid Ainsworthy from calling on me."

Vivian gave a little shudder and hugged the child closer, because Ainsworthy had been regarding her lately with an all-too-satisfied proprietary air, and yet he'd shown the baby no regard whatsoever.

Angela tucked her handkerchief back into her bodice. "No more talk of that wretched weasel. Let your husband and your son enjoy a little of each other's company."

Vivian accompanied her sister down the steps, saw her on her way, and found William reading his paper in the breakfast parlor.

"Good morning, William." She kissed his cheek and took a seat before he could rise and hold her chair. "I've brought a visitor."

William set his paper aside. "How is the lad this morning?"

"In good spirits." Vivian shifted the baby so William could see his face. "Would you like to hold him?"

"Come here, boy." William held out his arms.

"You'll be appalled at what our regent has done with your birthright lately." He took the child in his arms, and watching the old man and the new baby, Vivian felt a pang of such strong emotion that tears welled again. William had given her this child, and William was leaving her with this child.

William glanced up from the baby. "Waxing sentimental, Vivian?"

"Very." She looked around for the teapot, the toast rack, anything. "William, how are you feeling?"

He met her gaze, and some of his cheerful expression slipped. He patted her hand. "You must not be afraid. All will be well."

"You are not well," she rejoined, moving her hand to pour a cup of tea. "You smile and pat my knuckles and tease the baby, but, William…"

"I know, Vivian. We watched Muriel die, you and I. Do you think I don't know this is hard on you?"

"It doesn't seem hard on you," she said, some exasperation coming through. "I've never been a mother before, William, and I never expected to be a mother, not like this, not without…"

"Without a husband, a father to your child to raise him up with you," William finished the sentiment. "You must trust me, Vivian, to do what I can for the boy and for you. He's barely a month old, but I do love him. I love that he exists, and my regard for you, for what you did for the Longstreet succession, is greater than you know."

It was as close as he'd come to telling her he loved her, and Vivian's emotions shifted toward panic. From William, it was tantamount to a good-bye.

"Now"—William's tone became brisk—"take this great strapping lad from me, for he grows too heavy for these old arms. Will you be ready for the christening?"

"I will be. Angela will be as well, though I still say it will look peculiar not to have Jared for the godfather."

"Jared understands my choice," William said, passing the child back to her, "and I daresay you do too. Lindsey will make a proper job of it, and for reasons the world need not be privy to. I've written to him, you know."

"About?"

"The man has a son, Vivian." William said it very quietly, even though they were alone behind closed doors with only that son in attendance. "He deserves to know that your confinement has come to a happy conclusion, and he deserves to know that child and mother are doing well."

"This is not his son," Vivian said just as softly. "Legally, the man is nothing to the child."

William picked up his paper. "The very point of our elaborate fiction, but Darius Lindsey is a person, Vivian, a flesh-and-blood man, with feelings he probably doesn't even comprehend himself. I gather others have treated him as if he lacked those feelings, and I don't want to do him the same disrespect. Now, take his lordship here and explain to him he must behave at the christening, as the honor of the House of Longstreet rests in his chubby little hands."

William turned his attention back to the paper, silencing Vivian from further remonstrations.

She cuddled the baby closer. "My thanks for the diaries. I'll take the best care of them."

He folded down the paper to regard her and the

child. "I know you will, and of our son as well, but see that you allow some care to be taken of you too, Vivian." He returned to his paper on that cryptic note. Vivian took the baby back to the nursery and stayed there with him, reading diaries written decades earlier by a woman now dead.

Her peaceful day was interrupted by Dilquin's announcement that Mr. Ainsworthy was again swilling tea in the family parlor. Grateful that the baby slept— Vivian had yet to introduce her former stepfather to her son—she took her time tidying her hair.

"Vivian, dear girl." Ainsworthy took both her hands in his and spread them wide, so she was prevented from dodging his kiss to her forehead. "My dear, you look positively peaked. I am concerned for you."

"Newborns will wake one up frequently through the night," Vivian said. "If you'll keep your visit short, I'll have time for a nap before the baby wakes."

"Wouldn't it be wiser to employ a wet nurse, Vivian?" Ainsworthy contrived to look worried. "If our dear queen could do so for all fifteen of her offspring, you might consider it as well."

Vivian's chin came up half an inch. "He's my son and William's heir, and I am not the Queen. A wet nurse will not be necessary."

"Perhaps later." Ainsworthy seated himself and gestured to the place beside him on the sofa. "William can't think to tie you to that child for months and months."

Vivian took a separate chair, close enough that she could pour the tea, far enough away to avoid Ainsworthy's hands.

"I expect I'll be tied to that child for the rest of

his life," Vivian said, pouring herself tea, because Ainsworthy had helped himself before she'd arrived. "How is your family?"

"You are my family. You wound me when you suggest otherwise."

"I'm inquiring after Ariadne and her son. More tea?"

"Just a drop." Ainsworthy held out his cup. "Have you warned that sister of yours you'll be joining my household when William shuffles off this mortal coil?"

Vivian rose, fists clenched, fatigue, grief, and pure fury burning off her manners. "That kind of talk is inappropriate, callous, and unwelcome."

"Unwelcome? To offer you succor in your impending grief? To extend the arms of familial love and support in your hour of need? Vivian, childbirth has taxed your wits if you think I have anything but your best interests at heart."

Childbirth had not taxed her wits, but rather, sharpened them. "I beg leave to doubt the purity of your motivations, Thurgood, when my husband yet lives, and our household is celebrating the birth of William's heir. If you'll excuse me, I believe I'll go check on my son and perhaps take that nap you think I need so badly."

She swished out, closing the door softly only by exercise of will. The nerve of the man was appalling, and yet Vivian couldn't toss off Thurgood Ainsworthy as just an interfering busybody. He'd schemed to see Angela wed, and he'd schemed to induce Vivian's mother into holy matrimony, at substantial cost to the bride and her children.

"Dilquin." Vivian kept her voice low, because

Thurgood was no doubt intent on swilling his tea before he took himself off. "You will make sure that man leaves this house, and you will not allow him across the threshold again unless William is with me."

"Very good, my lady." Dilquin looked not the least perturbed by these directions, but his eyebrows flew up when one of the under footmen came running from the back of the house.

"My lady, come quick. His lordship's in a bad way!"

❧

"He's merely unconscious," Vivian said, seeing the rise and fall of William's chest. "Get him up to bed, but for God's sake, don't let Ainsworthy see you. Send for Dr. Garner, and bring paper and pen to his lordship's room so I can let my sister know as well."

Her orders were swiftly carried out, but Vivian's heart was pounding in her chest, for there was no such thing as *merely* unconscious for a man of William's years. Dilquin directed the footmen, who carried William to his bed then politely ejected Ainsworthy from the family parlor before the physician arrived.

By the time Doctor Garner was on hand, William was tucked up in bed and conscious, but he was alarmingly pale and weak. To Vivian's ear, her husband's voice was altered as well, his speech ever so slightly slurred.

The physician would not have picked that up, because he hadn't heard William's voice day in and day out for the past five years, but Vivian heard it, and her unease at William's condition grew apace.

Doctor Garner drew her aside, wearing a sympathetic

expression on aging Nordic features that looked both fierce and kindly.

"A mild apoplexy would be my guess, my lady," he said. "You must keep him comfortable and calm, though another seizure could occur at any time. He will be weak, possibly weaker on one side than the other, and he might have trouble recalling things or putting his thoughts into words. He's lucky. An apoplexy can be far more serious, leaving one without the ability to speak, move, or even swallow."

"He's lucky, and he can recover, can't he?"

"Some do," the physician said, folding the earpieces on his spectacles, then unfolding them. "Each case is different. Some go on and become as good as new, some fall victim to other illnesses, some are taken by another apoplexy within days, even hours."

And, Garner seemed to be saying, medicine played no role in altering those outcomes.

Vivian unclenched her fisted hands. "William's heir was just born a few weeks ago. His lordship has much to live for, and we will do all we can to keep him with us."

"I'd advise against such determination," the man said, tucking his spectacles into a vest pocket. "Clearly, my lady, you are devoted to your spouse, which does you credit, but he's very old, and being dependent on others for all assistance isn't easy for a man like Lord Longstreet. I've been his physician for years and had to have this same discussion with him when the late Lady Longstreet became so ill. If God is calling William home, who are we to demand William ignore that summons for our comfort?"

"When it was William's spouse dying"—Vivian had to pause on that word—"I understood such sentiments clearly, Doctor. I was closer to Muriel than to William at the time, of course, but now…"

Doctor Garner patted her arm. "Now you keep him as cheerful and comfortable as you can, and leave the rest in God's hands. Then too, you have a new baby, and your own health cannot be allowed to suffer because you're fretting over Lord Longstreet. Physically, he's not in much pain beyond what ails an old man. His discomfort is more likely caused by the injury to his dignity."

"Oh, that." Vivian's smile was rueful. "We Longstreets are always very much on our dignity."

"Sometimes dignity is all that's left to us. You'll send for me if there's any change in his condition?"

"Of course." Vivian showed him out and felt keenly the silence in the house in the wake of the morning's developments. She had to face her husband's approaching death, but how, exactly, did one face such a loss? She mentally put the question to her Maker, but no almighty answer rained down from the puffy clouds in the pretty September sky. Not knowing what else to do, Vivian fetched her son, had a rocking chair moved into William's room, and brought the baby with her so she could sit by William's bedside and pray for his full recovery.

❦

Valentine Windham had agreed to accompany Darius to the christening in exchange for Darius's promise to attend the opening concert of the symphony season. Darius had updated his wardrobe, procured a rattle in the shape of a scepter for the baby, and ordered flowers sent 'round to the new mother.

All that remained was to call upon Lord William—as a courtesy—the day before the christening. A simple social call had never caused a grown man so much trepidation or so much dithering over his attire.

"Good afternoon, sir," the butler said, handing Darius's hat and cane off to a footman. "The Honorable Mr. Darius Lindsey?"

"Yes. If you'd take my card to Lord Longstreet?"

"Lord Longstreet is likely not at home." The butler's brow puckered as he led Darius into the library. "Shall I let Lady Longstreet know you're here?"

"I don't want to bother her," Darius said. Calling on William was one thing; calling on Vivian just weeks after she'd given birth wasn't as easy to explain.

"You're sure?"

"I am." Darius took a minute to glance around the parlor. The wainscoting was dark, the walls done in a forest green, the gilt kept to a minimum. A comfortable, masculine room with well-padded chairs—probably William's preferred territory.

"If you'll just wait a moment, sir." The butler bowed slightly. "I'll retrieve your hat and cane."

"Certainly." Darius nodded, not at all displeased to have a few minutes to study this little piece of Vivian's world, and just perhaps, to hear the sound of a baby crying elsewhere in the house.

He heard the butler's dry tones and a softer voice, the words indistinct. Without warning, the door opened, and Vivian stood there, her expression surprised. "Mr. Lindsey?"

"Viv—my lady." He didn't approach her, but he wanted to. God in heaven, he wanted to. "A pleasure to see you." A pleasure and a towering relief, also the answer to myriad heartfelt prayers for the lady's well-being.

"I didn't know you'd come calling." She took a few steps into the room, paused, and turned to close the door. "Dilquin suggested William might like me to read something besides Muriel's diaries, but he neglected to mention we had a caller."

God bless Dilquin. "I thought a call the day before the christening might be courteous. I gather William is from home."

"He's… unavailable." Vivian looked away, her expression bleak. "Would you like some tea?"

"Tea sounds good." Bilge water would sound good, provided he could drink it in Vivian's parlor, in Vivian's company—though William's situation sounded not good at all. Darius held his ground while Vivian went to signal a footman. His eyes traveled over her as discreetly as he could manage, silently cataloging the changes: Her figure was once more in evidence, but more lush. The waistline of her dress was raised, though Darius could tell her breasts were fuller, her hips a little rounder, her backside a touch more generous.

The sight of her made his mouth go dry, she was so lovely. There was a softness about her, a maturity that made what had been pretty before beautiful now—despite the fatigue he could see in her eyes, and in the way she moved a little carefully to the sofa and took a seat.

She raised her gaze to his. "Will you join me?"

He could not tell if he was supposed to be Darius or Mr. Lindsey today, but he accepted the invitation and sat beside her, leaning close enough for a little whiff of her scent. "The baby is well?"

The exact right question to ask a new mother, and the answer a new father very much needed to know.

Vivian smiled broadly. "Healthy as a little piglet. He's perfect, Darius. Just… perfect, and when he smiles, it's impossible to believe there's misery or strife anywhere in God's creation."

"You're smitten with your own offspring," Darius accused, returning her smile. "He's keeping you up nights, I'd guess."

"He's growing." Vivian smoothed a hand down her skirts, and Darius was pleased to note that with him, she did not blush. "Growing boys need sustenance."

"You're not using a wet nurse?"

"My mother didn't endorse it, and neither does Angela, and all four of hers are thriving. I don't want to hand my son off to a stranger, not until I have to."

Our son, Darius mentally corrected her, though he hadn't the right. "What does that mean?"

"'Boys go into men's hands,'" she quoted, "though I have a few years before that happens."

She had those years, while Darius did not, and yet he didn't begrudge them to her—exactly. "I'm glad you're not using a wet nurse. If nature is any guide, it's a peculiar practice at best, but is there something you're not telling me, Vivvie?"

She was saved from answering by the arrival of the tea service, which gave Darius further opportunity to study her. There was an agitated quality to her, in her movements, around her eyes and mouth. He'd seen Vivian in many moods, from uncertain to angry to passionate, but she'd always had a quality of self-possession.

She passed him his tea, prepared with both cream and sugar, and Darius watched while she poured her own.

"You're tired, Vivvie," he said, "and maybe a little frayed around the edges from the birth and delivery. Was it very bad?"

"Bad?" She set the teapot down but kept her fingers wrapped around the handle, as if a little porcelain pot might steady her.

"I thought of you." He set his teacup aside and saw his hand was reaching forward to rub a slow circle on her shoulder. She looked in want of cuddling to him, in want of comfort. "I thought of you constantly. Childbirth is legendarily uncomfortable. That you suffered... I would wish it otherwise."

Was he the only man in all creation who would have borne a child to spare the mother her travail?

"I have a healthy son." She spoke as if reciting from a copybook. "William has his heir, and it was worth it. Angela said her first took twice as long as little Will did."

"You've named him William? The quintessential good English name. I like it."

"Wilhelm, actually." She turned a faint smile on him. Had she wondered what he'd think of the name? "Wilhelm Fordham Longstreet, after William's grandmother, Wilhelmina, who came over with the court of German George."

Darius's smile faded, though he didn't drop his hand, because Vivian wasn't protesting the contact. "Interesting middle name. Your idea?"

"William's." Vivian slanted a puzzled look at him over her shoulder. "He chose the names, and I like them. Your brother's eldest is named Ford, isn't he?"

"Fordham. After his uncle, Darius Fordham Lindsey."

"Oh."

She looked so completely nonplussed, Darius put aside the burning need to meet Vivian's son—his son, too, in a sense—and cast around for something, anything, to keep the conversational shuttlecock aloft. "Have you hired a nurse yet?"

"I'm borrowing one from Angela," Vivian said, looking relieved at the change in topic. "She's here only during the daylight hours, and a baby requires care 'round the clock."

"Vivvie, I know how this works, because I've been through it before. You want to be a good mother, and I know you are, but that means you're reluctant to let anybody, save perhaps your sister, deal with the child at all. Because you're not using a wet nurse, you must be up and down all night with him, and then you're trying to run William's household by day as well. This is how women end up with nervous exhaustion."

"You know too much." Vivian hunched forward, but she didn't shrug off his hand, so he continued to rub her back. "Angela scolds me similarly though."

"She isn't scolding. She's trying to look after you."

Vivian scowled at him over her shoulder. "You shouldn't be doing that." Now she aimed a look at his hand where it rested on her shoulder.

"I'll bargain with you. You nap at least in the afternoon when the child naps, and I'll leave off dunning you." Though of course, he had nothing to bargain with and wouldn't be on the premises to dun her—or rub her back or cuddle her or anything.

The current of bleakness common to all their dealings widened, threatening to engulf even his joy in being with her.

Until Vivian gave up a sigh, a tired sigh to Darius's ears. "I could. I could go to sleep right now, in fact."

"Is the baby asleep?"

"I hope so. You say John's mother went through this?"

"I had to practically move her bed into the nursery. She never really recovered from the childbirth, and she was terrified the child would not thrive."

Vivian nodded. "I can understand being terrified."

"For God's sake, Vivian, you've said the baby is healthy and growing, the delivery was uncomplicated, and you've got at least a day nurse." Darius sat forward to slide his arm around her waist. "You're a good mother, I'd stake my life on that, and all you need is a little more rest."

"I do." She let her head rest on his shoulder, and Darius rejoiced to offer her even that passing comfort. William should be doing this for her, restoring her spirits, assuring her of her competence, but he was likely too involved with the opening of the fall parliamentary session, or maybe too damned dignified.

"Will I see you tomorrow?" Darius asked.

"Of course, though I doubt William will attend."

"Not attend the christening of his heir?" Darius

shifted to consider Vivian more closely. The tension underlying her fatigue was William's doing, Darius would bet his horse on it. "He's unwell, then?"

Vivian nodded, so Darius waited, hoping she'd elaborate.

"Under the weather," was all she said. "He caught a cold this winter at Longchamps and struggled to throw it off for most of the spring. He's lost ground, Darius, and lately he's very weak."

"I was afraid he'd give up when the child arrived. It appears that's the case." The irony of it, that Darius should have spent years wishing his own father into the ground, and now grieve William Longstreet's imminent passing, was not lost on him.

"Give up?" Vivian lifted her cheek from his shoulder to regard him. "I could just... I'm not ready for him to leave me alone with this baby to raise, a huge estate to see to, several other properties. The title is old, Darius, and the properties are many and complicated, and then too, William had investments, and I don't know his man of business, and the solicitors are almost as old as William. I hardly know how to go on now as things stand, and if William dies..."

"When he dies"—Darius stroked her hair, hating the anxiety riding her so hard—"he'll have made generous provision for you in his will."

"He told you this?"

"He hasn't discussed it with me, no, but the man wasn't going to put you up to providing him an heir then ignore the magnitude of your sacrifice, Vivian."

"Sacrifice?" She snorted and got up to pace. "I should just ask him, I know that, and he'd tell me, but it seems so... callous, like something Portia would do."

"Portia Springer?" Darius rose too. "Not somebody whose company I'd seek. Come here, Vivian, and let me hold you a moment, and then I'll be on my way. It doesn't do for me to be closeted with you here for more than a few minutes, and you need to be napping in any case."

And didn't he just sound like the soul of avuncular wisdom, when what he wanted was to stand guard at her bedroom door, ensuring she wasn't disturbed until she damned well caught up on her rest.

He held her, the way he'd held John's mother when she was so tired and worn and bewildered as a new mother. The way he'd wished somebody had held him on more than one occasion.

"I'll wish you good day, then," Vivian murmured, though she remained quiet against him. Her shape was different than it had been over the summer. To Darius, it was wonderful in a whole new way. Still Vivvie, but even better, even more holdable, and worth cherishing.

"Walk me to the door, Vivvie," Darius said, dropping his arms. "Then go upstairs and take a damned nap. You'll feel worlds better, and the nurse will summon you if Will gets fretful."

Will, *his son*, named Wilhelm Fordham. Decent of Lord Longstreet to do that, beyond decent.

Vivian paused before they left the library. "I'm glad you came. More glad than you know. If the baby hadn't just gotten to sleep—"

"I'll see you tomorrow," Darius assured her. He'd see her tonight in his dreams too, of course. "You'll rest now. Promise me."

"I promise." Vivian tried for a smile, but it was a shy effort.

Darius kissed her cheek, only her cheek. "Get as much rest between then and now as you can."

She leaned in, her forehead on his chest as if she were drawing strength, then straightened and took his proffered arm. Dilquin met them at the door, handing Darius his cane and hat.

Darius eyed the older fellow. "I'm telling your butler you've promised to nap. I will trust his discretion to see you keep your word."

"The housekeeper and Mrs. Ventnor's nursery maid will abet me in this cause, sir," the butler volunteered. "Her ladyship will look in the pink tomorrow when she takes the baron about for the first time."

The baron. Darius's son already had a courtesy title and was going to sit in the Lords one day. It boggled the mind of a plain mister, it did, but Darius found himself smiling as he walked back to his rooms.

He could afford better now. Wilton's death not a month past had released some funds in trust, and Averett Hill was turning a steady profit. Then too, all the jewels Darius had been given—had *earned*—were of good quality and had been sold so the funds could be invested along with the final installment William had provided. All in all, Darius was well on his way to thriving financial health.

So he considered where a man ought to move, if he wanted quarters suitable for the occasional visit from his one and only… godson.

Seventeen

"YOU ARE AS NERVOUS AS A BRIDEGROOM," VALENTINE Windham said. "Hold still, or you'll be looking as tumbled as one."

"Men are not tumbled," Darius retorted, but he raised his chin so Val could retie the knot in Darius's cravat. "Nothing elaborate, if you please. This is a sober occasion."

"You're not the kind to show it when you fret." Val finished with the knot, then moved on to reposition the boutonniere gracing Darius's lapel. "What has you so nervous?"

Darius remained silent until Val had stepped back.

"This will sound... peculiar, but I feel as if I'm the one being christened." Darius surveyed himself in the mirror, finding a sober, reasonably good-looking fellow staring back at him. If Valentine thought that fellow daft, so be it. "This is the first thing I've done to participate in the proper rituals of Polite Society for many years. Maybe since I was a lad squirming in church. It matters to me."

They took his traveling coach—the only conveyance

Darius owned with pretensions to elegance—and all the way to St. George's, Darius pondered the pleasures of a life where he was free to act on the things that mattered to him.

This morning mattered a great deal.

He would see Vivian again.

And he would meet his godson.

His only child.

His and Vivian's child.

A feeling not unlike anxiety welled, but Darius considered it as they approached the church. Upon examination, worry was only part of the sentiment. The day was pretty, the air crisp, the sun warm. Not too cold a day for his son to be out greeting society. He spied Vivian holding the baby at the church door, her sister and likely her sister's husband at her elbow. When Vivian smiled at him, arms around their child, Darius put a name to what he was experiencing.

Joy.

Simple, uncomplicated joy, to be here this day, celebrating this event, particularly with this woman.

And more than joy, love.

He loved Vivian, loved her courage and integrity, her humor and passion, and loved her all the more because she would bring those qualities to being the mother of his child. He loved the child, sight unseen, loved the goodness inherent in all new life, the hope and potential.

He loved his own life, he reflected in some wonder as he made his way through the crowd gathered in anticipation of the service. There were regrets, of course, many and considerable, but right now, the gratitude far outweighed the sorrows.

"Lady Longstreet." There in front of half the titles in London, he leaned in and kissed her cheek. She beamed up at him, because such behavior was permitted on this most special occasion.

"Mr. Lindsey," Vivian replied, and while she still looked fatigued, she also looked happy. "May I do the introductions?" She did the pretty for her sister and Mr. Ventnor. Darius greeted the sister, a more matronly version of Vivian, and as for the brother-in-law, Ventnor was a handsome, dapper, dark-haired man in his prime, just a couple of inches shorter than Darius. His eyes were shrewd, but his manner was friendly enough.

"And will you introduce me to the young man in your arms?"

Vivian glanced down at the baby then up at Darius, her expression full of emotions shifting too quickly for him to read.

"I'll do better than that," she said, tucking up the child's receiving blankets. "He's a right little porker, in Dilquin's estimation, so you can relieve me of the burden of his weight. Darius Lindsey, may I make known to you Baron Longchamps, Master Wilhelm Fordham Zacharias Josef Longstreet." She passed the child to Darius, who received the little burden as carefully as he would the most precious of gifts.

Darius blinked down at the child, who was gurgling happily in his arms. He snugged the blankets around that cherubic little face and resisted mightily the urge to hug the infant in a crushing embrace. When he looked up, he saw Val Windham grinning at him from across the church's front terrace, and the sight was bracing.

"Greetings," Darius addressed the baby. *Welcome to life. I'm your father, and the luckiest, most blessed man alive.* He cleared his throat and tried again. "You look to be in good spirits today, my lord."

The baby caught Darius's nose in a little mitt, and while the other adults babbled on about God knew what, Darius stood there, falling in love and loving it.

Which, before such a crowd, would not do.

"He's strong," Darius said while Vivian reached over and removed the baby's hand.

"He's a little beast," Mrs. Ventnor agreed. "Viv spoils him terribly, but if we're not to while away the day on these steps, we'd best put the baron in his christening gown."

"We'll be along shortly," Ventnor promised. "Mind you don't rile the boy, as it will be a long day for him."

Mrs. Ventnor took the baby from Darius, and it was all he could do not to knock her aside and clutch the child to his chest. "Come, Viv," Mrs. Ventnor said. "We'll explain to the guest of honor he's not to cast his accounts all over Mr. Lindsey's lovely attire."

The women moved off, while Darius wondered how much of being a parent to Wilhelm Fordham was going to be about partings—from the boy, from his mother, from dreams and other possibilities.

For the service, Will was a little saint, going to sleep in his father's arms, the trust of such a thing being enough to fell Darius all over with its sweetness and gravity. Mrs. Ventnor had to nudge Darius to say his little parts, so fascinated was he by the baby he held. Vivvie had been right; the child was perfect.

Perfect, healthy, adorable, and asleep.

And so small. When it was over, Mrs. Ventnor excused herself to find her husband and sister, leaving Darius, lucky, lucky Darius, holding the baby.

"Makes a fellow pause," Val Windham said, peering down at the child. "To think you and I were once that small, that vulnerable."

"That innocent," Darius said. "That precious."

"I'm still precious," Val said, looking oddly sober. "To Their Graces, my siblings, their spouses and children, I'm precious to them, and they are to me."

This child and his mother were precious to Darius, and if God were merciful, Darius would have a chance to be a meaningful, if minor, presence in his child's life as well.

Precious. He could be a little precious to someone else, and even the idea was enough to make his chest hurt.

"Mr. Lindsey?" Angela Ventnor bustled up to him. "We're off to host the breakfast for the nearest and dearest at our townhouse. If you would see Viv and the baron back to Longstreet House, Viv said she'd try to convince the baby to nap so she could spend a little time off her feet with friends and family."

"I'd be happy to," Darius said. "Lord Val, will you accompany us?"

Val gave him a fleeting look of puzzlement, but nodded. "You carry Himself. He's been too good for too long, and there will be consequences."

"Viv brought extra nappies for the baron," Angela said, patting the baby's blanket. "You two gentlemen must come along with her and put your appetites to the test. Mr. Ventnor has laid in sufficient provisions for a campaigning army."

"It's always my fault." Ventnor smiled at his wife, a man in love ten years after speaking his vows. "Come along, my dear. Christenings work up an appetite."

Such casual domesticity, and yet to hear it and know these people would be part of Will's life was comforting. Darius lifted his gaze from the baby in his arms to see Val regarding him with a curious smile.

"Do not smirk at me, Windham. Go fetch my coach, and I'll retrieve Vivvie."

"Vivvie?" The smile turned into a grin, while Darius grimaced at his mistake.

"Her ladyship. We'll meet you outside."

Val peered down at the baby and back up at Darius, as if looking for resemblance. Darius bore the scrutiny, both dreading and hoping Val might see some.

"On second thought, give me the baron," Val said. "He and I will be outside, charming the ladies. This does not mean you are to be inside doing likewise."

"Go." Darius said, parting with his son—that he should give the boy into Valentine's keeping made it marginally less difficult. He spotted Vivian sitting at the back of the church. A nattily dressed middle-aged man was bent low, whispering in her ear, and Vivian's expression was carefully blank.

A parliamentary crony of William's, haranguing her over her husband's absence, perhaps? But no, Vivian would handle that easily. This had to be her stepfather. Darius quickened his pace.

"Lady Longstreet?" He inserted himself beside her pew, causing the man bothering her to take a step back. "If you're ready to go, the carriage and your son are waiting."

"I don't believe we've been introduced," the other man said. "I consider my daughter's welfare my concern, so all in her ambit are of interest to me."

Vivian rose and handled the introductions, but Darius barely heard her words. She was pale, more pale than she'd been earlier in the morning, and a mask was over her features that spoke more to upset than fatigue.

"If you'll excuse us, Mr. Ainsworthy." Darius tucked Vivian's hand over his arm. "Her ladyship is anxious to get the baron home."

"Vivian." Ainsworthy lifted her other hand and bowed over it, so each man had a grasp of one of her hands. "You will take my words to heart this time."

The fool made it sound like a scold, which was reason enough for Darius to loathe him.

"Thurgood. My thanks for your felicitations."

Darius led her away, though he could feel Ainsworthy's stare boring into his back. "What an unfortunate example of a stepfather," Darius remarked. "Is he always given to such melodrama?"

She ignored him, or hadn't heard him. Unease crept across the warmth in Darius's heart, an emotional cloud on an otherwise sunny morning. A superstitious man would have said somebody walked over his grave.

They collected the baby from Val, who elected to ride up with the coachy, and Darius situated mother and baby in his conveyance. He presumed on the day's benevolence by taking a place beside Vivian on the forward-facing seat.

"I can take the baby, Vivvie, and you can close your eyes for a bit."

Paternal of him, but William's admonition to look after mother and child rang in Darius's ears. He'd take care of them, he'd love them, and when the coach got to Longstreet House, he'd somehow find a way to say good-bye to them too.

"Darius—" Vivian turned her face into his shoulder.

He didn't think. He wrapped an arm around her, the only comfort he had to offer. "Don't cry, Vivvie. The day has been trying, I know, but we'll get you off your feet…"

She was shaking her head from side to side, and to Darius she didn't look like she was holding the baby so much as clutching the infant to her chest. Alarm threatened his composure, but he kept his voice steady. "Vivvie, talk to me. Tell me what's amiss."

"Thurgood. Thurgood recognized your coach. He knows I visited you last year, and he says you're Will's father. He says he *knows* you're Will's father, and, Darius, he'll use that knowledge to take this baby from me."

❧

Childbirth was painful, but that pain was productive, bringing forth a precious new life. The suffering that engulfed Vivian in that comfortable traveling coach had no purpose and no end.

She cried while Darius held her, and then cried because he *was* holding her, the child tucked between them. Her tears were for William, for Darius, and for herself—most of them were for herself.

Darius passed her a handkerchief, one with his soothing, exotic scent. She let him take the

child—perhaps the last time he'd hold his own son—
and tried to sit up.

"I can hold you both, Vivvie."

Vivvie. Nobody called her that, in just that caressing
tone, except Darius.

"I'm sorry. I'm not typically lachrymose." She
would be apologizing for a lot before she got out of
the coach.

"You are exhausted, William is dying, and your
reptile of a former stepfather has overset you. Talk
to me."

How fierce he sounded. That fierceness had drawn
her to him; it would let him hate her eventually. "I
understand something now."

He waited. He was ever patient with her.

"I understand how hard it was for you to turn away
from me, to show me indifference and disdain because
it was the only way you could protect me." She
glanced at the baby sleeping in the crook of Darius's
arm. "To protect the child."

"Our child." He spoke softly but not casually.

Vivian closed her eyes and inhaled Darius's scent.
The moment called for ruthlessness, not sentiment,
and certainly not honest sentiments like Darius had
just uttered.

"Thurgood has acquired literary aspirations. He is
penning a tale about an aging lord's young wife being
taken advantage of by her husband and a dashing rake.
He will share this tale with any number of publishers
and scandal sheets. He is considering drafting a second
version, about a young wife rescued by a noble old
peer from a dire fate, only to play her husband false.

When the truth of her selfish folly is revealed, all of Society condemns her, as well they should."

She expected Darius to withdraw his arm. If anything, his hold became more secure. This suggested he had yet to grasp her point.

"Darius, William told me last night that his will is written such that whomever I marry in the first three months following William's death will become Wilhelm's guardian. If I fail to marry in that time, Able becomes the guardian by default. William is confident Able will not take the child from me, but I think—" She stopped. *This was Darius.* "I *fear* William underestimates the mischief Portia could wreak. She became quite close with Thurgood during her stay in London."

A beat of quiet went by while the horses clip-clopped along. Vivian noticed they'd slowed to a sedate walk, indicating Darius had signaled the coachy at some point in her fit of the weeps.

"So you will permit Ainsworthy to choose your next husband, Vivian, is that it?"

Now his tone conveyed the detached consideration of a man who'd endured many beatings—all without flinching—while Vivian's throat ached with more tears. The consequences Ainsworthy would bring down on them all if she married Darius were unthinkable, and yet Darius was the only man she could envision sharing her life with.

"Thurgood says it will be a decent match, and unless my husband sets me aside, I'm likely to share a household with my son. If it means I see the child for fifteen minutes before tea each day, Darius, if it means

I get letters from him when he's at school… I will not abandon my son. I cannot."

"Our son." He imbued the words with a touch more steel. "It seems you have become a lioness, Vivian."

"I have become a mother." Darius had given her that, and now she must refuse him even the crumbs of the paternal banquet due a child's father.

More silence. The coach made yet another turn, confirming Vivian's suspicion they were walking in a circle.

"I have been a whore, Vivian"—the chill in Darius's voice was arctic—"and I have learned things plying my trade, so please heed me: your husband will be Thurgood's creature entirely. Thurgood will hold the man's vowels, his secrets, something, and through this husband of yours, all of your wealth and all of your happiness will rest in Thurgood's hands."

Darius paused and surveyed her with what looked like pity. "Your husband will resent that, and he will be the man to sire your other children. Count on that. He will couple with you because it is his right, and the only way he can compete with Thurgood's influence under his own roof. This is how sexual commerce works in the hands of those who trade in such things."

"You must not—"

He went on speaking with a precision and gravity that might have been gentle, except for the meaning of his words. "These men will control your fate, which may be your choice to make, but they will also control the welfare of an innocent child—his wealth, his happiness. We brought that child into the world, and his welfare is our responsibility."

Ah, God. She had bargained for this. She had chosen Darius Lindsey because he would protect his loved ones, and now she would destroy him as none of his harpies ever could.

"Darius, listen to me. Thurgood already has that control. He saw me getting out of this coach when I left Surrey. He knows this coach, he can describe the brass fittings on the lamps, and now he knows the coach is yours. If I thwart him, he will ruin you, me, William, and the child's entire life. I cannot allow that."

"So what you want is for me to slink away, a dog whipped by Thurgood's threats? A man who abandons the people entrusted to his care?"

She could not make her mouth form the word "yes," not when it struck her like a thunderclap that Darius had prostituted himself to provide for John and the collection of castoffs that formed the staff at Averett Hill. There was nothing, *nothing* Darius would not do to protect his loved ones.

"This is how it will be, Vivian: Someday, years hence, you will manage to get word to me that I might see the boy playing in the park with his governess. After lurking like a smuggler awaiting the wrecker's signal, I will have a few minutes to observe the child from a distance, and your husband will learn of it. You will not be punished directly—the child will be. Why do you think my father beat me so enthusiastically every time my mother danced with the wrong man?"

She turned her face into his shoulder, wishing she could bolt from the coach. The magnitude of the suffering he'd endured, the magnitude of the suffering he forecast, was unfathomable. "Then you must not lurk, and I must not signal you."

He heaved up a sigh. She knew, from their first month together, the exact contours and rhythm of his sighs. She both hoped and feared that his sigh had held the beginning of capitulation, maybe not total—the looming loss must be grieved—though it was the start of a consideration of surrender.

Why did she feel only despair where relief ought to be? "You can tell the coachy to take us home, Darius. I think we've said all there is to say on the matter." All they could bear to say.

He made no sign he'd heard her. He was instead regarding the baby, who'd whimpered with some baby-dream-induced distress.

"Hush, child." Darius cradled the child closer and ran his nose over Will's little cheek—when had she surrendered the baby into Darius's embrace? "You're safe. I'm here."

A heart could break over and over. Vivian had known that, watching William miss his beloved spouse, day after day, night after night. She'd gained a deeper understanding of it since meeting Darius, and today heartbreak pressed in on her from all sides.

"You trusted me, Vivian, as the man who could hold confidences that would affect the life of an innocent child." He glanced down at her, then back at the baby, his expression pensive. "You trusted me as your paramour. I think you trusted me as your friend—I hope you did."

What was he about? "I did—I do."

. Another silence, while Vivian wished and wished and told herself to give up wishing once and for all.

"Do you recall a certain night?" He swallowed and glanced away, out the window to where the lovely streets of Mayfair were showing to good advantage on a mild fall day.

She knew immediately where his thoughts had gone. "I gave you pleasure. You barely allowed it."

He nodded once. "That night, I could not allow it, because I was not worthy of such a gift. My shame was without limit, eating at me like a disease. As a sop to my pride—and isn't it curious how shame and pride can get along so well?—you pretended you were taking liberties. I knew better."

This had something to do with calling himself a prostitute and with a lurking accusation that Thurgood was going to back Vivian into the same role—the same fate.

"Go on."

"You were not on a casual erotic adventure, Vivian. You were making love to me. You were stating, in unequivocal terms, that no matter what I thought of *myself*, you would hold me in higher regard. I wanted, I want, that regard. Your generosity, your stubbornness, your goodness have prompted all manner of changes in my life—hard changes, but changes for the good. I am determined to be worthy of your regard, and for this reason—"

He closed his eyes. His throat worked. Vivian wanted to stop his words, and yet he spoke his truth to her, a truth she rejoiced to hear.

"For this reason, I can abandon neither the child

nor you to Thurgood's avarice and perversity. You trusted me before Vivian, in many regards, but can't you trust me as the father of your child?"

⁂

Vivian was watching his mouth, probably marveling at the fancies a grown man could spew when he was desperate and holding his only child for what could be the last time.

"What are you asking me, Darius? I would trust you with my life, and with Will's. I think William has done exactly that, but Thurgood is depraved. My mother couldn't see it, but he forged her signature on a power of attorney as casually as you'd scrawl your regrets to a Venetian breakfast."

And *that* was the man Vivian would entrust herself to for the sake of the child?

"I have consulted the finest legal minds in the City, Vivian. There is nothing Thurgood can do to affect Will's claim on the title. William posted a birth notice in every newspaper in the capital, signed birth announcements with his own hand, sent personal correspondence to his friends and familiars rejoicing at the birth of his son."

"How do you know this?"

"He wrote to me too, couching the letter as a request to serve as the boy's godfather, based on the friendship and respect earned in all our varied dealings." Those were William's words: *your honorable comportment in all our varied dealings*. Darius carried the letter with him everywhere and read it frequently.

"William said I was not to worry. I wish he'd told me."

Would she have agreed to such a letter? It argued loudly for allowing Darius to at least visit his godson, if nothing else.

"William does not want this child raised by a stranger of Thurgood's choosing." He had no right to add his own protestation, though it killed him to keep the words behind his teeth.

"We are going in circles, Darius. Angela and Jared will wonder if you've abducted me."

The thought had fleeting appeal. Darius thumped on the roof twice, and the horses shifted into a trot. He resettled his arm around Vivian's shoulders. "You'll allow me to deal with Thurgood?"

She was quiet for so long he wondered if she'd answer. Her gaze was on the child, who—bless the boy—had slept for the entire journey. "You love that child, Darius Lindsey. You just met him today, and you love him."

He loved the child and the child's mother. The two loves were tangled up, reinforcing each other and lighting dim places in a soul that had dwelt too long in shadows. To say such a thing to her in those words would be unfair, also unwise.

"I tried not to, Vivvie. You were a new roof. Will was fresh marl for all my pastures, and security for John. I find I am not as resolute in these matters as I ought to be."

A hint, the barest dawn-streak of a smile graced her features then faded. She spoke slowly, her gaze returning to the baby. "We have some time. William yet lives. Thurgood will do nothing while my husband is alive, and Dr. Garner assured me it's quite possible William will make a full recovery."

No, it was not. The handwriting and content of last month's letter from William had conveyed waning strength of will as much as waning health.

"We can but hope." That from a man who regarded hope as the last monster to escape from Pandora's box, at least until recently.

"No pistols or swords, Darius. Thurgood will not observe any rules of fair conduct. He'll have you stabbed in the back in some dark alley, and then be all sympathy and smiles at your bad fortune."

"He has no honor. I've learned to recognize the type." And he'd learned how to deal with them. "Promise me you won't be alone with him, Vivian. Not in your own front parlor, not on the steps of the church, nowhere. If he comes to call, then the baby is fussy and you cannot spare a moment from the nursery. Promise me."

The expression on her features reminded him of the day he'd stood behind her when she'd faced the mirror, forcing herself to truly see the hideous, calf-scours dress. "I will be from home, I will not let him accost me, and I will give you some time, Darius, to deal with him. I will give you whatever time William can spare us."

The coach bumped around the turn into the alley that led to the Longstreet mews, while Darius tried to content himself with a partial victory. Vivian did not want to put herself in Thurgood's hands, clearly. She wanted Darius to send the bounder packing, but she had to be a lioness in her decisions. Darius had only as long as William lived to find a way to rescue the lady and the child from the grasp of unrelenting evil.

As it happened, this meant he had no time at all.

❧

Muriel's death had been different, or maybe each death was different. When Muriel had died, Vivian's grief had been absorbed in concern for William and his sons. Vivian had been the one fretting over the surviving spouse, the one trying to tend to logistics so Muriel's family could manage their bereavement.

Now Vivian was stumbling through the day, seeing all the places William wasn't, hearing the silences that should have been filled with his voice or the sound of his shuffling gait. Letters of condolence poured in, and Vivian would have sat staring at them except that Darius's sister had shown up and taken Vivian in hand.

Leah, Countess of Bellefonte, embraced Vivian with the sturdy snugness Vivian had associated exclusively with Darius, whom she'd seen only fleetingly in the week since the christening. They'd arrived at Longstreet house to find Dilquin quietly distrait, William having slipped away during the christening itself.

Darius had managed the immediate, unthinkable logistics, instructed the servants to find the black armbands and air the crepe, ordered the death notice delayed by a day so as not to overshadow the christening, and arranged for Angela to come to Vivian's side.

And then he had disappeared, though Leah assured her he would attend the final services out in Oxfordshire.

This was some comfort, but not enough. Not when twice Vivian had remained above stairs while Dilquin had turned Thurgood away. The strictures applicable to early mourning meant she wouldn't be venturing onto the street such that he could waylay her in public, but even those strictures expected a woman to attend services.

Thurgood had already accosted her in a house of worship once, putting Vivian in mind of all the times the women Darius so loathed had come upon him without warning.

How had he borne it? How had he borne it without doing them bodily harm?

Vivian missed Darius terribly with a low, ferocious ache that included fear for his welfare and abject terror regarding the future. She missed William, too, even as she admitted relief that his suffering was at an end, and greater relief that Darius had sent Lady Leah and her exceptionally robust husband to stand watch over Vivian—and over the baby. From a woman, there was a different kind of comfort, and Vivian treasured the generosity of it.

Lady Leah made lists: There were notes to write, flowers to order, notices to send out, and crepe to arrange about the house on mirrors, portraits, and windows. Leah also oversaw the transformation of Vivian's wardrobe, and prevented the entire lot from being dyed an ugly, flat black.

She gave the servants orders Vivian could only guess at, and had Vivian's trunks packed for the journey to Longchamps, where William would be buried with his wife and sons.

❧

"This is perfect."

Thurgood Ainsworthy looked over the letter

supposedly sent by Mr. Able Springer, though the hand was Portia's.

"Did you say something, Good?" His wife rolled over and blinked innocent blue eyes at him, but at thirty-three, Ariadne was showing some wear. Fine lines radiated out from her eyes when the morning sun hit her face, and a softness would soon creep in under her chin.

Ah, well, another year or two and Thurgood could be looking for a bride elsewhere, his pockets full of the settlements Vivian would bring him when he sold her to her next spouse. A cit this time, or a nabob. Some grasping fellow who needed the cachet of a pretty, fertile, titled wife.

Thurgood set the letter aside and settled back among the pillows of a truly enormous bed. On more than one occasion—Ariadne occasionally visited her sister in Hampshire—Thurgood had been joined in that bed by no less than three other women at the same time. A man needed ingenuity to keep them all occupied, and Thurgood prided himself on an abundance of ingenuity.

He ran a hand over Ariadne's plump breast. "Would you mind if Vivian came to stay with us for a bit once William's will has been read? She's a new widow, and all the Longstreet properties hold sad memories for her. The boy will likely be in Able Springer's keeping, and Vivian will be at loose ends."

"Vivian?" Another blink. "Whatever you say, Good. You're decent to look out for her this way."

"She's family," Thurgood said, giving Ariadne's nipple a tweak. "Our duty is clear, and I wouldn't think of turning my back on her. Now, roll over, love, get that pillow under you, and spread your legs for me."

"My stomach, Good?" There was a hint of peevishness in her tone, just a hint.

"Unless you want more children to spoil your lovely figure, my sweet."

He'd realized long ago that his wife looked a little like Vivian, though Ariadne was afflicted with neither Vivian's independence of spirit nor much native intelligence. She could bear a prodigious grudge, though, which meant the marriage offered at least a nominal challenge to a man of broad and varied amorous interests.

Thurgood passed her a pillow, closed his eyes, pictured his stepdaughter's lush figure, and envisioned a pleasant and well-heeled future drawing ever closer—for him.

Eighteen

A TAP ON VIVIAN'S DOOR INTERRUPTED HER MIDPACE before her fire.

"Vivvie?" Very softly.

She went to the door and drew Darius into her sitting room by the wrist when he would have malingered in the corridor. For the three days since William's interment, the dratted man had lurked at Longchamps like a curate in training, barely addressing her and never lingering in the same room with her. She had stooped to desperate measures and put a note in his hand before retiring after dinner.

"I wasn't sure you would come, blast you and all your decorum." Perhaps a widow ought not to speak thus, and perhaps a widow ought not to plaster herself against a man with whom she was wroth.

His arms tightened around her with comforting speed. "Are you well, Vivvie? You barely said a word at tea. Is the baby all right?"

She put her hand over his mouth and resumed clinging to him. "You're leaving tomorrow. Were you simply going to bow over my hand and condole me on my loss again, Darius?"

In her own voice, Vivian heard exasperation bordering on panic. Even lionesses were entitled to exasperation.

He stepped back and kept his hands on her shoulders. "My condolences are sincere. You're up and down all night with the baby, you have my sister and her husband underfoot as guests, Thurgood lurks we know not where, and I would not trespass on your bereavement."

She searched his gaze, but he enfolded her against him before her scrutiny revealed any new insights. "You spend a great deal of time in the nursery, Darius."

"Nicholas does too. He likes babies." There was bemusement in this observation, suggesting the baby enjoyed having two grown men fuss at him.

"Will is sleeping more, going longer without waking at night."

Darius turned her under his arm and walked her toward her bedroom. "He's growing, so he can take more at a feeding, but you did not summon me here to brag about your son, Vivvie."

"You called him our son, not long ago."

Without her quite intending it, they ended up sitting on the bed. Or maybe she had intended, had wished for it—for almost a year.

Darius laced his fingers with hers. "In my heart, he is our son. He's William's son too, and yours. I have not yet put Thurgood to rout, Vivvie, if that's the point of this interview. I have plans in train, and I'm repairing to Town to see to their completion."

"I do not want a status report, Darius." She was

being cranky, like a teething baby, turning away every attempt at solace.

He pushed her braid back over her shoulder, not a caress, more of a comfort. "What do you want, Vivian?"

You.

She didn't apologize for the notion. William was gone, and while she had loved him, she'd never loved him the way a wife loved a husband. William—so devoted to his Muriel—was the last person who'd castigate her for her feelings.

"I want to see something in your eyes other than concern, Darius. I don't want you watching me carefully, as if I might lapse into strong hysterics over my tea." And damn the catch in her voice that said his concern wasn't misplaced. If Darius could not silence Thurgood and his threats, strong hysterics were a certainty.

"Your room is chilly, Vivvie. Let's get you under the covers." He rose off the bed all too easily.

He was attempting to cosset her. She was going to wallop him. "I'm not getting under these covers without you."

He paused in the act of lifting her covers. Paused and swallowed, then swung his gaze back to her face, carefully, as if not sure what he'd find there. "You're bereaved, Vivian. I would not want to take advantage."

His gaze moved over her, a blink-and-she'd-miss-it inventory that for just two consecutive instants revealed banked longing.

"You're grieving, too." That longing—so stark and sincere—had been a balm to Vivian's soul and restored to her heaps of patience and understanding she hadn't been able to locate a minute earlier. "All I'm asking is that you hold me, Darius."

She had the sense that was all she could ask, that if she begged him to take off his clothes, to bring the candles closer to the bed, to make passionate love to her, she would exceed the fragile limits of his self-imposed standards of… something.

Decency? For he was decent.

Or perhaps they were the standards of martyrdom—which thought made her ill on his behalf.

He moved around the room, dousing candles, banking the fire, pouring a glass of water from the pitcher and setting it on the night table while Vivian watched him.

Darius Lindsey was a man like any other, one whom exigencies had forced into indecent bargains, but underneath it all, a highly decent man, a painfully decent man. Maybe that was why she'd given her heart, her happiness, and the well-being of her child into his keeping.

"Come to bed, Darius. I will think you have taken me into dislike now that I am no longer married to another." The jest fell utterly flat, an occasion when bald truth arrived uninvited to the middle of a conversation.

He paused, two buttons away from removing his waistcoat. "Is that what you think? You think because I attempt to demonstrate my respect for your loss that my regard has changed?"

The idea intrigued him, clearly.

"I think I have lost William, and he was ready to go and deserving of a peaceful end, but I do not want—"

Oh, damn. Damn, and damn, and if she'd known any worse words, she would have thought them too. Bad enough when truth appeared uninvited in a conversation, how much worse when it popped up in the middle of a very sentence.

"Vivvie?" He was there next to her, that fear-of-strong-hysterics look replaced by simple, tender concern. "You can tell me, Vivvie. You can tell me anything."

She could. She could bear his child; she could put herself under his protection; she could give him her truths. "I do not want to lose you too. Not for anything, and yet Thurgood will ruin Will's life unless I give you up—unless we give each other up."

His reply was gratifyingly swift and certain. "You won't lose me." He lifted his waistcoat over his head, tossed it toward the clothespress, and started on his shirt buttons. "You will never, ever lose me. Even if you tried, you could not lose me. You shall not lose me."

Vows. He was spouting vows and tossing his clothing in all directions, both of which reassured Vivian mightily. "You should have a care for your clothing, Darius."

His stockings went sailing. One caught on a chair; the other landed on her vanity. "Hang the bloody clothing, Vivvie. I can afford new now. That dressing gown can go. Shall I help you with it?"

Would he also remove his breeches? "No, thank you."

She was out of her dressing gown and sitting on the bed by the time he stood before her, naked, beautiful, and smiling at her. "It's up to you, Vivvie. The nightgown can go or it can stay, but be assured, what's under it now is far more dear to me than what lay beneath it last December."

She looked away, deprived herself of all that masculine pulchritude in the interests of preserving a smidgen of dignity. "You are entirely too knowing, Mr. Lindsey. I have borne a child and am not—"

He stepped closer, close enough that the unique, soothing, spicy scent of him came to her, and close enough that his groin appeared in her line of sight. He was becoming aroused. This reassured too, but it intimidated a trifle as well.

"You're not," he said, tipping her chin up. "You're not that young woman, and I'm not that man. Did you find me attractive all those months ago, Vivian?"

"Yes." *Intimidatingly so.*

"Am I more attractive now? You know exactly the manner of person with whom I consorted, you know exactly how I allowed them to use me, you know what I took coin for, though it was arguably criminal of me to do so and certainly stupid. Am I attractive to you now?"

She did as she had once before, sat on the bed and wrapped her arms around his waist so she could press her face to the place beneath his heart. "If I knew more bad words, Darius Lindsey, I would be saying them to make you hush. You are not a criminal. You are not stupid. Yes, you are more attractive to me than ever. I look at you and lose my wits. I look at you and thank God you indulged in all those things you said—with me."

Confession enough, apparently. His hand landed on her nape. "Then, you ridiculous, lovely woman, do you think my desire for you could ever be less than consuming? You risked your life to bring my child into the world, Vivian. You are beautiful to me, and you always will be."

He was holding something back, though Vivian was too muddled to parse it out exactly. She let it go, lest he make an inspection tour of her lactating breasts, the slight belly she still sported, the circles of fatigue more prone to show up under her eyes. His argument could be made in the general case rather than example by example.

It was a convincing argument, she realized. He was dear to her in all his imperfections, and he was honest. The erection rising against the slope of her breast was convincing as well.

"Our son will be hounding you for sustenance soon enough, Vivian. Get under the covers."

"I like it when you talk like that," she said, doing as he'd bid. "You haven't acquired much shyness since last we shared a bed."

He climbed in after her, the feel of him spooned around her comforting, comfortable, and dear. "I have acquired one son, a far better addition to my treasures. Now tell me how long you can stand to have Leah and Nick underfoot."

He rubbed her back, he petted her hair, he let her talk and talk, and all the while, Vivian was aware of his arousal pressing against her from behind, warm, smooth, and wonderfully, undeniably hard.

❧

Darius told himself he was taking advantage, desperate, reckless advantage by being intimate with Vivian now, and yet, the dear, exasperating woman would not oblige him by falling asleep. She deserved comfort, and by God, he would comfort her.

She'd had time to heal physically from the birth— Darius had consulted both a physician and a midwife on those particulars—but she had dealt with so much.

The mill wheel of anxiety, hope, and gratitude that was his mind of late came to a halt when Vivian's fingers found his cock.

He could spend, just from having her touch him, he could spend.

God save him. "You need not trouble yourself with that, Vivian. If you aren't recovered from your lying in, you have only to say so, and I would not want you to think—" Not think he'd desired her every minute he'd been with her and every minute he hadn't? "I'm sorry, Vivvie, but William is dead, and we are not, and I just—"

He brushed his mouth over her nape. "Please, Vivvie for the love of God, say something." He was glad she couldn't see his face, though he desperately wanted to see hers, so he rearranged them on the mattress, facing each other.

"Darius Lindsey, I will not allow you to make love to me."

She sounded damnably determined on that point. Woe unto him who seeks to turn a lady into a lioness, and yet, he could not quite turn loose of her. She had invited him into bed, after all.

"Of course, you won't." He managed not to sound as emotionally strangled as he felt. She wanted him in her bed, but she did not want him intimately. This was what he deserved, for getting into so many beds where all that was wanted of him was a casual romp.

While he tried reciting the royal succession in the interests of his composure, Vivian wrested herself from his embrace, pushed him to his back, and straddled him.

God in heaven, she was magnificent. Mother, goddess, lady—and something more than all three rolled into one, and now—now—she was refusing his overtures.

Comfort for her, torment for him. A fair enough bargain.

Her lips grazed over his mouth. "You may not make love to me now, but I should be very pleased to make love to you, Mr. Lindsey."

The sense of her soft words, emphasized by that sweet kiss, sank in, and joy flooded his being despite the looming difficulties, despite all that remained unsettled.

I should be very pleased to make love to you, Mr. Lindsey. Very pleased.

For the first time in his life, Darius was going to be intimate with a woman he loved, a woman he adored, and could come to as a whole man, offering himself to her without conditions, reservations, or hesitation.

For a succession of moments, he was content to hold her, and she—wise lady—allowed it. She wore the scent he'd had blended for her. The realization was *very pleasing* to him, even as the subtle, spicy fragrance wafted into his awareness. Other impressions came to him, impressions he treasured because they marked a moment he wanted always to remember: her body under his caressing hand was different, of course, rounder, softer, and more lovely.

The room had grown cozy, which was good when

two people were likely to toss back the covers and make passionate love in the next moments. The hour was well past dark but not late, and that was good too, because the baby—their son, Will—would give them time to pursue their passions at length and at leisure.

Desire for her flared up as she kissed him again. "Will you allow me to make love to you, Darius?"

"You must do with me as you wish, Vivvie. I am your willing slave."

To be able to say those words, to let them occupy a place of uncomplicated flirtation between him and a woman who was intent on having her way with his person took a weight off his heart, and yet, Vivian shook her head.

"Not slave, Darius. Neither of us should be enslaved to the other, not ever. You are my love, and I am yours."

"Your *love*." The term was ardent, simple, and accurate. The last part of his heart, the part that had been trying to maintain some hold on sense and perspective, to think not of the night's passion but the cold possibilities of the coming dawn, tumbled into Vivian's keeping for all time.

She caressed his cock with her damp sex.

"Vivvie, I won't survive—"

Her smile as she used the end of her braid to tease his nipples was pure female mischief. "We'll get through this, Mr. Lindsey. You have my promise on that."

Her promise in exchange for his hands on her breasts. The bargains were improving.

Her breasts, lovely before, were fuller now. Her

figure had gone from perfect to the proportions of a goddess, and most spectacular of all, she was allowing him to gaze his fill, to note each change and all that was so wonderfully familiar.

"I have never, not ever, beheld so much beauty at once, Vivian. You are—"

Words failed. He was new at this, at making love as opposed to having relations. Oh, he'd made love to her before—from the first he'd been making love to her—but now she was to make love to him.

She leaned close enough to kiss his cheek. He used her braid to bring her down onto his chest, where he could hold her for a moment and catch his emotional breath.

He was nervous, as anxious as he was aroused, and yet, there was no reason for it. Vivian wanted only to give to him, and he to her. This was not a realization; rather, it bore the luminosity of revelation.

"You mustn't be too fierce with me, Vivvie. Be careful and tender. There's time for unbridled passion later." He prayed there would be, but a man didn't presume, not when his name was Darius Lindsey, and Thurgood Ainsworthy was lurking like the bad fairy in a child's storybook tale.

She levered up to eye him curiously. "Because it's the first time after the birth?"

He answered a question with a question. "I was your first, wasn't I, Vivvie? Your very first?"

He dreaded her reply—hadn't ever wanted to ask her for this truth because either answer was fraught with emotional peril.

"You were, and I'm glad you were. Very glad."

He loved her, he trusted her, and he'd asked for her trust in return. He shifted to lay his hands on the pillow on either side of his head, to be vulnerable. When she laced her fingers with his, he had to close his eyes. "I'm glad too, because this is my first time. Right now, with you. My very first."

He did not dare open his eyes for fear she was laughing at him. The notion was ridiculous, that he could be unsullied by his past, but she didn't laugh. She didn't tease or mock. Darius felt her hand smoothing over his heart like a benediction. "You have the right of it, Darius. We will be tender with each other."

As many different ways as he'd made love with her the previous year—every way he'd known how to, and a few he'd stumbled upon only with her—this time was different. Vivian kept him on his back, the position in which he had the least to do, except to use his hands, and mouth, and body as he pleased.

He mapped her treasures with his fingers and palms, then again with his mouth. He gave her all the soft words and silly promises; he teased and even tickled, though that came to a halt when she tickled him back.

They were unhurried, and while shadows lurked in the room, they weren't the shadows of a permanent parting, or of guilt, remorse, or self-loathing. They were shadows many couples faced: the unknown, the challenges lying between them and a happily ever after, the worry any parents would feel for their child.

Vivian straddled Darius's hips and took his swollen shaft in her hand. "You've stalled long enough, my love. I must have you now." Her eyes had a feline glitter, determination and tenderness combined.

"Then put me where you want me, Vivian. Put me where I need to be."

Her control was impressive—also damnably frustrating. She braced herself over him, joining their bodies by the merest lazy increments. Darius watched himself disappearing into her heat and felt his sanity evaporating as they became more and more intimate.

"Faster, Vivvie, please."

She complied, though not by much. From some reserve of female wisdom, she was going to hold back, and hold back, until—

He did not groan, he *shouted*, the hoarse surrender of a man thrown headlong into pleasures of a nigh terrifying depth. While Vivian rocked and keened with him, Darius felt as if his body were becoming weightless, a pure light that merged with Vivian until they were one incandescent being, without end, without name, without limit.

And very nearly without breath.

As he panted in counterpoint with his lover—his *lover*—Darius had the satisfaction of realizing she was as wrung out as he was. And yet, they'd been tender—excruciatingly, wonderfully, miraculously tender. A whole new variety of tenderness formerly beyond his ken, one he never wanted to lose his grasp of.

He kissed her temple. "Are you all right?"

She swiped her tongue over his nipple—just the once. *Yes.* While Vivian fell asleep on his chest, Darius treated himself to another inventory of her person. Her hair was a wonder, thicker and even softer than it had been a year ago. This was supposedly a function of childbearing, though Darius hoped excellent nutrition and adequate rest had played a role too.

Her features were a trifle sharper—he could confirm with his touch what his eyes had suggested—and her breasts were both heavier and more sensitive than they had been before she'd conceived.

What he ought to have done was tuck her in, then leave her alone to catch up on much needed sleep before the nurse brought Will in for a middle-of-the-night feeding. What he ought to have done was blow out all the candles Vivian had left burning—the better to display her wares for him—and slip away.

He was never going to slip away again. If he had the pleasure of sharing her bed again, he would not leave her unless it was after a proper good night. This resolution bore the clarity of a vow, one he made happily to himself and to Vivian—despite all of Ainsworthy's schemes to the contrary.

He eased their bodies apart, spooned himself around her, and fell asleep holding his lover, the mother of his child.

❧

Vivian cocked her head, regarding Darius over her teacup. "You look different to me." He'd wanted to accompany her to the nursery for both night feedings, but grudgingly agreed to keep the bed warm for her when she pointed out that three footmen and a nursery maid would see him escorting her through the house.

"I am without my clothes," Darius said. "One hopes that to be a change from my usual condition."

He sounded—chipper. Not merely brisk and

energetic, but eager for the day, which was both novel and intriguing.

"Are you going to leave me any breakfast at all, Mr. Lindsey?"

"I'll have another tray sent up when I take my leave of you, but, Vivvie, I must know your position on the question of the day."

He passed her half a buttered scone and—just when she might have taken a bite—snatched it away and slathered it with raspberry jam.

"Which question?" This time, she took the scone from his hand. "I seem to recall refusing your offer of lovemaking last night."

And the devastation in his eyes when he'd thought she was refusing *him* had been heart wrenching. Soldiers too long at war had eyes with that bleak look, women who grieved for their children… "You are asking for my leave to deal with Ainsworthy, aren't you? It's why you must repair to Town before the will is read."

Darius topped up her teacup—the tray was resting across his thighs—and settled back against the pillows.

And everlasting God, did she like the look of him in her bed.

"I will deal with Ainsworthy, with or without your permission, Vivvie. I'd rather have your permission."

Deal with, when uttered by Darius in those tones, with that light in his eyes, was not a pleasant prospect at all—for Ainsworthy. The day was getting off to a lovely start indeed. "Not the pistols or swords sort of 'deal with,' Darius. I haven't budged on that. I cannot condone killing."

Nor could she condone any notion that lessened

the chances she and Darius might eventually share a future with their child.

He slathered butter on yet another scone—one had to wonder if the kitchen weren't already privy to the number of the bedroom's occupants—and looked thoughtful. "I can promise you I will not kill him. He has a wife and a stepson, and they are innocent of his schemes."

Vivian thought back to Darius's words from the night before, his eyes closed, his hands clasping hers tightly, "…because it's my first time."

Her lover was courageous to a fault, dear, and determined—also the father of their child—and he was *asking* for Vivian's blessing. He could all too easily have sneaked away and proceeded without consulting her.

"You can't trust him, Darius, but I trust you." Simple, simple words, but so very well deserved.

The scone was receiving not a dollop of butter—it would hold no more—but some careful, artistic arrangement of the entire pat with flourishes of the knife edge. "And you can accept the means I propose to bring him to heel? This is not honorable, and the people who have supplied me with the necessary information are not highly regarded. I wouldn't want you to be any more ashamed of me than necessary."

Vivian forgot to chew. He hadn't undertaken this scheme, which had required rubbing elbows with all manner of unfortunates and scoundrels, lightly, and he hadn't shared it with her lightly.

When Darius Lindsey trusted, though, he trusted as fiercely as he cared.

"Darius, you haunt yourself with doubts for no reason. You are the most honorable man I know." At his startled expression, she went on. "I am not ashamed of you, Darius, I am *proud* of you. You found a way to cut those leech-women loose when another man would have turned to violence. You're doing the same with Thurgood, and when dealing with such as these, you have to fashion weapons they understand. I am proud of you, do you hear me?"

He studied her for a moment, then his lips turned up. "I think half the house might have heard you."

She had, indeed, become emphatic in expressing her sentiments. "*Let them*. To answer your question, I do trust you, Darius. I trust Ainsworthy to be cunning, determined, and self-interested. You will best him, because while you are cunning and determined, your motivation is—continues to be—the regard you have for your loved ones."

His smile became a shimmering, glowing embodiment of happiness, and then he surged over her like a slow tide, and once again, very tenderly, made love with her. Before it was over, there was raspberry jam in unlikely locations, much laughter, crumbs between the sheets, butter on the tip of Vivian's nose—Darius licked it away—and a thoroughly agreed-upon plan for dealing with Ainsworthy.

Nineteen

"You might consider warning a man before you have mail delivered to his office." Worth Kettering passed Darius several letters as he spoke.

"I might." Darius took an elegant Louis XIV chair and sorted through the missives. "Except I'm a bit at sixes and sevens these days. My thanks, though. I think this one is the one we've been waiting for." He opened the single folded piece of paper and scanned the contents.

"Game, set, and match." He passed it to Kettering, who took the second seat. "She identifies Ainsworthy right down to the scar on his left earlobe where he tried to pierce himself at the age of sixteen. She says there's another scar on the tip of his..."

Kettering's smile was not nice. "I can read it. The lady has a memory for detail."

"'Hell hath no fury,'" Darius quoted, feeling the first sense of relief he'd known in days. "That's two of them, and I'm ready to confront the man."

"And if he calls you out?" Kettering's tone could not have been more casual. He crossed his feet at the ankles, making the little chair creak. "One doesn't like to brag on such a thing, but I make a fine second."

"I've promised Vivvie I won't meet him over pistols or swords, but if he challenges me, my choice of weapons would be these trusty appendages, and the timing as immediate as I can arrange." Darius held up two clenched fists and met Kettering's gaze.

"You would have made a fine barrister, Lindsey."

"And you mean that as a compliment." Darius abandoned his seat—it had precious little padding for all its elegance—and helped himself to a drop of Kettering's brandy. "This is an interesting letter from Able Springer—it arrived to my address this morning and explains some forged marriage lines he found reposing in his wife's workbasket." He passed the epistle over to Kettering and sipped his drink, finding it very fine potation, indeed.

When he finished reading, Kettering looked up. "Are you ready to take on Longchamps as well as Averett Hill if the man emigrates to America?"

Darius set his glass down and rolled his shoulders. "One feels for Mr. Springer. William didn't tell me Springer's mother was married when she gave birth, which means Able is technically the legitimate issue of some other fellow."

Kettering refolded the letter and set it aside, his expression suggesting he expected it to sprout eight hairy legs momentarily. "So the unfortunate Mr. Springer is married to a woman who forged marriage lines between Longstreet and Springer's mother. I suppose the intended effect was to posthumously label Vivian's son a bastard and visit the viscountcy on Springer."

For which Portia ought to hang, there having been not one dishonorable bone in William Longstreet's body. "Portia was also apparently in ignorance of the circumstances of her husband's birth. The result of her efforts would have been to make Able's mother the bigamist, any marriage between William and her invalid, and William's subsequent marriages would have remained entirely legal. I do not envy you your profession, Kettering, if issues like these are your daily bread."

Kettering spared the letter another chary glance, got up, and made a circuit of the room. While Darius took another sip of brandy, Kettering came to rest with his backside against the windowsill, arms folded. "What will you do?"

He would see that Ainsworthy was effectively silenced, marry Vivvie, and devote himself to raising up their child—their children, God willing.

"I would like to say I'll manage Longchamps for the baron until he's in a position to take it on himself, but that decision still rests in his mother's lovely hands. She has another several weeks to make up her mind about who Will's guardian will be. In those weeks, I shall deal with Ainsworthy in as decisive a manner as possible."

≈

"Your literary aspirations are threatening Vivian's peace of mind, Ainsworthy." Before his guest was seated, Darius closed the parlor-door latch with a soft snick. "Or do we call you Thurmont Ainsward, or perhaps Torvald Ainsely?"

Ainsworthy took a seat amid the comfortable opulence of Wilton House, the London residence of the late, unlamented Earl of Wilton, and present abode of nobody in particular.

"My name is Thurgood Ainsworthy. Says so on my marriage lines, and I'm not threatening anything. I've merely been doing some creative writing and attempting to turn a coin or two on it. I've a wife and child to support. Surely you can understand how that goes, Lindsey? Or do I forget? You had only yourself to support, and yet you still took coin where you could find it."

"Prove that," Darius said easily. "I'm happy to prove you're a scheming bigamist, whatever your name is."

Ainsworthy plucked at some imaginary lint on his sleeve, his self-possession likely the natural by-product of having no conscience. "Names can be very similar. England is a big place, and I'm sure those other fellows don't look a thing like me. Now, how much are you willing to offer should my writing talents be put aside, Lindsey? I'm sure Ventnor would contribute—the cits are inordinately sensitive about these little social tempests. Then, too, I am loathe to queer Vivian's marital prospects unnecessarily. One does, after all, feel some familial loyalty, and scandal could perhaps be profitably avoided."

"Familial loyalty?" Nigh six and a half well-muscled feet of Trenton Lindsey, Earl of Wilton, sauntered into the room. "We understand that, don't we, Darius? Did I hear this man attempt to blackmail you?"

"You did," Darius said, "except he alluded to a

familial connection with Vivian Longstreet, with whom it has not yet been my privilege to form a legal union. Unfortunately for Thoroughgoing Arsewipe here, he was married when he took his vows with Vivian and Angela's widowed mother. This makes his marriage to the countess invalid, his use of her funds fraudulent, his contracting marriage on Angela's behalf equally fraudulent, and the farthest thing from a display of family loyalty."

"Unfortunate," Trent mused. "You know, the magistrate might have caught wind of this. I understand he's signing warrants for the arrest of one... what were all those names you said? I happened to glance at the documents when information was laid, and there were at least five names on them."

"Who is this?" Ainsworthy's tone was dismissive, but his eyes betrayed the first hint of uncertainty.

"Wilton." Trent bowed graciously. "Earl of, at your service, whoever you are. Are you going to call him out, Dare?"

Darius cocked his head. "He's got literary aspirations. I might accidentally blow off his fingers and damage his writing hand rather than put a ball through his black heart."

Ainsworthy rose. "There's no need for violence. This is all a simple misunderstanding, probably the work of some jilted wife who married a man with a name like mine. Or several wives, getting up to nonsense because they aren't properly supervised."

"Is that so?" Nicholas Haddonfield emerged from the hallway. "Several wives, acting in concert, all with husbands who have names like yours?"

"Right." Ainsworthy swallowed audibly at the sight of Nick, who topped Trent by a couple of inches of height and at least two stone of brawn. "If you get descriptions, you'll see the error of your conclusions."

"Nicholas, Earl of Bellefonte." Nick grinned menacingly. "Perhaps the man has a point, Darius. You can't be calling a fellow out on mere whim and speculation."

"Heaven forefend," Trent added, "that any brother of mine react so cavalierly when a man's good name, much less the arrangement of his face, his ability to walk, and possibly his ability to sire children hang in the balance."

"Well, then." Darius lifted a document from the sideboard. "Nick, perhaps you'd assist the man out of his breeches? We can clear this up easily enough."

"Out of my breeches?"

"Rhymes with screeches," Nick said, approaching Ainsworthy. "Interestingly enough. We'll settle this right now, and I'm sure Mr. Lindsey will offer apologies all around if he's wrong."

Trent grimaced, taking Ainsworthy's other arm. "One does wonder how a man would acquire such a scar."

"His wife says"—Darius peered at the document— "his current wife and two previous wives, anyway, say he has a scar on the tip of his cock in the shape of the letter L, running from… what?" He looked over at Ainsworthy, who'd blanched white as ghost.

"Who said I have such a scar?"

"Your present wife, for starters," Darius said slowly, as if the man were simple. "Bellefonte chatted her up with an officer of the court on hand to take her statement. Sweet woman, if a little too trusting, though Bellefonte's charm is legendary. She described your scars, the exact shape of various intimate attributes, and a few other details only a wife would know. And by sheerest coincidence, two other women describe their husbands having precisely the same characteristics. Moreover, we went to the trouble of bringing witnesses to those marriages up to Town, Ainsworthy, and they each identified you by sight as the errant husband.

"Now the strangest coincidence of all." Darius paused, and his tone became flat. "Each woman was well set up until she married you. Her fortune, or as much as she turned over to your keeping, disappeared with you."

"And correct me if I'm wrong," Trent said, "but didn't those women have children to support?"

Nick gave Ainsworthy's arm a nasty little shake. "And wasn't one of them expecting when her dear spouse accompanied the entire harvest of wool into London, never to be seen again?"

"All right!" Ainsworthy glanced nervously from one man to another. "I've been unlucky in love. It's not a crime to leave your wife."

"It isn't," Darius agreed, "though whether you leave or not, she's still your wife, and it is a crime to marry again while the first wife is extant. Moreover, you owe your deserted wife support at all times during the marriage, and you surely owe your own child the same."

"You cannot expect me to sit here and listen to this nonsense," Ainsworthy sputtered.

"You can read the sworn statements," Darius said, "but you won't convince us we're in error without dropping your breeches. You can let him go, gentlemen, though I'd guard the exits."

Nick took one doorway, Trent the other.

Ainsworthy rose, tugging down his waistcoat with a righteous jerk. "Name your seconds, Lindsey. I am at your service."

"Present company. Yours?"

Ainsworthy's chin came up. "That will take some time. Honorable challenges must be handled delicately."

"Well, then, the choice of weapons is mine, I believe. But then, perhaps you'd know more about this than I would?"

"I know about it," Nick said cheerfully. "Choice of weapons goes to the challenged. Time and date at the mutual convenience of the parties, location generally chosen by the seconds for discretion. I'm feeling very discreet right here and now."

"This is a premeditated assault, nothing more," Ainsworthy spat. "Three against one, and the two of you titled and immune from prosecution."

"We're not immune, are we?" Nick looked adorably confused to ponder such a thing.

"Why, no," Trent replied. "We're prosecuted in the Lords, if we're caught, except I'm not sure what our crime would be, since we're not touching the man, are we?"

"I'm not." Nick shrugged massive shoulders. "Darius, what's your pleasure?"

"Either wave the goods before witnesses, Ainsworthy, or name your seconds. Makes no difference to me."

It took another hour, but two men eventually posted from the nearest club, and the matter was taken out to the mews.

"Rules of engagement?" one of Ainsworthy's reluctant seconds asked.

"I won't kill him," Darius said. "Trent, you'll make sure I don't?"

Trent's expression became considering. "You might regret letting him live," he said quietly. "He preys on women and children."

"Don't let me kill him," Darius said, his gaze going from Nick to Trent and back. "Vivvie deserves better than a man who kills with his bare hands, whatever other crimes I've committed."

"All right," Ainsworthy's man said. "You fight until one man is done in, by agreement of the seconds. I have to say, I can't like this."

"You think I'd give him a chance to tamper with my guns?" Darius asked as he began to strip from the waist up. "Or disappear with his present wife's remaining funds? She has a child, by the way, much like her predecessors, though the boy isn't Ainsworthy's get."

"One hopes it wouldn't come to that," the man replied.

"And one hopes it needn't be said," Darius added, "but this is a bare-knuckle fight, no weapons. Not knives, not cravats used to strangle, not rings used to cut."

"A clean fight." The fellow hustled over to Ainsworthy and gestured for Darius's opponent to remove his several rings.

The circle was drawn in the cold dirt, and as will happen, the stable boys from the nearby mews soon gathered, then some other men coming to fetch their horses, until the circle was ringed with male spectators. Oddly enough, no one was willing to bet against Darius, and the crowd became strangely silent as Nick and one of Ainsworthy's seconds gave the signal to come out swinging.

Darius toyed with his opponent silently, letting Ainsworthy start with a glancing blow to Darius's ribs. The pain was a trifling thing, not enough to make a man intent on his objective blink.

A series of blows in rapid succession all over Ainsworthy's lily-white midsection conveyed Darius's initial sentiments.

"Damn, he's quick."

"Accurate too."

"Blighter's mad," another man said. "Look at them eyes. Barkin' bloody mad."

Nick and Trent exchanged a look at that comment. Darius's response was to land a single blow to the jaw that left Ainsworthy staggering. Darius backed away, despite all instinct screaming to the contrary, until the man was righted by the spectators and turned back into the circle.

When Ainsworthy was pawing the air with his fists again, Darius started in once more. For Vivvie, for the baron, for Angela, for the wives, their children, for William... Blow after blow fell, the sound and feel of each reverberating through Darius's soul like a tocsin.

"Relentless as a mill wheel, that one."

"A damned maniac."

"Look at his eyes, lad. He'll kill the idiot, see if he don't."

"Poor bastard shouldn't have crossed that mad bugger."

Another single hard right, only this time Ainsworthy went down. Darius didn't back away immediately but hovered, until Nick and Trent marched him backward, while the rest of the crowd tried to jeer Ainsworthy to his feet.

"Have some damned pride, man!"

"On your feet, boyo. You've yet to land a decent shot."

"Stay down, unless ye want him to finish ye for certain."

The seconds conferred while Ainsworthy hung on all fours, lungs heaving. When he managed to get to his feet, he spat in Darius's direction.

"Bad form!"

"Make him pay for that. This is me own mews he spat on!"

"Fetch the parson. The skinny bastard's done for now."

Darius waited, letting Ainsworthy weave closer, then closer still. With exaggerated care, Ainsworthy pulled back an arm, and while he was choosing his moment—a scientific fighter, clearly—Darius hit him with a right jab that sent him into the dirt again, unable to rise.

"Show's over," Nick said meaningfully. "Back to work, lads, before the King's man reads us the Riot Act."

Somebody tossed a cold bucket of water on Ainsworthy, while Trent threw his greatcoat over Darius's naked shoulders.

"Trent?"

Trent put an arm around his brother and bent close. "I'm here."

"Get me away from this place," Darius said, chest

working like a bellows. "I want to kill him. I want to put my hands around his miserable throat and choke the life from him. I want to kill them all."

Trent started walking Darius toward the townhouse. "Kill who-all?"

"The damned skulking, bastard predators," Darius panted. "Ainsworthy, Wilton, even the women."

"I know." Trent hugged his brother closer. "But you didn't, Dare. You wouldn't let yourself."

"Trent?"

"Love?"

"It felt good to beat the shit out of him. It felt wonderful. I want to do it all over again. I'm going to be sick."

❧

Trent hovered, despite having obligations out at Crossbridge, and Darius let him hover for two days.

On the third day, they rose and went to the docks to watch as Ainsworthy scurried onto a ship bound for Boston.

"How many warrants did you say were drawn up against him?" Trent posed the question as the gangplank was raised and the ship drifted out toward the current in midchannel.

"Five felonies at last count, and at least three angry women are out for his blood. Ariadne seemed mostly relieved, but her fortune was still largely intact."

Darius stood beside his brother, the bracing wind off the river slapping ropes against hulls and making unfurled sails luff madly. For a few minutes, they watched the ship slip farther from the dock.

"Does it help, to know you've hounded him out of the country?"

"It helps."

To see the ship depart helped a great deal, like weight taken from Darius's chest, like somebody had turned up the lamps and opened a window. Beating the stuffing out of Ainsworthy had helped too, as had having Trent and Nick's unquestioning support. It all helped—but not enough.

"You're for Longchamps?" Trent asked.

Darius nodded as Ainsworthy's vessel caught the current and began to turn downriver.

"You have a special license?"

Another nod.

"Then what the bloody hell are you waiting for?"

⤞⤝

"It's like this." Darius addressed the small bundle in his arms—though perhaps not quite as small as even a few weeks ago. "I can't very well ask permission of anybody else, but I feel the need to ask permission of somebody, and you're the only fellow on hand."

The baby gurgled happily and grabbed Darius's nose.

"None of that strong-arm business now." Darius retrieved the paternal beak from the child's grasp. "This is serious stuff, your lordship. Baby Baron, your mama calls you, and you probably like it, don't you?"

The infant made another swipe at Darius's nose, but Darius was getting wise to his son's tricks.

"So you won't mind too much if I marry your mama?" He settled into a rocking chair with the baby.

"You won't get colicky and difficult because I love you both until I'm mad with it? You have scared years off my life, boy, just by being precious and dear. Say something, why don't you?"

Except Darius knew damned good and well the baby was far too young to offer any words of comfort or encouragement. A child this young didn't even understand—

"By God, you're smiling at me," he whispered. "You're grinning like a sailor hitting his first tavern on shore leave. You, sir, are a rascal."

The child beamed at him some more, and the toothless grin was the greatest blessing a man bent on courtship might have wished for.

Vivian deserved better than the not-always-so-very-Honorable Darius Lindsey, there was no arguing that, but she was at least fond of her lover. She understood him, and the comfort of that was immeasurable.

"You have to know something," Darius said to the child now drowsing in his arms. "I'm going to be a papa to you in every way that counts, provided your mama will have me. When you are a grown fellow, we may have to explain a few oddments to you, about why you resemble me but inherited all manner of wealth and consequence from dear William. He loved you too, and he loved your mama. I'd stake my life on that."

Darius fell silent, sending up a prayer that William was reunited with Muriel and their sons, and beaming down from some happy cloud.

"Your mother and I will muddle through those details as best we can at the time—if she'll have me."

The child fell asleep, and Darius lingered a long while, admiring his son—and gathering his courage.

~~~

A new mother got used to the prodding of instinct, even in the middle of the night—maybe especially in the middle of the night. Vivian rose from her nice warm bed, slipped into her mules and night robe, and headed for the nursery down the hall. A glance at the eight-day clock told her Will had nursed not two hours earlier, but some awareness tickling at the back of her mind had awakened her.

She opened the door to the nursery and was greeted by a current of cozy air. The fire was kept going here, lest Baby Baron take a chill.

Baby Baron had taken something worse than a chill, for the child was not in his bassinet. Panic sent Vivian's heart hammering against her ribs in an instant—until she noticed a long, dark form sprawled on the daybed against a shadowed wall.

Darius Lindsey lay fully clothed but for his boots, fast asleep without so much as a blanket to cover him. His hand cradled a small bundle on his chest, one wrapped in a pale receiving blanket with an embroidered hem of peacock feathers.

Her menfolk, no doubt worn out from exchanging confidences. The sight of them in slumber, both with hair of the exact same dark shade, did something queer to her heart.

"You have been out carousing on your papa's chest long enough," she crooned to the baby. She would have lifted him into her arms, except the instant she touched the child, Darius's eyes flew open, and his grip on the child became implacable.

Then, "Vivvie." He bundled the infant up and passed him to her. "I was telling Will a story. He wore me out."

The baby yawned, a mighty effort from such a wee lad, and subsided into sleep.

"You're worn out from riding out from London by moonlight," Vivian chided. She took the rocking chair, while Darius rolled to his side and propped his head on his fist.

"What woke you?"

"You."

"Should I have sent another note, Vivvie?"

"I rather liked the note you did send, and I wish I could have seen Ainsworthy off on his travels myself. Five felonies has a nice, permanently inspiring ring to it."

Darius rolled to his back, his gaze on the ceiling until he turned his head to spear her with a look. "A permanently intimidating ring to it, I hope. I put out his lights first, Vivvie. Rather decisively, and he won't be scribbling any fiction for the foreseeable future."

This recitation of violence was another one of Darius's tests of her understanding. Vivian cuddled the baby closer before she answered. "I hope you landed a few blows for me and for Angela. I should have liked to kick Ainsworthy in a particular location when you already had him retching in the dirt."

Darius's brows twitched. "Would you really?"

"Hard, repeatedly."

He shifted around on the bed, sat up, and visually

located his boots but didn't put them on. "Why, Vivvie? You are the one person who was able to dodge Thurgood's schemes, to outwit him and to equip yourself with allies who could best him."

Vivian wanted to cuddle the baby closer, and then realized she'd commit the mortal sin of Waking the Baby if she didn't put the little fellow in his bassinet soon. "Will you tuck him in?"

Darius rose and prowled out of the shadows to regard Vivian in the rocker. "He looks very content where he is. One is loathe to disturb a fellow at his pleasures."

"One had best do as the fellow's mother asks," Vivian replied, handing Darius the baby, "unless one wants to answer for the consequences."

Darius accepted the bundle of baby and cuddled him close enough to run his nose over a sleeping-baby cheek. "He bears your scent, Vivvie. I am jealous of a mere scrap of a lad."

The tenderness of Darius's smile as he beheld that lad was enough to break Vivian's heart all over again. She had never thought to behold such a thing, not in the middle of the night, Darius in his stocking feet and looking so tousled and dear she could weep with it.

"If you two fellows are going to be up until all hours, I am not going to be a part of your folly." She struggled to her feet, only to find Darius's hand under her elbow.

He stood there next to her, the baby cradled against his chest, his expression unfathomable. "Vivvie, will you marry me?"

She sat right back down.

"You ask me that now? Here?" It was all she could think to say in reply, though he'd spoken words she'd longed to hear.

"I had to ask the baron's permission—and there was that business with Ainsworthy." Darius did not put the child in the bassinet, but rather, took up residence with the infant on the footstool beside Vivian's rocker. "Our situation is all backward, you see, and the child was the only one I could think to ask."

"For my hand?"

"For permission to court you, yes. You and I were intimate, though I could not court you. I hope we became friends, then the baby arrived, and we are lovers—you said that—and it's all muddled, but I have the sense if you'll marry me and be patient with me, then I can get it turned right at last."

He fell silent, kissed the baby's forehead, and said again more softly, "I can get myself turned right at last."

Vivian stroked a hand over his hair. There was a flaw in his reasoning, somewhere, somewhere... but not in his conclusion.

Insight struck, but she took a minute to gather her courage. "Tuck the baby in, Darius."

Darius rose, gently laid the child in his bassinet, and tucked in the blankets. "Good night, little baron. Sweet dreams, and know your papa loves you." Rather than resume his perch on Vivian's stool, Darius picked up his boots with his left hand and winged his right arm. "I will see you tucked in too, my lady. The hour is late, and you should be abed."

What did that mean? She took his arm. She did not intend to simply capitulate, though it was tempting.

If they got to expressing themselves emphatically over this will-you-marry-me business, then they needed privacy.

The corridor was chilly, and Vivian's room not much warmer. "Come to bed, Darius, and we will discuss your latest question."

"My proposal?" He sat on the side of the bed to pull off his stockings. "When you invite a fellow to bed to discuss his proposal, you do know he's inclined to be encouraged?"

But cautious, too. The caution, the hesitation to presume, was there in his eyes.

"I cannot be held responsible for a new father's queer starts." Vivian took off both her night robe and her nightgown, and hopped onto the bed in a state of complete undress. In a moment, Darius joined her, equally unclad.

He made no move to take her in his arms. "Talk to me, Vivvie."

Beneath the covers, Vivian reached across the cool expanse of the mattress and took his hand in hers. "I am the daughter of an earl. You are the son of an earl. A match between us would be seen as appropriate, if precipitous, given William's recent death. I am a widow with a child to rear. You're a spare. Nobody would raise an eyebrow at your becoming Will's guardian, particularly not when Viscount Longstreet himself chose you for the child's godfather."

Darius's fingers laced with hers. "You're naked in bed with me, Vivvie, and spouting logic. I am not encouraged by that at all."

"Hear me out, because you are inclined to spout

logic, sir, to do the sensible, selfless thing when it makes no sense at all."

She was getting ahead of herself. Vivian turned on her side to face him, keeping her hand in his. "You love your son. I have every conviction you loved the child before he was born, loved the idea of him and the possibility of him. Fiercely, without limit."

A cautious nod, then Darius rolled to his side to face her too. "Go on."

"If you are offering marriage to me because it ensures you become Will's guardian, then be at peace, Darius, because Able will not contest your right to serve in his stead. He assured me of this before he and Portia took ship. If you are marrying me to keep me safe from Ainsworthy, then I think we need not fret he'll trouble me from points unknown. If you are marrying me out of duty, as William did, then I can promise you, I have no interest in that sort of union, even with my lover."

Darius traced her hairline with one finger. "I am not marrying you for any of those reasons, though they are sound enough, and I considered them. I hope you consider them too when you give me your answer."

"Why do you want to marry me, Darius Lindsey?"

He brushed the pad of his thumb over her lips. "My reasons are selfish, Vivian. For once in my life, I must be selfish—purely self-interested. I have to be with you. You keep me safe from my worst impulses, from bad judgments and poor choices. You've hauled me out of a thicket where every turn was a wrong turn and I was contemplating dire alternatives far too soberly. I was so lost—"

He stopped and kissed her fingers one by one, and she waited for him to sort himself out.

"I cannot be the man I am supposed to be without you, Vivian. Unless I can love you, I will remain lost. I tried making my way on my own, relying solely on my own wits and wiles, and it was… you saw what I became. Please, Vivvie, let me love you. Let me be the one to love you as your husband, as your friend, as your lover, as anything—" He stopped and swallowed, closed his eyes, then opened them and looked straight at her. "I love you. I'm begging you to marry me because I love you and only because I love you."

This time, his thumb brushed a tear from Vivian's cheek. She scooted across the mattress, into his arms, and addressed the muscular expanse of his chest.

"I married William because he was my only option, and I was his best hope of companionship in his declining years. I married for duty and expedience. I could not bear another such marriage, Darius, not even with you. I was a biddable, unpaid nurse-companion in an ugly dress. I am not… I am not the woman I am supposed to be, unless I am with you. I had no courage. I had no fortitude. I had no trust. I was nobody's mother, nobody's lioness, nobody's lover."

She had to pause while he used the edge of the sheet to wipe her tears. "I want to marry you, Mr. Lindsey, desperately, to be all those things you showed me how to be, and to be your friend too, but mostly"—another pause, while she forced herself to look up and meet his gaze—"mostly, I want to marry you—I *need* to marry you—because you are the man I love, and the man who loves me."

His embrace was fierce and cherishing as he shifted over her. "I do love you. I love you past all reason, to madness and past madness to unshakable sanity." He kissed her forehead and her eyebrows. "I love you until I want to shout with it, until I could beat my chest for all to see." He kissed her mouth, her nose, and again, more lingeringly, her mouth. "I love you until I could weep with it, Vivvie. I love you, I love—"

She kissed him, tenderly, using means other than words to match his verbal effusions.

In the hours, days, and years to follow, they resorted to words, and to those other means frequently, until the baron had three sisters and four brothers, until both Averett Hill and Longchamps were known for their generous hospitality and comfort, until even young people who thought themselves quite expert on the subject declared that The Honorable Darius Lindsey and his Lady Vivian carried on well into their golden years like a pair of newly besotted lovers.

Which, in fact, they did, each day and night of their marriage—exactly like a pair of newly besotted lovers.

Acknowledgments

Darius's story is something of a departure from my usual path, though like all my books, it deals with reclaiming parts of the soul thought lost. My editor, Deb Werksman, spotted this story lurking in the shadows of my personal slush pile, yanked it into the light, and let me know early in our dealings that this tale merited further attention. If you've enjoyed the read at all, Deb should get the credit.

Thanks go as well—as always—to the wonderful people at Sourcebooks, Inc., who treat each of my books as if their name went on the cover: Skye, Cat, Susie, Danielle, and our fearless leader, Dominique Raccah. Writing books with the support of a team like this is a pleasure and a privilege.

About the Author

New York Times and *USA Today* bestselling author Grace Burrowes hit the bestseller lists with her debut, *The Heir*, followed by *The Soldier* and *Lady Maggie's Secret Scandal*. *The Heir* was a *Publishers Weekly* Best Book of 2010, *The Soldier* was a *Publishers Weekly* Best Spring Romance of 2011, and *Lady Sophie's Christmas Wish* won Best Historical Romance of the Year in 2011 from *RT* Reviewers' Choice Awards. All of her Regency romances have received extensive praise, including starred reviews from *Publishers Weekly* and *Booklist*. Grace is branching out into novellas, and her first Scottish Victorian romance, *The Bridegroom Wore Plaid*, was named a *Publishers Weekly* Best Book for 2012.

Grace is a practicing attorney specializing in family law and lives in rural Maryland. She loves to hear from her readers and can be reached through her website at graceburrowes.com.